EARTH Y4K
BLOOD, OIL, AND TEARS

A SAPPHIC ACTION DVENTURE

L. FERGUS

ARTICLE94

Contents

For those who love the BattleTech and MechWarrior universe like I do.

WAR CAT

Ornamental Break from Vecteezy.com

WAR CAT

K ITA HUDDLED IN HER bunk, clutching her pillow while burying her face in the thin stuffing. The pillow wasn't absorbent enough to catch her tears. Instead, falling to the ratty blanket. Her despairing cries grew longer every day after she returned from the grueling training ritual. She cried not for herself but for her friends and the choices she made, leading them to such a hellhole.

The door buzzer sounded. *It's not for me. Just Jabak's idiot friends.* Jabak was her roommate. Every woman in the Aven Foreign Legion was assigned a male. According to legion doctrine, females performed better under male supervision.

On her first night in the Legion, Kita made it clear to Jabak that she would do everything legion doctrine required, but if he touched her, she'd kill him. Jabak scoffed at her, reciting Aven's holy texts that partaking in a woman's flesh was sinful and dirty. The arrangement worked for a week until he returned from the Men's Club, woke her, and demanded that she do his laundry after spilling beer down his front. She jumped out of bed, grabbed the front of his shirt, yanked it over his head, then smashed his forehead against the bunk leg. In the morning, they came to an uneasy truce. He'd let her do what she needed, and she wouldn't say how he got the bruises.

The door buzzed again.

"You going to get that?" Jabak asked from the top bunk.

"Your friends. You get it."

"How's it going to look if I answer the door? You're the woman. Do your duty."

Kita bit her lip, rubbed her face on her pillow to dry her eyes, then tossed it aside. She swung her bare feet out with a huff and touched the cold metal floor.

"While you're up, the room could use a cleaning."

Before Kita could retort, the door buzzed again. *Impatient bastards.* Ignoring Jabak's order, Kita went to the door and hit the OPEN button, revealing Kimmy. Her face contorted with infinite rage, and a few tears leaked from the corner of her eyes. In her hands was her mech helmet.

"Love, what's wrong?" said Kita pulling her partner inside and putting an arm around her. She slammed her fist on the CLOSE button.

Kita was pushing legion doctrine by using Kimmy's pet name—homosexuality wasn't allowed in the Legion...for females. Kita wasn't sure what the men did.

"Ahhhh," Kimmy roared, slipping from under Kita's arm to throw her helmet against Jabak's locker with a loud *bang*.

"What the fuck, woman?" he yelled down from his bunk.

"Go to hell, you cock worshiping troglodyte. I should chop your nuts off and nail them to the flagpole."

"Bitch. You will show me the respect I'm owed," snarled Jabak as he slid off his bunk.

There wasn't much space, but Kimmy brought her right foot up and slammed it on the side of Jabak's knee with an audible *pop*. He collapsed, swearing while holding his injured leg. "Fucking bitch. I'll have you sent to the mines for this!"

"They already have, asshole. What do I care?" Kimmy snarled at him.

"Ah, love, what happened?" asked Kita, ignoring Jabak and putting a hand on Kimmy's shoulder.

"I hate this place," Kimmy wailed as tears fell down her face. "I'm sorry. I tried. But...but...that creatin Colonel Masterson volunteered me for the Baby Factory. He said my eggs would make excellent pilots."

Air hissed between Kita's teeth as she hugged Kimmy. None of the Angels were in the same training troop. The group was split according to legion doctrine when they joined. Kita learned to survive by not attracting attention—her mech piloting marks were average for a reason. It was out of character, but experience was a harsh teacher. She would prove she was the best where it mattered—on the battlefield. But Kimmy wanted to prove to the legion brass that women were as good as men. It appeared the Aven Federation valued Kimmy's DNA more than her skills as a pilot.

"I'll get you out of here," said Kita.

"I know you will. That's why I came. But we have to hurry. I'm supposed to leave on the evening shuttle. What are we going to do?"

Kita sighed. "I'll think of—"

"You two are going to the mines," Jabak huffed as he tried to use the bunk to stand.

Kimmy snarled and kicked Jabak in his wounded knee, causing him to fall to the floor. She savagely kicked him across the face, knocking Jabak flat on his back.

"I told you, asshole, I'm already going there," Kimmy snarled.

So much for that plan. The plan was to become mech pilots and take the giant robots—known by the slang term *mech*, short for mechion—Into battle. The Aven Federation, through the Aven Foreign Legion, was the only government that allowed subjects—a noncitizen of any of the many multi-planetary governments spread across the galaxy—to become pilots. After completing training and a five-year hitch with the Legion, the Angels would be granted citizenship in Aven—the caveat being the Aven Federation military was all male. Female citizens were only permitted to serve in the Blood Witches, a renowned all-female mech unit. When the Angels gained veteran status, they could pick any government or private mech unit. *Now, what are we going to do?*

Kita had one option to talk to the other Angels. Ultraviolet, an Angel hive mind, assimilated several key personnel around the base. The Angels used them to communicate, and Ultraviolet did what she could to protect the flock.

"We need to find UV," Kita whispered in Kimmy's ear. "She can get you to Alientown."

Alientown was the slum where the nonhuman Angels and Jynx were living.

"Ok," nodded Kimmy.

Kita guided her partner toward the door.

"Where the hell are you going?" yelled Jabak.

Kita looked at him and sneered. "To get you help. Should I tell them you fell getting out of your bunk?"

"Bitch. I'll have you both sent to the mines."

Kita shrugged. "You're welcome to try." She opened the door and waved Kimmy out.

In the hallway, Kita hurried through the barracks to the communications panel next to the main door. She brought up a list of cadre names and found one of her assimilated instructors. She tapped the name, and the communicator placed the call.

"Yes?" The screen displayed a picture of Sergeant Frek.

"Sergeant Frek. This is Recruit Roosevelt. I need you to inspect my quarters, and there's a medical emergency. My overseer has fallen and injured his knee."

"I understand, Recruit. I will meet you at your quarters with a medical team."

"Thank you."

Frek killed the connection. Kita and Kimmy returned to Kita's quarters to find Jabak sitting on Kita's bunk.

"Feeling better?" quipped Kimmy harshly.

"Sergeant Frek is on his way with a medical team," said Kita in a gentler tone.

"You're both finished," Jabak hissed through his teeth.

"Sounds like it hurts," said Kimmy. "I can break your other leg to take your mind off it."

"Who the fuck are you?" gasped Jabak. "You should have been thrown in the mines with the rest of the useless women."

"Well," said Kita, "I guess it doesn't make a difference now...This is Kimmy Roosevelt—my partner."

"How the fuck did two queer dykes get in the legion?"

"As compared to a peter-puffer wannabe like you?" yelled Kimmy.

"Male masculinity has been proven far superior to weak, emotional females," spat Jabak. "It's been proven by Aven scientists."

"Right," replied Kimmy rolling her eyes. "I'm sure that was a double-blind study."

The door buzzed. Kita—closest to it—hit the OPEN button.

Sergeant Frek, a tall, lanky man, stood with a pair of men wearing white armbands with red crosses carrying medic bags on their backs.

Frek stepped inside. "Recruit Roosevelt, Recruit Roosevelt, follow me. Sergeant Moore, see to Recruit Jabak."

"Sergeant!" cried Jabak. "I need to tell you what happened, and these two recruits are dykes."

Frek raised an eyebrow. "You let me worry about them. As far as what happened, you slipped, getting down from your bunk. That's what happened, isn't it?"

"That one attacked me!" Jabak pointed at Kimmy.

Frek clenched his hands behind his back. "Are you saying a woman struck you hard enough to injure you? I will have to file a report."

Jabak pressed his lips together. "No, Sergeant. I missed the bottom bunk when climbing down and fell. I landed on my knee."

Frek nodded. "I'll make a note. Female recruits, follow me."

He exited the room, and Kita and Kimmy fell in behind him. They walked through the barracks, out the door, and toward the towering wall surrounding the training compound. Frek stopped and faced Kita and Kimmy when they were away from everyone else.

"It seems we both have urgent news." Frek's eyes glowed ultraviolet to show the others Ultraviolet was in direct control of him.

"What's happened to you?" said Kita, concerned. *It can't be good if UV can't solve the problem.*

"An instructor I assimilated in training troop A has been brought in for evaluation."

"Have they discovered you?" said Kimmy, sounding worried.

"Not yet. Depending on how extensive an evaluation they do, they will."

"Can you remove yourself from the body?" asked Kimmy.

Ultraviolet shook her head. "We release an inhaled spore that attaches to the brain stem. The only way to remove the spore is surgically—and there is a high probability that removing the spore will kill the host."

Kita grunted. "At least that's something, but it's all the more reason to get off this rock."

"What happened to you?" asked Ultraviolet.

"They want to send Kimmy to the Baby Factory. I'm sure the mines afterward."

"Over my dead body," snarled Kimmy. "I've harvested a few eggs before, and that was bad enough. No way I'm letting them have all of them. I may still want another kid."

Kita winced inwardly. *First I've heard of that.* Kita didn't fear the Baby Factory. She'd removed her eggs long ago. "You don't have to worry, love. We'll get you out of here. It sounds like we need to get us all out."

"Yeah, but how?"

"Maybe Flexi can steal a shuttle or—"

"We have an idea," said Ultraviolet.

"That's good," said Kita, "because I don't have any."

"There is an assault ship in port—with several mechs aboard. The ship contains everything we would need to run our own mech unit. I can assimilate the crew and have it ready for launch. We just need to get the flock there."

Kita exchanged looks with Kimmy. "That sounds perfect."

"The ship has room for two troops. We thought we could steal some of the trainers' mechs. They might not be great on the battlefield, but they would give us some cash flow."

"Sounds good," said Kita.

"Yeah, but where would we go?" said Kimmy, sounding unsure.

"It would have to be outside Aven's reach."

"Ash'a has studied the frontier and believes there is enough work to sustain a small operation," said Ultraviolet. "It will be hard getting parts and supplies."

"The ship can reach there?" said Kimmy.

"We have researched the Apollo class assault ship and believe it can take us anywhere in the galaxy. We will make sure it is completely fueled and stocked."

"How long will that take?" said Kita.

"We have been working on it for two days."

Kimmy gasped. "How long have you had this problem?"

"For three days. We didn't want to bring it to you until we had a solution."

"I love that you think like I do," said Kita. "It sounds like our best option. Thank you."

"We are trying to help the flock as best we can."

"You do an excellent job," said Kimmy.

"W AIT HERE," SAID THE sergeant—his eyes glowing ultraviolet—as he closed the door to the small pilot's ready room.

Kita stared at the floor, unable to look at the other Angels.

"Everyone agrees this place sucks, right?" said Karen. She looked gaunt and haggard—her hands chapped and split, her normally gorgeous dark chocolate skin ashy, and her gorgeous black hair shaved.

Tears formed in Kita's eyes. She brought the others here. *I hope they haven't been treated as poorly as Kimmy.* "I'm sorry," Kita said as loudly as she could muster.

Everyone looked at her.

"I'm sorry," Kita said again, trying to be louder as the pit in her stomach grew.

"It's not your fault," said Zhi. The Angel looked slightly better than Karen. She had her hair, but her face was puffy and discolored. "No one knew this place was full of racist women-haters."

"Racist?" whispered Kita as she gulped hard. "What happened?"

"You didn't notice they're all pale men?" said Karen.

"I never noticed. What did they do?"

"Let's just say I have no fear of getting sent to the Baby Factory," said Zhi.

"I better understand what my ancestors went through," replied Karen.

"What happened?" said Kimmy, her eyes wide and angry.

"If they raped you, I will kill them," said Anna.

Karen shook her head. "No fear of that. But..." She turned, unzipped her mech suit, and shrugged off the top to expose the keloids of scar tissue across her back. A pair were still healing.

"My god, Karen!" Kimmy exclaimed. "Why didn't you say something?"

Karen shrugged her mech suit back on. "I'm a big girl. I can take it. I didn't want to ruin it for everyone else."

"You're not alone," said Zhi. "I got the lash a couple of times. This week is my first without a black eye."

"Why the hell didn't UV tell us? We would have gotten you both out," cried Kimmy.

"I told her not to say anything," said Karen. "I wanted to be a pilot as bad as everyone else. I'll take a little pain to get it."

"That's not a little pain," replied Nicole looking at Lizzy. "That's horrifying."

"Yeah. You should have told us," Lizzy said with an unhappy look. "I was one barracks away. I would have come over and kicked the shit out of them. Let's see how well they take a swift kick in the nuts."

"The guys here can't take a discouraging word, let alone a shot, to their precious jewels."

Nicole and Lizzy exchanged a fist bump.

Kita slumped against the wall and slid to the floor, resting her head on her knees while silently sobbing. *This is all my fault.* "I'm sorry," she blubbered into her knees. "I didn't mean to bring everyone into this nightmare."

Kimmy and Nicole knelt in front of Kita. Gently Kimmy stroked Kita's braid.

"Angel, it's not your fault. We all agreed to come. But now that we've seen what they're like, I'd rather die fighting my way out than live another day with these assholes."

"Agreed," said Anna, her blue eyes burning savagely.

"Yes," said Nicole. "I know I went through hell—I can't imagine what Karen and Zhi went through."

"It hurts and sucks," said Karen. "But I know it's only temporary."

"Still, after I find my axiom, I'm going to poison the fuck out of some Avenions," replied Zhi.

Where are the axioms? They're supposed to find us when we're in trouble. Each Angel had an axiom that held her powers, abilities, and Angel DNA. When disguised as Humans, they only had their Human DNA.

"But you're my friends," sobbed Kita. "I'm supposed to take care of you and protect you."

"We're big girls," said Nicole. "This has been a hard lesson—one we won't forget. But Karen is right. It's only temporary. No matter what, we get to go home."

"Come on, Kita," said Kimmy, lifting her partner by the arm. "We need our heads straight if we're going to pull this off. No one's blaming you, but we need you. I'm going to have a chat with UV. The treatment of Karen and Zhi shouldn't have happened—no matter how well they can take the punishment. I know I'd be in tears."

"Who says I wasn't?" said Karen with a chuckle. "But I didn't let them see me cry."

"I didn't cry," said Zhi, "but I did make my male's life miserable."

Kimmy and Nicole pulled Kita to her feet. Gently, Kimmy dried Kita's eyes and hugged her.

After a few breaths, Kita calmed herself but couldn't get rid of the pit in her stomach. Her friends seemed willing to forgive her, but she couldn't forgive herself. *I should have researched the people more...not just looked at the recruiting poster. I never want this to happen again.*

Kita broke from Kimmy and went to Karen and Zhi. "I want to hug you...but I don't want to cause you any more pain."

Karen and Zhi laughed.

"After four months, any affection is worth the pain," said Zhi as they hugged Kita.

"Don't forget the rest of us," said Lizzy.

The Angels shared a group hug that lifted Kita's spirits.

"I needed that," said Karen as she squeezed Anna.

"*Da*," said Anna. "Four months is too long without sex or companionship."

"I'm sure your male was willing to give it to you," chuckled Zhi.

"He was an uncouth pig happy in his filth. These men know nothing of sex with women—or men. They want a milking machine."

"They seem happy just to stick it in a hole and blow their load," Nicole said with a cringe.

"Can we not talk about that?" Kita grimaced. "Sex seems so distant—I've shut everything off. I'm looking forward to some much-needed affection."

"Cuddling sounds wonderful," said Kimmy.

The other Angels agreed.

The door opened, and the sergeant stepped inside. "Follow me, ladies." He led the Angels into the mech hangar. It was small, with just enough room for the cadre's twelve training mechs—all scorpion class—and the base commander's mech—a badger class. The maintenance crews moved along the scaffolding, allowing access to the various mechs' limbs, torsos, and cockpit. Six of the mechs looked to be down for maintenance. The six scorpions they would take had most of their scaffolding removed, except for the ones leading to the cockpits. The sergeant halted Kita's group in front of an assembly of instructors with glowing eyes and a sheet-covered table with seven lumps.

"Alright, ladies," said the lead instructor, Sergeant Bloome. "Today will be a live-fire exercise. To do that, you'll need these."

He removed the sheet, revealing seven mech helmets. The training helmets Kita and the others used were configured for the simulator and training mechs—not usable for live fire. Kita was still a month away from the live-fire training module.

"Each of you grab the helmet with your name on it and join your instructor. Two of you will have to double up. Sorry, half the training mechs are down. When you get in your mech, you will sit in the observation jump seat, plug into the mech, observe what your instructor does, and they will explain what they are doing. This is not a piloting exercise. At no time will you be allowed to pilot the mechs. Is that clear?"

"Yes, Sergeant," the Angels answered.

"Good. Grab your helmets and an instructor."

Kita and the others broke formation and descended on the table. Each helmet was painted different colors. *Matching each angel's wing color. How nice of UV.* Kita found hers—a black and baby pink helmet with FALLEN ANGEL stenciled across the front. The others each had their angelic names. Grabbing hers, Kita stood next to an instructor—Sergeant Norman—and nodded to him. She noticed Nicole and Lizzy were the pair doubling up.

She leaned into Norman and whispered, "UV, we need to talk about the treatment of Zhi and Karen."

"We understand you're upset. Kimmy is too. We will explain, but most of it was out of our control."

Kita nodded.

"Mount your mechs," ordered Bloome.

Kita followed Norman across the hangar to bay six. He saluted the chief mechanic and guided Kita into the elevator. The platform rose three stories to the top level of the aged dock scaffolding, mottled with peeling yellow paint. The scorpion mech was a bipedal scissor-legged design with a large cockpit and a boxy left and right torso that could carry missiles, beams, or cannons. Its stubby arms held beam weapons. The entire thing was painted a patchwork of baby blue and yellow. They followed the grated platform to the hatch on the front of the mech.

The cockpit of the scorpion was large. The main pilot sat in a command chair with a stick and throttle. On the other arm was an array of buttons and switches controlling ammunition settings, weapons groupings, and other systems. In front of the chair was a console displaying coolant, outer armor, internal structure, ammunition levels, gyro, and additional information about the mech. Behind the command chair was the observation jump seat, allowing the observer to see over the pilot's shoulder. There was a receptacle for her helmet so Kita could see the Heads-Up Display that gave her information like distance to target, weapon grouping, data on the target, targeting reticle, and other information about the target and the scorpion.

Norman climbed into the command chair, and Kita strapped into the jump seat. Undoing the cord from the back of her helmet, she plugged into the observation receptacle.

"Strapped in and plugged in," Kita announced to Norman.

"Excellent." He hit a button on the armrest, and the hatch closed.

Outside, amber rotating warning lights turned as the gantry retracted and the scaffolding swung open. The bay doors retracted, and the bright red sun burst through, momentarily blinding Kita.

"Good morning," chuckled Norman activating the dimmer on the canopy. Nodding, he pressed forward on the control stick. "Here we go."

Kita leaned to one side so she could see through the bottom canopy. As their mech took its first step, a ground guide with lighted wands waved them forward. Norman followed the guide through the massive bay door onto the tarmac.

The mechs lined up behind a pilot car and followed it across the tarmac to the base's back gate. Once outside, the pilot car pulled to one side, letting the mechs continue. At a fork, the mechs followed the path around the base instead of to the live-fire range.

"Kita," said Ultraviolet through Norman.

Kita tore herself away from watching Norman drive. "Yeah?"

"We have to go through the city to reach the shuttleport. We've assimilated the assault ship's crew and are ready for launch. We have installed Athena, who is taking over the ship's computers. We will be able to launch as soon as we arrive...Kita, we are sorry about Karen and Zhi. We did our best, but we did not know they were in such danger. We sent away a sergeant we caught beating Zhi. They just now told us it was other recruits attacking them. They didn't tell us earlier, or we would have stopped it. We are sorry for our failings in protecting them."

Kita rubbed her chin. "It's not your fault. You were doing the best you could. I'm upset with myself for bringing them here and putting them in danger."

"But you did not know!"

"I should have checked out the Legion and the people more. I saw the recruiting posters for the Blood Witches and thought: It's an all-women unit. It'll be a safe place. Now that I've experienced the Legion, I wonder about the Blood Witches. What must they be like if they survived the Legion for five years? What did they sacrifice or do to get there? If this is what I—and my friends—have to do to join their ranks, is it worth it? I'm leaning toward no."

"We promise we will make up for our mistake. We will have the medical bay ready for Karen and Zhi. We will do whatever we must to—"

"It's ok, UV. Everyone makes mistakes. You did what you could with the information you had. Karen and Zhi didn't want to ruin it for the rest of us. I understand their reasons, even though I don't agree with them. It's one thing to put me in danger and suffer at the hands of others—it's another for my family and friends to suffer. I—with your help—will make it right. Stealing this assault ship is the first step in righting the wrong—and helping us realize our dreams of being mech pilots."

"We wish we were as good a leader as you," replied Ultraviolet with longing in her voice.

"You're an awesome leader. I may create universes, but I've never ruled one."

"You've ruled a planet and Reality. That is not an easy achievement."

"Yeah, but you make it look easy."

"We had great friends who made it possible."

Kita leaned her head against the shoulder of the command chair. "I couldn't have done it without my friends either. May they rest in peace."

"Someday, we will bring them back."

"Someday..." Kita looked out the canopy, not seeing the wall but the faces of those lost to Directive 77 when Galina purged the Angels many universes ago.

"Kita, are you alright?" said Ultraviolet, sounding worried.

"Just ghosts of the past."

The mechs followed the towering wall and entered the city surrounding the base on three sides. As they moved up the wide street, locals came out to move vehicles and other items they didn't want to be stepped on.

The street opened onto a wide plaza lined with trees. The column of mechs filed in, forming a line on the near side. On the far side of the plaza was a mech Kita didn't recognize. Norman zoomed in on the mysterious mech, revealing no markings or identification.

"Hey, about time you girls showed up. I was afraid I'd have to start this party without you."

"Flexi?" Karen answered.

"You got it. I've got Chelsea, UV, and Ash'a with me. So, what do you think? I built it myself."

"I helped!" exclaimed Chelsea. "So did Knockout."

"They did. I'm making your girl into quite the wrench-turner."

"You made that?" exclaimed Kimmy.

"I mean, I don't have any weapons mounted, but I've got plenty of hard-points for ballistics, missiles, and beams. The arms are reinforced, and I can land a devastating melee blow."

"Wow," remarked Zhi. "Your baby looks awesome."

"See how it is in a fight," said Lizzy.

"Hey, I'll take you all on. I can take a lot of punishment."

The computer didn't recognize Flexi's mech. It did rate it as a fifty-five-ton medium mech—thirty tons more than the scorpion's rating. Kita would make it her mission to get it armed once they were free.

The scorpion carried a twenty-millimeter cannon, a Short-Range Missile two-pack, and a pair of medium-power beams—not a great loadout for a fight, but it did give the pilot familiarity with all three major weapon types.

"Jynxie," called Kita, "How are you?"

"Covered in grease was just how I wanted to spend my leave from West Point."

"Love you, kiddo. I'm glad you're safe."

"I'm doing ok. Flexi's been teaching me how to drive. And Knockout has been teaching me all the mech's systems."

"That's great, sweetie," said Kimmy.

"Where are the Morphicons?" said Kita.

"Velositi took the others to sneak onto the shuttleport," said Flexi. "She said she wanted to get aboard before Kita wrecked the place."

The Morphicons hid in Alientown among the local populous, observing and helping the Angels who weren't in military training.

Kita chuckled. "I hope we can walk in and get aboard."

"Can we get out of here?" said Zhi. "I feel like a sitting duck."

"Yes," said Ultraviolet to everyone. "If you would like to switch places, you can drive."

"Are you serious?" said Nicole.

"You all need the practice more than me."

Norman undid the safety harness and slid into the back. Enthusiastically, Kita hit the release on her harness and jumped into the command seat. After strapping herself in, she familiarized herself with the controls. The layout resembled the simulator, but there were a few extra switches. Pushing on the throttle, the mech took a step forward.

"Wee! This is so much fun," exclaimed Karen.

"Bunch of noobs," laughed Flexi. "Come on, follow me to the shuttleport."

Using the stick and throttle, Kita stomped across the stone-paved plaza toward Flexi. She fell in behind the much bigger mech. They exited onto a wide dusty street, ignoring the traffic doing its best to pull to one side. Not far away was the shuttleport, the assault ship hidden by the wall protecting the compound.

"So...UV said the Aven Foreign Legion was an eight-up soup sandwich," called Flexi to the other Angels.

"I've never seen such a shit show," replied Karen. "Their training sucked, and treatment of women and other races is deplorable."

"All they care about is sucking each other off," grumbled Nicole.

"I caught my male and his buddy doing it in my bed," huffed Lizzy.

"Did you make him wash the sheets?" chuckled Zhi.

"He'd die first. I did make him pull out and get the hell off. Told him they could go to one of the all-male dorms to do that. I was pissed, but it was funny as hell. I don't think they knew what they were doing."

"Just learning to fit in," laughed Flexi.

"They aren't supposed to do that," said Ultraviolet. "We have learned from the people we assimilate that most male pilots that come to the Legion aren't homosexual, and this is their first experience with the Aven lifestyle. We will stress this is different from the normal male homosexual lifestyle found throughout the rest of our experiences—in this universe or others. Their Lover-Beloved bond is strong, and they pair for life, but most aren't homosexuals. From what the assimilated tell us, many are asexual."

"I know, right?" laughed Zhi. "I mean, these idiots are nothing like the gay guys I've known. They knew how to treat a lady and have fun."

"I, ah, did some research on the Avenions," said Jynx somberly. "They were founded by a group who worshipped ancient Greek culture and gods and followed the Apollo Manifesto. I read it...it's mostly nonsense about how Human pale—vanilla males are what they call themselves—males are superior to other races in the galaxy. Human women are supposed to be inferior and subservient. It rambles on how pale human males are destined to rule the galaxy and are the pinnacle of Zeus' creation. They're the coming of something called the Apollo Epiphany—I don't know what that means. But they believe other races are genetic trash—failed attempts at making Humans. Why would anyone believe such garbage, Mom?"

"Because men are stupid," snarled Anna.

"Ryan's not. He's cool and treats Sarah well—and the rest of us."

"I don't know, sweetie," said Kimmy.

"The great masses of the people will more easily fall victim to a big lie than to a small one—Adolf Hitler," interjected Kita.

"What I don't get," said Chelsea, "is if they hate women so much, why have the Blood Witches?"

"I heard rumors all Blood Witches must go to the Baby Factory," said Nicole.

"What's the Baby Factory?"

"I only know rumors and what they told me," replied Kimmy. "It's a place they send women to harvest their eggs. I believe it is also where they fertilize, sex, alter, and gestate the zygotes. It's how they replenish their population."

"Gross," huffed Chelsea.

"Technically, I did the same thing to make you," replied Kita.

"Yeah, but…you had Mom's permission, and…and you did it for love—not hate."

Kita chuckled. "We did do it for that."

"I missed you. It sucks they wouldn't let me join."

"Better you didn't," said Nicole.

"Definitely not a place for teenagers," said Karen.

"You learned more with Flexi than we did with these asshole lovers," replied Zhi.

"We both did," interjected Ash'a.

"Hey, Ash'a," said Lizzy. "Where have you been hiding?"

The Aurorian laughed. "More hanging on for dear life."

"My driving's not that bad," muttered Flexi.

"Yeah, Ash'a helped," added Chelsea.

"Did UV give you a helmet, Ash'a?" asked Karen.

Ash'a chuckled. "She did—it even says Alliance on the front. I don't know how much I'll use it, but it'll look nice on my desk. I did turn a few wrenches in between learning about how the galaxy operates. I've got a good idea of running the business end of our new venture."

"Awesome," remarked Zhi.

"That's been a worry at the back of my mind," admitted Kita.

"I knew someday we'd be in business for ourselves—UV had me put my curiosity into practice over the last few days. I've made some contacts and nosed around the Mnet and DarkNet looking at contracts…both legitimate and pirate—I wasn't sure which we would go for. I should be able to make it work."

"That's incredible, Ash'a!" exclaimed Kimmy.

"Just doing my part. If it were easy, you would do it instead of pulling a trigger."

The other Angels laughed.

"How are you girls doing? No problems? No one harassing you?" asked Kita.

"We eked out a living repairing stuff at our shop in Alientown," said Flexi with a grunt.

"Not a lot of food, and we had to barter to get parts," said Ash'a, filling in Flexi's grunt. "I did make the mistake of leaving Alientown without Chelsea and was jumped by a goon squad, but after a day, I was fine. After that, anytime we left, we brought Chelsea."

"It was weird," huffed the teenager. "I had to pretend I owned them. People kept coming up wanting to touch them."

"Should've seen them jump when I answered in Common," laughed Flexi.

Kita wanted to hang her head but didn't feel confident with the controls not to run into Flexi. "I'm so sorry," said Kita sadly. "I hate that I didn't know this place was so bad."

"What's a little adversity?" cooed Flexi.

"It's good to experience the worst," said Ash'a. "It'll make us appreciate life when it gets better."

"It does keep one honest," remarked Zhi. "Still not as bad as flight school. They can call me slanty-eye all they want as long as they don't call me mud-fish."

"I swear I will come back and burn this place into oblivion. Aven is next," hissed Kita.

"How would that go down in the history books?" said Nicole. "Lesbian destroys gay nation for giving homosexuality a bad name."

The other Angels chuckled.

"I would recruit an army of gay men to prove it wasn't just me."

"You would probably get help from the larger galactic community," said Ash'a. "Aven has no allies. Only their army of hoplite mechs keeps the rest of the galaxy at bay. The fact they occupy Earth and restrict pilgrims and other Humans from returning is a major sticking point among the Human-based civilizations."

"Hmmm," mused Kita. "I just might have to start a war."

"With six scorpions and Flexi?" teased Kimmy.

"I've started with less."

"How about we worry about getting away first?" interjected Nicole.

"Shuttleport coming up," announced Flexi.

The wall around the shuttleport wasn't as tall as the base. It was still taller than most mechs and required them to go through a gate guarded by a pair of turrets mounted on the gatehouse towers. More turrets sat on the corners overwatching like modern gargoyles.

"UV, you have control of the facility?" said Kita.

"Yes. We have control of everything. Athena and we have fueled the ship and made it ready for liftoff. All that is required is to load your mechs, but I can only do two at a time."

"Ok, ladies, you heard UV. Nicole, Anna, you'll go first once we get into the shuttleport. The rest of us will form a defensive perimeter in case someone notices we borrowed their toys."

"Roger," everyone acknowledged.

Flexi led the convoy through the gate, past several buildings, to an open yard with three compacted dirt shuttlepads lining three sides. Large cylindrical fuel tanks stood in the corner near the wall. The only ship in port was a large gray shuttle with large open eight-story doors on the side. The mech hangars inside looked ready for them.

"Nicole, Lizzy, Anna, go," ordered Kita.

The mechs broke ranks and stomped up the shuttle's ramp, disappearing inside.

"Everyone else, spread out and cover the gate." Kita took a position closest to the entrance. She planned on being the last to board in case they needed to get away in a hurry—or she had to stay behind.

"Kita," said UV, "we detect a force of several light vehicles moving toward the shuttleport at a high rate of speed. They have Aven Foreign Legion markings. Do you want us to open fire?"

"Not yet. Stall them at the gate the best you can. I don't want to expose you more than you already are."

"Understood."

"Ladies, listen up," Kita called to the other Angels. "We've got AFL forces incoming. UV is going to hold them at the gate as long as possible. Be ready to fight a group of toe-poppers."

"I guess we'll find out if they blow up like they do in the simulator," chuckled Karen.

Kita spent ample time in the simulator and concluded that a bunch of testosterone-raging teenage males programmed it. Everything blew up in spectacular explosions, and impressive kills were replayed in slow motion. It was unlike any simulator she'd ever been in—more like a bad video game. She hoped they accurately modeled the mech controls.

"Kita," said Ultraviolet, "the commander of the AFL force is threatening to blow up the gate if we do not let them in."

The gate was raised, keeping Kita from seeing the AFL vehicles. She didn't have long-range missiles allowing her to shoot over the gate. Her SRMs were direct fire only—the same for the beam and ballistics.

"UV, lower the gate so I can get a shot and have your turrets ready."

"The AFL vehicles are inside our firing arc. We have shots from the corner towers for the vehicles in the rear."

"Perfect. Take them out, and we'll trap the others."

The gate lowered into the ground. Kita put her targeting reticle on where she thought the enemy vehicle was. Flipping the toggles on the various weapon groups, she armed her twenty-millimeter cannon and beams. *That should be enough to take out a light vehicle.*

The lowering gate revealed a six-wheeled armored personnel carrier with a double cannon turret. Flipping her SRM toggle, Kita waited for the computer to signal it was locked on. *I need to talk to UV about what a* light vehicle *is. An APC carrying the same gun I do is not light.*

A high-pitched tone sounded in her ear. Kita wasn't experienced enough to fire on instinct—she had to think about it. Squeezing the trigger, she sent an alpha strike at the APC. The beams arrived first, striking the front of the APC and burning holes through the metal armor. Her twenty-millimeter round struck the armored turret, punching through, causing the twin guns to sink and rest onto the APC's front deck.

The armor-piercing SRMs streaked toward the target. The missile tips contained a thermal detonator that burned through the metal armor and launched a shaped charge through the hole to destroy the interior. The missiles struck, pushing into the APC and detonating the interior. The vehicle jumped into the air as the turret blew off and landed out of sight.

"First kill!" Kita announced with glee.

"Doesn't count," scoffed Flexi. "You gotta kill a big one for it to count. The little ones you can step on."

On the corner towers, the turrets opened fire on something hidden from view. One turret was a quad-mounted thirty-millimeter cannon array, and the other mounted ten SRMs. The missiles and cannons fired several times, lighting the shuttleport's interior with orange and yellow.

"I think UV gets the most," chuckled Zhi.

"The front gate is blocked," announced Ultraviolet. "We are ready for the next pair."

"Karen, Zhi, get aboard," ordered Kita. "And then report to the medical bay and get those lashes and bruises taken care of."

"Roger," said Karen.

"Oscar Mike," responded Zhi.

The mechs broke ranks and jogged toward the shuttle's hangar door.

As the pair walked up the ramp, Ultraviolet tapped Kita on the shoulder. "We're detecting a mech approaching the shuttleport. It is a badger class—equipped with thrusters. We will open fire, but we won't be able to keep it out."

"Send it our way," hollered Flexi.

"Be careful, Flexi," said Kimmy. "A badger sports a six-pack of SRMs and four medium beams. It can do a lot of damage."

"Its weakness is heat," added Kita. "Two or three shots from those beams, and it's going to need to cool down."

"Lucky for me, throwing punches doesn't generate heat," Flexi replied enthusiastically.

"If you can survive getting close enough to throw one," replied Kimmy.

"That's what I have you for."

The four turrets on the wall opened fire on something outside.

"Ok, girls," Kita prodded the others, "that badger is coming."

"We scored some hits, but it jumped," announced Ultraviolet.

"Everybody, back up and spread out," ordered Kita as she moved the throttle back. A camera on her console let her see the landing pad behind her. She stopped next to the empty dirt platform and scanned the sky, looking for the badger.

A squat, angular mech appeared over the wall, trailing smoke from its thrusters. Kita laid her targeting reticle over the badger and waited for the targeting computer to identify and lock on. As she waited, she selected her cannon and beams. The SRMs didn't have a lock, and the badger was moving too fast for them to be useful. When the targeting *warble* sounded in her helmet, Kita pulled the trigger. The *thunk* of the cannon firing punctuated the silence of the beams.

The targeting reticle flashed green, then violet, informing Kita the three weapons scored hits. The badger's left torso turned yellow on her console, pinpointing where the weapons had struck. The target icon in the HUD flashed again, indicating someone else had hit the badger. *Kimmy proving why she's better than the boys.*

The badger twisted, trying to land and take a shot at Kimmy. As it flared its thrusters, Flexi sprinted forward.

"Eat this!" she yelled as her mech's arm retracted, then launched forward, slamming into the badger's central torso just above the cockpit.

The badger's legs dipped as the mech's gyro compensated for the impact and kept the machine upright. Its torso squared, aiming the four beams in its right arm and right torso at Flexi.

"Flexi! Look out," yelled Kita as the badger fired an alpha strike. *I hope that thing is as armored as Flexi says.*

The bright flash of the badger's beams was blocked by the smoke of the six SRMs slamming into Flexi's central torso. Flexi's machine didn't compensate for the blast. Rocking backward, it fell, sending up a cloud of dust as it hit the ground.

"Flexi! Are you ok?" cried Kimmy.

"We're ok," said Ash'a. "Just a little shaken."

"I, ah, couldn't find a gyro," announced Flexi sheepishly.

"Kimmy! We need to draw his attention before he takes a kill shot," yelled Kita.

"Lining up the shot now."

Kimmy's angle was too wide, and the best she could do was savage the badger's left arm. She took the shot anyway. Kita was impressed her partner could rapid-cycle her twenty-millimeter cannon to fire two shots instead of one. This was a technique of veteran pilots. If done correctly, you got double the penetration, but it was hard to control the climb of the cannon. Often, for inexperienced pilots, the second shot went high.

Not for Kimmy.

Kita's HUD flashed and reported that Kimmy didn't hit the left arm. Instead, she hit the cockpit, even her second cannon shot. *That'll get the pilot's attention.* The target cockpit was a tiny circle near the top center of the icon. It flashed red, indicating Kimmy had damaged the area a lot. *I wish I was that good a shot. How am I going to take advantage of that?*

Kita didn't have time to puzzle it out. She took a snap shot, not giving the computer enough time to lock on, but she thought she was close enough that aiming wasn't an issue—and she had to keep the badger off Flexi. The HUD registered her shot—hitting the badger in the right torso and left leg.

The badger turned toward Kimmy. Kita moved to the left toward the badger's rear while giving time for her weapons to reload, charge, and reset. The missile rack in her left arm was connected to an ammo pod in her left torso, requiring time to get the projectiles loaded. Every time the cannon fired, the barrel climbed, requiring the computer to reload and aim the gun. Beam weapons didn't have projectiles to load but did require time to recharge their capacitors and cool. Depending on the weapons' systems, this time requirement left the mech vulnerable to attack. The best defense was to move out of your enemy's firing arc. Barring that, you turned the mech's most armored areas toward the enemy.

"Flexi! You've got to get up!" encouraged Kita as the big mech struggled to stand without a gyro system to stabilize the weight.

"I'm trying. I've got to do the weight distribution by hand."

Mechs carried internal liquid tanks allowing them to shift weight around like a human body. Normally, a computer linked to a gyro handled it. Without a gyro, Flexi would have to direct the computer.

As the badger charged Kimmy, Kita put herself between it and Flexi. Kimmy fired, hitting the oncoming badger in the right torso, followed by an electrical explosion.

"Got them!" whooped Kimmy.

On Kita's console, two of the badger's beams were destroyed. A tone in her helmet, reinforced by a flashing light in her HUD, said her weapons were ready. Kita targeted the weak armor of the back of the badger. Not waiting for tone, instead hoping to spare Kimmy a full assault, she pulled the trigger. The back of the badger exploded as her cannon found the badger's left arm, her SRMs hit the rear left torso, and the beams struck the center torso.

It wasn't enough to kill the badger, but alarms had to be sounding. On Kita's console, the rear left torso was blinking. *That's two spots—I doubt I could hit the cockpit.*

"Kita!" called Ultraviolet. "We're ready for the next two."

"Roger. Flexi, Kimmy, get aboard. I'll handle him."

"Kita," Kimmy protested, "You're closer. Go. I can finish him."

"We must hurry," interjected Ultraviolet. "Kita, more mechs and vehicles—some appear to be Long Range Missile carriers—are moving through the city."

"Those could take out the ship," gasped Kita.

"Kita, go!" ordered Kimmy.

"No. You go. You're better. Someone will have to lead if I don't make it."

"It's my honor!"

"It's my mistake," retorted Kita. "I made the bad choice to bring you all here. I'm going to get you out. If I have to sacrifice myself, so you're safe, I will. Now, go!"

"Momma, come with us," yelled Chelsea.

"I plan on it—but you and your mom must get aboard first."

"Mom, let's go," Chelsea pleaded.

"Not until Flexi is ready."

"I've almost got it."

Kimmy moved to the right, exposing her left arm. The badger fired, his six SRMs slamming into the appendage, highlighted by the burns from the pair of beams. The damage penetrated her missile pod and set off a chain reaction of exploding ammunition into her left torso, blowing that section's armor off her mech.

"I've got alarms all over," Kimmy reported.

"Get aboard!" Kita yelled.

"Get him off me, and I'll go."

Kita's cannon was the only weapon system ready. She lined up on the badger's damaged rear left torso. *I hope this is a magic bullet.* She pulled the trigger, but the round struck the rear right torso instead of the left, but it did get the badger's attention.

The badger pilot must know he's in a bad spot. Trapped between two mechs—one to the front and one to the rear—with no discernable way out...*except*... The badger fired his thrusters, leaping over Kita. He landed in her rear arc near the shuttleport's fuel tanks. *Well...bloody moons.*

Kita grabbed the control stick and jerked it hard to the right, putting her better-armored right side to the enemy—just as a salvo of SRMs and beams hit her right arm and leg. Her console damage screen lit, her yellow right leg indicated damage to her outer armor, and her orange arm, with damage to the external armor and internal structural damage. *The repair crew won't like that.*

"I'm up," reported Flexi.

"Get aboard, both of you," Kita ordered.

"Right. Headed there now. I, ah, guess this thing wasn't battle-ready."

"It will be, but we must get out of here first."

"I've got her back," said Kimmy.

But who's got yours, love? "I'll cover you."

Kita turned her mech, keeping herself between the badger and the others. Bringing herself to face the badger, she moved her targeting reticle toward where she thought the enemy mech should be. Instead of being near the fuel tanks that she could blow up, it was on top of her. The *thud* of the badger's arm slamming into her mech reverberated throughout her machine. An alarm sounded as her console reported her left torso suffered internal damage.

The badger filled Kita's view—she had so much target she didn't know where to aim. Slamming the control stick backward, her scorpion took a few steps back, bringing the badger into focus. Kita pulled the trigger without a lock. *I'm so close. Who needs to aim?* Kita's scorpion fired an alpha strike. To her dismay, the cannon shot high, the beams hit the badger's right leg, and the SRMs hit the badger's left torso and left leg. *Ok, so maybe I'm not as good as the computer…yet.*

Jamming her throttle to maximum, Kita guided her scorpion to the left, trying to keep out of the badger's firing arc while putting some distance between them. She didn't dare turn her back on the heavier badger. It outweighed her twenty-five-ton scorpion by ten tons.

"Power down the mech, woman, and surrender—or I'll blow the ship," said a low, gravelly voice in Kita's ear.

Kita recognized Colonel Masterson's voice. *Bloody moons, he must be spotting for the LRM carriers outside.* Kita looked at Sergeant Norman. "UV, please tell me you can take out the LRM carriers?"

"They turned down some side streets and have taken cover behind the buildings. The other vehicles have pulled into defensive positions around them."

They can rain down hell, and there's no way to stop them. The assault ship is built to take punishment but not that much…and even less for me.

There was one way to stop them. Kita set her target reticle over Masterson's cockpit. On her console, the tiny area blinked red, damaged by Kimmy. Around the targeting reticle was a circle. It started wide and closed around the reticle. When the computer had a lock, it flashed green.

Waiting for the computer left Kita open to receive damage. Moving was her only defense. However, keeping the targeting reticle where she wanted required piloting skills she had yet to acquire. She did her best, moving backward while keeping the targeting reticle where she wanted.

A flash and trails of smoke caused Kita to grimace. She hit the button to brace her mech against the incoming SRMs. Bracing a mech told the computer to prepare for impact: noncritical systems shut down, ammo pods disconnected, weapons sealed, and the gyro prepared to keep the mech upright by adjusting weight and reconfiguring the leg joints.

Bracing did little to dampen the impact. The explosion threw Kita sideways in her seat. As Kita righted herself, her console lit up, and alarms sounded in her helmet. *To the Crushing Depths…* According to the computer, Kita was missing her right arm and torso—a foot or two to her left, and he would have detonated her power plant—core. *I don't need to be cored my first time out.*

Kita released her mech from its brace and retrained her targeting reticle on Masterson's badger cockpit. The lock circle closed as Kita walked back until she ran out of room. Her scorpion's foot hit the pile of compacted soil of the far shuttlepad. The dirt was too unstable and steep to climb. *Well...nuts. What do I do now?*

Masterson, seeing Kita was stuck, charged.

Dammit. Come on, you stupid computer...faster!

Masterson fired six SRMs and beams on the run.

Kita gritted her teeth. She was going to have to take this round on the chin. If she braced again, she'd lose her targeting. *Of course, if he hits me like last time, I'll lose it anyway. Come on, you bastards—miss!*

Kita's scorpion shook as two of the six missiles struck—the rest blasted fountains of dirt into the air. A new alarm sounded. Kita's leg was blinking on her console. The missiles punched through her right leg's outer armor and damaged the internal components. The computer didn't tell her what was damaged, but redundancy was the watchword for mech designers.

Through the impact, Kita kept her reticle on Masterson—even as he charged. The lock circle closed around the reticle, and there was a *ping* in Kita's ears. After double-checking the reticle to make sure, she pulled the trigger. The SRMs leaped from the pod and streaked toward their target. The cannon let out a loud *thunk*. The silent beams cut into Masterson's thin cockpit armor.

Masterson's cockpit disappeared in a cloud of smoke and fire. The badger stopped mid-step and collapsed face-first into the dirt.

"Yes!" Kita whooped as she turned and exchanged a high-five with Ultraviolet.

"Excellent kill, Kita," exclaimed Ultraviolet. "The ship is ready for you, and we must hurry. The LRMs may have lost their spotter, but they can fire blind."

Kita pushed her stick forward, but her scorpion moved with a noticeable limp. *No sprinting for me...I can barely walk.*

Fountains of dirt erupted in front of Kita, blasting large holes in the ground. Kita pushed her stick hard to the right to dodge a smoking pothole. The last thing she wanted was to get her stricken mech stuck and have to abandon it... *If I even can.*

Pushing the stick to the left, Kita navigated the hole and plotted a course around another hole between her and the ship's ramp. She willed the wounded scorpion forward, hoping her mental energies would give her a boost.

Kita straightened her stick as she navigated the next hole. She had thirty yards—thirty seconds—to the ship's ramp as the next missile barrage struck in a medley of dirt and fire. Clods exploded against her cockpit while a smokey haze obscured the ramp. As Kita struggled to see, she kept her stick pushed forward and her throttle at maximum—the computer limited her speed. Kita didn't know how to override it.

The battered scorpion took another step and tilted wildly as the foot plunged two feet into an unseen crater. The mech swayed as the gyro indicator lit, showing it was trying to compensate for the sudden drop and angle change.

As Kita struggled with the stick and throttle, the mech swayed violently. "By the Crushing Depths, what do I do?" This had never been covered in training. *I'm finding out many things were left out of the training regime.*

"Here," said Ultraviolet as she leaned over Kita's shoulder, flipped a series of switches, and lowered a slider bar on the console. The mech squatted, and the swaying stopped. "That is the gyro override."

"Oh, good. I was afraid we were going to fall flat on our face."

Ultraviolet chuckled. "We know enough to not let that happen. The ship has a simulator. We will talk to Athena about updating it with advanced training for you. It will allow us to pass on the knowledge we have acquired as instructors. It doesn't do us any good."

"Don't be so quick to dismiss. We may still need you in the field."

"We don't want to ruin your dream, but we could run a support troop for you."

"The more warriors we have, the better."

"We may spend some time in the simulator then," UV smiled as she leaned back and sat in her seat. "Push the slider to maximum to stand up and then move forward normally."

Kita did as instructed. Her limping scorpion took a few unsteady steps to climb out of the hole. Once on solid ground, Kita pushed the stick forward and the throttle to maximum.

Looking over her shoulder at Ultraviolet, Kita said, "How do I make it go faster?"

"That would be unwise. The computer has calculated a safe speed that will not damage the mech's systems further."

"If we don't go faster and get out of here, the next missile barrage might come down on our head."

"True." Ultraviolet leaned forward and flipped a switch on the command chair. When a screen appeared on the console, she tapped the override button. "You do realize this will most likely damage the structure of the leg further, and we have to make the repairs?"

"If it saves our asses, I'm sure Kimmy will kiss you for saving me."

Ultraviolet chirped laughter. "We have never been kissed. We look forward to the experience."

Kita's eyebrows went up. "Yeah, but...you must have assimilated billions of people who have kissed."

"Yes, but those are their memories—not mine. We have come to enjoy the love and affection we get from the Angels. But this is a discussion for another time. We are not currently Angels and not indestructible. As Zhi would say, shut up and drive."

Kita peered through the smoke and haze, but the air was so thick she couldn't see the ground or the shuttle. *If I back off the throttle, we'll never get there, but I don't want to fall into another hole.* "UV, is there a way to see through this smoke?"

UV leaned over Kita's shoulder and hit a switch on the arm of the command chair.

In Kita's HUD, a graphical overlay showed her the ship, ramp, and ground. When she looked to her right, she saw the rest of the shuttleport. It wasn't in great detail, but enough that she could discern objects and obstacles.

"This is the LiDAR," explained Ultraviolet. "It's what the computer uses to 'see.' You can add other sensors, but this is the basic overlay and should get us to the ship."

The ramp was fifteen yards away. Kita pushed the throttle as much as she dared, hoping her scorpion's leg would hold together long enough to get aboard. Kita grimaced with every step. A flashing light lit the console. Kita tapped the warning, which expanded to show the mech's right knee, and the hydraulic fluid level had dropped to dangerous levels.

"We have to reduce our speed," said Ultraviolet. "Or we'll lock the joint."

Out the cockpit, Kita assessed the ground left to cover and the ramp. She had ten yards to get inside. The scorpion shook violently as explosions blasted around them. Kita slammed the throttle to maximum. *I'm coming home with my shield or on it.*

The scorpion limped up the ship's ramp. The lights of the interior cut through the haze and smoke, guiding Kita like a beacon.

"Come on...Come on," Kita urged her injured mech.

The scorpion crossed the threshold into the ship's mech bay. An alarm sounded, and the console flashed a warning the right knee joint seized. Kita turned to look back at Ultraviolet when the mech creaked and fell forward, slamming into the bay's deck.

"Kita, are you alright?" asked Ultraviolet.

"I'm fine. Get the ship out of here."

"We will liftoff momentarily. We can have a crew free you as soon as we're in orbit."

Kita hit her harness release and fell out of the command chair onto the cockpit glass.

"Kita," protested Ultraviolet. "You need to stay seated for liftoff."

"Too late now," Kita grumbled. "I'll be fine. Get us out of here before they target the ship."

"Warning! All crew brace for emergency liftoff. Repeat. Brace for emergency liftoff."

Athena. Kita pushed against the cockpit hatch. The thick shatterproof glass weighed a ton as Kita pushed, moving it only a fraction. As she grunted, Ultraviolet helped push. Together they lifted the hatch enough to wiggle through.

Kita jumped to the deck as the ship lifted off with a terrible vibration, the g-forces dragging Kita to her knees. The acceleration kept Kita down as warning lights flashed.

The feeling of her stomach jumping into her throat was followed by the ship switching to artificial gravity. Kita pushed on her knee to stand. Around her towered five scorpion mechs and Flexi's homebrew. Each was parked in a bay caged by scaffolding.

"Welcome to the Aetos, Mom," said Athena from the ship's speakers mounted around the cavernous mech bay.

Kita wrinkled her nose. "What's an Aetos?"

"It means eagle in Greek."

"Oh...yuck. Can we change it?"

Athena laughed. "Of course, once we're outside Aven space. What do you have in mind?"

Kita stroked her braid as she scanned her memory. A white and gray face appeared with a cute nose and ears. His cat's smile brought a tear to her eye. *Sarge.* "How about War Cat?"

"Your current partner might not like you naming the ship after your ex," quipped Athena.

Kita laughed. "No, not Snowy. Sarge."

"Ah. I will update the ship's registry when it's safe. And...like I have to guess...what flag would you like to fly?"

Kita clicked her tongue, bemused by her daughter. "Raise the black flag."

"Naturally. Ash'a has some contracts on the frontier to discuss. I will set a course if you want."

"Yes," Kita replied emphatically. "Let's get the Crushing Depths out of here."

EARTH Y4K

BLOOD·OIL·AND·TEARS

Hardcover ISBN: 978-1-949789-20-1

Paperback ISBN: 978-1-949789-21-8

@FallenAngelKita

http://FallenAngelKita.com

Cover art by Mrinmoy Kar

Ornamental Break from Vecteezy.com

CHAPTER 01

ASTARI IIIa
DEFIN MINING COLONY
LUNAR BIOME
¥51,834
1, OCTOBER 4003

*T*HUD. *THUD. THUD.* THE sound of Kimmy's mech's footfalls didn't come through the atmosphere—as the tiny moon had none—but courtesy of the poor engineering of her ocelot. Every step reverberated through the mech's chassis and rattled the cockpit. After her first patrol, she'd returned to their assault ship, War Cat, and had a mouth guard made, so she didn't lose any teeth.

She led her wingmate, Nicole, over the lip of the crater where the small mining facility owned by Defin Industries lay. They'd been hired to guard the facility and the water crystals it produced.

Turning around, Kimmy looked down through the lower cockpit glass, scanning the far side of the deep crater. The perfect impressions of her footprints in the moondust followed her like a ghost. The razor-sharp dust was murder on filters and armor, getting into everything, degrading parts and performance. Ultraviolet's maintenance teams were constantly vacuuming it out of the mechs' chassis.

"War Cat Main, Apocalypse. We've reached checkpoint alpha. Same shitty view as yesterday," Kimmy called to Athena. The AI Digital Angel was the mission coordinator for the Angel's mech troops.

"But the stars are pretty," the AI replied.

The band of stars making up the galaxy crossed the sky in a giant cloud. They didn't twinkle and reminded Kimmy of their lousy predicament. "They look the same as yesterday. We're moving toward bravo."

Their course would take them along the crater's southern rim in search of pirates who viciously plagued Defin. Kimmy and her mercenary company had been on the ground for a month but found nothing. Kimmy would have complained, but Defin was happy and honoring their side of the contract. Including supplying needed knowledge on how to operate in the moonscape environment.

So, Kimmy kept grumbling about the lack of action to herself. Kita, her partner, also shared her frustration, but like always, Kita could turn any situation to her advantage. The tiny moon proved an excellent environment to train the other Angels on the mechs' piloting and gunnery skills in live fire exercises—Defin didn't mind if they blew up moon rocks. She focused on their daughter Chelsea, who didn't get the basic training the other Angels had in the Aven Foreign Legion. War Cat had a simulator—reprogrammed by Athena to get rid of the childish programming of the Avenions—and Chelsea made good use of it, but nothing beat practical experience.

Kimmy turned her mech to the south and followed the trail around the crater's southernmost point.

"How was the game last night, Nemesis?" Kimmy called to Nicole as their mechs plodded along.

"It's a little unfair when the entire opposing team is controlled by one person. I'm impressed by how fast UV learned basketball. How was home life?"

"What homelife? Kita and Chelsea spent the night in the mech bays while I was on the bridge with Athena, working out today's mission and going over scouting reports. I think Defin making the pirates up—but the money's good, so..."

"I'm with you. I think these pirates are a myth."

"We've got another month, so get used to it. I know it's boring—hell, I want action, too—but I'll also take an easy payday. With this, we should be able to have a down payment on a new medium-class mech—"

"If we can find one in this backwater."

Kimmy grumped. That was the problem. The mine was on the periphery where very little people and material from the established states reached—but it made a good hiding place and was as far as they could get from the Aven Federation.

"Flash override," announced Athena in a calm voice. "Unknown enemy sighted in sector Zulu. Fallen Angel and Jynx are engaging."

"Pirates at last," cooed Nicole.

Kimmy wasn't so sure. "It could be a moon slug," she muttered as she flipped her radio from the patrol net to the command net.

There was a hiss of static and then, "Momma! I'm coming to help."

"Jynxie, stay back," Kita ordered. "Find your mo—" Static cut her off.

"Momma! I can help! I can get behind them!"

"Go!" Kita roared. "I will—" Kita's radio cut, and only a slow hiss remained.

"Momma! Momma!" Chelsea screamed over the radio.

Shit. What the hell did they run into? "Come on, Nicole. We've got to get over there."

"This is Main," announced Athena. "War Cat is preparing for immediate lift off. We have three boggy ships coming in fast. All mechs are advised to seek shelter and avoid contact. Whoever these intruders are, they're not the local pirates. I will contact you once we break contact and avoid our pursuers."

Kimmy turned her torso to the right in time to see War Cat blast off, leaving a trail of dust and fire in her wake. *Athena must have slammed the doors and put everyone on the floor to liftoff so fast.* Over the horizon, a pair of fighters streaked in low before pulling up to give chase to the assault ship. *How are Athena and UV going to outrun those?* War Cat carried few weapons.

Pushing her throttle to the maximum, Kimmy couldn't worry about the assault ship. She had to save her daughter and partner...and probably herself.

Keying her mic, Kimmy tried to raise her daughter. "Jynx, Apocalypse. Nemesis and I are approaching from the west toward your last known position. Where are you?"

"Mom! Mom! They're after me! They blew up Momma!"

A pit the size of the black hole at the galaxy's center appeared in Kimmy's stomach. Her only hope was her A'ahegre—an alien lifeform bonded to her. Kita and Chelsea were, as well. The A'ahegre gave each unique abilities and could sense each another. Kimmy felt her partner and daughter. *Kita must be alive. Maybe she ejected, or it's just her mech's legs...*

"Ok, Jynx, listen to me. You need to come to us. Do you have a lock on them?"

"No, Mom. I see them on the radar behind me, but I—" A loud static hiss was followed by Chelsea screaming over the radio. "Mom! They shot my legs. I can't move!"

"Chelsea! Get out!" Kimmy screamed. "Grab your life preserver helmet and get out. Let them have the mech. Nicole and I are coming as fast as we can!"

It was a long way around the crater to the north side. Kimmy pushed her ocelot to the redline as Nicole's faster firefly mech jogged alongside.

"Poison, Venom, are you girls moving?" Kimmy called to the other Angels guarding Defin.

"Roger," said Karen, known by the call sign Poison. "We're climbing out of the crater now."

"Get me a line of sight, and I'll light them up," announced Zhi, call sign Venom.

"You'll get there first," replied Kimmy. Her ocelot was slow for a light mech. "Nemesis, sprint ahead and see if you can get a lock for our Long-Range Missiles, but stay out of their range."

"Roger."

Nicole's firefly accelerated toward the unknown.

Kimmy's mind filled with hundreds of scenarios—none good—that could have befallen her daughter and partner. Pushing herself to concentrate on the task at hand, she armed her LRMs and charged her particle cannon. Both effective long-range weapons and combined with her gunnery skills, she could take down bigger mechs.

On Kimmy's radar, two silhouettes appeared—an indirect fire indicator, meaning her computer couldn't see them, but someone else in her troop could. *It must be Nicole.* The computers didn't share target information, only location. It was an upgrade Athena was working on. Still, even the AI struggled to get the different mech computers to talk to each other.

A red ring closed around both targets in Kimmy's Head's Up Display. The targets were behind a long ridge and out of her direct line of sight, but Kimmy's computer could see them, thanks to Nicole. What Kimmy couldn't do with an indirect fire attack was target specific parts of the enemy mech. She would have to fire blind. *Still, it'll be enough to get their attention.* She pulled her trigger, and a pod of five LRMs burst from their tubes and streaked through the atmosphereless sky up and over the ridge, disappearing behind it.

Kimmy didn't get the damage report from her computer, but Nicole squawked over the radio, "Nice shot, Apocalypse. I'm hunkered down on the far west end of the ridge, and I've got eyes on two andra class mechs with Blood Witch markings. They're holding position over Jynx's downed mech. Let me know when you want me to slime them."

Oh shit. How did they find us? The Blood Witches were an all-female mech unit in service to the Aven Federation. Kimmy and the rest of the Angels' original goal had been to complete the five-year hitch in the Aven Foreign

Legion and then join the Blood Witches. However, the Avenions' treatment of women, non-vanilla Humans—those without pale skin—and alien races led to the Angels stealing an assault ship and forming their own mercenary unit.

"Nemesis, what're the specs on those?" Kimmy didn't want to wait for her computer to get in range.

"Seventy-five-ton heavies. Armed with particle cannons and large, medium, and small beams. They pack a punch. I'm staying out of range and haven't fired yet, but your shot will wake them up and let them know someone's out here."

Someone is, but not enough. Kimmy ran the battle in her head, and no matter how she played it, her four light mechs wouldn't be enough to take down two heavies—but there was no place to retreat. What few reinforcements they had—the living metal Morphicons—were on War Cat, and they had as much or more trouble with the moondust than the mechs did. *It doesn't matter. They're not here.*

"Apocalypse, Poison. We're climbing the ridge and have two enemy mechs on radar. We're headed toward them now."

"Roger. Did you copy Nemesis' scout report?"

"Roger. What's the plan of attack for these big girls?"

I'm thinking about it. No option was good, but one was better than the others. "Our best bet is for your troop to get them into a Circle of Death while my troop snipes from a distance."

"Sounds good. We'll crest the ridge and start our attack."

Kimmy bit her lip while admiring Karen's and Zhi's bravery. *Still, taking a pair of light mechs against a pair of heavies...that's valor.* The pair were fighter pilots trained in Kimmy's Imperial Navy, and she expected nothing less. In another universe, Kimmy ruled over a different Earth—Earth 832—as empress.

On Kimmy's radar, Karen and Zhi moved to engage the Blood Witches. She had one trick up her sleeve. When they arrived on the periphery, they'd bought a broken Gavion Sparkler from a junk merchant. Sprokkit, a Morphicon medic and scientist, tinkered with the device and got it working along with an upgrade. It was mounted on Nicole's firefly, waiting for an opportunity to be put to use. *No better time than now.*

As Karen and Zhi disappeared over the ridge, the Blood witches changed direction on the radar to engage the newcomers. Kimmy pulled her trigger, firing another salvo of missiles to give her side some cover while they closed the distance.

"Nemesis, hit it," ordered Kimmy. She hoped the jammer worked. In theory, it would disable the Blood Witches' computers' radars and HUDs, keeping them from helping aim and locating their attackers. If the Blood Witches carried missiles, it would keep them from locking on their targets.

On the radar, the Blood Witches stopped, appearing to have lost their targets.

"Attacking now," reported Karen.

Kimmy wished her mech would move faster. She was at the ridge base when a tone in her helmet alerted her that her missiles were ready to fire. Pulling the trigger, the bright lights of the rockets streaked by her cockpit.

"Apocalypse," called Nicole, "do you want me to open fire?"

Kimmy hit the switch for the radar's terrain overlay. It displayed her on the back side of the ridge and Nicole far to the west, outside the Blood Witches' radar. One of Sprokkit's sparkler upgrades gave Nicole an extra wide radar view, allowing her to see the enemy undetected.

"Do you have a lock?"

"Sure do."

Nicole's firefly carried one pod of fifteen LRMs. Speed was her saving grace, as she would be useless in a stand-up fight. Seeing how far Nicole was from the Blood Witches, Kimmy didn't think she was in much danger, especially with Zhi and Karen attacking at close range.

"Nemesis, bring the rain, then scoot. See if you can get behind them."

From her left, bright orange streaks blocked the stars as the deadly stream of missiles streaked toward their target. LRMs were a tradeoff of fuel and warhead. A single LRM warhead was small, but its fuel capacity gave them a long range. Entire mech loadouts were built around the idea of swarming targets with LRMs to knock them over or cause catastrophic damage.

"Mom?" called Jynx in a weak and scared voice.

"Jynx!" Kimmy nearly shouted. "What are you still doing in your mech? I told you to get out!"

"I'm scared, Mommy. I can feel their footsteps and…and I don't want to go outside. What if they step on me?"

Kimmy let out a sigh parents reserve for their kids when they don't listen. "Jynx, it's too late now. You're going to have to sit tight. Poison and Venom are almost to you and will drive off the Blood Witches. Are you buckled into your seat?"

"Yes, Mommy...I just...I don't...want to..."

I've never heard her sound so scared. "Jynx, listen to me. We'll get you out, but I need you to be brave. You need to do what Momma taught you about controlling your emotions and actions. Remember what they taught you at West Point about being under enemy fire? This is the same thing. Dig deep and screw your courage to the sticking place. We will come for you, understand?"

Chelsea took a deep breath and was silent until she replied, "Yes, Mom."

Sounds like I woke her up.

"Ok, Jynx, we'll be there as soon as we can."

"Ok, Mom. I'll strap in and wait."

Kimmy sighed again. *Kids. I thought she was mature enough to handle this.* Dealing with Chelsea's fear didn't alleviate Kimmy's, even though she had put it aside—mostly. She was scared for both Chelsea and Kita. That Kita could be dead haunted the edge of Kimmy's mind. Only the need to rescue Chelsea and get rid of the Blood Witches kept her from breaking into tears. Kimmy couldn't do that. She needed to lead the Angels into battle.

"Here we go!" whooped Zhi.

On the radar, Zhi's and Karen's mechs circled the Blood Witches in a Circle Of Death maneuver. This was a favorite technique of light mech pilots, allowing them to use their speed and rapid weapon cycling rate to their advantage. The constant movement and changing of direction made it hard to target the nimble light mechs while they punished their target with their smaller weapons.

Damn. I wish I could see what they were doing. Kimmy would have to wait until her computer had line-of-sight on the mechs before she would get telemetry data. *By then, it could be too late.*

Knowing there was little she could do to influence the battle. She watched the countdown timer on her missile pod. Once it hit zero, it was reloaded and ready. She cursed both the timer and mech to go faster. The timer reached zero with hundreds of yards to go. She pulled the trigger, hoping her missiles would be a nasty surprise for the recipient Blood Witch.

"Watch out! Hot tamale!" crowed Zhi.

Sounds like they're getting some hits in.

"Splash in," reported Nicole, meaning Kimmy's missiles hit their target.

Kimmy fired another salvo of missiles. "What's the enemy status? Has anyone taken any damage?"

"Negative on damage," answered Nicole. "I'm about to their backside."

"I'm hitting them with everything I've got," said Karen. "Target one shows yellow across the left leg, left arm, right arm, and right torso. Target two is showing yellow in the left arm, left torso, and its temperature is rising. I've taken a few shots from their short and medium beams, but the damage is only superficial."

"I'm concentrating my flamers on target two and getting her coolant temp up," announced Zhi. "That should keep them from firing at us."

Kimmy nodded. If the mech's core temperature reached a critical threshold, it could not fire its weapons without causing internal damage to the mech or damage to the weapons. The flamers mounted on Zhi's widow maker aimed to force the enemy into a shutdown where critical strikes could be made to cripple or kill the mech.

"I've had minor beam burns that scuffed and gouged my armor, but I'm alright," said Zhi. "They're too dizzy to get a proper shot off."

"Keep that napalm flowing," ordered Kimmy. "These Blood Witches—for some reason—brought beam weapons to a moon. If we can overheat them, we can kill them."

"Kill them?" retorted Karen. "We should salvage them."

The thought hadn't crossed Kimmy's mind. A pair of heavy mechs—even one—would boost their combat power. Kimmy shook her head. *Easy girl. We have to rescue Chelsea and Kita first. We'll worry about salvage later—if we can bring them down…a big if.*

"We need to rescue Jynx and Fallen Angel—that's our mission. If we get them to retreat, I'll be happy."

Kimmy fired a missile salvo with the ridge top in sight. Once there, she should have nice sightlines toward the Blood Witch mechs. She would have to monitor her heat buildup, as her particle cannon generated a fair amount. But the heat-to-damage ratio was worth it. To ensure she wouldn't run into heat problems, she cycled her coolant—a toxic brew circling throughout the mech to keep weapons and the engine cool. Cycling would swap her active coolant for the cooler reserve. It took time but would be completed by the time she crested the ridge.

The Blood Witches made a tactical error using high heat-generating beam weapons in a lunar biome. The lack of atmosphere reduced heat sink effectiveness by twenty-five percent. This oversight meant the Blood Witches' firing rate would be reduced to prevent overheating.

"Apocalypse," Nicole radioed. "I'm on the north side of the ridge and have both targets lit. I've got a rear arc shot on bogey one and a left-side arc shot on bogey two. Who do you want me to target?"

Kimmy frowned. *I wish I had the Blood Witches' damage reports.* Calling for the report would take valuable time and take the other pilots' attention away from the fight. She would have to gamble and go with what should pay the highest dividends.

"Nemesis, shoot the bogey in the rear. Hopefully, it'll scare it off."

Most mech armor was thinnest in the rear to save on weight. The thin rear torso armor offered a quick and easy path to the engine, ammo storage, and weapons that were heavily armored if you attacked from the front.

"Roger. Splash out."

Kimmy didn't see the splash, even as her cockpit crested the ridge top. She took another twenty steps before easing back on the throttle to let her and her computer see the battle below.

The Blood Witch pair was on either side of Chelsea's downed mech. *From the looks of it, they shot out her legs.* Zhi and Karen were circling the two larger mechs, firing. The left Blood Witch mech glowed red across its torso and legs from Zhi's napalm. The other Blood Witch mech had its right side exposed. Both seemed to try to time shots as the nimble light mechs ran by. When they did fire, their light and medium beams would show in Kimmy's HUD.

Time to let them know I've arrived.

Kimmy's HUD lit up with information when the computer finished analyzing the scene. The left Blood Witch mech covered in napalm showed orange across the entire mech, and its temperature was near the red line. The right Blood Witch mech had taken less damage. Most of it was yellow or orange—damaged by Karen's beams and machine guns—and its temperature was dangerously high from firing its beams trying to hit the Angels.

The high temperature explains their lack of fighting back.

Moving the targeting reticle over the left Blood Witch mech, Kimmy locked on to the mech's central torso. It was the most heavily armored area on a mech, but the area was orange, and the particle cannon Kimmy wielded could do substantial damage. The particle cannon charges caused an Electronic Magnetic Pulse when they struck, shutting down the target's electrical components and stunning them. Kimmy pulled the trigger when the computer beeped that it had a lock, firing both her missiles and particle cannon.

Missiles roared by on her left, and a sparkling blue cloud of charged particles traveling at the speed of light flew down the front of the ridge and struck the wounded mech. Kimmy's computer registered the particle strike and ensuing EMP. The missiles slammed into the stricken mech's torso. The badly injured mech stopped moving and kneeled in a defensive crouch while its systems rebooted.

"Girls! The west Blood Witch is stunned. Take it down!" ordered Kimmy.

"Coming around on its rear now," replied Karen. "Preparing an alpha strike."

Kimmy hoped Karen's soldier mech's mix of medium and light lasers could punch through the Blood Witch's damaged rear armor. She carried four Short-Range Missiles—unlike LRMs, the stubby SRMs carried large armor-piercing payloads which could blast through inches of armor like a shotgun.

"Incoming!" warned Nicole. "We've got an Aven recovery ship coming in."

Shit. What in the hell are they going to do? A recovery ship was used to salvage damaged and destroyed mechs. Kimmy didn't want to lose her heavy mech prize, but it seemed odd the Blood Witches would call it in with the battle still underway.

"Nemesis! Target that recovery ship. See if you can scare it off."

"Roger. I'm locking on now. Will be ready to fire in thirty seconds."

Kimmy grit her teeth. In this type of battle, thirty seconds was a lifetime. Checking her weapons, charging her particle cannon would take almost as long. Her missiles would be ready sooner, and she moved her targeting reticle over the slow-moving ship.

"Nemesis, does that ship have an odd course?"

"What do you mean? Looks like it's headed to the Blood Witches."

Kimmy guessed it was hard to tell from Nicole's vantage point. From her position on the ridge, the recovery ship wasn't headed to either Blood Witch but between them. *Why would they...OH SHIT! CHELSEA!*

"Girls! Shoot the ship! They're after Jynx!"

"No shot," replied Karen.

"It's out of my arc," reported Zhi.

"Apocalypse, you and Nemesis take aim at the ship," suggested Karen. "Venom and I will keep pressure on the Blood Witches."

Kimmy's ears burned red from being countermanded. *Karen is a Navy captain. She's got way more experience than I do at leading combat forces.* A feeling of helplessness overcame her as the recovery ship hovered over the battle—directly above Chelsea.

"Jynx," Kimmy called, fighting back tears and the million-pound weight on her chest. "Chelsea—know that Momma and I love you, and whatever happens, we will find you and rescue you. I'm sorry—I love you—it's going to be alright...just..."

"Mom? What's going on?" cried Chelsea.

Kimmy's computer beeped, telling her she was locked on. Pulling the trigger, Kimmy hoped the attack would scare away the ship. Recovery ships weren't meant to be used during the battle but after and had thin armor. Someone was gambling with the machine. The knot in Kimmy's stomach told her they held the high cards—even if all of Kimmy's mechs fired on the ship, it would take more than they had to bring it down fast enough to save Chelsea.

When the recovery ship's belly doors opened and the magnetic hoist lowered, dread crept up Kimmy's back. It made her dark, wavy hair tingle. She had never suffered such a loss or the feeling of helplessness so total. Her child—her baby—was about to be taken from her, and there was nothing she could do. Tears flooded her eyes, and a chest-wrenching sob escaped her lips. Out of desperation, she jammed the throttle forward, sending her ocelot sprinting down the ridge, ignoring the weapon's ready tone in her ear.

Something, instinct probably, caused her to pull the trigger, but she'd never selected a target, and the computer did it for her. Set to target the most damaged first, the computer locked onto the left Blood Witch and fired an alpha strike. Kimmy's missiles and particles slammed into the unguarded and disengaged mech's torso with an explosion of fire, smoke, and sparks.

The damaged mech fell forward, crumpling into the moondust. Its center torso crumpled from the damage. The recovery ship's magnets settled on Chelsea's mech.

"Nice shot!" whooped Zhi as she maneuvered around the downed heavy mech, turning her torso to aim her weapons at the remaining Blood Witch.

Kimmy didn't hear her. In her roiling emotions, she knew only one thing: she had to get to Chelsea.

"Uh-oh...shit. I'm in the dirt," reported Karen.

The remaining Blood Witch had stuck out her arm and clotheslined Karen's much smaller mech.

"I'm coming," replied Zhi.

The pair had, until now, pulled off a textbook COD: both running opposite each other, keeping their weapons trained on their targets while maintaining their high speed. Now, Karen was on her back, struggling to stand while the Blood Witch positioned herself to step on the downed mech.

Kimmy focused solely on her daughter. The computer calculated over a hundred yards to go. She didn't care about the rest of the battle. She would save Chelsea or die trying, even as the recovery ship's lines pulled tight and lifted Chelsea's mech out of the moondust.

"Mom! Mom! What's happening?" yelled Chelsea.

"I'm sorry! I'm sorry! I'm sorry," Kimmy wailed as she repeatedly pulled the trigger, desperately trying to make her weapons respond.

"Mommy! I'm going up! Mommy! What's going on? Don't let them take me!"

Kimmy couldn't answer as her breaths came in ragged gasps and sobs. Through her tears, she kept her mech aimed at where Chelsea had been. Lifting her head, she focused the targeting reticle on the recovery ship. But dared not fire now that Chelsea was aboard.

Chelsea and her mech were hoisted aboard as Kimmy reached where her daughter had been. Striking the console in frustration mixed with an emotional cacophony, Kimmy jerked her control stick to the right, taking aim at the only thing she could take her fear, rage, and pain out on.

With a metallic *thud*, Kimmy slammed her ocelot into the back of the Blood Witch, assaulting Karen.

The Blood Witch stomped on Karen several times while ignoring the damage by Zhi. Kimmy hit the heavy mech as it raised its leg. The blow was enough to destabilize the Blood Witch's advanced gyros, sending her toppling into the moondust.

"Wow!" yelled Zhi. "I'm calling my shot!"

Kimmy tore off her helmet and buried her face in her hands. Her console switched to show the gyro working to stabilize her mech, and her left arm and torso blinked yellow, showing the damage from the collision.

"I'm...sorry...so...sorry," she wailed into her tear-slicked palms. "I...failed..." Undoing her safety harness, Kimmy slumped forward onto her console, thumping her forehead on the plastic display. Kimmy's mech sensed she was out of her chair and lowered the mech into a defensive posture.

"Apocalypse? What are you doing?" asked Zhi, her voice coming from the cockpit speaker.

Kimmy's reply died in her throat and was replaced by a sob.

"Let her be...for now," ordered Karen. "Nemesis, Venom, concentrate fire on the remaining mech. We have to kill it while it's down."

"Roger," said Zhi. "My flamers are dry, but I've got enough ammo in my twenties and machine guns to do some damage. I've been saving my beams. They're nice and cool."

"Hit her with everything you got."

"Splash out," reported Nicole.

"Splash in," replied Karen. "Nice shot, rear center torso."

"All Angel elements, this is War Cat Main. The enemy's taken flight, and we're headed back to your location."

"Negative, War Cat Main," replied Karen. "Fallen Angel needs to be recovered ASAP. Her status is unknown."

"Roger. Wilco. We'll find her and retrieve her. Do you want us to drop off the other troops to reinforce you?"

"Roger. The fighting might be over by the time they get here, but we don't know if they'll be back."

"Do you have Fallen Angel's location?"

"She went down somewhere on the northwest side of the crater. Our location is just north of the ridge on the west side of the crater."

"Roger. We'll keep you informed."

Kimmy hadn't realized she was holding her breath until a big sob struck her. In her desperation to save Chelsea, she'd forgotten about Kita. Her universe came crashing down. Her daughter and her partner were both in danger, and there was nothing she could do. With a series of loud sobs, each ripping a chunk of her heart out, she curled up in her chair and wished the world would end.

"Apocalypse?" called Nicole gently. "Kimmy, are you ok?"

The sounds of a mech outside barely registered through Kimmy's tears, heartbreak, and mental fog. The mech stopped in front, and the torso turned to face her.

"I see her, Poison," reported Nicole. "She's got her helmet off and not strapped into her chair."

"Roger. There's not much we can do for her here. We need to get the battlefield policed and decide what to do."

"Roger. I will secure the Blood Witches and make sure they don't get squirrelly."

"War Cat Main, Poison," called Karen.

"Yes?"

"When you finish recov—rescuing Fallen Angel, I need you to pick up Apocalypse. She seems incapacitated by events."

"Oh, dear. We will pick her up and then get the fallen mechs. Rivet, Sapper, Cardinal, and the Morphicons are standing by to help with security."

"Roger. Watch the scopes to see if they come back."

"So far, the group that attacked us has fled."

"Tell the other Angels to standby—maybe for combat, but for sure, we have a wounded Angel, and she's going to need help."

"Roger. I will tell the girls to be ready."

Kimmy reached down the side of her chair, grabbed the first thing she could find—a flare—and threw it at the console, trying to get it to shut up. The other Angels' chatter only reinforced her loss.

"Fallen Angel rescued," announced Athena. "Moving toward the battle-field to pick up Apocalypse."

Kimmy's eyes filled with tears as she dove onto the bare metal floor behind her chair. She curled into a ball and covered her head with her arms. The sobs that racked her body made her struggle for air. The unknown condition of Kita—her partner and soulmate—was more than she could bear. Living without her was unthinkable. She'd faced the idea of Kita's death, but that was always abstract. Today it was real. The unthinkable had happened, and Kimmy wasn't prepared. *Would I ever be prepared?*

Another thought punctuated Kimmy's grief over Kita—Chelsea. Her daughter was gone, and there was nothing she could do. The grief over both battled and intertwined, creating a chaotic emotional hurricane Kimmy couldn't bring to heel. It swirled, tearing at her soul—her whole life was falling apart, and there was nothing she could do.

The metal *bang* of the magnetic hoist was lost in Kimmy's overwhelming sorrow. The force of going up and the swaying only upset her.

"NO!" Kimmy screamed at the metal and plastic cockpit. "I don't want to go! I can't face her." Slouching back against the rear of the cockpit, Kita's face—her floor-length blonde hair and captivating blue eyes—floated in front of Kimmy.

Kimmy's ocelot settled on the deck in a mech bay aboard War Cat. Out the window, scaffolding moved into position around the mech.

Sniffing and weeping, Kimmy didn't hear the cockpit hatch open.

"Hey, I got her!" yelled Lizzy.

The young Army officer entered the cockpit. Lizzy kneeled next to her friend and one-time rival and touched Kimmy's hand.

"Hey," she whispered. "They pulled Kita from her mech and rushed her to medbay."

Only a word penetrated Kimmy's fog. "Kita?" she whispered around broken sobs and quick breaths.

Lizzy put her arms around Kimmy. "Yeah, that tough old bird is hard to kill. UV's people have her in medbay. I guess Kita's messed up pretty bad."

The sound Kimmy emanated was something between a gasp and a gulp. She leaned her tear-slicked face against Lizzy's shoulder. She didn't know how to react. Kita was alive...but for how long? And what would be her condition? The uncertainty swirled in her chest and gripped her heart like an icy hand. The unknown multiplied her grief.

Lizzy held Kimmy until Anna stuck her head in the hatch.

"Is she dead?" The Russian assassin asked.

"No," replied Lizzy gently, contrasting Anna's harsh tone. "Just heartbroken."

"Crying over one's mate and child is fine, but not here. The service crews need to work."

"Such compassion," teased Lizzy.

"Kita would understand."

"Help me get her out." Lizzy nudged Kimmy. "Hey, we need to clear the mech. We can go to the lounge if you want."

Kimmy didn't resist as Lizzy picked her up and guided her to Anna and the hatch. The Angels helped Kimmy through the hatch onto the scaffolding. The ocelot was only twenty-three feet, and the elevator ride to the bay floor was short.

At the opening to the mech bay, all available Angels stood waiting. Lizzy guided Kimmy to the others. The first in line was Velositi.

"Oh, Kimmy, I am so sorry," the Morphicon leader said, wrapping her arms around Kimmy.

A cold numbness befell Kimmy from when she was in Lizzy's arms to Velositi's. She was still crying, but being pressed against Velositi's warm metal exterior was comforting. It was the first time she'd ever been comforted by Velositi. Kimmy now understood why Kita liked it.

A sob escaped Kimmy's throat, bringing the rest of the Angels in for a hug. Kimmy wasn't sure who was there, but she was buried in arms and sympathy, making her feel warm and safe. Whatever happened, she was with people who cared and would do everything they could to heal Kita and get Chelsea back.

CHAPTER 02

ASTARI IIIa
WAR CAT ASSAULT SHIP
LUNAR BIOME
¥51,834
1, OCTOBER 4003

K IMMY SAT, LEANING HER head against Velositi's arm in War Cat's lounge, surrounded by her friends. But life in a mercenary unit never stopped. A troop of Angels returned to patrolling the area around the mine, and those with Kimmy were prepared to deploy if trouble erupted.

Having brought her emotions under control with the others' help, Kimmy was numb as uncertainty ate at her. It was all she could do not to grab Ultraviolet and shake her for a status update on Kita. She knew the hive mind was busy doing her best, controlling the doctors and techs working to save Kita. The Angel didn't need Kimmy hanging over her shoulder.

"Kimmy, you ok?" said Velositi. "You have gone quiet."

Kimmy blinked. "I'm numb. I'm scared of what will happen to Kita and not knowing about Chelsea eats at my stomach."

Lizzy kneeled in front of Kimmy and gave her a hug. Her bright blue eyes portrayed her youthful exuberance and optimism. "Come on, don't worry. Kita will be bouncing off the walls in no time. Then, those Blood Wenches better look out. She will hunt them down and beat them to death with their own mechs to get Chelsea back. Shit. It'll happen so quick Sprokkit won't have time to fix the mechs you smoked out of them."

A slight smile crossed Kimmy's lips. *If anyone can do that, Kita can.* Still, this was the first time one of them had been seriously wounded in their adventures. They'd suffered serious setbacks before, but they always overcame them—together. The thought of Kita tearing around the universe, kicking down doors, and killing those in her way brought comfort to Kimmy's heart. That her partner would know how to get Chelsea back and could make it happen made her feel better.

"I thought my duty lay in the group," grumped Sprokkit from across the room. "I can evaluate the damage and see what needs to be done. It is not like I am doing anything useful here."

"You will stay," ordered Velositi as she pointed the larger Morphicon to his corner. "We are here for Kimmy. To comfort, support, and be with her in her time of need. Once Kita is attended to, and Kimmy settled, we will continue our missions."

"Hey, what if more of those creepos show up?" asked Bernoot. "We missed all the fun last time. I wanna blast some metal."

Velositi leaned into Kimmy. "Is it ok if I let them go? I do not want them to bring you down with their complaining."

Kimmy chuckled dryly. "It's fine. Nobody has to stay if they don't want to. I know you all have things to do. And I am feeling...better. I'm sure my spirits will soar when Kita gets out of surgery."

"I guess that's permission for you boys to move along," said Ash'a, the golden scales on her head and back moving in patterns to show her amusement. "But I better come with you, Sprokkit, so I can get a list of parts we'll need to repair our catch."

The Aurorian stood, wearing a black jumpsuit with the arms tied around her waist, exposing her back and head full of colorful scales. A matching black bikini top covered her breasts. She wore a pair of boots with a five-inch heel. Aurorians never walked flat-footed and loved fashion.

Ash'a gave Kimmy a hug and a kiss on the cheek. "Here's wishing on the stars that Kita recovers quickly and rejoins the flock. I can't help but feel somewhat responsible that I couldn't get her a better mech."

Kimmy gasped. "Ash'a, don't think that way. You found us the best hardware we could buy. I—I never told you how impressed I was at the price you got for the scorpions. What you got bought us the best the periphery had to offer."

"I know, but the comet is the worst medium mech—no army fields it. I should have done better, found something else—"

"Ash'a, you did the best you could, and you know Kita. She had to have the biggest, even if it was junk. That's not your fault. We took what we could get. It's no one's fault...well, maybe Kita thinking she could go up against two heavy mechs by herself. I know she was trying to protect Chelsea, but..."

Kimmy shook her head. Kita always had to be the best—and she almost always was. If not, she threw a fit and stormed off. This time it cost her—them. *And I'll do everything I can to ensure she returns to form.*

Kimmy took Ash'a hands. "Don't blame yourself. It's no one's fault. All we can do is regroup and move forward. When Kita's better, we'll figure out a plan for Chelsea. We have another twenty-seven days on our contract. That should be plenty of time."

"I thought you'd want to go after Chelsea right away," said Nicole.

"Every fiber in my body wants to," replied Kimmy, "but we're going to need Kita. Until then, we regroup and get our resources ready."

"We have an issue," announced Ultraviolet.

Kimmy raised an eyebrow while trying to read the Mi Prii's body language. It was unnerving how Ultraviolet sat on the couch, legs crossed, hands in her lap with a cheerful look on her face while she controlled over two hundred minds on the ship with ease. She and Kita got on amazingly well. If there was a dynamic between sociopath and hive mind, Kimmy wasn't aware of it.

"What is it?" asked Kimmy, deciding the only way she would get the needed information was to ask.

"We are conducting after-action inspections on the ship, and my engineers have discovered damage to the FTL drive coupling. It's the piece that joins to the jump rod so that when it goes faster-than-light, we go with it."

Kimmy looked between Athena, the AI in control of the ship, and Ultraviolet trying to gauge how serious the problem was. But Athena was just as impossible to read as Ultraviolet.

"The ship sustained some damage from evading the Aven Foreign Legion ships," admitted Athena. "Internal checks show minor damage that would not interfere with normal operation of the ship, but I have not run a test on the FTL drive. I will do so now."

At least she's forthcoming. "UV, do we have a spare coupling on the ship?"

Ultraviolet uncrossed her deer-like legs, putting her split hooves together. "No. Most of the spare parts War Cat carries are for the mechs. We do not have many spare parts for the ship. The Aven Federation would return the ship to ground-side dock or a construction ship for repairs."

We don't have that option. Kimmy turned to Ash'a. "I hate to put one more thing on your plate, but can you find the part?"

The Aurorian's scales rippled, displaying a rainbow of colors around her head and down her back. "I would need a description and a part number. As I have no idea what I'm looking for."

"Any idea how much this is going to cost?" asked Kimmy, knowing the unit had just over fifty thousand credits left after selling the scorpion trainer mechs they stole along with War Cat.

"It's not a simple part to be replaced," said Ultraviolet. "It requires calibration and precision. Otherwise, we could jump straight to the Void if it's done wrong."

"Could you help with that, Sprokkit?" Velositi prodded the scientist. "You repaired our ship."

Sprokkit grunted, then sighed. "I could if I knew what I was doing."

"Instructions shouldn't be hard to find," said Ash'a.

"Our knowledge base says the government usually supplies the part," interjected Ultraviolet. "But its per item cost in the Aven Federation parts manual is nearly a million credits."

Kimmy choked, trying to fight back tears. *How are we going to make that much out here?* Defin was only paying them sixty-five thousand for two months, and that was before everything that had to be paid for. "Can—can we even make that much out here?" Kimmy looked at Ash'a, who acted as the group's business manager.

"Ah...the short answer is no, at least not with the contracts Kita instructed me to take. There are more lucrative jobs, but they require bigger mechs, and the risk is substantial. Not only to life and equipment but angering the states is a real possibility."

In a pinch, Ash'a was also the political advisor, but Kimmy was no stranger to governments, having run her own global empire. Unlike Ash'a, Kimmy spent more time in the cockpit than studying intergalactic politics. *But I might have to start...including which state to align with? And if we did, would they pay for the repairs? Question is, what would they want in return? I can see us getting every shitty mission they can dream up.*

Kimmy laid her worries aside. "Ash'a, get with UV and see if you can find the part locally or if they can deliver it."

"How are we going to cover the cost?" asked Ash'a.

"Credit? Beyond that, I don't know. We could do some work in exchange."

"This limits us to the local area," reminded Ash'a. "The jump ships in the area link about a dozen systems, but again, hitching a ride will cost us."

A tingling chill crawled up Kimmy's back as she tried to shut down her mind. She didn't want to deal with this now—not with Kita in surgery. But the others were looking at her for leadership and to make decisions Kita would normally make.

"Let's see about finding the part and how much it'll cost first," said Kimmy, trying to narrow down what she had to worry about.

"Yes," said Velositi. "Let us not heap all our troubles on Kimmy. She has her own worries. We can deal with whatever issues the attack has caused at the command meeting."

Kimmy pressed the side of her head against Velositi to say *thanks*. Velositi had been with Kita and Kimmy since the beginning and was the third link in their throuple. And right now, with Kita's condition unknown, Kimmy was thankful Velositi was there.

"We apologize," said Ultraviolet. "We are sorry if we disrupted your grieving."

Kimmy shook her head. "It's ok. I just...I just need to know about Kita and her status. Once I know that we can plan on what to do next."

"If her injuries are so severe, maybe we should send her home," said Sprokkit.

Fear gripped Kimmy. She didn't want to live without Kita. Going back to the Reality Computer would heal whatever injuries Kita had sustained. "I don't know what's possible after Leaf didn't come back. The only way out is to die and that could be permadeath. Ryan can pull us out but only Kita can contact him to tell him."

"Unfortunately, she is unconscious," interjected Ultraviolet.

Kimmy exchanged a look with Velositi. "And I know Kita. She won't want to go back until we find Chelsea. She'll do everything in her power to free her."

"That might not be much."

Kimmy froze. "What do you mean?"

Ultraviolet crossed her legs. "The injuries she sustained were catastrophic."

"What?"

Ultraviolet smiled and stood. "Perhaps it is best we show you. The autodoc is finishing up. We can go to the observation window while the nurses and doctors dress the wounds. This will take some time."

A lump in Kimmy's throat nearly choked her. She grabbed Velositi's arm and squeezed, causing the Morphicon to put an arm around her.

"Ultraviolet," said Velositi.

"Hmm, yes?"

"Be gentle. Kita is our partner, and it has already been an emotional day."

"We apologize. We do not wish to cause you or anyone any undue stress or grief. Just know we have done the best we can with the facilities on the ship."

A tear trickled down Kimmy's cheek. *That doesn't sound good.*

"Come," said Velositi. "Let's go see Kita."

The robot-like Morphicon stood, helping Kimmy up by the arm. Kimmy clung to Velositi, her warm metallic body radiating a sense of calm through her.

Velositi escorted Kimmy through the ship, ducking her eight-foot frame through the human-sized doors and bulkheads. It was an inconvenience for the light-framed Morphicon but a problem for Sprokkit, who stood twelve feet tall and kept him from certain areas of the ship—like the medbay.

"I will go down to the mech bay," announced Sprokkit.

"You can watch from there," ordered Velositi.

"If I must."

"Remember, you are a part of this team and family. One of us is injured and needs our compassion and sympathy. You can spare thirty minutes."

His blue eyes glowed intently. "Thirty minutes I could spend working on something useful—like new heat sinks for the teams' mechs." Sprokkit stomped down the hallway in the direction of the mech bay.

"I wonder what he'd be like if Kita had given him emotions," Kimmy said with a chuckle.

"I am sure he would be more miserable and insufferable than he is now," Velositi sighed.

"We can't all be emotional pillars. At least he wants to do what he can for the team."

"He is most happy when he is at his workbench, puttering on a project."

Kimmy laughed. "You make him sound like he's an old man."

Velositi's eyes lit—how they showed emotion. "He is much older than I am. The elders sent him with me to be a voice of reason and restraint—I do not think he likes that I have matured and he no longer has the sway he once did."

"He seems to have put his energy into the triplets."

Velositi chirped laughter. "Yes, they are always in a hurry to get away from him, except Stunner. She finds him fascinating, and in return, he teaches and encourages her—much like Ryan."

Kimmy remembered when Ryan and Sprokkit first met. The pair were inseparable and always working on something. Now, Ryan led the Universe Room back home on Roost, trying to recreate a stable universe in hopes of one day recreating the original universe, Universe Zero.

When they reached the medbay, Ultraviolet moved to the front as the ship's doctor came to the door with ultraviolet-glowing eyes. He didn't say a word, just stood like he was waiting for a command.

"Please, we hope you will understand," said Ultraviolet. "The ship has limited ability to treat the wounds sustained by Kita."

Kimmy gulped as dread crept up from her toes. "What happened to her?"

"The Blood Witches struck her core and ruptured her coolant system. The corrosive and toxic coolant flooded her cockpit. Parts of her body were submerged in the liquid for some time. What wasn't was exposed to the extreme temperatures of the core melting down. As they say, it is a miracle she is alive—it may also be a tragedy that she is."

Kimmy squeezed Velositi's hand so hard she thought she might deform the biometal. "I have to see her."

Ultraviolet nodded. "Kita is under heavy sedation and will be for a while as her body accepts the skin grafts."

Kimmy pressed her lips together, trying to imagine her partner's state. "Please. Let me see her."

"Of course." Ultraviolet led the group through the small medbay, past the autodoc room, to one of four patient recovery rooms. A door to room three opened, revealing a lump obscured by a medical tent. Ultraviolet touched a monitor on the wall, and Sprokkit appeared. "Excuse the tent. Kita's immune system is compromised, and we must do all we can to prevent infection."

Kimmy released Velositi's hand and took six shaky steps to the head of the bed. Kita was covered in bandages. Her fabled floor-length hair was gone. Skin grafts covered her torso, her left arm, and—"UV, where are Kita's legs and right arm?" she exclaimed, alarmed.

"They were the parts submerged in the coolant. By the time we rescued her, the liquid had eaten away the flesh and bone. Unfortunately, medbay is not equipped to handle amputees. We have no prosthetics for her. Normally, someone with her injuries would be transferred to an Aven Federation hospital ship equipped to treat such injuries."

"What happened that her entire body requires skin grafts?" asked Velositi.

"It was thermal damage. Her exposed skin was burned off, and her clothing melted to her. The autodoc removed it, but she had no skin. The skin grafts will act as skin for her."

"Will she always require them?" said Kimmy in a shaky voice.

"Yes. They are synthetic. We do not have the technology to grow her natural skin." Ultraviolet bowed her head. "We are sorry, Kimmy. We did the best we could with what was available. This medbay is only meant to be the first response, and more advanced treatments are given later in a proper facility. Please, we did everything we were able with what we had—"

Kimmy put an arm around the distraught Mi Prii. "UV, it's not your fault. You did the best you could with what we had. We'll figure something out. I just—it's just…" Tears leaked from the corner of her eyes as she glanced at Kita. "I'm not seeing Kita. I see a lump…which is probably a good thing that I can't connect what I see and what I know. It'll make helping her easier, as I won't be as emotionally stricken." She faced the Angels gathered in the room and out the door. "We need to have a command meeting as soon as possible."

"The next patrol arrives in twenty-five minutes," said Ash'a.

"If I may interject," said Sprokkit.

"Yes?" said Kimmy.

"Until we can get proper prosthetics for Kita, I may be able to make something so she can have some mobility."

"That would be fantastic," said Velositi. "I know how much Kita values mobility."

"I will add it to my list," Sprokkit said gruffly.

"Let's go to the lounge," announced Kimmy. "We have a lot we need to discuss."

ASTARI IIIa
WAR CAT ASSAULT SHIP
LUNAR BIOME
Y51,834
1, OCTOBER 4003

KIMMY SAT NEXT TO Velositi in the lounge, staring at her reflection in her coffee. A series of ripples in the dark liquid disrupted her image and replaced it with her daughter's. Kimmy winced and closed her eyes, but Chelsea's face appeared on the back of her eyelids. Opening her eyes with a start, Kimmy took a long pull from her mug.

"Are you ok?" asked Velositi, putting an arm across Kimmy's shoulders.

"Just hoping Chelsea's ok. I know the horrors the Avenions can inflict on a female."

The Aven Foreign Legion training commander thought Kimmy would serve them better as an egg donor at the Baby Factory than as a mech pilot. The realization that the fate she escaped now could befall her daughter turned Kimmy's insides to knots. *I wish I'd known. I'd gladly trade places.*

"Chelsea is strong and smart," said Velositi. "This will be a test for her, which is a good thing. In the hottest forges, the best biometal is made."

"I just hope we've done enough to prepare her. She's much younger than when Kita or I were put through this kind of test."

"From Kita's stories, she seems to have started at an early age."

Kimmy let out a knowing sigh. But Kita always had a safety net—her mother—when she was younger. Here, Kimmy lacked the resources and reach to save Chelsea. That feeling of unpreparedness led to hopelessness. *Please let her make wise decisions and not be like Kita.* In her heart, she knew that wouldn't be the case. Chelsea idolized Kita and wanted to be like her momma—flaws and all.

"We're all here," announced Ash'a from the center of the room.

The room was filled with the Angels that could fit. The others on patrol or in other parts of the ship appeared on a screen to Kimmy's left.

Kimmy bit her lip, debating how best to break the news. "I have some news on Kita." Her voice caught in her throat, and she slopped coffee out of her cup. Kimmy wanted to panic and run.

"Kimmy, are you ok?" asked Velositi.

Kimmy shook her head and waved at Velositi to continue for her.

"Kita...Kita...I...I am sorry..." Velositi's blue eyes dimmed. "UV, if you please."

Ultraviolet sat on a couch with a warm smile that seemed out of place for all but her. She uncrossed her legs and stood, moving to the center of the room.

"Hello, everyone," the Mi Prii began. "During the battle with the Blood Witches, Kita's mech was cored—" Being *cored* is when a mech's engine core is destroyed and usually means instantaneous death.

"Hot damn," exclaimed Lizzy from the screen. She was on patrol. "Of course, Kita survived that. I bet you slapped a bandage on her, and she'll be good by dinnertime."

"Kita's recovery will not be so simple," replied Ultraviolet.

"The heat from the engine burned away her skin. Her limbs were submerged in coolant that ate flesh and bone."

"Oh, fuck me," gasped Nicole. "What's that mean?"

Ultraviolet faced the screen with the concerned pilots. "Kita required three amputations to her legs and left arm. We did the best we could with the resources aboard the ship, but this ship's medbay is not designed for the long-term care Kita will need. Normally, if this was a state vessel, she would be transferred to a hospital ship or a planetary facility. We currently do not have the funds to purchase the care and supplies Kita requires. We can keep her alive and functioning, but we do not believe life like that would be better than death."

Ultraviolet's closing statement was like a dagger to Kimmy's heart. She swallowed hard, trying to suppress her emotions. She set her coffee on the deck between her legs and looked at her feet, drawing strength from her love of Velositi and Kita. When she looked up, her face was stone. She switched to the persona she used on her homeworld, Earth 832, as the Empress.

Kimmy removed Velositi's arm and stood. "No," she said firmly. "We don't kill our friends and loved ones just because we know what's on the other side. We came here to live as mortals—not gods among mortals. If Kita wanted that, she would have died in the cockpit. Instead, she fought to stay alive—because that's what she wants to experience, life. She knows death—she's died more times than all of us put together. We will do what we must to give her the best life possible. If we have to take extra contracts to pay for her recovery, we will. If no one else is willing, then I will, alone. We knew the risks when we came—this is a part of life, as ugly and painful as it is...and we haven't started yet. Kita's not awake. If she decides to go home, that's up to her. But I'm not going to send her there because I don't want anyone to send me home if I was in her place. I will do whatever is necessary to give my partner and friend the best care possible."

"Yeah, but what if Momma-K never wakes up?" said Bombshell, the first Morphicon triplet daughter of Kita and Velositi.

"She will wake up," said Ultraviolet. "She's being kept under sedation, so the grafts and amputations heal without causing discomfort."

"How long will that be?" said Knockout, the second triplet daughter.

"Most likely weeks," replied Ultraviolet.

Ash'a approached Kimmy. "I believe I speak for everyone when I say we will do whatever is necessary to help Kita. She's our friend and has helped all of us. At the very least, we can return the favor. But our predicament leaves us with limited options. We're still under contract. War Cat is damaged, and this region of space offers limited employment."

"Whoa, back up," cried Flexi from the screen. She was out on patrol. "What's wrong with the ship?"

Ultraviolet turned toward the screen. "The ship was damaged evading Aven forces during the battle."

"Yeah, I was onboard for the ride. You've got to let me drive this thing. But what's wrong with it?"

"The FTL coupler was damaged and won't engage the FTL drive."

Flexi's quills along her muzzle rippled. "Can't bang that out in the mech bay."

"I've checked," said Sprokkit. "The part's tolerances require more than what we can do here."

Kimmy grimaced inwardly. If her two best mechanics said they couldn't do it, it was broken beyond repair.

"Ash'a's already searching for the part," said Kimmy. "We also have another problem. They took Chelsea during the battle."

"And here I thought you sent her to her room," quipped Flexi.

The comment fell flat.

"Hey, I'll lead the charge to get her back," announced Flexi somberly.

"I already have someone in mind," said Kimmy. She crossed the room to Anna. The spy was sipping her tea, taking in the conversation. Kimmy kneeled before her. "Anna, I know you like to live your own life, but I have a favor to ask. You're the best at what you do, but I know you came here to be a mech pilot. I wouldn't ask, but as a mother, I'm truly desperate. Will you please find Chelsea and bring her home? I'll give you all the money and supplies I can...just, please, bring my baby back to me."

Anna put her cup and saucer aside on the bench and interlaced her hands over her knees. "Of course, *mat'*," she purred, her words accented from growing up in Russia. "I wondered how long it would take you to ask when I heard Kita was injured. I will find Chelsea and make these Aven dogs pay."

"Thank you." Kimmy bowed her head to the other Angel.

"You're my friend and have shown me nothing but kindness—though I might ask a favor in return."

Kimmy raised an eyebrow. "If you want Kita, she is mine."

"I do not want her forever...a night is plenty."

"You're welcome to spend a night by her bedside. That's where I'll be."

Anna smiled. "I can make her forget her pain."

Kimmy stood, eyeing the assassin. "Produce my daughter, and my only stipulation is that I'm included."

Anna didn't react but said, "I will find Chelsea and bring her home. I promise."

Kimmy returned to the center of the room.

"Anna, that's totally inappropriate," exclaimed Nicole.

Kimmy raised a hand to her friend. "It's ok. If that's what I must do to get Chelsea back—"

"I mean no disrespect to you," said Anna calmly.

Kimmy knew she wasn't lying—an ability provided by her A'ahegre—and that Anna had a thing for Kita. However, Kimmy knew how to handle sociopaths—like Anna and Kita. Kimmy could tell her stipulation rattled Anna, probably not enough to dissuade her from Kita, but enough to make her think about what she wanted. But, to be sure, "Remember, Kita's with me for a reason."

Anna's emotionless smile hinted she'd gotten the message.

"I hate to interrupt," said Karen, "we're on the south side of the crater, and radar is showing two troops inbound."

"About time the pirates showed themselves," said Nicole.

"Track and evade," ordered Kimmy, "until the rest of us get out there. Bernoot, Flexi, move around to the south side to reinforce Karen and Zhi. Velositi, take the Morphicons and block the entrances to the crater. We can't let them reach the mine. We'll back you up as soon as we mount up. Once we're up to strength, we'll move south and catch them in a pincer."

"Maybe we should engage them when they get close to keep them occupied," suggested Karen.

Kimmy thought about it. "Engage them only after Flexi and Bernoot get there. I don't want you getting encircled and shot to pieces."

"Roger," said Karen. "Flexi, where are you?"

"Northwest side."

"You come down the west side, we'll draw them to the east, and you can attack their flank."

"Gotcha. We're moving."

"Ok, everyone, let's mount up and earn our paycheck," said Kimmy. "Athena, you have operational command and control."

"Yes. We're updating the map with the information from Karen's mech. It's not much, but from it, her plan seems sound. We need to invest in better equipment."

Kimmy rolled her eyes at the AI. "I'll add that to the shopping list."

"The better the equipment, the better I can do my part."

"Let's get through the battle first. Let's go."

CHAPTER 03

ASTARI IIIa
DEFIN MINING COLONY
LUNAR BIOME
¥51,834
1, OCTOBER 4003

KIMMY'S OCELOT JOGGED AROUND the southwestern area of the Defin crater with Velositi, Sprokkit, and Anna in her mouse. On the other side of the crater, Nicole led another troop with Lizzy, Knockout, and Bombshell. Zhi and Karen had retreated to the southern edge of the crater and turned their sensors to passive mode to not alert the pirates.

"Either these guys are uber-confident or uber stupid running with their radars lit," commented Zhi.

Kimmy didn't respond and hoped no one else would, either. Everyone on her side was supposed to have their radars off to achieve maximum surprise. The pirates may not detect their active radar transmissions but could—if they had the right communications equipment—detect radio transmissions. Kimmy's group was encrypted, so the pirates may not know what was being said, but they could detect if someone was there.

After this morning's battle, Kimmy wasn't about to be overconfident. With Zhi and Karen's radar off, they couldn't report the mech's size or makeup. They could only report on location—and right now, that was due south moving north, but slower than Kimmy expected. *Either they're bringing heavy and attack mechs or being smart and moving forward cautiously. I hope it's just a bunch of trashcans moving forward tactically.*

"Coming within range, Apocalypse," reported Karen. "Holding tight until we get a clean shot. Then we'll retreat and draw them towards the east."

"Roger," said Kimmy. "We'll move in behind them."

Kimmy went through her pre-fight checklist, ensuring her particle cannon and beams were charged, and her LRM system was ready. She wished the ocelot was faster and debated trading armor for speed, but the nagging part of her brain said armor would keep her alive. To make up for the slow speed, she had thrusters that would launch her seventy yards, more than enough to put her behind an opponent or get her out of trouble.

"We have a course deviation," reported Karen. "A troop of three mechs is moving west. The other troop of four mechs is turning east. What do you want to do, Apocalypse?"

Kimmy wiggled her nose as she thought about what to do. If she let Karen and Zhi reveal themselves, they could be caught in a pincer and wouldn't last long against seven mechs. The better alternative was to have her pincer troops stop, take up defensive positions, and divide the enemy forces. It would divide her forces, but Karen and Zhi could close behind the larger force and attack from the rear. Her troop could hold the smaller pirate troop until Nicole's troop could finish the larger pirate troop and attack the smaller pirate troop in the rear. *If we can hang on that long.* The best thing for Kimmy's troop would be to engage at range and trade space for time. *The only problem, I'm the only mech with range weapons. Well, we'll figure it out.*

"Poison, let the troops split. Nemesis, pull your troop into defensive positions and attack the larger pirate troop coming at you when you have a shot. My troop will engage and fight a withdrawal with the smaller pirate troop. Poison and Venom attack the larger pirate troop in the rear once they engage Nemesis' troop. Flexi and Bernoot move around the west side to support Nemesis' troop. Nemesis, once you've destroyed the enemy troop, you bring everyone and attack what's left of the smaller pirate troop. Roger?"

Kimmy received a round of affirmatives while she planned her troop's defenses.

"Velositi, Sprokkit, I want you to skirt the crater's rim and flank the incoming pirate troop—try your best to get behind them. Cardinal, I want you to sweep wide and flank them. I will engage them at range and draw their attention. I'll do my best to keep them at range."

"Yes, Apocalypse," replied Velositi. "Be careful."

Hey, I'm an empress. I'm used to being the center of attention. On Kimmy's radar, her troop executed her orders. She found a crater that protected her legs and part of her torso. The position gave her a free field of fire. On her radar, the indirect mech icons provided by Karen and Zhi showed her the pirates moving toward her position.

The three pirate mechs didn't take long to get within range. Using the imager, Kimmy brought up the three to see if she could visually identify them. One was an ocelot, like hers, and the other was an uber—known as a trashcan. It was short and squat but armed with a thirty-millimeter cannon and two medium beams. The third was much larger, and Kimmy didn't recognize it.

Kimmy was known for being a helluva shot, and now she was going to prove it. Keeping her radar off and only using her HUD, she manually aimed her particle cannon and LRMs at the other ocelot, knowing it could reach out and touch her. She'd worry about the others later.

Laying the target reticle over the ocelot, she used the imager to zoom in on the cockpit. The targeting ring closed around the reticle and let out a series of beeps, letting Kimmy know it was locked on. Taking a quick breath, Kimmy pulled the trigger. Her LRMs burst from their pod as the glittery glob of charged particles raced toward the unsuspecting pirate at the speed of light.

The pirate ocelot's cockpit exploded in sparkles, followed by five LRMs exploding in or around the cockpit's window. The ocelot took another step, then fell flat on its face.

Kimmy flipped a switch and directed her mech into a crouch, hoping the crater was deep enough to conceal her. She let the breath she was holding out as she charged her particle cannon and made sure the autoloader filled her missile pods. When she was ready, she stood and searched for the pirates.

She found the remaining pirates moving forward. Her radar showed them pinging the area—turning up the radar's power, hoping to find something. Kimmy obliged them by turning on her radar to get information about them and draw their attention so the rest of her troop could get flank and rear shots.

As the computer analyzed the enemy mechs, Kimmy aimed at her next target, the uber. The little mech sported heavy armor...including an armored cockpit. Its weakness was its legs—and that's where Kimmy aimed, hoping to knock it down.

As Kimmy pulled the trigger, the computer beeped, letting her know its analysis was done. Kimmy ducked her mech into the crater and tapped her console to bring up what the computer found.

By the Void...they're junk. The two downed pirate mechs' condition were rated yellow and orange—the pair were in such disrepair they shouldn't be functioning. Their weapons were still operable and could do damage, but the armor was tinfoil—except for the mech Kimmy didn't know.

She'd never heard of a fat max before. It was rated as a fifty-ton medium mech heavily armed with two forty-millimeter cannons, two machine guns, and two six-packs of SRMs. Its armor condition was green. *I've got to keep my distance from him.*

Kimmy kept her radar on as the fat max homed in on her. Deciding she couldn't stay in her hole, Kimmy flipped off her radar and backed up. With the fat max throwing so much energy into the air, it was easy to track him passively. The pilot reached the outer limits of his cannons and could be dangerous if they could shoot straight. *So far, I'm not impressed.*

As Kimmy crested the rim of her crater, she moved the targeting reticle over the fat max and let the computer get a lock. As she waited, her ocelot bucked like someone had punched it. Her mech status on the console blinked, her left leg flashed orange, and her left arm—bare of weapons—was yellow. *Shit. Who knew these guys could shoot?*

Kimmy moved the throttle to max as she moved backward, but an angry vibration shook her mech. Bringing up the damage report on her leg, Kimmy made a frustrated sound. The knee actuator was damaged, and if she kept going, there was a good possibility she could tear the gears to shreds. Kimmy lowered the throttle until the vibration was nearly gone, but she was only doing quarter speed. *I should have stayed in my hole.*

Kimmy let the computer handle the recharge and reload as she concentrated on maneuvering her mech using the rearview camera. For her, this was one of the hardest things to master when learning to drive a mech. Growing up as Princess of the Empire of the United States, she'd done little driving.

Her mech contorted and shook as her damage report sounded a warning in her helmet. Kimmy looked from the rearview camera to the console. Her right torso took two shots from the pirates' forty-millimeter cannons, blasting through her armor and tearing up her internal frame. *Does this guy have speed loaders?*

"Hey, Velositi, I could use a little help," Kimmy called to the rest of her troop.

"Roger. We're coming around him now."

I can't wait. Kimmy's particle cannon and LRMs were still reloading, but the pirate was now within range of her medium beams. The lasers did minor damage but were pinpoint accurate and, in the right hands, could act like a scalpel.

Kimmy lined up the shot with her imager on the fat max's left leg knee joint. She hoped to cripple the mech for salvage. *We could use an upgrade.* It was dangerous, but a skilled pilot could do it.

When the computer sounded it had a lock, Kimmy pulled the trigger. The two beams showed up in her HUD and the imager. On the pirate mech, there were two perfect circles where the beams melted through the leg's armor. *I hope you got to the good stuff.*

Kimmy jerked the control stick to the right to ruin any shot the pirate was lining up. Still moving backward slowly, she diverted power to her beams to charge them faster.

Two flashes behind the pirate's mech signaled Velositi and Sprokkit had engaged the enemy.

"Shoot the legs!" Kimmy instructed her troop.

From the right came Anna in her mouse. Tiny but fast, it packed SRMs and beams. The mouse was much shorter than the fat max—only coming up to its mid-torso—but Anna was a stellar pilot. She maneuvered herself inside the fat max weapons arcs and shot at the pirate mech's legs.

Anna's quartet of beams showed brightly in Kimmy's HUD as they burned their way into the armor of the right leg, softening it up for what came next. Three of the four SRMs Anna fired struck the fat max's right leg, while the fourth missile left a fiery trail to crash down somewhere on the moon.

The fat max responded by turning its torso and peppering Anna with a hundred rounds of machine gun fire. The Armor-Piercing rounds chipped away at a mech's armor, leaving it cratered and weakened. *I hope she can get out of there.*

A *chirp* sounded in Kimmy's ear, letting her know her weapons were ready. *Good. I can help Anna.* Kimmy didn't wait to take a precise shot. Instead, she pointed her targeting reticle center mass of the fat max and let the computer select the target. When a *ping* sounded in her ear, she pulled the trigger. All her weapons fired, slamming into the pirate mech's center torso, turning it from green to yellow. Not a lot of damage, but it pulled the pirate's attention from Anna to her.

Rapid blue flashes behind the pirate mech announced Velositi and Sprokkit were dug in and engaging. Velositi's morphed arm was a double cannon, firing like a machine gun. Though each plasma burst did less damage than Sprokkit's large single cannon, her rate of fire made up for it. Their plasma cannons could blast their way through most mech armor. And now, they were working on the thin rear armor of the fat max.

The pirate seemed more interested in Kimmy than the rest of her troop. He brought his weapons to bear on Kimmy. She saw the flash of his SRMs and yanked her torso around to expose her damaged left arm. The forty-millimeter cannons arrived first, blasting through her arm into her left torso. The SRMs slammed into what was left of her arm, blowing it off. Some minor damage reached her left torso, causing the loader to report the missile feeder was knocked out of line.

Kimmy flipped through several screens on her console to the loader, bringing up a display of the mechanism—the feeder was flashing red. Kimmy tapped it and brought up the calibration and reset menu. She instructed the computer to recalibrate the feeder by ejecting the ammo, resetting the connections, and reloading the system.

While Kimmy tried to fix her mech, she received the weapons' ready tone in her ear. While she initiated repairs, she lined up her next shot. The pirate mech was now close enough that Kimmy didn't need the imager and used the HUD to lay her reticle on the pirate's damaged knee. When the red lock circle closed around the reticle, she pulled the trigger, firing her beams and particle cannon.

There was no explosion to mark her success, but the fat max stumbled and fell face-first into the moondust—leaving Kimmy no shot at the other leg. Already, the pirate was going through the procedure to stand.

"Troop, take out the right leg," Kimmy ordered as she changed course to get a shot.

Anna fired an alpha strike into the limb. From the rear, Velositi and Sprokkit fired rapidly at the downed mech. Kimmy's computer updated the downed mech's damage analysis and reported that the pirate's right leg was severely damaged but functional.

Kimmy jogged around the fat max for a clear shot. Her LRMs would be no good, but the rest of her weapons would be effective. She targeted the damaged knee and fired. Visually, nothing happened, but the pirate mech ceased trying to stand and lay motionless in the lunar soil.

Flipping to an open channel, Kimmy ordered the pirate, "Seal and lock all weapons. Power down put on your survival gear, and exit the mech."

"I don't have any survival gear," came a gruff growl.

"Then you get to sit in there until our ship comes to get you." Kimmy kept her weapons aimed at the downed pirate while she called her troop. "I'll guard him. Check the others to see if the pilots are still alive." She changed frequencies to the command net. "Poison, how's it going?"

"Mopping up. We have three trashed—and they weren't much to begin with—mechs. I doubt we'll get much for them, but we might try selling them by the pound."

Kimmy chuckled. "War Cat Main, we have a prisoner for pickup, maybe more, and some mechs to be recovered."

"Roger, Apocalypse. We'll get the ship moving."

ASTARI IIIa
WAR CAT ASSAULT SHIP
LUNAR BIOME
Y51,834
1, OCTOBER 4003

B OMBSHELL OPENED THE CELL door—one of a dozen on War Cat to hold enemy mech pilots—and stuck her head in while morphing her arm into a cannon. There was a flash as she fired a plasma burst at the floor. "Hey, wake up, slimeball," yelled the teenage Morphicon.

"What in the Void are you?" came a gruff reply.

"The girl that's going to beat you into a pulp. Now, sit up. Empress Apocalypse wants to talk to you."

Bombshell withdrew her head, and her eyes glowed pink at Kimmy. "He's all yours."

"Thanks, Bomb."

Kimmy was accompanied by Ash'a and Athena's holographic body unit. She entered the cell and looked down at the pirate leader.

"Damn, honey, aren't you a sight for sore eyes? How'd you know it's been a while?"

Asha and Athena filed in behind Kimmy.

"What the Void are they?" he said, looking between Ash'a and Athena.

"Girls," growled Kimmy. She wished for her empress regalia—namely her tomahawks, so she could slam one between his legs. Instead, she wore the formal version of Kita's black military uniform. "Who are you?"

The pirate straightened, doing his best to smooth his mech pilot suit. "General Pierre Dupont, commander of the Astari Defense Force."

"Why do pirates always claim to be defending when they're stealing?" asked Ash'a snidely.

"Those miners haven't paid their taxes," retorted Dupont.

"Uh-huh. Last I checked, there wasn't a government on Astari—just pi-rates."

"Listen, I'll make you a deal," offered Dupont. "You let me out, and I'll let you in on a secret. You seem to have the resources to get places, and I know of a place where we could both get rich."

Kimmy's eyebrows lowered. Money was what she needed, but...*Hidden treasure?* "What's stopping me from taking it?"

"Only I know the route, honey. I—"

Kimmy brought her leg up and kicked out, catching Dupont's throat between her three-inch block heel and her foot, slamming his head against the plastic wall with a *thud*. Twisting her foot, she snarled, "I *am* Empress Apocalypse. You are nothing but the dirt—"

Dupont raised his cuffed hands and grabbed Kimmy's ankle. She frowned and applied more pressure, but when Dupont twisted his arms and lifted her, he sent Kimmy crashing to the ground.

He looked at her and said with a grin, "Nice thing about sexy women is they're light."

Bombshell rushed in. Both her arms morphed into cannons. "You want me to shoot him?"

Kimmy thought about it as Ash'a helped her up. She needed him alive to tell her where his base was so they could raid it. The treasure would be nice, but she wouldn't bank on it.

"No. Go get Ultraviolet and tell her to bring me one of her assimilated."

The young Morphicon morphed her cannons back into hands and hurried out the door.

"I've seen a lot of aliens in the universe, never saw one like her," quipped Dupont as he looked at Kimmy, grinning.

Kimmy said nothing but the triplets' wild color pattern of hot pink and turquoise covering their android-like bodies was unique.

Ash'a lowered her tablet from her chest and asked Dupont, "What are the details of this treasure?"

Dupont turned up his nose. "I'm not telling you, goldie. I want paroled and seventy-five percent of what we find."

Ash'a's scales rippled as she said, "You can tell me now, or Ultraviolet will tell me."

"I wasn't talking to you. I was telling *Her Highness*."

Kimmy took a slow breath to keep calm and let Dupont think he had the upper hand.

"Yeah, getting thrown to the floor is humiliating," he chuckled.

"Yes, Kimmy?"

Kimmy turned as Ultraviolet entered the room, followed by a guard in combat armor and glowing ultraviolet eyes.

"Are we the only Humans on this ship?" exclaimed Dupont at seeing Ultraviolet.

The Mi Prii Angel wiggled her dear-like nose and stroked her horn, showing worry and unhappiness.

"I'm not Human," Kimmy said flatly. "I'm an Angel...disguised to look Human. All the Humans on this ship are like him." She pointed to the guard.

"He might want to see an eye doctor, or is that some cosplay effect."

"That is to show we have assimilated him," said Ultraviolet.

Dupont's confident exterior cracked. "What the Void does that mean?"

"My friend, Ultraviolet, is a hive mind," explained Kimmy. "She releases a spore—" In Ultraviolet's hand a glowing ultraviolet sphere appeared "—and it attaches to the spinal cord of any sentient being, giving her complete control over its mind and body." Kimmy eyed Dupont. "And you know she's doing it, and there is nothing you can do. Your will, mind, and body become hers to do as she wishes. Now, you have a choice. You can tell me what I want, or you can become one of her drones."

"Slave, you mean?" said Dupont, his face morphing from confident to defiant.

Kimmy shrugged. "Not my problem...yours. So, which do you prefer?"

"If I tell you...you give me parole—I'll even drive a mech for you—and I get fifty percent."

Kimmy laughed. "You're in no position to make demands. You tell me, and she—" Kimmy waved at Ultraviolet "—doesn't get into your head."

"Ah, come on! You've got to give me something."

"Answer Ash'a's question. Tell me what we're getting, and I'll take the cuffs off."

"I won't do anything, I swear. I'm not a pirate—not really. I'm a merc that got stuck on this rock and proved I was the best pilot."

Kimmy smirked. "You're an ok pilot that can't lead for shit. The state of your troops was pathetic."

"What do you expect with no resources on this rock? I've been doing what I can with nothing except raiding mining settlements for scraps."

"Let me guess, after the Blood Witches tore us up, you thought you'd come pick at the pieces and maybe take our ship to get you out of here?"

Dupont grimaced. "Those were Blood Witches?"

Kimmy nodded. "I killed one, and I killed you."

"You must be pretty good then."

"Better than you. So, tell Ash'a what she wants to know."

Dupont looked at the Aurorian and sighed. "I, ah, have the first part of the map—"

Kimmy spun on her heel. "UV, he's—"

"Wait! Hear me out. It's the first piece of three and leads to an ancient UEE base—"

Kimmy leaned into Dupont. "What does UEE stand for?"

The man cocked his head. "United Earth Empire—I think. They've been gone for a thousand years, but their tech is unbelievable. They had hidden war caches across the universe. This is supposed to be one of those caches."

Kimmy's head felt like floating away. This could give her the firepower to save Chelsea and the tech to help Kita...if they could get the FTL fixed—and if it were true.

"Where's the map?" demanded Ash'a.

Dupont grinned. "Stored on a secret drive back at my base. You'll need me to access it. I encrypted it, just in case."

Athena laughed. "Nothing a Human has built that I can't crack."

"Is that enough to get me out?" asked Dupont as he looked at Kimmy.

Bombshell stuck her head in. "Hey, Momma-Kim, Administrator Toi is here."

Kimmy looked at Dupont. "I'll take the cuffs off. You stay here until we're ready to go." She motioned to Bombshell to take the cuffs off. "Come on, ladies. Let's go see what our employer wants."

ASTARI IIIa
WAR CAT ASSAULT SHIP
LUNAR BIOME
Y51,834
1, OCTOBER 4003

"A DMINISTRATOR TOI, WELCOME. PLEASE have a seat." Kimmy waved to a pair of seats around a large table in the lounge.

Toi and his assistant took them with a formal nod.

Their overalls are spotless. I bet they've never seen the inside of their mine.

With their guests seated, Kimmy nodded to Ash'a and Athena. She and the Aurorian took their seats while the AI remained standing.

"I apologize Commander Kita couldn't be here," said Kimmy. "She was injured in the raid on our troop."

Toi steepled his fingers. "Yes. I understand you had a busy day dying gloriously for your paycheck."

Kimmy wanted to roll her eyes so hard they'd fall out of her head and escape across the floor. Instead, her smile faded. "Commander Kita sacrificed herself to protect your mining operation. You may not respect what we do, but you need us...or would you prefer going back to being raided every few months when the pirates get bored?"

Toi waved Kimmy off. "I understand you've solved our pirate problem."

"We engaged two pirate troops and defeated them. We were about to move on the pirate base."

Toi scoffed. "We will take care of that once we collect our share of the salvage. Then you can go."

"Our engineers and techs are going through the salvage now. Once we decide what we want, we'll release the rest to you. I considered the base salvage, and we get first choice as stipulated by our contract."

Toi leaned back and folded his arms. "Yes, your contract. The situation has changed, and we no longer require you. We're willing to offer generous terms for renegotiating your departure contract. My assistant will give it to you."

Toi's unnamed assistant reached into his pocket, pulled out a data module, and flipped it haphazardly to Kimmy.

Showing her dexterity, Kimmy caught the drive and handed it to Ash'a. The Aurorian put the module in her tablet and read what Toi offered.

Kimmy pushed away from the table and went to the door, ignoring the look Toi gave her. Grabbing a crewmember with ultraviolet eyes, she pulled the tech to her and whispered, "UV, I need you to get Bombshell and Knock-out and bring them to the lounge. I have a situation that requires you girls."

"Done," said the tech.

"Thanks," said Kimmy.

She returned to the table and sat, resting her elbows on the table. She looked at Ash'a curiously as the Aurorian flipped through her tablet rapidly.

Kimmy looked at Toi warily. "This doesn't look good."

Toi's brow furrowed like he was annoyed.

"Are you in a hurry?"

"I can sum it up for you," he replied in a condescending tone.

"I—"

Ultraviolet, Bombshell, and Knockout entered the lounge. The Morphicons grabbed chairs from another table, turned them around, and sat on either side of Kimmy and Ash'a. Ultraviolet stood to one side of the table, looking superior.

"What do you want, Mamma-Kim?" said Bombshell.

"I want to hear what Administrator Toi was about to say. I'm afraid I will not like it. I think he thinks we have no bargaining leverage and will have to accept whatever deal he gives us. I want you to show him our leverage."

"You mean these?"

The two girls morphed their arms into cannons.

Knockout pointed hers at Toi. "Want to see what comes out the end?"

Toi gave her a dismissive shrug. "Go back to the planet you crawled out of, metal freak."

Knockout looked at Kimmy. "Can I shoot him?"

"That would make a mess—"

Toi snarled, "We do not permit personal weapons on Defin Industries' properties."

"I'd like to see you take them away," quipped Kimmy.

"Violating company policies negates your contract."

Ash'a's head snapped up from her tablet. "Good, we don't owe you for docking and fuel fees."

Kimmy looked at the Aurorian. "In the original contract, that was covered."

"In this new proposal, we owe them over a month's docking fees, fuel, and maintenance, and they get first pick of salvage we generate on the battlefield."

Kimmy wrinkled her nose in disgust.

"And they owe us ten thousand credits to be paid toward what we owe them."

Kimmy cocked her head. "Now that there's no threat of pirates, you think you can kick us out and not pay us? I should file a complaint with MerkNet."

Toi scoffed. "You think MerkNet will side with a ragtag bunch of mercs over an intergalactic company? You don't have the credits to take us to court."

Kimmy pulled her dark braid around and stroked it, a habit she learned from Kita. "No. I have something better. I was going to have Knockout and Bombshell escort you off my ship—roughly—and make sure we're fueled so we could leave. All the salvage we collected is aboard the ship, and you don't have the firepower to take it—"

"I can deny you permission to leave, and when my new mercenaries arrive, you will hand over our property."

"You hired new mercenaries to deal with your old ones? Maybe I should send them a letter on how Defin Industries does business with mercs. But I don't have time. Maybe there's something you're forgetting: Mercenaries expect to get paid. If we don't, I carry a skull and crossbones flag for this type of situation. What will Defin Industries say when my troops destroy their mining equipment and cart off what's valuable over some administrator trying to save sixty-five thousand credits? I bet the new merc cost ten times that."

"They're already here," spat Toi.

Kimmy grinned. "I guess I get to add to my kill count. Did you offer them a death benefit? You didn't with us. As much as I relish going into combat for a third time today, I'll give you a choice: you can pay us what we're owed and let us fly away, or everything that is yours belongs to her," Kimmy pointed to Ultraviolet, "and we still fly away with what you owe us."

The Mi Prii opened her hands, creating two glowing ultraviolet spores.

Toi jumped to his feet. "What is this thing?" He pointed at Ultraviolet.

"She is Mi—a hive mind in a Prii's body—a sentient creature from her planet. I don't think either exists in this universe, but that doesn't mean she's any less effective. UV, I'm tired of waiting. I want to know what he's done and what he's planning."

"Yes, with pleasure." A glowing spore flew from Ultraviolet's hand and up Toi's nose.

Toi's assistant flailed his arms, falling backward. He untangled his legs from the chair and sprinted toward the door.

Bombshell sprang to her feet and stepped into the fleeing man's path. Sticking out her arm, she clotheslined him, and he landed with a *smack* on his back. The Morphicon put her foot on his chest and morphed her arm into a cannon, pointing it at his head.

"Move, and I'm a happy girl."

Purplish light shown from Toi's mouth, nose, and eyes. His face dropped the angry look and went placid. He stood with dull eyes and a slack jaw as Ultraviolet did whatever she did.

"A troop of Devil Wolves is escorting a Defin Industries convoy to the pirate's base. A message arrived two days ago stating the pirates owned valuable information that could lead them to an ancient technology cache. We were to engage the pirates and clear the way for them."

"Well, shit. Athena! Sound general quarters. We'll move War Cat to Dupont's hideout and engage. Tell the others to get ready. I want everybody for this—including Dupont."

"What should I do with them?" said Ultraviolet.

"Take them back to the mine and do whatever you can to disrupt their plans for the cache. I don't care if you have to assimilate the entire mine. If you do, see if you can get us some funds."

"Can I go after the entire company?"

Kimmy grinned. "If you can. I feel they won't stop until someone finds the cache."

"I may not be able to get War Cat repaired at this facility, but Defin Industries must have a place on the periphery."

"Yes. Do it. Come on, girls. We have a treasure map to find."

CHAPTER 04

ASTARI IIIa
NEAR PIRATE HIDEOUT
LUNAR BIOME
¥51,834
1, OCTOBER 4003

"Convoy located," announced Athena over the command net. "They're moving away from the pirate hideout."

"Hot damn!" exclaimed Dupont from his mech. "No one gave them permission to go through my stuff."

"If they weren't going to, I was," replied Kimmy. "And going to make you standing there."

"Not like I got much. Been a long time since a woman's seen my man cave."

There were snickers from the other Angels.

"What's so funny?" demanded Dupont.

"What you got don't impress me much," sang Lizzy.

"I'm not trying to impress a woman out here."

"That's not what Apocalypse told us," Nicole said with a chuckle.

"I've never been in a unit with so many women. What happened to the men?"

"Ok, cut the chatter," ordered Kimmy. "Survive this, and you might find out. Are we ready to drop, Athena?"

"Yes. Drop in sixty seconds for Apocalypse Troop."

"Radars off, everyone. Nemesis will be our eyes."

Kimmy and her ocelot stood next to the drop bay door. Once her troop was free, War Cat would drop Karen's troop and the Morphicons ahead of the convoy.

The roar of War Cat's engines sent vibrations up Kimmy's ocelot. Her poor mech still had the battle wounds from the earlier day's engagements. Ultraviolet's mech technicians worked feverishly to repair the damaged knee and returned it to mostly functional. Her troop also contained Dupont and his fat max. It received just enough attention to make it functional but not battle worthy. Kimmy wasn't sure how far she could trust him and wanted to core him—if needed.

Flexi and Nicole rounded out her troop. Both carried LRMs, so the troop could attack at range. Flexi would be their defense if the enemy closed. Her homebrew mech was heavily armored. Kita scrounged several weapons systems for it, including a large thirty-millimeter cannon, enough to blow through four inches of armor.

The drop bay doors opened, and Kimmy pushed her throttle forward, guiding her mech onto the lunar surface. She walked to the end of the bay doors, allowing her troop to file in behind her.

"Everyone dirt side," said Athena as she spooled up the engines, creating a swirling dust storm around the newly released mechs.

"Let's get out of the dust," said Kimmy as she throttled forward, leading the others toward their target.

"Target acquired Apocalypse," announced Nicole.

Kimmy's radar displayed five mechs and a pair of vehicles but no data about them. "What do we have, Nemesis?"

"Looks like two leopards, two rexes, and a snow tiger guarding a cargo truck and a command vehicle."

"Sounds like what we're here for. Let's cut off the retreat."

Kimmy's troop had been dropped behind the Defin Industries convoy to attack the rear, while Karen's troop and the Morphicons blocked the way forward.

"So, what do you gals do for downtime?" asked Dupont.

Kimmy was about to snap at him to cut the chatter, but Flexi retorted, "What's a *gals*?"

"Women?" he replied, sounding unsure.

"I'm not a woman," huffed Flexi.

Kimmy and Nicole snickered. Dupont hadn't met Flexi before mounting up.

"Ok, I'm not stupid enough to walk into a trap—"

"But you're doing so well," quipped Nicole.

"Are...are you female?"

"Yes," the others answered in unison.

"Ok. What do you females prefer to be called?"

"Huh," Nicole said with a laugh. "He may not be stupid."

"Girls," answered Kimmy. "Kita doesn't like being called a woman—she, and we, are not derived from men. Now, be quiet and watch for the enemy."

"But there's nothing out here," whined Dupont.

"You know that for sure? Remember, one hit and your mech faceplants."

"Ok. But, ah, one question—who is Kita?"

Kimmy sucked in a breath and let out a heavy sigh. "She's my—"

"She's our leader," replied Nicole firmly.

"Look forward to meeting her...especially if she's like the rest of you."

"What would you like on your tombstone?" replied Nicole in a harsh, deadpan voice.

"Kita doesn't put up with stupid males. It's a fast way to the grave," explained Flexi.

"You can let me off at the next transfer station," grumbled Dupont. "I'm not about to work for some hard-ass feminist man-eater."

"And your treasure?" replied Kimmy coldly.

"I expect you to do the honorable thing and leave the map with me."

"For your information, Kita is my partner. We are bad meets evil, and I will kill you just as fast as she will—the only difference, I will do it with a smile. If you want your share of the treasure, I suggest you quit being macho and acting like the pitiful oppressed male and start being a smart team player and a better mech pilot than I've seen. So, shut up and do what I tell you."

"How'd I get mixed up with a dy—"

"Don't say it," warned Nicole. "Unless you want a ship full of them nailing your nuts to the wall."

"Shit," groaned Dupont.

"You could be considerate, debonair, and suave."

"Or," growled Kimmy, "he could not be an asshole and think of my pussy first and the rest of me never."

"Hey, I'm a nice guy. It's just been a while since I've seen a...a girl. Getting laid would be nice, but I'd be happy being in the presence of a girl after two years with pirates."

"Gotta remember, Kimmy," said Nicole, "guys think with their dick first when they've had a bit of a dry spell."

"A bit?" huffed Dupont.

"Well, he's in for an even longer one."

"Wait...is every girl a...a..."

"Lesbian works," cooed Nicole.

"Lesbian?"

"Could try Karen or Zhi...not sure Chelsea should have you as her first experience."

"Touch my daughter, and I will gut and flail you," snarled Kimmy. "I'm going to throw him to Anna."

Nicole grunted. "You want a real man-eater, Dupont? She's your girl."

"I just want a girl to take out, have a good time, and maybe get some," whined Dupont.

"You should have led with that. It would have gotten you a lot farther than I'm horny, and I want to get my dick wet."

"I thought you girls would be just as hard up, being cooped up on that assault shuttle—"

"War Cat," hissed Kimmy.

"The name holds special meaning to Kita," explained Nicole. "When I get horny, I go find Lizzy."

"Are you two back together?" asked Kimmy.

Nicole let out a deflated sigh. "No. I tried before we came, but she's only interested in an open relationship, e.g., sex. I'll take sex and cuddling. They fill the need, but I want an actual relationship."

"Sorry. I wish she hadn't gotten torched when she was younger."

"Hey, my fault. I left—"

"Kita's fault, too. She dumped her for me."

"Sounds like drama city," chuckled Dupont.

"Hey, you're never getting laid on War Cat," huffed Nicole.

"Just trying to be funny."

"It's not funny," yelled Kimmy. "It's mine and my friends' lives, not some sitcom for you."

"Apocalypse, why don't we worry about what we're doing," said Nicole. "War Cat has dropped Poison and Velositi's troops."

"Roger," huffed Kimmy. *Sometimes I hate having so many high-ranking military officers in my command and as my friends.* "Let's head toward them, but no one fire until they're engaged."

Kimmy pushed her throttle to half speed, letting her mech climb up and down the lunar landscape full of craters.

As they reached the edge of the enemy radar, Kimmy halted and allowed her indirect fire LRMs to lock onto an enemy leopard. "Nemesis, hold on the jammer until I give the word." Kimmy wished for a bigger surprise—like a missile boat mech—to hit the enemy instead of her thirty missiles, but she would go with what she had.

Pulling down her viewer, Kimmy zoomed in on the battle five hundred yards away. Anna and her mouse were on the enemy's flank, shooting them with her small number of SRMs and beams. Zhi, Lizzy, and Karen were holding the line and concentrating fire on a Devil Wolf rex. The Morphicons guarded Karen's flanks. Bombshell and Knockout were morphed into tanks, blasting away with their plasma cannons to keep the remaining Devil Wolves busy.

Though smaller than a mech, the Morphicons could take a lot of punishment and, as long as they had power, could regenerate. The triplets had a library of vehicles they could morph into, except most were ineffective in a lunar environment. The lack of uranium to make the vehicle shells limited them to their energy-based plasma cannons.

Bombshell fired, a bright blue energy blast lighting up the lunar surface. The plasma bolt slammed into the left arm of a leopard, blowing through layers of the mech's armor. The Devil Wolf ignored her and fired at Karen. Kimmy flipped her radio to Karen's troop net.

"...I'm backing out to find cover. I'm blinking red all over the place," announced Karen to her troop.

"We'll cover you," replied Lizzy.

"I'm pinned down by two of them," said Zhi.

"It's too much," yelled Karen. "I'll call Apocalypse."

Kimmy heard her cue. "Poison, we're coming." She switched radio nets to her troop. "Everyone, open fire. Nemesis fire up the sparkler. All missiles target D-W-three."

She received a round of affirmatives as she pulled the trigger and sent her five missiles toward the battle. Her missiles were joined by ten from Flexi and fifteen from Nicole. The swarm slammed into the back of a Devil Wolf targeting Karen. Kimmy pushed the throttle forward to close the gap between sides.

"Blade," Kimmy called to Dupont, "get those big guns firing and see if you can get some shots in the back of D-W-three."

"From this range?"

"If my friends die, I'm taking it out of your share of the treasure and your hide."

"Do my best."

"If you fail, I'll blow a hole through you."

"Ok, ok. You don't have to be a bitch."

Kimmy pressed her lips together as she gritted her teeth, trying to let the comment go and hope Dupont's actions would make up for his mouth. As she did her best to regain her self-control, her particle cannon lit, letting her know it was in range. She still had DW3 selected, and its back was turned to her.

They must not have thought much of our missile barrage if they ignored us or were confused by the jamming. Probably both.

Kimmy pulled the trigger and fired her particle cannon. The charged particles slammed into the target's back, already ravaged by the missile attack. An enormous explosion engulfed the mech, followed by one behind it. *Uh-oh, what happened?*

She scanned the battlefield and saw an ejection chute floating toward the ground, but the marking on the chute was Devil Wolf. *Must have gotten DW3.*

"Apocalypse, Venom. Poison's had to eject."

Shit. Explains the second explosion. "Roger, Venom. We're coming in fast. Do your best to hold the line."

"We're taking a pounding. The faster you get here, the better."

There's not much I can do until we get in range. "We're almost in range of our medium beams. We've got time for another salvo of missiles. Just do your best to—"

There was a big explosion to Kimmy's right.

"Shit. I'm flashing red all over. I'm punching out!" cried Zhi.

Dammit. "Venom?"

"She's gone, Apocalypse," replied Lizzy. "I'm taking fire from three sides."

"We're coming," exclaimed Kimmy. "My troop, prepare to fire on D-W-two."

It was still too far for beams, but her particle cannon and missiles were ready to fire. When she received affirmatives from her troop, she ordered, "Fire!"

LRMs from Kimmy's center torso were joined by LRMs from her left by Flexi and Nicole. To her immediate left was a flash from Dupont as he fired his twin thirty-millimeter cannons. She admired him for having the balls to join the firing line and take the shot.

The Devil Wolf's back in the center of the enemy line erupted in fire. Kimmy's radar was off, so she couldn't tell the extent of the damage, but the wounded Devil Wolf turned ninety degrees to its left, bringing its left side around for protection. *We must have hit hard.* This would keep the enemy pilot busy guarding his rear and keep from being able to bring all his weapons to bear.

"Hey, look what I found," exclaimed Dupont. "Got some Defin Industries vehicles hiding in a crater."

"Good," said Kimmy. "Don't let them get away. You hit anything at this range?"

"I'll damn sure try."

Kimmy shrugged. That was the best she was going to get from him. "Then target D-W-four and get it knocked out so Velositi and troop can roll up the line."

"Sure thing."

As Kimmy moved forward, her beam weapons lit on the console—in range, charged, and ready to fire.

"Rivet, all your weapons hot?" Kimmy called Flexi.

"Just tell me what you want to shoot."

"Let's see if we can punch through D-W-two's arm and blow its core."

"Void, yeah! Ready when you are." Flexi's homebrew mech had a thirty-millimeter cannon, two medium beams, and a ten-pack of LRMs.

Kimmy aimed her weapons at the exposed left side of DW2. "Fire!"

The projectiles and beams slammed into DW2, blowing off the arm.

"Nice shot," reported Nicole. "Let me help you out."

Farther down Kimmy's line, Nicole's mech spit fire as the LRMs streaked toward the wounded mech.

"Boom!" exclaimed Nicole. "Right arm and right torso are gone. We've got medium damage to center torso."

The damaged mech lowered to the ground and braced. The mech to its right, DW5 in a snow tiger, disengaged from Lizzy and charged Kimmy's troop.

"Looks like we've attracted the snow tiger," Kimmy informed her troop. "Covers blown. Light him up."

Tapping a few buttons on her console, Kimmy changed her radar from passive to active. The passive mechs on her screen changed from ghostly silhouettes to silhouettes of the identified mechs. In her HUD, the computer gave her data about the mech, including heat, armor rating, damage, weapons, and range. The snow tiger was beam heavy, packing a large beam, three medium beams, and a small beam. That also meant it would run hot in the lunar environment.

"Nemesis, Rivet, finish off D-W-two. I'll handle D-W-five."

Kimmy steered her ocelot toward the snow tiger, trying to draw its attention. As she waited for her weapons to charge and reload, she kept her targeting reticle on DW5 so her computer would maintain its lock.

It was a race between mechs to see whose weapons would come up first, and Kimmy lost. She didn't feel the beams hit her, but the computer alerted her to damage in her right torso, right arm, and left leg.

Shit. Those aren't even repaired yet. Her left leg flashed red. It was holding together, but barely.

A *ping* in Kimmy's ear signaled her weapons were ready. Her targeting reticle was locked, and she pulled the trigger. Her own beams and particle cannon fired, punctuated by her five missiles slamming into the snow tiger.

Kimmy was less than enthusiastic about the damage done. Her computer reported yellow status for the snow tiger's left and center torso. *That won't slow him down any.*

Kimmy's forward velocity slowed to a crawl as her mech tried to walk on the damaged leg without injuring it further. The snow tiger charged. Kimmy turned her mech to decrease the chance of the snow tiger hitting her leg. She knew his weapons would be ready before hers. To add to her defensive posture, she braced for the impact that would come.

The drumming of the SRMs on her right arm shook her cockpit. When the arm separated—taking her particle cannon and beams with it—the damage to her right torso reverberated through the entire mech. Kimmy twisted on the control stick to bring her torso around to aim at the snow tiger and leave her legs in place to protect them.

On the display console, a countdown let her know how much time she had before her LRMs would be ready. She was barely outside the minimum effective. Kimmy tapped on the control stick while raising her mech from its crouch. When she heard the *ping,* she fired.

The missiles streaked toward their target, slamming into the conical-like center torso of the snow tiger. Kimmy hoped for a lucky shot, but her computer reported minimum damage to the fifty-five-ton medium mech—it wouldn't be a fair fight even if Kimmy's mech was healthy—But Kimmy knew little in war is fair.

Kimmy twisted her torso forward and tapped on her console to put the mech back in a crouch. Two loud booms shook her mech. The console blinked wildly as Kimmy's seat straps tightened. The tipping of the mech to the left was followed by her falling straight back with a *thud*. Looking out the window, all Kimmy saw were stars.

What hit me? Kimmy tapped on the console, closing the warning messages, and found her left leg had been hit and collapsed. She flipped screens to start the standup procedure, but the mech's computer refused and brought up the damage diagnostic screen. The leg was gone.

"Poor baby," Kimmy sighed and patted her ocelot.

A shadow fell over her mech.

Well, shit. I've never died before. I guess I get to experience my first time. I hope Ryan can reinsert me. I don't want to leave—

"Hey, Empress," cooed Dupont.

His mech appeared in Kimmy's window and fired.

"Come on, big boy. Come pick on somebody your own size."

Kimmy grabbed her mic. "Blade! Don't engage him. One shot, and you're cored!"

"Well, I guess I won't get hit. Don't worry, Empress, this isn't my first rodeo."

Has he even been to a rodeo? Hell. I never should have told him that. How am I ever going to live this down?

Kimmy undid her helmet and set it aside. Ruffling her hair, she let out a sigh, knowing the battle had passed her by. Her radar updated her on the status of the others. In short order, DW5 and DW2 went down. Kimmy wasn't sure who got the kills, but her troop moved on to take out the remaining Devil Wolves. Both were injured fighting the Morphicons.

Giving up on the radar, Kimmy thumped her head against her chair and sighed. Being out of the action was not something she was used to. Thoughts of failure drifted to thoughts of Kita, and tears trickled down her face.

She already missed her partner. She tried to work around the lump of guilt and regret plaguing her all day. *If only I'd been there or gotten there sooner...Or not let them go alone. Why weren't we warned? Defin had to know the Blood Witches were in the area.*

Visions of Kita and Chelsea appeared through her tears. "I'm sorry!" Kimmy yelled at her empty cockpit. She flailed her arms and pounded them against the armrests in a teary fury. A wave of frustration swept over her, and doubt about her skills as a pilot, leader, partner, and mother made her want to crawl into a hole and die.

Her hand went to her safety harness' release latch when a small voice called out to her through her fog of self-loathing, doubt, and guilt.

"Hey, Empress Apocalypse, area clear."

God, I hate that voice. At this moment, Dupont represented everything she wanted and should be.

Kimmy wasn't ready to face the others and ignored her helmet. Wrapping her arms around herself, she hugged herself tightly, trying to free herself from the black pit she'd gone down.

I can't do this. I can't lead, fight, and worry about them...does that make me a coward? Kimmy wished for Kita's arms and council. She never doubted herself and always had a plan. *Am I grasping at straws...Treasure? Hidden UEE caches? Who am I kidding? There's nothing out there. There's nothing that can be done for Chelsea and Kita. I failed them, and I'm alone.* Kimmy slammed her head against the side of her command chair, hoping to knock herself out and escape her mind, but the soft cushion bounced her head back without so much as a headache to distract her.

"Kimmy?"

Rubbing her nose, Kimmy sniffed, her mental collapse pierced by Nicole's voice. She fumbled around her cockpit and found her helmet. With a sad sigh, she put it on cockeyed and spoke, "N—Nicole?"

"Hey, we haven't heard from you in a while. You ok?"

Kimmy sniffed, and a sob escaped her lips. "No. I need a hug."

"Hey, we all get shot down," Dupont said with a chuckle. "Happens to the best of us. No need to get upset."

"Shut up!" Kimmy screamed as she tore off her helmet and threw it across her cockpit.

"Kimmy! Kimmy?" Nicole pleaded.

Kimmy turned in her seat and curled up in a ball.

ORBITING ASTARI IIIa
WAR CAT ASSULT SHIP
SPACE BIOME
¥51,834
1, OCTOBER 4003

K IMMY'S COCKPIT HATCH OPENED with a *creak,* illuminating the inside with yellow light from War Cat's mech bay.

"Kimmy, are you alright?" said a voice she didn't recognize.

Kimmy raised her head from her chair's arm and rubbed her forehead to get rid of the red spot she was sure to have. Her hands drifted from her forehead to her eyes to get rid of the tears. *I really have to stop doing this in here.* Of course, War Cat offered few places to cry in private.

Grabbing her helmet, Kimmy looked behind her chair to see a pair of glowing ultraviolet eyes. Kimmy sighed in relief.

"Hi, UV. I'm ok. I just needed time to collect myself."

"Would you like to talk to someone? We have a doctor onboard. Psychology isn't his specialty, but we can prescribe you medication."

Kimmy unplugged her helmet. *My poor mech.* "I should talk to you girls. I don't think I need meds...at least not yet. Did we get the map?"

"We captured the Defin vehicles but haven't had time to question the crews or search the vehicles. As soon as the mechs are aboard, we will find the map. What would you like to do with the damaged mechs?"

"They can't be repaired?"

"They could, but we do not have enough bays. We thought the priority would be the mechs we captured from the Blood Witches and the Devil Wolves. They are all better mechs than we have."

"How long to repair them?"

"Two weeks."

"And the rest of the mechs?"

"Zhi's widow maker and Karen's soldier would be better sold for salvage, as we would need substantial parts to repair them. The fat max will take several days, as will your ocelot."

Kimmy stumbled as she tried to get around her command chair to the hatch. She stumbled and was caught by the mech tech.

"Let us help you out."

I guess I do need help. Kimmy allowed the tech to take her arm and guide her from the hatch onto the catwalk.

"I can manage from here," said Kimmy as she took the yellow rail and shuffled to the elevator.

On the bay floor, she met the other pilots.

"Kimmy!" exclaimed Nicole. The Empire of the United States Air Force colonel rushed over and hugged Kimmy. "Are you ok? I was worried when you didn't answer."

Kimmy rested her head on Nicole's shoulder as tears built up in her eyes. "No," she whispered. "I'll be happy when the day is over."

"Oh, Kimberly. Girls!" Nicole called to the others standing around.

The other Angels gathered around, squeezing Kimmy in a big group hug.

"Oh, thank you," Kimmy blubbered as tears fell down her face. "I don't know what I'd do if I didn't have you."

"Cry in your cockpit," said Zhi as she gave Kimmy a kiss on the cheek.

"We're here for you," said Karen. "We know it will be hard on you with Kita injured and Chelsea gone. But we're here for you. Anything you need—a hug, a shoulder to cry on, someone to sit with you and Kita—we're all here for you."

"You don't have to face it alone," said Lizzy.

"It hurts so much," admitted Kimmy. "And not having Kita—" she burst into tears "—and Chelsea taken to god knows where—"

"I will get her back," assured Anna. "There is nowhere they can hide."

"Thank you, Anna. Thank you, thank you. The hope you give me lets me carry on."

"While I hunt, you do what is necessary to heal Kita and fix our ship."

"I will. I promise. I have an announcement about why we attacked the Devil Wolves and Defin Industries."

"I thought it was to get back at them for screwing us," chuckled Nicole.

"There is that," admitted Kimmy. "But the pirate we captured has a map to—"

"Treasure!" whooped Lizzy.

Kimmy laughed through the remains of her tears. "Well, sort of, it's a—"

"Damn. All these sexy girls go with the beautiful voices over the radio? Woah, nelly."

The knot of Angels split to reveal Kimmy in the center.

"Who are you?" snarled Anna.

"Just the luckiest guy this side of the periphery. Name's Pierre Dupont. I, ah, saved Her Highness earlier. Now, there's no need to thank me. I'm just doing my part as a team player."

Anna's face twisted into an icy vixen. Kimmy had seen her use it when she was hunting her target. Using a well-practiced routine, she sauntered up to Dupont and placed a hand inside his mech suit.

"You saved Kimmy?" she asked in a sultry voice.

"Wow," said Dupont. "You don't have to thank me—here."

Anna whipped her leg back and brought her knee up into his crotch. As Dupont doubled over, Anna spun and smashed her boot across his face, collapsing him to the deck. She turned and strode back to the other Angels with a savage look on her face.

Karen and Zhi stood over Dupont.

"Team players don't expect a reward for saving a teammate," said Karen in her harshest command voice.

"We're here to fight," snarled Zhi, "not stroke an idiot's ego."

Kimmy stood between them and looked down at Dupont. "I warned you. I thought you were smarter than this."

"Has he been sliming on you?" Lizzy asked Kimmy, putting a hand on her arm.

"Nothing I can't handle—"

Lizzy pulled her KA-BAR combat knife from her belt and stepped toward Dupont. Kimmy jumped in front of her.

"Lizzy, it's ok. He's just a hard-headed male idiot, and I need him in one piece right now."

Lizzy juggled her knife while she said, "He steps out of line. I'll shove this through his spine."

Kimmy looked at Dupont. "These are the Angels. They're combat veterans and know how to kill you in a hundred different ways. No one is interested in you beyond taking us where the first piece of the map leads. You can bunk with Ultraviolet's crew and use their heads. You can eat in the galley with everyone else and hang out in the lounge. If you can't keep your mouth shut, one of these girls will shut it for you. Understand?" Kimmy offered Dupont a hand.

He took it but couldn't stand up straight.

"Come to medbay," said Ultraviolet. "We will get you some ice and explain the life you find yourself in."

"I'm just trying to be friendly," admitted Dupont.

Ultraviolet cocked her head. "Then try 'hello.' It worked for me."

"I will help," said Athena, coming around the group of Angels. Unlike most of the Angels, she had her wings.

"Is this what you girls normally look like?" asked Dupont.

"They don't have gray skin or blue wings," replied Athena. "I'm a digital Angel—the AI that runs War Cat. The other Angels have their normal skin tone, and each Angel's wing color is as individualistic as she is."

"How do you get wings...and why be human?"

"You will never have wings. Kita would have to die and give up Reality before that happens. We look Human to blend in with the rest of the universe. In some universes, we keep our wings, but this universe has proven averse to non-human races. Our goal was to explore the far future and become mech pilots."

"You should have stayed where you came from. This universe is hell."

"As we're finding out," said Kimmy. "Go get taken care of. Everyone else, get ready for the After-Action Review. UV, see if you can find Dupont's drive."

ORBITING ASTARI IIIa
WAR CAT ASSULT SHIP
SPACE BIOME
¥51,834
1, OCTOBER 4003

"So, what'd you find?" asked Kimmy as she entered the ship's bridge with Karen, Ash'a, and Nicole.

"We found five data modules," said Ultraviolet.

"I have asked Lizzy and Anna to bring Pierre here so he can tell us the correct one," said Athena. "They should arrive momentarily."

Kimmy crossed her arms. "I hope this isn't a wild snipe hunt."

"I could scan the drives if you wish," offered Athena. "But if this data is encrypted or hidden, it could take me longer to find it than it—"

Lizzy entered the compartment lit by ambient light from the computers, leading Dupont and Anna. Dupont kept looking back at Anna.

"We brought him as requested," said Lizzy.

Dupont looked uncertain as he glanced at the Angels.

"I promise they won't hurt you," said Kimmy, reading the worried look on Dupont's face. "I apologize for Anna damaging your jewels. I hope Ultraviolet eased the pain and swelling."

Dupont cocked his head, looking perplexed. "I, ah, yeah, she gave me some ice and pain meds. I can walk."

"I didn't intend any permanent harm, only issue a warning that we are not girls he can take advantage of," said Anna formally. She glared at the back of Dupont's head. "If I wanted to castrate him, I would have."

"Yeah, look, I'm sorry I came off wrong. I was trying to be friendly and give you girls a compliment."

Kimmy held up a hand. "I understand, but to be fair, men have traumatized some of these girls, and they regard any attention with suspicion. I've talked to several and related our initial encounter to them. You're deemed a threat by many of them. I'm not against you becoming a member of our team. Keep helping. It'll go a long way to gaining my trust. Gaining the other girls' trust will be harder. I suggest giving up the role of macho mech pilot. The girls will respond to a male who is considerate, caring, and does not objectify us. Compliments are nice, but not as come-ons. If you don't think you can hack it, I'll give you some money and drop you at the transfer station when we drop off Anna. Ok?"

"I...I'm sorry. I didn't know about the girls' past. I didn't mean to stir up painful memories. I acted like I did when I served with the Urseval Army Rangers. I—"

"It's ok," said Karen. "We are new to the world of mechs, but many of us have served in military units and know what life is like and what behavior is appropriate. The problem was you misread the situation. We were not having a celebratory group hug. The group was consoling Kimmy over the kidnapping of her daughter, Chelsea, and the grave wounding of her partner, Kita. As a group, we are hurting, and your gesture, mixed with previous experiences, wounded instead of lifted spirits. I apologize as well for the physical attack. That wasn't necessary."

Anna spun on her heel and left.

"Don't mind her," said Kimmy. "She's one of the girls hurting, so you won't get an apology from her."

"So am I," said Nicole, "but I'll apologize. It wasn't fair to you not knowing the whole situation."

Dupont rubbed the back of his neck. "Ah, thanks. I'm a nice guy...as far as guys go. I just wanted to compliment everyone and tell you how impressed I was taking on a Devil Wolf troop...especially with the light mechs you have. I want to be part of the team and help find the treasure. You haven't cut me out, have you, Kimmy?"

Kimmy shook her head. "No. You'll get twenty-five percent...if you help us find it. Speaking of which, Ultraviolet found five data modules. We need you to tell us which one has the map."

Dupont pursed his lips. "You, ah, haven't looked at them, have you?"

"No."

"Can I see them?"

Ultraviolet stepped forward with the five drives in her hand.

"Ah, that one. The red one...but don't judge me on what's on the drive."

Kimmy raised an eyebrow. "Porn?"

Athena took the module and plugged it into her computer.

Dupont blushed. "Yeah."

"If it's any good, I might have to snag a copy," said Nicole.

Dupont's head whipped around as he did a double take.

"What?" said Nicole. "You think you're the only one? I'm interested to see what porn looks like in the year four thousand."

Dupont's jaw dropped. "I, ah, just...I...Don't take this wrong...you're gorgeous girls. What do you need porn for?"

"Why thank you, but I still get horny and Lizzy...more often than not, isn't available. So, I'm left with a good vid and a dildo."

Lizzy shrugged. "I stop by when I'm home. I'm not opposed if you go elsewhere."

Nicole nodded somberly.

Dupont's jaw was slack.

"I think you blew his mind," quipped Kimmy.

"I just...never...girls..."

The collection of Angels laughed.

"I can't say I use it," said Karen with a shrug. "Looking at pictures of naked men isn't the same as the real thing. Something about holding a cock in your hands is a turn-on."

Kimmy shrugged. "Kita has no problem being naked, but we have watched porn together. She likes to play copycat."

"What's that?" said Nicole.

"Where you do what's on-screen to your partner. Never lasts long as we get into each other."

"I think I've entered another dimension," Dupont gasped.

Nicole laughed. "You didn't know girls talk about sex as much or more than guys? Trust me, a guy fails to please a girl, and every girl will know in hours. Do it right, and you wonder why some guys get all the girls."

"What do I have to do to do it right?"

The girls laughed.

"You'll have to talk to Karen," said Nicole. "You've got an outie, not an innie."

Karen raised an eyebrow. "Maybe. We'll see how he does around here. It has been a while."

"Kimmy, I found it," said Athena from the PA system on the wall by the door.

The group moved to the screen above several racks of computers.

"Excuse the image on the screen," said Athena.

Kimmy raised an eyebrow at Dupont. "And here I was, prepared for something exotic. She's pretty."

Dupont blushed in the dim light. "I, ah, she's my favorite."

"The map is embedded in the image file," said Athena.

"You found it that fast?" exclaimed Dupont. "It took me forever to get it in there."

"Even with this ship's meager computer resources, I'm still one of the most advanced AI's the UEE ever created up to that point in their existence. Because I'm of UEE construction, it helps to know what I'm looking for."

"I don't get it," said Nicole.

Athena laughed. "The map is encoded in a UEE image algorithm. I'm used to working with them, and they're easy to spot. I'm sure for most analysts searching, they would bypass this as gibberish."

"Takes one to know one," said Dupont.

"Exactly."

The image on screen separated as a star chart appeared over the naked woman.

"I don't recognize the names or the stars involved," said Athena. "I will have to run them through my UEE database to decode them."

Dupont squinted at the screen. "What's it written in?"

"That's what I'm saying," said Athena. "It's written in a version of UEE Common. Not the same as I knew, but similar. I can decode it, but it will take time—time we could use to repair War Cat."

"I'll need to talk to UV and Ash'a," said Kimmy.

"Ok, so how long would it take for Defin or somebody else to decode the map without you?" said Lizzy to Athena.

"That would require finding it and then decoding the language. I would say three to five years...if they had a sample of UEE Common and a supercomputer running nonstop. Without the language sample, it may be decades."

"Damn. I'm glad Kita found you."

Athena smiled. "I have been with Kita for a very long time."

"And you just run the computers?" asked Dupont.

Athena chuckled. "You might say I keep Kita's life in order. As an Angel, Kita has a computer in her head more powerful than any built in this universe, but she uses it differently than what I'm structured to do. They originally developed me to run the city of Gaia on Kita's homeworld. Since then, I've run Kita's empire of Hades and Kita's global conglomerate. I now run Roost and the world outside it. I am also partnered to Kita's daughter, Quill, making me Kita's daughter-in-law. Kita has extended my purpose, and I think I am the second most powerful computer system next to hers—though mine is far more complex than hers."

"I thought AIs were illegal, but it sounds like you've had some adventures."

"Throughout this universe, AIs are illegal, but I won't tell if you won't. And yes, I do. Maybe some night I will tell you."

"Athena's programming is so good she can pass as a Human if she looks like one," said Kimmy.

"And lose my humanity," quipped Athena.

"Even you can fake it for a few hours. Ash'a, UV, let's go see what we can do about finding the part we need and a place to do the repairs. Everyone else, thanks for the help. Karen, can you get Pierre settled somewhere nicer than he currently is?"

"Sure thing. There are spare bunks in the pilots' quarters."

"I don't want to intrude on you girls," Dupont replied humbly.

"Eh, there's a head for you. The girls have been using it as overflow. After the Aven Foreign Legion, we're all used to bunking with men...just be more considerate than they were."

"You girls were in the Legion?" Dupont replied with respect and awe.

"For a while. I'll tell you the story. Lizzy, you coming?"

She looked at Dupont, and her lip curled. "I'm going to the simulator. I want to review today's battle. I'll meet you for dinner." She added under her breath, "God, eating sucks," before she left.

"Guess it's you and me," Karen said to Dupont. "See you at chow time, Kimmy." She led him out, leaving Kimmy with Ash'a, Athena, and Ultraviolet.

"Ok, ladies, please tell me you have good news for me," said Kimmy.

"I've found a part," said Ash'a. "It's five systems over and two hundred and fifty thousand credits plus another one hundred and fifty to have it installed. The Astari system ship hauler can make the jump for twenty thousand credits for each jump, so a hundred thousand total. To have it delivered is two hundred thousand credits, but we must find someone to install it."

Kimmy leaned her butt against a workstation while she chewed on a knuckle. When Ash'a finished, she said, "Any chance we can get a loan?"

Ash'a's scales rippled in a rainbow of colors. "I've tried, but we don't have the credit rating or the cash flow. I'm sorry, Kimmy. I can delve into the BlackNet and see if I can find something there."

Kimmy looked at Ultraviolet. "Anything with Defin Industries?"

Ultraviolet wiggled her deer-like nose. "I have identified an installation that can do the work and get the part, but I do not have control of it, and it could be many months until I can. It's on the other side of the periphery. I do not have control of a person with enough stature to send us money or float us a contract. To do that would require us changing our name so as not to raise suspicion with the bean counters as Defin has blacklisted us."

"Great," huffed Kimmy. She wished for Kita and her partner's amazing ability to always have a plan for any situation. "What are the chances of finding work in the Astari system, Ash'a?"

The Aurorian shook her head. "No legit jobs. There is a smash job on BlackNet—" Kimmy knew of the mercenary underworld job posting site. "—On Astari Two, the gold mining operation Jungle Cat Mining wants something bad to happen to a rival mining company. I can contact them for details."

"How much?"

"Forty thousand."

"Tell them we'll do it for a hundred."

"All start that as our first offer. How low are you willing to go? Forty is enough to cover our monthly expenses—without purchasing any mech supplies."

"I'll do eighty, and we get priority salvage," said Kimmy, tapping a nail against her teeth.

"I'll contact them."

"And see what rates you can get from a BlackNet loan shark. UV, do your best to get Defin under your control."

"Can I widen my assimilation network to outside beings?"

Kimmy wiggled her nose. "Not yet. Defin is dangerous enough. I don't want to be on the run if you're discovered."

"We are careful."

"I know, and I trust you. Ok, I'm going to go visit Kita."

"We will escort you," offered Ultraviolet.

Kimmy followed the Mi Prii across the ship to medbay. After the door slid back, Kimmy entered Kita's suite and frowned at the tent that contained her partner.

"We will leave you," said Ultraviolet, taking Kimmy's hand. "If you need anything, find us."

"Thank you," Kimmy said solemnly.

She moved to the head of the bed, where she could see inside the tent. Pulling up a chair, she sat, wishing to hold Kita's hand.

"Hey, angel," Kimmy whispered at the head covered in artificial skin that looked nothing like Kita. A tear slid down her cheek, and she buried her face in her hands. An overwhelming weight—her problems, worries, and loneliness—dropped on her shoulders and increased her tears from a trickle to a torrent.

Kimmy raised her head, wiping the tears from her eyes and face. "I'm sorry. You're the one with the tragic injuries. I know I should be strong. I'm an empress, for Void's sake. But... how do I do it without you? You've always been there supporting and guiding me. Taking over the world didn't look as daunting as this...and...and I have to do it alone, without you. How can I do it? I'm scared...for you and Chelsea...what if I make a mistake? It could cost me both of you...and I don't want to fail. I've never failed at anything...but I've always had you by my side. I love you, angel. You mean everything to me, and seeing you like this breaks my heart. What am I going to do?"

Kimmy gazed into the space where Kita's eyes should have been. She gulped hard. When there was a *smack* inside the tent, she jumped and fell out of her chair. Looking at the bed, Kita's arm was resting on the plastic tent.

"By the Void, Kita," Kimmy gasped. "You have got to be the strongest-willed person I've ever met...but of course you are. Who else becomes the God of Evil and takes over Reality?" Kimmy bowed her head to her partner. "Thank you, Kita. I know you're with me...maybe not in body, but in spirit. I can do this, and I will...no matter what I have to do. I will save you and Chelsea. I love you—more than anything in Reality."

Kimmy placed her fingertips against Kita's and drew on her partner for courage, resilience, and determination. *I will do this. I have to. Failure is not an option. I will save Kita, Chelsea, and the rest of the Angels.*

CHAPTER 05

K IMMY NAVIGATED HER DAWNBREAKER mech through the jungle trees, carving a path for the smaller mechs. The dawnbreaker was a refurbished andra mech salvaged from the Blood Witches. Ultraviolet's team cannibalized the second salvaged andra to repair the other. Kimmy changed the name, not wanting anything to identify them with the Blood Witches, Aven Foreign Legion, or Aven Federation. Through the creative use of armor and changing the weapons layout, Ultraviolet's mech techs created a new silhouette for the mech.

"Ack, man, this jungle's thicker than a...a...jungle," remarked Dupont.

"At least it's not the kind that grows super-fast and swallows you whole," replied Flexi.

"There are jungles that do that?"

"I saw them when I was a pup aboard the Diamock frigate Canine. We had people armed with herbicides constantly spraying the jungle to keep it back. I saw people wrapped up and swallowed by the vegetation."

"Let's avoid those worlds."

"Should have unleashed a horde of Verisom princesses on it and told them it was a delicacy," chuckled Kimmy, speaking to the legendary appetites of the herbivores.

"Yeah, I know they can do it," said Flexi with a longing sigh.

"Sorry, I didn't mean to make you miss your princess."

"Princess? Who's a princess?" demanded Dupont.

"I was," cooed Kimmy. "But Flexi was partnered to an Angel Verisom princess, Catnip. She died protecting some other Angels."

"Sorry," said Dupont. "My condolences, Flexi."

Dupont had dropped his flamboyant macho attitude, and most of the Angels warmed up to him. As far as Kimmy knew, none had slept with him.

"Ok," said Kimmy, "I have the mine's tailing piles and settling ponds in view. Venom, Rivet, I will paint a target on the settling pools dam. When I'm ready, I'll tell you to fire."

Kimmy put her targeting reticle on the dam and fired a medium laser at low power. The missiles Zhi and Flexi carried detected the energy given off by the laser and followed the path of light to the target.

After receiving readies from the other pilots, Kimmy ordered, "Fire!"

Zhi's rex and Flexi's dwarf homebrew carried a ten-pack of LRMs. The missiles streaked out of the jungle canopy toward the target.

This strike, and Kimmy's height, was to be a distraction while Karen and her troop attacked through the jungle on the opposite side.

The missiles struck the earthen dam, blasting dirt, mud, and rock into the air. The water, sediment, and sludge on the bottom rushed out, carving a path through the jungle.

Kimmy increased her throttle and moved out of the jungle into the clearing upstream from the pond. A series of pipes fed the pond from the sluicing process. Kimmy followed the pipe up the hillside to a giant gold mining sluice box. A front loader poured dirt into the hopper.

Checking her radar, Kimmy didn't pick up any mechs. It was possible they were powered down and hidden in the jungle. She frowned over having to destroy the miners' hard work. This wasn't an industrial setup like the group that hired them. She didn't see any static defenses either.

The front loader stopped, and the cab door opened. The operator put a foot on the ladder and looked at Kimmy's dawnbreaker. Panicking, the man grabbed a radio from his overalls and called his boss, Kimmy assumed.

Hmmm, I have an idea. "Poison, where are you?"

"Nearing phase line lion. The jungle is hampering our movement, but we should be there in five minutes."

"When you reach lion, I want you to hold. We've begun our attack and reached the mining operation, but there are no defenses, and I don't detect any mechs. I'll try talking to these guys and see if they'll pay us to go away."

"Weren't we hired to destroy them?" said Lizzy.

"We're not mercs on this outing. We're pirates, and pirates go where the money is. I'm trying to get double paid for this job."

Flexi chuckled. "You've been hanging around Kita too long."

"Thought you were an empress, not a pirate," commented Dupont with a laugh.

Kimmy huffed at the playful ribbing. "I'll be the empress of the pirates if that's what it takes to get Chelsea and heal Kita."

Kimmy flipped her radio from internal to external and spoke to the front loader operator. "I want to speak to the boss. We'll level the operation if he doesn't arrive in ten minutes."

The operator spoke into his radio. He waved to her after he exchanged words with someone. Kimmy hoped that someone could pay. She flipped her radio to internal and found the others in the middle of a moral discussion.

"Stealing from these poor miners isn't right," argued Nicole. "It's no better than destroying their livelihood. Wouldn't it be better if we walked away? As a group, we're better than this. We should destroy the corporate thugs that hired us to destroy this independent mine."

"Unfortunately, we need the money," replied Kimmy sternly.

"We can make more money some other way. I can't be alone in this. Poison, Venom, you girls are officers. Doesn't this go against what we were trained?"

"Like you, I took an oath to obey and defend the Empress of the Empire of the United States," said Karen. "If she wants to double-cross our employer—I hope she got paid upfront. It's wrong, but it's on her. She is the Empress."

"We also have a hierarchy of oaths," replied Zhi. "We're honor bound to serve, protect, and obey Kita, and she needs our help. I'll do whatever is needed to save her because of my oath and because she is my friend."

"We're not on Earth Eight-Thirty-two," Nicole shot back. "We don't owe Kita or Kimmy any oaths beyond friendship and doing what's right in our hearts. This is not right—not the destruction or shaking down of this mine. These are hard-working people doing the same thing we're doing, trying to get by and make a living."

"It's not the same," huffed Kimmy. "I've got a kidnapped child and a severely injured partner. If these people can't protect what they have, that's their mistake."

"How are miners going to afford security mechs? We don't even know if they have any money. It's not right, Kimmy."

"Neither is having Chelsea taken and Kita in a protective tent keeping me from being able to touch her. Life isn't fair, and today it's the miners' turn."

"I won't be a part of this," said Nicole firmly.

"Fine. You and anybody else can move to the pickup location."

"Sapper, you with me?" Nicole called to Lizzy.

"I, ah, made the same oath as Poison and Venom to Kita when I became leader of her Commandos. That oath was for more than Earth Eight-Thirty-two. That was personal to Kita. She's my friend, and I don't see any other way. If there was, I'd take it. I'm glad we're not destroying the mine. I don't see what's wrong with asking them to pay us to go away, especially when we tell them why we're here. I see it as we're keeping the other guys from doing it again."

"But it's not right! You have to see that. As officers, we were taught to do what's right for our country and by our honor."

"My honor belongs to Kita," said Karen.

"How can you sleep at night?" yelled Nicole. "You know what Kita is—Kimmy is becoming just like her—and what she's done. You're all better than this. I know you are. I promise we can find a better way. Let's take the money we have and go."

"Sometimes you got to do what you got to do," said Dupont. "It does seem wrong stealing from the little guy."

"Weren't you just doing that?" said Karen.

"Yeah, but I had no choice if I didn't want to starve. We already got money from this job. I know we need a fair bit, but...why don't we ask instead of demand?"

"When it's your family, I hope your friends don't have a moral discussion over what's right and wrong to save them," Kimmy snarled. "I'd do everything in my power to help if it was one of you."

"We could go back to Roost," replied Nicole coldly.

"I will not give up!" screamed Kimmy. "And I can't pull Chelsea out if I don't know where she is! I won't abandon my child! How dare you suggest such a thing!"

"Calm down, Apocalypse," said Karen. "That's not what Nemesis meant. We would never abandon Chelsea or Kita. And we're not abandoning you. It's your choice what you want to do. I will back you regardless."

"Me, too," said Zhi.

"Anyone who doesn't want to be part of this can go to the pickup point," directed Karen. "No hard feelings. We understand why and respect it. I just ask that you do the same for those of us who stay."

"I'm going," said Nicole icily.

"I'll go with you," said Lizzy. "Kita would understand why."

"I'll sit this one out, too," said Dupont. "I'm a pilot, not a pirate, honest."

"Fallen Angel's my ship captain, and Apocalypse is the XO," retorted Flexi. "I'll do what they command."

"They're your friends, too," said Karen.

"Yes, I mean no disrespect by not including that."

A pickup-style vehicle pulled up next to the front loader, and the driver leaned out the passenger side window. The operator pointed at Kimmy's mech, and the driver looked out his window at the mech, acting like this was the first time he'd seen it.

Kimmy switched her radio to external. "There is a comm panel on my right middle toe, left side," she directed.

The driver exited the pickup and walked toward Kimmy while looking at her five-story tall mech. He seemed to know where the communications portal was, opened it, and his face appeared on Kimmy's console.

"Ah, who's this?" said a man with a weather-beaten face who looked like he should be retired.

"I'm Kimberly Roosevelt, leader of the Fallen Angels Merc Company. I'm here to destroy your operation—as you can see from your settling pond. That'll be the beginning—unless you want to cut a deal. Mister?"

"And here I thought Jake screwed up the dam. Jonny Henry Senior, ma'am. What do you want?" He spoke with a long drawl behind something he was chewing on.

"A hundred thousand credits will make us go away and leave you with just the dam breach."

Jonny ran his forearm across his brow, mopping the sweat. "I ain't got that. Wouldn't give it to you if I had it."

"How much does a front loader cost? Especially out here?" Kimmy trained her firing reticle on the red piece of machinery. Her torso angled slightly, aiming the thirty-millimeter cannon.

"You can turn it to scrap," Jonny said with a shrug, "but it won't get you nothin'. I ain't got nothin' to give."

"This is a gold mine, right?" demanded Kimmy. "I'll take that."

"We ain't got much. My operation just started washin' rocks a couple of weeks ago. I'd say we got about ten grand in credits. Not enough to keep your outfit goin', I reckon. Not enough to keep us going, that's for damn sure. Listen, I know you're here to wipe us out, and if ya do, that's your prerogative.

We've got no way to stop ya. The only thing ya be doing is destroying my life savings and leave me stuck in this godforsaken hellhole."

Kimmy grit her teeth. Her A'ahegre enabled her to detect lies, and Jonny wasn't. She didn't want to destroy their operation, but she had little choice except...*I've got one weapon left.*

"I don't want to," said Kimmy as she drew upon her emotions to get the tears flowing, "but...but...I need help. Please. My ship was damaged, trapping my friends and me here...I don't have any money for repairs...and my partner is...is...gravely injured after her mech was destroyed by the Blood Witches when they kidnapped my daughter...I don't know what I'm going to do. I have no options. We have no money...I...just want to save my family. Please..." Kimmy sniffed while wiping the tears from her eyes. She hadn't lied and hoped a damsel in distress routine might get her somewhere.

Jonny swallowed hard and looked down. "Listen, I'm powerfully sorry about your family. You have my best wishes and sincerest condolences. I'm learnin' life out here on the periphery is mighty hard, but I don't got anything—everythin' belongs to the bank. My boys haven't been paid yet. I can't rightfully give away their paycheck. I'm sorry, I don't have nothin' to give you...even if I wanted to."

Screw it. I will save Kita and Chelsea. I don't care who gets in my way. Kimmy sneered at Jonny as she pulled the trigger, firing a thirty-millimeter round into his front loader's engine, blowing the back end up and over the front.

"How's that for *best wishes and sincerest condolences*?" she screamed at Jonny. "Didn't they teach you not to get in the way of a desperate woman?"

Jonny turned to the screen, his face pale and sweating. "Alright! Alright! I don't want no trouble. It's just money, not worth anybody's life. You can have the gold we got. I'll take you to the office up the road. That's where I keep the take. Follow me in my truck. I promise no funny business—just don't shoot up anything else or kill anyone. You kill one of my boys, and the deal's off."

"Get in the truck and let's go," Kimmy said sternly.

"Sure thing." Jonny closed the communications panel and walked to his truck.

"Girls," Kimmy called to those left, "I'm going to the office. Step out into the clearing so they can see we mean business. Athena, I'll need you to come down and drop Bombshell so she can pick up what they give us."

"Roger. I'm maneuvering the ship now. What are they giving us?"

"It better be gold. Have Ash'a run the exchange rate and find a place to cash in."

"Wilco. We'll be over the site shortly."

"Roger. I'm following the mine boss now. Have UV prepare to drop the mouse mech that's in storage. We'll give it to them if the price is right. Ask Ash'a what's the price of a mouse in working condition?"

"Who's going to buy that out here?" replied Athena, sounding confused.

"I'm desperate, but I won't be a thief. I'll give it to the miners if their offer is enough." Kimmy followed Jonny up a winding, jungle-lined path.

"Ash'a says ninety-five thousand on the mech market. She said to add forty thousand for our location. Do you want it stripped?"

"No. If they can figure out how to pilot it, they can use it for defense."

"Then she said, add another twenty."

"One fifty-five. Got it. Ok, I see the miner's camp."

"Roger. I have you on the scope and am coming in. We'll hover at five hundred feet. Bombshell is ready to drop."

"We're in the encampment now." Kimmy steered her mech into a large clearing with five white inflatable domes and tire tracks that belonged to trucks like Jonny's. Jonny parked next to a larger inflatable dome—Kimmy assumed it was his office. He went into the dome as War Cat hovered overhead. The drop bay opened, and Bombshell jumped into the hot, muggy air.

The Morphicon Angel spread her wings and caught an updraft. She circled the miner's camp, descending until she landed next to Jonny's truck. Jonny came out carrying a small tub and set it on the hood of his truck. He saw Bombshell and did a double take at the Angel. Kimmy couldn't hear what she said, but he went inside and returned with another tub. Jonny made three more trips.

Kimmy changed her radio to external. "Bomb, open a container and see what's inside."

The Angel pulled out a jar and held it up for Kimmy. Pulling down her viewer, Kimmy looked at the golden contains.

Son-of-a-bitch. The man wasn't lying. The only thing Jonny left out was how much he had. And that was a type of lie Kimmy couldn't detect. Kimmy took a few steps forward to put her right foot near Bombshell so she could use the communications panel.

"Hey, Kimmy. This guy's like your Fort Knox."

Kimmy chuckled. Jonny didn't have that much gold, but it was a lot. "Make sure it's all gold and do your best to get a weight." She flipped her radio back to internal and called War Cat. "Bomb's checking the goods now. I don't know how much we've got, but it's a lot. Prepare to drop the mouse mech."

"Roger. One of UV's training pilots will make the drop."

Jonny brought out the last tub and spoke to Bombshell. She pointed to the communications panel. He appeared on Kimmy's console with a haggard expression.

"That's all of it. One thousand, two hundred, and thirty-four ounces."

Kimmy turned her radio to War Cat. "Athena, he's got over twelve hundred ounces. How much is that worth?"

"The current exchange rate is two thousand and twelve credits per ounce. So, roughly two point four million credits?"

Kimmy sucked in a deep breath. That was more than she thought the miners had. She couldn't in good conscience take it all...but that much money would pay for the repair and could go a long way in outfitting them and keeping the operation going. Kimmy thought she was generously giving them the mouse...and there was the destroyed front loader.

"Jonny," said Kimmy to get the man's attention.

"Yeah? I know you want to gloat, but I got to get back to work. Take it and go."

"I won't take all your money, just most of it. I am going to give you a mech for security—"

"Lot of good that does me. I ain't got no pilot. We're miners."

Kimmy rubbed her chin as she flipped the radio to War Cat. "Athena, tell Bombshell to load a thousand ounces—Jonny can keep the rest—and then put UV on."

"Yes?" said the hive mind.

"UV, I want the pilot bringing down the mouse to stay and protect the miners. They're not to be assimilated, just protected."

"It won't be long before the Jungle Cat Mining Company tries to destroy these guys again," said Athena. "A mouse won't be much protection."

Kimmy tapped the side of her helmet as Bombshell lifted four tubs off Jonny's truck and took flight back to War Cat. "Then we'll stop at Jungle Cat and convince them to help Jonny and his crew." She flipped the radio to Jonny. "Jonny, I'm going to give you one of my pilots. You don't have to pay him—I'll do that—just feed him, give him a place to sleep, and when he's not in, the mech can help your operation. I'll also take my crew to Jungle Cat and chat with the supervisor about leaving you alone. You may even get some help from them. That's the best offer I can make."

To Kimmy's left, the mouse landed and stepped out of the drop ring. The ring flared its jets and flew to War Cat. The light mech drove over and stood next to Kimmy.

"Jonny, this is..." Kimmy switched radio nets and called the light mech. "UV, who is that driving?"

"Frak Foren. He was a training pilot at the AFL."

"My guess is the Aven Foreign Legion won't be popular. We need a new name and back story. These guys seem very down-to-earth and hardworking...Earl..."

"McGovern? He was a pilot with the Gavion Consortium. Everyone likes them."

"Sounds good."

Kimmy switched to Jonny. "...This is Earl McGovern. He's a hard worker and willing to help you. He served six years in the Gavion Consortium. He's one of my best pilots and doesn't mind getting his hands dirty. If you have any problems, talk to him, and he can contact me. I owe you a favor, and I'm going to start by having a word with your competition that hired us."

Jonny raised an eyebrow, but his face was stoic. "What good are you to me? You ain't my friend, just a thief. Take my gold and get."

"I know it looks that way, but I don't forget those who help me. I'm in dire straits now, but I promise I'll repay you when I get back on my feet."

"Pretty words from a pretty girl don't mean shit. I don't need you to make me feel better about you robbing me. Get."

"I wouldn't lie, Jonny. I promise to replace your loader."

"You know what it took to get that here? No way you're replacing it. I don't know what I'm going to do."

"Earl will shovel the dirt by hand—if he has to—but I promise you'll get a new loader."

Jonny waved Kimmy off as he walked away.

Kimmy contacted War Cat. *I keep doing this, and my head is going to spin.* "UV, you there?"

"Yes?"

"Take the mouse to the destroyed front loader and start moving the dirt by hand."

"We'll need more people if we want to move the pile before the end of time."

"I know, but it's a show of good faith to Jonny until we get to Jungle Cat and have them send him a loader."

"How are we going to do that?" said Athena.

Kimmy chuckled. "UV's going into the mining business."

"We have run mining operations before...but never on such a small scale."

"We're doing this for Jonny, not trying to supply a universe. If you make us a profit, all the better."

The mouse jogged down the dirt road. Kimmy followed Jonny up. Jonny picked up the remaining tub and held it up to Kimmy. She changed the radio to external.

"It's yours. I'm not taking it—it's more than I need. Thank you for helping me. I promise I'll repay you."

Jonny spun on his heel and took the tub inside his office.

Kimmy sighed. *I promise I'll repay you in this life or even if I have to give you a second life.* She maneuvered her mech out of the miner's camp and trotted down the path to the mining operation. She passed "Earl" already loading the pay dirt by hand. After navigating the empty settling pond, she entered the jungle to meet her team.

"How'd it go?" said Karen when Kimmy found them among the foliage.

"We netted around two million credits."

"Holy shit," exclaimed Zhi. "These backcountry miners had that much?"

"Yes, and I gave them the mouse and said I would return the favor—starting by talking to Jungle Cat."

"I doubt they're going to be helpful."

"Oh, I'm not thinking of asking politely...more of a hostile takeover."

ASTARI II
JUNGLE CAT MINE
JUNGLE BIOME
Y51,834
1000 oz. GOLD
12, OCTOBER 4003

KIMMY, ASH'A, AND ULTRAVIOLET stepped onto the compact dirt landing pad of Jungle Cat Mining Corp, followed by Karen's troop of mechs. As War Cat lifted off, Kimmy bowed her head against the dust and heat.

"Come on, girls. Let's go have a chat," Kimmy said into her radio to the mechs. She waved to the others, and they walked across the landing pad and out of the dust. A ramp led to a two-story office building surrounded by small outbuildings and a protective half-dome protecting a piece of equipment being serviced.

Karen spread her four mechs around the encampment. She was in dawn-breaker and the others in Kimmy's biggest mechs. The thumping of the mechs' steps alerted the miners to their arrival. The mechanics left the half-dome, pointing and gawking at the towering mechs.

Several trucks with Jungle Cat logos sat parked around the office building. Bounding up the metal steps, Kimmy jerked open the door and stepped inside the dingy office. Ash'a and Ultraviolet followed.

"Place stinks of oil and dirt," said Ultraviolet, wiggling her leathery nose.

A man behind an L-shaped desk piled high with computers and papers looked from the window to the new arrivals. "Those things with you?" he asked, sounding dumbfounded.

"Yes," replied Kimmy tartly. "We're here to see the boss."

"Ah, who are you?"

"Empress Kimmy Roosevelt, leader of the mercenaries he hired to get rid of his competition."

Above them, the sound of footfalls came through the cheap prefabricated ceiling. They went to the back of the structure and down a narrow stairwell hidden behind some shelves. A twenty-something-year-old stepped into the room. His sandy blond hair was pushed to one side, revealing blue eyes. He wore a flannel shirt, jeans, and heavy leather work boots.

"She with the mechs outside?" he demanded.

"The mechs are with me," Kimmy retorted.

The young man ran a hand through his hair. "Who are you, and what do you want?"

"I'm Empress Kimberly Roosevelt, leader of the Fallen Angels. I'm here to tell you we completed the job you hired us for."

"What in the Void are you doing here? You're supposed to send pictures through a secure server...not show up and implicate us!"

"Let's say we got a better offer."

"From old man Henry? He ain't got no cash. What'd he offer?"

Kimmy shrugged. "Between him and me—"

"I already paid you, and I ain't payin' you no more. You shoot up my operation, and Lover will send more mercs than you've ever seen to hunt you down. You won't be able to take a shit without a mech crawling up your ass."

Kimmy wrinkled her nose. "Pleasant, but we had something else in mind, UV?"

Ultraviolet spread her ultraviolet-colored wings. Opening her hands, she grew two glowing spores in her hands. "Your minds are ours."

The spores flew into the mouths of the supervisor and his assistant. Light burst from their mouths, nose, and eyes as the spores wiggled their way to the brain stem and attached themselves. Both men's faces went slack, and their eyes glowed.

"As soon as the spores are ready, we will assimilate the rest of Aaron's crew," announced Ultraviolet.

"Do they have any gold on site?" said Kimmy.

"Yes. Five hundred ounces in the safe." She pointed to a large gray safe in the room's far corner, half hidden by boxes. "Aaron's crew has not been as successful as Jonny's."

"We'll take three hundred ounces and leave the rest for you to run the operation."

Aaron and his assistant opened the safe. They removed several jars and took them to a scale where they weighed out what Kimmy wanted.

"UV, get Ash'a into their computers." Kimmy smiled at the Aurorian. "I want to see if you can improve their operation. This could be a lucrative side hustle."

"I'll see what I can do. I keep this up, and I'll qualify for my diplomatic business certification."

Kimmy chuckled. The Aurorians saw everything as a negotiation and lived for diplomacy. Many roamed the galaxy, living on the periphery.

Ash'a went to the computer. The office assistant offered his seat.

Ash'a's scales rippled as she turned up her nose at the dirt and grease-stained upholstery. She rolled it away with her foot. "No thanks, UV. I don't want to get my overalls dirty." She bent over the computer and plugged in her tablet.

"We will go get the one from upstairs," said Ultraviolet as Aaron ran upstairs.

Ash'a looked up from her tablet and said, "Athena, can you get me in?"

Kimmy let her friends work and stepped back outside to talk to Karen.

"Poison, we're good. UV has the supervisor and his assistant. She'll have the entire camp by tomorrow. I snagged us another three hundred ounces."

"Wow, awesome. That should keep us going. We'll pull back to the landing pad and wait until you're ready."

"Roger. It shouldn't be long. Ash'a is going through their business records and hooking them into Athena's network."

"Sounds good."

Kimmy waved at Karen, then went back inside.

"I found an interesting analysis," said Ash'a. She had two computers open. "Someone did a soil analysis of Jungle Cat's claim. It's not rich. Somehow Aaron acquired the analysis of Jonny's claim, and it's significantly richer. I think Aaron was going to claim jump Jonny after we destroyed his operation."

"From the payout we received from both, I see why. Do you have what you need?"

"Yes. I'm linked into the Jungle Cat network. I've identified ways to make the claim more profitable, but I can't do anything about what's in the dirt."

Kimmy shrugged. "We have enough. This is supposed to be extra." She looked at Ultraviolet. "Do your best to pull gold out of the ground and help Jonny. I need you to deliver a front loader to him to replace the one I shot up."

"We might be able to salvage that one," said Ash'a. "Jungle Cat doesn't have a spare, so we'll be short the tools we need."

"Do what you have to do. Helping Jonny is paramount. If you're finished, let's go. Ultraviolet can finish assimilating the miners on the way to getting War Cat repaired."

ASTARI SYSTEM
NEAR ASTARI TRANSFER STATION
SPACE BIOME
¥51,834
1,300 oz. GOLD
14, OCTOBER 4003

KIMMY ANGLED HER DAWNBREAKER through the hip-deep water toward the beach, and a pair of expo heavy mechs engaging the rest of Kimmy's troop. Her HUD announced a lock on an expo's back right torso. Squeezing the trigger, Kimmy unleashed an alpha strike on the weakly defended area.

She didn't need so much firepower to blast through the armor, but she was experimenting with the dawnbreaker's capabilities and didn't want to not kill the expo. Her attack blew through the armor, and the cascading damage destroyed the center torso. The stricken mech fell and disappeared into the jungle fauna.

Kimmy trained every free chance she had to gain experience with heavy mechs. She was learning there was so much more that required her attention. The weapons loadout was three times what she was used to, and learning to balance the reload times and heat took much of her concentration. *We have got to get a better computer system. A good VI or AI would make us way more effective.* It was a dream Athena was working on, but she lacked the computer hardware to develop what was needed. The lack of resources didn't stop the AI from working on the problem. She co-opted the simulator whenever it was not in use—sometimes running her software in the bots to test. But the simulator hardware had limits.

"Kimmy?" said Athena through the simulator's messaging system.

Kimmy tapped the flashing box, and the words *PAUSE* appeared on the simulator screen. "Yes?"

"Kita is awake. I thought you'd like to see her."

"Oh, Void, yes. I'll be there in a minute. Can you shut the simulator down?"

"Of course."

Kimmy undid her harness and helmet as the simulator canopy rose. Ducking around the command chair, Kimmy opened the hatch in the back and hopped onto the platform. She raced down the stairs—the metal *clanging* of her boots showing her excitement—at the bottom, she swung around the rail and rushed for the door, thoughts of Kita dancing in her head.

Every day Kimmy visited Kita, hoping for some improvement. The inability to touch her partner was heartbreaking. She knew even if Kita wasn't in the tent, the synthetic skin wouldn't be like Kita's usual smooth skin. But even being able to talk to her sent Kimmy's heart soaring.

With a lighthearted step, Kimmy entered the medbay and was greeted by a nurse.

"How is she?" Kimmy couldn't contain her excitement.

Ultraviolet smiled. "She is awake. We explained what happened. She hasn't spoken since."

"I'm sure she's confused. I bet a familiar face will cheer her up."

"Follow me."

Kimmy followed Ultraviolet to a recovery suite. The hive mind Angel opened the door, and Kimmy stepped inside cautiously upon seeing the tent. She could see Kita's arm and stomach through a clear section. Creeping to the head of the bed so as not to startle Kita, her stomach filled with butterflies. Kita's head, wrapped in synthetic skin with no eyes, made Kimmy uneasy.

"Angel," Kimmy said in a gentle tone but loud enough to be heard. "It's me, Kimmy. I'm so excited you're awake."

Inside the tent, Kita's head rolled toward Kimmy.

"Oh, angel. I'm so glad you're awake. I've missed you so much."

Kita's mouth moved.

Kimmy couldn't hear, nor could she read Kita's damaged lips. She took a guess and said, "I love you, too, angel."

Kita's wrinkled, plastic-looking skin contorted, giving her an angry expression. Her chest inhaled, and she let out a whisper of a shout, "Let me die."

Kimmy recoiled in shock and fear. That was the last thing she expected to hear, and her insides exploded with a new set of fear and anxiety. In theory, she and Kita could die in a level one Reality and be transported back to their level three Reality. From there, they could go back to Roost, a level two Reality, and be reinserted into the level one Reality. But it had never been tested. The only time an Angel died in a level one Reality was Leaf, and she suffered permadeath. Kimmy wasn't willing to risk Kita unless she absolutely had to. The risk was even greater since they were in a universe's far future. No universe had ever run this long, and no one knew the risks. All the trial universes crashed around 3500 C.E. Kita, in her exuberance, had thrown caution to the wind and wanted to see what the future held. Kimmy was willing to risk a lot, but not the love of her life.

"Let me die!" Kita whispered in rage. She lifted her good arm and slammed it against the tent.

"Kita! Calm down," pleaded Kimmy as Ultraviolet rushed in. "I know it's bad, but I'm doing my best to save you. I...I—"

"Save me from what?"

"I...I'm working on a plan to get you better treatment. It's going to take some—"

"What happened to me?" Kita shrieked in a whisper.

"I'm sorry, angel. You lost your legs, arm, and sight when the Blood Witches cored you."

"No! Let me die!"

"Kita, listen. This isn't permanent. I'm working on getting the money."

Kita arched her back, slamming it against the bed. She twisted back and forth, slamming her good arm against the tent, causing it to collapse.

Ultraviolet pushed Kimmy aside and grabbed Kita's IV line. She pulled a syringe from her pocket and pushed the needle into the IV's injection port. Kita collapsed, tangled in the tent.

Another nurse and doctor rushed in. Kimmy stepped aside to let them work while she wiped tears from her eyes. Seeing Ultraviolet was going to be busy, Kimmy left.

"She's going to be out for a while," Ultraviolet called after Kimmy.

Kimmy sniffed. Her heart broken she didn't know what to do.

"Kimmy, are you alright?" said Velositi from behind.

Kimmy threw her arms around her girlfriend. Sobbing, she pressed her cheek against Velositi's warm metal stomach.

"Oh, Velositi. I've never seen her like this before. She's always optimistic and can deal with any situation. I've never seen her give up. She's...she's never rejected me before."

Velositi put her arms and wings around Kimmy. "I am sure waking up to what has happened to her is a shock. Kita has always relied on her physical abilities, and the sudden loss must be painful and depressing. I know she has been without eyesight before, but she had a way of compensating. As far as I know, she has never been without her legs and arms for any length of time. The closest is when she died and had to learn to walk and fight again. She may see that in her future, and it scares her."

"But why did she reject me?"

"I am sure she is scared. I will talk to her."

Kimmy shook her head, smearing tears across Velositi's black stomach. "UV put her back under."

"Oh...nuts. I was hoping to get to talk to Kita. Oh, well. Another time, perhaps. Come, you and I can talk and cuddle to make us feel better. Kita will come around. She always does. We need to be patient."

Kimmy looked at Velositi and nodded. "That sounds good. I could use some quality time with something that's not...well...a mech."

Velositi chirped laughter. "Put an AI in them, and they could be the unwanted bastard stepchildren of the Morphicons."

Kimmy shook her head. "They'd lack soul."

CHAPTER 06

ASTARI SYSTEM
ASTARI TRANSFER STATION
SPACE BIOME
Y51,834
1,300 oz. GOLD
21, OCTOBER 4003

"THANKS, ANNA. I CAN'T tell you how much this means to me—us. I know Kita would be grateful," said Kimmy as she hugged Anna at the personnel terminal of the Astari Transfer Station.

"It is my pleasure, *mat'*. I will find young Chelsea and bring her home. If I can, I will destroy those who took her."

Kimmy bowed her head. "If you can, or the flock will deal with them when we catch up to you."

"They will discover their grave mistake. The Aven fools should have let us go. Now, those pathetic men will know the wraith of women."

"Leave some for the rest of us," said Zhi. "I owe them a few shots for the scars on my back."

"Me, too," admitted Karen.

Kimmy winced inwardly. She knew the gashes from the lashes had healed, but it seemed the psychological damage went deep—as much as Karen and Zhi didn't want to admit it.

Kimmy reached into her pocket and pulled out a credit chit. "Here, Anna. It's all the liquid currency we have. I hope it will get you where you need to go."

Anna looked at the chit and frowned. "*Mat'*, I do not need to take the flock's money. If I need money, I will get it."

Kimmy pressed her lips together. She knew Anna was a capable spy but was willing to pay any amount to get Chelsea back. She placed her hand on Anna's, giving her the chit. "I know, but I want you to have the fastest, best chance. So many days have passed, and each day she gets farther away. I hope this will speed your journey and prevent Chelsea from suffering some horrific punishment. She doesn't deserve to pay for her parent's mistake."

"It wasn't your fault," interjected Nicole.

"I couldn't save her," Kimmy whispered, tears collecting at the corner of her eyes.

"You did the best you could," said Karen.

"And we've got the best people finder in the universe," said Flexi.

"When Anna finds her, we'll go scorched earth and desecrate Aven," added Zhi.

How to get Anna and Chelsea out of the Aven Federation hadn't crossed Kimmy's mind. She wasn't sure how, but she knew Anna would think of a way. Kimmy had no desire to take on the Aven Federation and their army of hoplite mechs.

"I already know where I must go," said Anna. "I have little doubt those despicable creatures will not deviate from their favorite course of action for Human vanilla females."

"Oh, Void," gasped Kimmy. "Please don't let them take Chelsea to the Baby Factory."

As an all-male society, the Avens could only reproduce by synthetic means. The fertile, vanilla women who came into their clutches were sent to the Baby Factory to have their eggs harvested. The commander of the Aven Federation Foreign Legion had ordered Kimmy there when she was a trainee. It's why the Angels stole War Cat and fled to the periphery.

"I will do everything in my power to keep her from their despicable exploitation—even if I must destroy it."

"You'd be doing the universe a favor," said Zhi.

An announcement over the speaker alerted everyone that Anna's shuttle was ready to board.

"Oh, group hug," said Kimmy as the other Angels stepped in and shared a warm embrace. "If you need anything, don't hesitate to call."

"If I need help, send Kita after me," Anna replied with a wink.

Kimmy smiled as the knot of Angels broke up.

Anna picked up her duffle bag and waved to the others as she walked to the gate.

"I can't help but think we've unleashed a demon to raise hell," said Zhi.

"But she's our demon," replied Ash'a.

"Yeah, she won't hurt us," said Flexi.

Kimmy shrugged. She believed Anna wouldn't hurt the flock. *I guess we'll have to wait and see. She's never done it before.* "Come on, ladies. Let's go cash out."

Karen, Zhi, and Flexi shouldered bags containing the "borrowed" gold.

"Girls ready?" said Dupont as he stood from a nearby seat.

"Not a hugger?" teased Kimmy as she led the group onto the concourse.

Dupont blushed. "I, ah, didn't want to have to take my nuts back to medbay."

Kimmy smiled. "Sorry about that. Anna is protective of the flock. I'd say wait until you get to know her, but I don't know her that well. She stays by herself. I think only Kita has gotten to know her. They share professional and psychological interests."

"Psychological?"

"Both are sociopaths. I think Kita is helping Anna learn to be more personable and understanding of regular people."

"I...wow. Never heard that before. And you're partnered with one? I always heard they were...unsavory."

"She has her moments, but we make it work with some firm ground rules and some education for me. There's no one I love more in the world."

"Yeah, but I've heard sociopaths don't love. Does she reciprocate?"

"Of course she does...in her own way. She gives me what I need, and I fulfill her needs and desires."

"You should see them together," said Lizzy. "Mushy central."

"I thought that was your problem with Kita. She wasn't mushy enough."

"Nah, my problem was when I learned she was so old."

Kimmy and the other Angels laughed. Kita never divulged her age, and Kimmy was fairly certain she'd lost track.

The group entered the main concourse of the transfer station. It formed a large loop through commercial, military, and personal docks and gates. As the economic center of the Astari system, most business for the system was conducted here—including currency exchange. From there, getting War Cat signed up for the next FTL transfer ship was a quick walk. It would take five jumps to reach their destination, the Kliene system, and the part needed to fix War Cat.

As Kimmy led the group, she found Dupont on her right.

"I apologize for not being chattier since you came aboard, Pierre. Life's been hectic."

"Hey, it's no sweat. You aren't keeping me in the brig and rooming with you girls—Angels?—is pretty nice. I mean, it smells better than most barracks."

"You can call us Angels. I don't think anyone will mind."

"Wait until he sees our wings," chuckled Karen.

"You Angels have cosplay wings and halos?" Dupont asked with a smile.

"I don't think any of us have halos," chuckled Zhi. "But the wings are real. We don't have them, so we fit in. If we find our Axioms, then, buddy, watch out. There's nothing this pilot hates more than being grounded."

"Hey, I like thrusters as much as the next pilot," Dupont said with a shrug.

Karen and Zhi laughed. "Mech piloting is ok, but wait until you strap into a fighter."

"Nothing like your afterburners throwing you into the seat as you hit Mach-two," said Zhi with longing in her voice.

"You mean starfighters?" asked Dupont.

Both Karen's and Zhi's ears pricked up. "Starfighters?"

"Yeah. They get launched into space."

Karen and Zhi shared a look of excitement, then looked at Kimmy.

"I can't get you, girls, into one at the moment...but let's see where Pierre's map takes us."

"That would be so cool!" said Zhi, clapping her hands, then throwing her arms around Karen. "Can you imagine flying in space?"

Karen looked at Kimmy. "You got her hopes up. Too late to back out now."

Kimmy smiled. "I lack those kinds of resources."

Zhi looked up from Karen's shoulder and back at Ultraviolet. "Hey, UV, think you can conquer one of these states for us? Karen and I want to fly a starfighter."

The Mi Prii Angel glided up with Ash'a. "I could. Which do you want?"

"We're not taking over a state," said Kimmy angrily. "I would be the one left to govern it, and I have enough on my plate. Be happy with the new mechs."

"Sorry, Kimmy. We don't mean to add more stress to you. But flying in space sounds tantalizing. Maybe not this time, but another time."

"Have you conversed with the Angel Jammer in the Memorial Hallway?" said Ultraviolet.

Karen and Zhi shook their heads.

"She was a starfighter pilot for Kita. She has many stories of flying in space as an electronic warfare pilot."

"When we go home, I'll have to talk to her," said Zhi.

"Is this a place on War Cat I haven't been?" said Dupont.

"Someone will explain it later. We're here." Kimmy stopped in front of a small sign that read CURRENCY EXCHANGE. A shabby-looking door that didn't close had a handwritten sign reading HUMANS ONLY. Kimmy let out a frustrated sigh. *Goddamnit. Why can't the universe be decent? All I want is for this to go smoothly.*

She called for Velositi. "Hey, can you take charge of everyone while I take Zhi, Karen, and Pierre into the exchange?"

"Yes, of course. Is there a problem?"

"The proprietor doesn't like non-Humans." She moved aside so Velositi could see the sign.

The matriarch Morphicon's eyes dimmed.

"Is there a better place?" said Bombshell as she handed her bag to Karen.

"Oof," grumbled Karen as she put the bag of gold on her shoulder. "I miss my Angel strength."

"This was the only one listed," replied Kimmy to her stepdaughter.

"They give you trouble we'll come shoot up the place," said Knockout.

"We should go with them," said Bombshell. Sparkles spread across her body as she morphed into a blonde Human dressed in a miniskirt, heels, and a cut-off shirt. Her sister copied her.

Kimmy recognized the look from the pinup poster in the mech bay.

"Here, you can have this back," said Karen, handing the gold back to Bombshell.

I wonder if they have a white male? That would be the easiest way. Kimmy shrugged the thought away. She wouldn't push the girls into something they weren't comfortable with.

"Did you know they could do that?" Dupont said to Karen.

"They're daughters of Kita. I wouldn't be surprised if they morphed into hill giants flinging fireballs out their butts while solving universal hunger and conquering the galaxy."

"Ok," said Kimmy, rolling her eyes at Karen's bizarre description of the triplets. She was curious to see Dupont's reaction when he learned there was a third.

Kimmy pushed open the door with a *creak* and stepped inside the tiny room divided by a narrow counter. On the far side was a slim desk with a tablet, scale, and cash box. On the walls were the exchange rates of the various currencies and pictures of Earth wilderness scenes mixed with Aven Federation propaganda posters.

A door to the right opened, and a young white man who looked to be trying to grow a beard stepped out. His scraggly blond hair was hidden under a dirty cap. He wore jeans, work boots, and a flannel shirt. The man stopped behind his desk, leaned on his knuckles, glowered, and said, "We don't want no nigos or slanty yellows in here. Get the Void out. If you want to do business, bring a male with you."

"I did," said Kimmy hotly as she pointed to Dupont.

"That ain't no male. That's a nigo. Get it out of here before it pollutes my establishment."

Dupont stepped up to the counter. "Son, I will pound the racism right out of you. Let the woman do what she needs, and we'll leave."

"All I want is to exchange my gold, and we'll be gone," said Kimmy. "I'll send the others out, and you can deal with me. I'm white, your white—I served time in the Aven Foreign Legion to protect the fatherland. I even donated my eggs."

The young man's eyebrows went up. "Fine. You can stay. The rest of you degenerates, get out."

Kimmy turned to the others. "Ok, you heard him. Everyone out."

The others left, grumbling.

"You want us to leave, Momma-Kim?" said Bombshell.

Kimmy nodded. "Yes. The fewer people in here, the smoother this will go."

"Ok," said Knockout, "he gives you any problems, you come get us."

"I will, girls."

Those carrying bags dropped them on the counter. Kimmy dug into one and pulled out a jar full of yellow metal.

"Nice hall. I haven't heard of a female working the mines. What mine are you from?" the man asked as he took the jar.

"Kimmy Roosevelt. I recently acquired the Jungle Cat Mine and got a favor from Jonny Henry."

The jar hit the table with a *thump*. "No way Aaron would sell to a female. If this is his gold, you stole it. And we have ways of dealing with thieves." The man reached under the table and pulled out a pistol—illegal on the transfer station, but Kimmy saw the rules only applied to outsiders.

"Call him," said Kimmy. "He'll tell you who I am and where I got the gold. Some came from the Jungle Cat Mine, most from Jonny Henry's mine. I was hired to destroy Henry's mine by Aaron—"

"Mister Astolt, to you, female."

Kimmy let out a frustrated sigh. She'd experienced some bigotry as a lesbian on her homeworld, but this was next-level bullshit.

"Then you will address me as Empress Roosevelt."

"Empress?" he scoffed. "Of what?"

"Earth Eight Thirty-two."

"Where the Void is that? The only Earth I know belongs to the Aven Federation."

"That would be Earth Eight Ninety-two. You keep up this misogynistic bullshit, and I will conquer it, too. Now, Mister Astolt and I have come to an understanding of ownership. You can message him—"

"Only if you're paying."

"I just spent my last credit. All I've got is gold."

"How much?"

"Thirteen hundred ounces."

The man's eyebrows went up. "It ain't the end of the season. No mine has got that much."

"Like I said, most came from Henry's mine as payment and the rest from Mister Astolt as my share of the mine's profits."

"No way Aaron would let a female in."

"I offered him something he couldn't get, mechs and protection."

"No way. If Aaron needed protection, he'd call his Lover, and they'd send an army of hoplites."

"Or, they sent me. Because I'm closer and could handle it. I'm foreign legion, remember?"

The man scratched his chin. "Ok, I'll see what I can do. Unload the bags, and I'll weigh it."

Kimmy released a silent sigh of relief. She opened each bag and pulled out ten jars, lining them up on the counter.

The man zeroed the scale with a bowl attached. One by one, he emptied the jars, forming a large golden mound.

"Alright, you've got three point eight one ounces over thirteen hundred."

Kimmy leaned over the counter to check. Craning her neck to look at the exchange rate, she did the math. *Two thousand and five credits per ounce. So that should be two million, six hundred and fourteen thousand, and some change. More than enough to get us to the Kliene system and fix War Cat. Maybe we can even find some medical treatment for Kita!*

"Excuse you!" said the man as he planted his hand firmly on Kimmy's forehead and pushed her back.

As Kimmy huffed over the manhandling, he opened a drawer, pulled out a credit chit, and inserted it into his tablet.

"Who do I make it out to?"

Kimmy rolled her eyes but gave him the benefit of the doubt that he'd not heard her name. "K-I-M-M-Y-R-O-O-S-E-V-E-L-T."

The man tapped on his tablet, then withdrew the chit. He handed it over. "Here you go. Now, get out. I don't need a female stinking up the place."

Kimmy checked the balance. *Three hundred sixty-five thousand and nine hundred and seventy-nine credits? What the!* "Hey!" she squawked. "I gave you over thirteen hundred ounces! That should be over two point six million credits!" She pointed at the rate board.

"That's the preferred client rate. You received the AFL rate minus the undesirable penalty."

"Undesirable?" Kimmy shouted. "Who's your boss—who owns this place?"

The man puffed up his chest and grabbed his pistol. "You got your credits. Now get out. I'm not giving you more."

"It's not enough!" cried Kimmy. "I've got to get to the Kliene system and pay for ship repairs! My partner needs medical treatment. She might die if she doesn't get it!"

The man wrinkled his nose. "Ew. Get out, beaver-eater. I don't want your sick foul pollution in here."

Tears filled Kimmy's eyes. "Dammit. I played by your rules. I did everything you wanted. Why can't you be a decent human being?"

"Beaver-eater, you don't leave, I'm putting a bullet in you."

As Kimmy wiped her eyes, she fled the exchange. She rushed hurried onto the concourse and ran into Velositi's wing.

Turning, Velositi let out an, "Oh! Kimmy! What's wrong?" Her exclamation brought the attention of the other Angels and Dupont.

Kimmy looked at Velositi, wringing her hands, then exclaimed, "Oh, shit!" through her tears. Defeated and embarrassed, she wrapped her arms around Velositi and cried into her armored middle.

"What happened?" said Karen.

"I bet it was that asshat," said Bombshell. "Come on, sis. Let's go teach him some manners."

"What a second, girls," ordered Velositi. "Let us find out what happened first. Then we will decide on a course of action." She rubbed Kimmy's back a few times, calming Kimmy. "Kimmy, what happened?"

"Shit!" squawked Kimmy. "I've got to go back in there." The idea brought fresh tears to her eyes.

"Not without us," said Zhi.

"Why?" asked Velositi. "Did you not exchange the gold?"

"I lost the chit," sniffed Kimmy.

"We'll go get it," said Knockout.

"We'll take his head off, too," added Bombshell.

Velositi's eyes dimmed. "Girls, what have I told you about rushing into things? Let us tend to Kimmy, then we will take a course of action to retrieve the chit. It may be as simple as walking in and picking it up off the floor."

Feeling foolish, Kimmy turned in Velositi's arm and faced the other Angels.

I can't believe I let that creep get to me. I was doing what he wanted and...and that's what he wanted. He knew he would never give me all the money. He probably pocketed the rest. Shit. I should tell UV to expect a call from Aaron about stolen gold.

How am I going to get the money back? I could unleash the triplets or UV...but that makes me as bad as him. What do bullies fear most? People standing up to them—and I have many people willing to stand up to this guy. Kimmy stepped out of Velositi's arms and wiped her eyes.

"Everyone, sorry for my outburst. The stress is getting to me. Bomb, Knock, thanks, but if we blow his head off, we're no better than him. But I have an idea. Everyone, come with me. It'll be tight inside, but remember, he doesn't have that many bullets."

The Angels laughed, but Dupont looked uneasy.

"Why are we charging down a gun?" he asked.

"Nothing to be scared of," said Nicole. "You can stand behind me if you're worried."

"I'm not scared, but it *is* a gun."

"Pssst," said Zhi as she waved it away. "Guns aren't nothing—at least, a pistol, anyway."

"We're going inside to face down a bully," said Kimmy. "Most bullies are too scared to use their guns, anyway. And if he shoots, he doesn't have enough bullets to take us all down. Those left standing can pummel the shit out of him."

"Yeah!" said Bombshell.

"You cannot kill him," said Velositi. "Kimmy needs him alive to get the credits we are owed."

"Nuts. Oh, well. Cracking some skulls is just as fun."

"Come on, everyone," said Kimmy as she waved the group to the exchange door. She opened it, and the Angels and Dupont filed inside. Kimmy, threading her way through the group to the counter, heard, "What the Jiminy are you freaks doing in here? Get the Void out! No one wants to smell your non-Human stink."

"You better watch your mouth, asshat," said Bombshell. "You don't know what I am or capable of."

"I don't care if you're God himself—"

The room erupted into laughter.

"Excuse me, Bomb, can I get by?" said Kimmy. She traded places with the Morphicon and rested her arms on the counter. She looked at the man and sighed. "It's *herself*. And god *herself* is standing in front of you. I'm one of two entities that make up the God of Reality. I doubt you worship us, and I hope I don't disappoint. Now, did anyone pick up my credit chit?"

"There was nothing on the floor when I came in," said Nicole.

There was some shuffling as the others checked under their feet and hooves.

"Nothing," said Karen as she looked around at the others.

Kimmy turned to the man. "I believe you have two somethings of mine."

"Any lost property left or otherwise, is property of the finder."

"Really?" said Kimmy, aghast. "Then what's keeping me from *finding* this place is mine?"

"Sorry, female. You lost it. Go cry somewhere else."

Kimmy jumped over the counter, landing behind the narrow table. "Hey, girls, look what I found. They have no name. I mean, my credit chit has my name as proof of ownership, so these must not belong to anybody." She grabbed the cashbox and tablet and tossed them to Bombshell and Knockout.

"Hey! Give those back!" The man lunged across the counter at Bombshell, but Nicole grabbed him by the arm and back of the pants and pulled him into the Angels. He landed with a *thud* on the dirty carpet.

"Don't get too close," snarled Lizzy. "You don't want my stink on you."

The man struggled to stand until Velositi's large angular foot came down on his back.

"And what would you like to call me, Human?" said Velositi as she morphed her right arm into a cannon.

"Hey, Mom!" cried Bombshell. "What was that lecture you gave us?"

Velositi's eyes lit as she smiled at her daughters. "It's my girlfriend he made cry. I'm protecting her honor."

Knockout scoffed. "See what Momma-K has to say about that."

"Bomb, give that tablet to Ash'a to see if she can unlock it. Knock, open the cashbox. I want a count to prove we didn't take anything." Kimmy climbed onto the counter. She sat, letting her legs dangle. Looking at the man, she said, "So, how's it feel to be oppressed?"

"Take the cashbox! Take anything you want. Just don't kill me!"

Kimmy cocked her head and played with her dark, wavy hair. "Weren't you listening? I'm not here to steal. Just get back what's mine—all two million six hundred fourteen thousand and one hundred thirty-nine of it. Let's start with my credit chit. Where is that?"

"No idea. Maybe the auto-vac got it."

"An auto-vac hasn't touched this floor since you were born, son," said Dupont.

"If you don't produce it, Lizzy and Nicole will ooze all over you until they find it."

"We will?" Lizzy made a disgusted face.

"Or I can. Nothing I haven't done before. I should be glad Kita isn't awake to hear about this." Kimmy slid off the counter, landing next to the man. She checked his shirt pocket. Finding it empty, Kimmy checked his pants pockets, pressing the flat of her hand against him as much as possible. She found the missing chit in his back pocket. "So, going to explain how this got back there?"

"To the Void with you!" he cried. "Help! Help! I'm being robbed!"

"As loud as this station is, you will not be heard," said Velositi. Kimmy raised an eyebrow as the Morphicon adjusted her foot. "Think about your head cracking like a melon instead."

Kimmy turned to Ash'a. "Any luck?"

"Yes, I'm in. The password was written on the tablet. I'm searching the accounts for the missing money."

Kimmy pushed Velositi's foot aside. Gently, she helped him sit up. "You, ok?"

The man sat hunched over, looking to be expecting the worst.

"We won't hurt you—well, maybe the Morphicons, but they're only protecting the rest of us. Now, what is your name?"

"My—my Lover is rich and powerful. He'll send the hoplites after you."

Kimmy chuckled. "That seems to be the going threat among the Beloved—my Lover this, my Lover that...don't you *men* stand on your own two feet? I know it's nice to feel protected, but, like now, they're half a galaxy away. Doesn't do you a lot of good. I could kill you, won't be my first, but I'm trying to be nice. I want you to be courteous and treat me respectfully so I can get my business done. Isn't that what you want? To make a little money?"

"His Lover is giving him all the money he needs and probably more," scoffed Nicole.

"As long as he gets down on his knees—" added Lizzy.

"Girls," scolded Kimmy. "We don't make fun of his sexual preferences as long as he doesn't comment on ours."

"Beaver-eater," coughed Zhi.

"There is that," Kimmy said with a sigh. "Fine, if you don't want to be helpful, sit there and be quiet, or I'll let the Morphicons have you."

"Where's the pistol?" said Dupont.

"It wasn't on him," replied Kimmy.

Dupont jumped the counter and looked through the desk. "I don't want that thing coming back to haunt us," he explained as he searched.

Kimmy looked down at the man. "Where is it? If you don't tell me, I will let Velositi have you. I won't endanger my friends."

"Kimmy," called Ash'a.

Kimmy turned to the Aurorian. "Yeah?"

"I'm not finding any money transfers beyond what's on the credit chit. I am finding a bunch of love letters to Aaron Astolt. Apparently, our friend Caleb wants to run away with Aaron and live off the gold he took from you."

Kimmy looked at Caleb and burst out laughing. She looked at Ultraviolet. "Did you get that note?"

"We did. We're ignoring it...unless you want us to reply, but we don't know what to say."

"I don't think you have to say anything." Kimmy looked at Caleb. "Did you know you've been in a relationship with her for the last few weeks?" She waved Ultraviolet forward so Caleb could see.

"By the Void! What the fuck is that?" cried Caleb as he tried to scoot away from the Mi Prii Angel.

Kimmy wedged her foot under Caleb so he couldn't get away. "Tsk-tsk. Be nice. Ultraviolet's a Mi Angel in a Prii's body. She's friendly. I'm sorry she hasn't responded to your love notes. I don't think she knew she needed to. With great sadness, I must inform you that Aaron is in a new long-term relationship with her."

"Aaron wouldn't leave me!" cried Caleb.

"He had little choice," said Lizzy with a grin.

"Once UV gets into your brain, you belong to her," agreed Kimmy. "Sorry, but you can always go back to your Lover."

Kimmy wasn't sure how the Lover-Beloved relationship worked in Aven. She knew an older, established male chose or fell in love with a younger one. The Lover, or older male, was responsible for the wellbeing of the Beloved or younger male. She was sure there was a sexual component but not sure if it was an open relationship. It seemed from Caleb's note they were planning on ditching their Lovers to run off and be together.

Caleb grumbled something, then looked at Kimmy defiantly with a tear in his eye.

Kimmy shrugged. "Sorry to ruin your love life. I guess you know how I felt when I left."

"Pierre," called Ash'a. "Can you look for the gold in the backroom? I can process it and give us the rest of what we're owed."

Dupont was under the desk and gave a muffled reply.

"I'll get it," said Lizzy. She and Nicole jumped the counter and pushed open the door leading to the back.

"Kimmy, do you want these letters?" said Ash'a.

"Sure, we can use some leverage on Caleb. Sounds like he doesn't want his Lover to know about him and Aaron."

Ash'a tapped on her tablet and then on Caleb's. "All set. I need your chit to move the money."

As Kimmy dug the chit from her pocket, Nicole and Lizzy came out of the backroom carrying the jars of gold in the bags they'd used to carry it earlier.

"Here you go, Ash'a," said Nicole as they set the jars on the scale.

"I think we found it all," said Lizzy. "Not just what he cashed out for us."

"Help me over?" Ash'a asked Bombshell and Knockout. The Morphicons helped her over the counter, where Ash'a opened a jar and poured it on the scale. Entering the results on Caleb's pad.

There was a *thump* followed by a *bonk* from under the table. "Son-of-a-bitch," exclaimed Dupont. "But I got it. Coming out."

"Why, hello," said Nicole, looking down between her legs.

"Whoops! Sorry," Dupont replied with a chuckle. "Don't mean to be intrusive."

"I guess I can say I've had a guy between my legs." She moved out of the way and helped Dupont up.

He broke down the pistol, pocketing the firing pin. "There. That should keep us from getting shot in the back."

"What were you doing?" asked Lizzy.

"Defeating the gunlock. Not hard, just required a screwdriver." He patted an upper arm pocket that contained handles to several tools.

"Why do you have a screwdriver?"

"To adjust the mech's throttle and control stick. New mechs are stiff and old ones are looser than a hooker's...ah...you know."

"Never been with a hooker," Lizzy said with a shrug.

"A hot dog down a hallway?" Dupont replied, scratching the back of his neck.

The Human Angels laughed.

"I don't think any of us have to worry about that," said Karen.

"I mean, what kind of sex are you having, Pierre?" asked Zhi with a sympathetic look.

He shrugged. "Beggars can't be choosers."

Kimmy and the rest of the girls looked sympathetic.

"Don't worry," said Bombshell, "we'll find you somebody nice."

"How about a toy?" suggested Knockout. "Most of the girls have theirs."

Dupont blushed. "I, ah...never...I'll...stick to the shower."

Kimmy came to his rescue. "That's enough, girls. Not everyone is comfortable talking about their sex lives."

"Not sure how I would have sex," said Knockout. "I mean, it's just energy storage and armor down there."

Bombshell giggled. "Ask Mom. She would know."

The two young Morphicons looked at Velositi.

"I have only had sex with Human females. I would not know about Human males. You will have to explore on your own."

Zhi looked at Kimmy. "So...you and her or you, her, Kita...How's that work?"

Kimmy winked at her friend. "Both. Her fingers are quite dexterous, and she never gets tired."

"I might have to teach one of these kids."

Kimmy shrugged as Ash'a announced, "Got it weighted and entered. Let's see, ah, there's a standard five percent surcharge and...my...lots of deductions. Here we go. Aven Federation citizen gets the full ninety-five percent share, or the Aven Foreign Legion gets a ninety percent share. What do you want?"

Kimmy tossed her hair. "Let's go with AFL. I don't want to look like we're stealing from them."

"Hey," whispered Flexi loudly from the back, "We do have the manager tied up on the floor."

"Details."

"All set!" Ash'a set the chit on the counter.

Kimmy picked it up and checked the balance—two million, three hundred and fifty-two thousand and seven hundred and twenty-five credits. "Outstanding! Come on, everyone. Let's go get our ship on the jump ship manifest." She pulled Caleb to his feet. "Thanks for your help. I'll do you a favor and have Ash'a wipe that tablet to get rid of your correspondence with Aaron. If you contact him, you'll end up with UV." She guided his head to the right Angel. When Caleb winced, Kimmy said, "You need to be more open-minded. She's one of the most powerful creatures in the universe—able to take over entire planets in days...took me years to take over mine. She's very nice and sweet. You don't know what you're missing."

Caleb looked at Kimmy. "Is Aaron dead?"

"Of course not!" Kimmy replied, aghast. "He's assimilated by UV, though."

"If you write him, we will reply," said Ultraviolet. "But know his heart is one with mine."

Caleb looked perplexed.

"Write him," said Kimmy. "See what you get. Ok, everyone out."

The Angels filed out as those behind the counter helped each other over. Kimmy was the last to leave. She stopped at the door.

"Thanks for your help. Write Aaron. Love is a funny thing. You never know what you're going to get."

Ducking out, she caught up with the back of her group.

"Why didn't we shoot him?" said Flexi.

"Because I wanted to be better than them," said Kimmy. "Plus, it's messy when I don't have Kita to clean up the body."

"Think he'll write Aaron?" Lizzy said with a chuckle.

"We'll see. I'm sure UV will tell us if she enters a relationship."

K IMMY CREPT INTO KITA's medical suite. She didn't want to wake Kita and upset her, but she wanted to be near her partner. The tent was gone, and Kita was asleep.

Sitting in the chair by the side of the bed, Kimmy heaved a tired sigh. War Cat was docked with the FTL jump ship, and the journey would begin shortly. It would be a series of five FTL jumps. At each jump, the FTL ship would load and offload ships, requiring their voyage to take three days.

"Can you sigh any louder?" Kita's voice was ragged and angry. "I can't save you. I can't save myself."

"Kita!" Kimmy exclaimed. "I...I...How are you feeling?"

"I'm just as fucked as you, probably worse. You won't let me die. I could be better!" Her scream came out hoarse.

Kimmy spun from her chair onto her knees, grasping for any part of Kita she could touch. Her hand found her partner's hip. "No, Kita, you can't die. I won't lose you. You need to be patient. I have money, and I can get you the medical care you need...I just need to fix War Cat first. Please, Kita, hold on. I know it's hard...but...but Sprokkit is working on prosthetics for you. You'll be able to walk—"

"Like a damn cripple!" Kita's scream ended in a coughing fit.

Kimmy sprang to her feet and pulled Kita to a sitting position, careful of the synthetic skin. She wasn't sure what it would take to tear it or if that would cause Kita any pain.

"Kita, I'm sorry. I know it's not what you want, but please give us a chance. I know it'll be a few months...but...but...I have a map to a UEE compound. It can save us."

Kita flopped onto her pillow, causing her to cough more. She spoke around coughs, sounding weak. "Save...yourself. Let...me...die. I'll...come...back."

"No. You don't know that. Leaf didn't come back. We don't know for sure that'll happen, and I won't risk it."

"What good am I?" Kita hissed. "KILL ME! Let me come back as someone useful."

Tears flooded Kimmy's eyes. "No," she whispered. "I won't take that chance...unless it's the only chance. You're here and alive. I think we can fix you. You might not be the same, but something is better than nothing."

"I won't be this way!" Kita's scream was airy and hollow.

"Kita, please, you're going to injure yourself."

"How can I do anything with this?" Kita held up her good arm. "I can't even kill myself. I'm a useless waste you keep around to spare yourself from your own guilt. Kill me! Let me come back as the person who can save you. That's what you want, isn't it?"

"No," Kimmy whispered. "I love you, and I won't lose you. I can save us. We don't need you to. I would rather have a piece of you than none of you. I promise it'll get better."

"Bah. Go away. Let me wither and die."

Kimmy backed away from the bed. "I love you. I'm sorry this happened to you, but I will do my best to make you as whole as I can. Just give me a chance, please?"

Kita chuckled and coughed. "You don't love me. I'm just a pile of useless, putrid flesh. An object for your pity after what happened to your daughter. Kill me. In death, I always come back a...little stranger."

Kimmy shook her head, tussling her dark hair. "No. I won't risk it. You'll learn to be happy. Once we get you the care you need. I don't care how long it takes, I'll wait, and while I do, I'll rescue Chelsea. I love you. Please feel better." She rushed from the suite, tears in her eyes.

Crossing the medical bay, Velositi put out an arm and corralled Kimmy.

"Kimmy, what is the matter?"

Kimmy sniffed and rubbed her nose. "I...Kita wants me to hate her."

Velositi pressed Kimmy against her. "No. She is scared you will leave her."

"What? No! I told her I love her and would help her. I'd do anything for her."

"I know, but yours is not the mind of a sociopath. Kita sees everything as a balance, a quid pro quo. You offer her things she desires, and she has things you desire. In her mind, that balance has drastically altered away from her favor. She is desperate to get it back, to get you back. I may have mistakenly told her about Pierre and that you seemed friendly with him."

"Friendly, yes, but I would never leave her for him! Yuck. The whole idea of being with a man is mortifying."

"In her conspiracy-addled mind, anything is possible. She loves you and will do anything to keep you. If she were mobile, I would tell Ultraviolet to guard Pierre."

"On, no. What do I tell her to reassure her I love her?"

"The easiest way would be to send her back to Reality...if we could. But that way remains blocked by the parameters set for this universe. Killing her would—theoretically—take her back to Reality—"

"I won't do it," Kimmy said firmly. "I won't risk her not coming back. Leaf didn't come back. I won't lose Kita, and I would rather have her as she is than nothing at all. I know we can repair most of the damage."

"That might not regain the balance in Kita's eyes."

"What balance? She said she loves me, and I love her. What more balance do we need?"

Velositi stepped back, holding Kimmy at arm's length. "You know Kita does not think in intangibles. In her mind, you love her because of the things she has, is, or can offer. You have things she desires. What those are, you will have to ask her. But it appears from her outbursts with you her body is a great asset to her, and the loss hurts a great deal.

"Remember, she is an assassin, an incredible gymnast, and a great beauty. She has lost the means to protect you, and her skills are useless. She feels she can contribute nothing to the cause. To her, death...even absolute death...is preferable to her existence now."

Kimmy cocked her head. "How do you know?"

"I talk to her. She has been withdrawn and made known her desire for death when we talk, but her desire is not so absolute or demanding. I think that is because she thinks I think of her differently than she perceives you."

"How does she perceive us? Why the difference?"

"To her, I am a caretaker, consoler, guardian, and mentor. I will always see her as little Kita—a beautiful creature that needs help. Now, I love her via the same mechanism as you. I do not see our relationship as a scale—I love her for who she is if she's little Kita like now, or god Kita when she's not in a universe."

"But I love her for who she is, too. I don't care if she's little Kita or god Kita—she's still Kita."

"Yes, but in her mind, she must always be god Kita—to protect, love, even turn you on. If she cannot be that way, she would rather die."

"I don't care what she looks like. I love that twisted, broken body and will do anything to make her feel better. That's all I want to do—take away her pain and heal her. I want to give her back her mobility. I don't care if she can't do a backflip or swing a sword. I just want her."

Velositi's eyes dimmed. "She does not see it the same way. Remember, everything is a balance. If the balance is disturbed too much, it can destroy her self-image. Her self-image and self-worth are defined by what she can do, offer to others, and what she can get in return. At the moment, she feels she has nothing to offer you. It will be rough going forward, but it will improve as we increase her mobility. I think being able to walk will help."

Kimmy stepped out of Velositi's arms and rushed to Kita's bedside.

"Kita, listen to me. I love you—no matter what. I don't care if you don't have legs or can backflip or swing a sword. You are mine. It's your wonderful, sexy brain—it's you—that keeps me wanting more. I don't care if you're brain is in a jar on my desk talking to me through a tiny speaker. You always told me knowledge is power. If you want to know what you offer that outweighs anything I can give you, it's the knowledge you possess. I can never match that. The only thing I can offer that possibly outweighs it is my love. Please, I know you're in a lot of physical and mental pain, but I'm here for you and will do anything to ease your suffering."

Kimmy kissed Kita's wrinkly artificial skin. It felt wrong, but Kimmy didn't care. She would get used to kissing it if she had to. It was Kita, and that was all that mattered.

"You never give up. That's one thing I will always love about you," Kita whispered.

"Kita?"

Kita turned her patchwork of pale skin covering her head away.

Kimmy lowered her head. "I won't give up until I've saved you and our daughter. Sleep. Heal. I won't save myself. I will save us. I love you."

Kimmy walked back to Velositi.

"No drama this time," said Velositi, her eyes alight.

"I had to tell her the one thing she has that I find more valuable than anything."

"What is that?"

"Her knowledge. No one I've ever met has weaponized knowledge like she has."

Velositi smiled. "I knew you were a good match for Kita."

"I think the three of us are a good match. I don't think I could handle Kita on my own."

Velositi put an arm around Kimmy. "You could, but I make it easier."

Kimmy looked into Velositi's bright eyes and said, "Who knew all those psychology books you read would be this useful?"

Velositi chirped laughter. "Kita doesn't have the knowledge market cornered."

Kimmy put an arm around Velositi's armored middle. "Let's go cuddle. I need to bleed off some stress—I'll do it naked if you want."

Velositi's eyes grew brighter. "You are a pleasure to look at, and I always find great joy in it."

"I wish I had something sexy or alluring to wear for you."

"Someday, we must stop at a developed world and go shopping. Until then, you naked is exquisite. Do you want me to do you?"

Kimmy debated, "Maybe. Let's see how it goes. I will take being admired and adored—and relax in the arms of someone who cares."

CHAPTER 07

KLIENE SYSTEM
KLIENE SHIPYARD
SPACE BIOME
¥2,252,725
24, OCTOBER 4003

K IMMY ENTERED WAR CAT'S command deck with Ultraviolet, Ash'a, and Athena, trying to talk over the noise and vibration of the repair crew. Through the window, the gray and yellow scaffolding wrapped around the ship. Repairs were scheduled to take a week, and work went around the clock. Ultraviolet's crew didn't mind, but the pilots grumbled about interrupted sleep.

"So, what do you have, Athena?" asked Kimmy. She'd come from the simulators, the quietest place on the ship.

In the center of the room, a screen appeared on the holotable, displaying a cipher of letters and words. One side was Common, and the other was a mixture of lines and swirls. Next to the alien characters, another similar line of characters appeared.

"This looks like you translated the map or have a key to the translation. The other alien language is the UEE language you know?"

"Yes. Kita would know it too, but even without her help, I've decoded the map. I thought it would be more impressive if I showed my work."

Kimmy chuckled. "So, where are we going?"

"You don't want to hear about how I broke down each letter and compared it to the map, then ran a statistical analysis on the probability of the letter being correct—"

"Athena!" barked Kimmy. "Sweetie, I love you, but we are not Kita and do not have the computer background to understand what you're telling us. I love you did it, but how is lost on me."

"Actually, it's linguistics. Studying the differences in the UEE language across different universes would be fascinating. It's amazing how similar they are. I—"

"Why don't you ask Ryan for samples?"

"Oh! But I'm not allowed into the Universe Room. Kita said it was strictly forbidden in case of another Harbinger Incident."

Kimmy vaguely knew about the Harbingers. They were a neighboring universe to Kita's. They tried to take over by simplifying their equations to fool Kita's universe into allowing them in. She didn't understand how the ancient universes worked, but Kita and Leaf built the new universes and Reality from them.

"I'm sure we can pull the data safely and pass it to you."

"I'm excited to see their computers when we get there. I bet with this Rosetta Stone, I can run on their machines without a virtual interface."

"What's the difference?" said Ash'a.

"Now, I'm running a virtual machine that translates my commands and passes them to the operating system. With this, I can control computers on the machine level—increasing power and speed."

"So, you can't control War Cat's computers?"

"I can...sort of. I am learning the Aven's computer language—I identify it as language core five-three-seven-November-foxtrot-six-eight. Learning this language allows me further access into the computers, but I haven't learned most of it. When I do, I will have complete control and access over War Cat and the mechs."

"Sounds like you want my job in the pilot's seat," teased Kimmy.

"No. I wouldn't take the joy of pulling the trigger from you. But I could increase the efficiency of the mech's computers by thirty percent and the different systems on the mechs by twenty percent or more. I've run some basic trials in the simulator—but the simulator code is simpler and different from the language used by the mechs and War Cat."

Kimmy put her hand on Athena's shoulder. "You figure it out, you tell me. That's a massive buff that would let us dominate our opponent."

"It is high on my ten to the eleven million seven—"

"Athena, I don't need to know the exact number. We understand you have a lot to do." Kimmy hugged the hologram, which felt like hugging sand.

"I understand its necessity," admitted Athena. "I have made it a high priority."

"What could we do to make it faster?" said Ash'a.

"Fast, powerful computers I could gain full access to. Nothing around here qualifies, and I wouldn't waste our money."

"Ok," said Kimmy, trying to turn the conversation back to what the AI had uncovered. "So, you uncoded the map, right?"

"Yes. This map leads to a United Earth Empire relay station on a remote icy world twenty-seven light-years from Earth, located in Sasari Confederation space. I'm assuming the station has the next piece of the map. The map mentions a cache." Athena highlighted the words on the map. "The UEE—and the Bush family specifically—I believe you would have liked Kasey, Kimmy...except she was dating Kita at the time—"

"—Who wasn't?" retorted Kimmy with a sigh.

Athena smiled and said, "Katalina. Anyway, the UEE was twitchy after other nations attacked and conquered the United States of America. After the UEE returned and conquered Earth, they expanded throughout the galaxy. They were a paranoid lot. They built a dozen weapons and technology caches throughout their domain. You can ask Kita about the caches the Legion, and Red Legion had around our homeworld. I'm interpolating this cache is like those caches. If we find it, a wealth of riches is ours."

"Twenty-seven light years. That's all our fuel reserves to get there," said Ash'a. "I suggest we refuel before we get there so we don't have a fiasco like Astari-Three-A."

"I will plot a course that takes us to a Sasari Confederation station."

Kimmy liked that idea. "Good. Can you bring up the moon?"

"This way." Athena led the group to the navigation computer. It shimmered and blinked before bringing up a moon named Veri-II-b. An icon blinked in the northern polar region.

Ash'a tapped the hologram and brought up a synopsis of the moon. "It says the equatorial belt is a game preserve and the polar regions are seasonal recreational centers. Currently, the north polar region is off-season. Kimmy, I will prepare the necessary visas and transit paperwork. Depending on what we find, we may owe the Sasarians something. I'll have to check on their treasure-hunting laws."

Kimmy rolled her eyes at the amount of work Ash'a was going to have to do. "What's wrong with just going and getting it—without telling them?"

"That's a good way to get us blasted to space dust or forfeit everything we find. Let me handle it. I've read the Sasarians are a friendly group. They do have a powerful military being neighbors to Aven."

Kimmy shuddered. "Too soon to return there. What would I do without you, Ash'a? Both of you?"

"Have you heard the Angel Dev?" Athena replied with a chuckle. "She found interesting solutions to problems. She taught Kita the importance of management and governing. Becoming the bureaucracy was easier than killing everyone...too many bureaucrats to kill."

Kimmy and Ash'a laughed.

"Someday, I will have to get her to tell me how she became a god."

"Even I don't know the entire story. I believe all those who do are dead."

"Amazing to live such a long life," said Ash'a, her scales rippled, displaying a rainbow refraction.

"If you two are satisfied with what you need to do, I need to get away from this noise," remarked Kimmy.

ZILIO ARCOLOGY
SPACE BIOME
¥1,802,725
2, NOVEMBER 4003

"OK, EVERYONE, WELCOME TO Zilio Arcology," Kimmy said as she and her friends entered the ship's servicing concourse. Zilio was the largest space station in the Sasari Confederation, containing over a million people and a trade hub for Sasari and its neighbors. "We have six hours to find cold weather gear to keep hands, feet, and hooves warm. According to the brochure, if it can't be found on Zilio, it doesn't exist. So, go have some fun, shop, and prepare for snow and ice."

The Angels split into groups and went their separate ways. Kimmy was with Velositi, Ash'a, Karen, Zhi, and Dupont. She followed signs out of the servicing concourse toward the main loop promenade.

"So, is this your subtle way of telling us where we're going?" asked Dupont as they walked along a corridor lined with spinning triangles, creating an elaborate piece of art.

"Just be prepared for cold, snow, and ice," retorted Kimmy. Only Ash'a and Athena knew their destination. Kimmy trusted the Angels, but the fewer people who knew the complete picture, the better.

"Ah, come on. It's my map."

"My map," said Kimmy tersely. "You're still under parole, and I haven't forgotten your share. But if you don't let me get us there, you won't get it."

"Ok, no sweat. Glad you haven't forgotten. I'd hate to be used for my good looks."

Kimmy rolled her eyes. "You'll be told when we get there."

"Why so paranoid?"

"You have not met Kita," replied Velositi with a chirp of laughter.

"I *am* the State," replied Kimmy, turning up her nose. "I know and understand the reasons behind operational security."

"If you think she's bad, Pierre, try Kita," said Karen.

"Yeah," said Zhi. "If Kimmy isn't telling us, she has her reasons. Come on, I want to find a cute jacket."

"I'm going to miss being an Angel for this, aren't I?" said Karen to Kimmy.

"The internal thermal regulation is nice. This will remind us what it's like to be Human."

"Always been Human," said Dupont. "What am I missing?"

"Lots," said Karen, taking his arm. "Come on. I'm hungry, and you can let Kimmy get on with what she needs to do—besides answer your questions." She pulled Dupont away, with Zhi following with an unhappy look. "Bye, girls! Let us know if you find an adventure outfitter store."

"Should be lots," muttered Kimmy as the trio entered the promenade.

"This place is enormous," said Velositi as she looked around at the circular promenade.

Unlike the Tetrahedron, which Kimmy had visited and was built like a layered cake, Zilio was a giant enclosed ring. The people lived and shopped on the inside, while docks encompassed the outside. The ring was ten miles in diameter, but you could see the far side from any point.

"It feels like a giant pip wheel," said Ash'a, referring to the tiny animals Ultraviolet kept on Roost in the ultraviolet forest.

The promenade was lush. Water features, grass, rocks, and plants from around the galaxy were prominently displayed and brightened the station. Artificial light came from top and bottom, giving the feeling of a bright spring day.

Kimmy pulled her communicator from her belt. It was connected to the station's network. She typed in cold weather gear, and a dozen stores blinked on the map. She showed it to Ash'a and Velositi.

"I wonder if they have anything in my size?" Velositi laughed.

"Do you need cold weather gear?" said Ash'a.

"No, but it helps conserve energy. Kimmy...I do not suppose there is a store to find you something?" Her eyes lit brightly.

Kimmy chuckled, remembering the orgasms from earlier. *I guess I should get her something special.* "Hmmm, I'm sure they do. Do you have something in mind?"

"I think watching you try on a few pieces would be nice. We do not have to buy anything."

Kimmy gave Velositi a wry smile. "Kita doesn't do this for you, does she?"

Velositi's eyes dimmed. "No. She does not like wearing lingerie. She prefers to be naked...but likes revealing clothes...but not lace."

Kimmy laughed. "Her body is a weapon, and she knows it. She doesn't like being sexy for me, either. Though I have made her sweat with some pieces I've brought home."

"I am glad you like wearing it. I hate to ask."

Kimmy giggled. "I like it...especially if it makes my girls happy."

"Maybe they'll have something for me," said Ash'a.

"I would be interested in seeing you," said Velositi. "I have not seen an Aurorian before."

Ash'a shrugged. "I didn't think I would have someone who would appreciate it. I like to explore different styles from different races. The stuff on Aurori is so...plain, and I like to be prepared."

"In case you find another Aurorian?" said Velositi.

Ash'a laughed. "It doesn't have to be an Aurorian. Technically, anyone I can get DNA from, but I'm not interested in birthing. Anyone with finger-like appendages will do the trick."

"I know Aurorians require sex to ease anxiety and stress," said Kimmy. "If you don't mind me asking, what have you been doing to keep yourself sane?"

Ash'a giggled. "Myself. I was hoping to get a turn with Pierre, but he seems interested in Karen."

"You are not the only one disappointed," said Velositi. "Zhi does not seem happy with the arrangement."

"I thought Karen and Zhi were together."

"I think they are, but not sexually," said Kimmy.

"I would have to ask, but I may be of service," said Velositi.

"Is that your way of asking me?" Kimmy retorted with a chuckle.

"I do not have the relationship with Ash'a that I do with you. I feel I have a unique skill that I could offer."

"You just want to see her naked."

"Well, yes."

Kimmy looked at Ash'a and shrugged. "Up to you. I don't know how you go, but she knows how to hit all the right spots. Velositi, since you seem busy taking appointments, schedule me again. I could use a good release."

"I do not mean to take myself away from you. You and Kita will always have priority."

Ash'a smiled. "I guess I owe you, Kimmy. I've seen you naked. If a balance in your relationship must be maintained, I'm not opposed to you seeing me naked or sex."

Kimmy's mind raced, trying to remember when Ash'a had seen her naked. It came to her. She'd finished having sex with Kita and was asleep on Kita when Ash'a came in with an important call.

"I'm committed to Kita and Velositi, but I won't say no if Velositi approves. I've never gone lingerie shopping with other girls before." *I could use some affection and attention. Velositi is great, but she admits she can only do so much. And she'll be there. So, it's not like I'm cheating. Kita won't mind and would understand. She's had sex with lots of people. It's just friendly sex. I don't want a relationship. It's bound to happen that we visit all these universes. We're going to have sex with other people.*

"I don't mind, as long as you don't mind me being there. Perhaps we can find you an entire ensemble you can take off?" suggested Velositi.

Kimmy rolled her eyes playfully at the Morphicon. "I'm in for a penny. Might as well go for a pound."

ZILIO ARCOLOGY
ALICE'S FIXATION
SPACE BIOME
Y1,802,725
2, NOVEMBER 4003

"T A-DA!" SAID KIMMY AS she pulled back the dressing room curtain and stepped onto the viewing platform. She wore the future's idea of a red lace teddy, matching stockings, and heels. They'd stopped by a restroom to get prettied up for the occasion. Kimmy chose a red and silver makeup style she'd learned from a makeup artist on Earth 832.

"Wow!" said Velositi. "You look fantastic."

"I think the best is in the back." Kimmy turned and wiggled her butt to show off what was there and what wasn't. "I really like this. It shows off my ass without being up my ass."

"I am confused," said Velositi. "I have never seen clothing that went up someone's butt."

Kimmy giggled. "Not like that. I'm talking underwear like thongs and G-strings. I like them for sex and special occasions—remember the dress I wore for Kita and mine's engagement party?"

"Yes. You were...and I will quote Bernoot...a stone-cold stunner."

"I wouldn't say I'm that. God Kita is. I would say she's a Greek goddess."

"She is god."

Kimmy turned in the mirrors, admiring her butt and the rest of her. The teddy made her butt look good. It ran between her legs, across her cheeks, and connected to the front above her hip. Small strips of lace covered part of her cheek, and the rest was open.

"I think I will take this one home." Kimmy ran her hands down her front, feeling the lace against her skin.

"That would be wonderful," said Velositi, her eyes alight.

"Don't take it off until I can see," called Ash'a from the other dressing room in their private viewing area.

Kimmy smiled as she pulled at the top of her matching lace stocking. The front went up her thigh to connect to the teddy. The back went across her leg just above the knee. *I guess I'm ready to be admired. We should have gone somewhere to get our hair and nails done. I guess Ash'a doesn't look her best, either.*

She went to Velositi and twirled in front of her. "You like? Can I sit?" she motioned to Velositi's lap.

"Of course. I do. It shows off all that makes you beautiful. I am always amazed how clothes can make you more gorgeous."

"You make me feel good."

"You have doubts?"

"Always."

"But you are gorgeous."

Kimmy sat in Velositi's lap, enjoying the warmth of the Morphicon. "That doesn't quiet the voice in my head. I wish I had Kita's overabundance of confidence."

"You look amazing," said Ash'a, sticking her head through the curtains. "I think it'll be great fun to take off you."

Kimmy blushed. "Did you find something you like?"

"I did. Human fashion is wonderfully diverse. I swear, whatever they dream up, they make."

"It is not like that on Aurora?" asked Velositi.

"No. Clothing on Aurora is regimented. As much as we have sex, we don't have special clothes for it."

"Now I'm dying to see what you picked," said Kimmy with a smile.

"I hope you like it." She pulled the curtain back and stepped out wearing black five-inch stiletto heels. The shoes matched the rest of the outfit. It was a simple lace bikini top that didn't cover much. Ribbons ran around her breasts, ending in red bows on the bikini string. More ribbon crisscrossed around her middle, ending in a red bow. The G-string was lace with a bow on top. A black stocking with red bows was on her left leg, and a ribbon with a bow went around her right thigh.

I can see why it took her so long to get it on. "It's...ah...wow." Kimmy felt her skin flush. "That looks spectacular on you." It was more than that. It made her yearn to be touched. Her body liked it, too, as she felt wet.

Ash'a laughed. "I was hoping to look as good as the model."

"You, ah, surpassed that. I, ah, shit. If I wasn't going to buy this before, I will have to buy it now."

"You don't have to buy it for me. It's just fun to try on."

Kimmy laughed. "Not what I meant, but I will buy both."

"You like it that much?"

Kimmy nodded.

"How much?" Ash'a sauntered over and leaned over Kimmy, letting her breasts hang. "We have to take it off to pay for it."

"Here?" exclaimed Kimmy. "I don't think here is a good spot to teach each other."

Ash'a giggled. "You don't have to do me...at least here. I know I'll have to teach you. I've watched Human porn. I'm interested in practicing what I've learned." She placed a hand on Kimmy's cheek and stroked it with her thumb.

"I...ah..."

"You said you would not say no," said Velositi, her eyes glowing.

"I did say that."

"Don't worry," said Ash'a. "We can start here and finish on the ship." She leaned in and kissed Kimmy.

Damn. When an Aurorian wants it, they don't play around. Ash'a said she was hard up, and if she doesn't get it, she could have medical issues. I'm helping her out and ensuring we're both at peak performance. She's not the only one who could use a release.

Kimmy liked to think she had a skilled tongue, but Ash'a's was almost prehensile, the way she stroked and caressed Kimmy's. She moaned lightly when Ash'a sucked on her tongue.

"Oh," Kimmy sighed as Ash'a sucked on the tip of her tongue while playing with it with hers. "Damn. Your tongue is incredible."

The scales on Ash'a's head rippled. "I'm not that good. Some Aurorians will tie you in knots."

"I don't think my tongue could do that," Kimmy chuckled.

"Your tongue was divine, and the taste sends ripples up my scales."

Ok. Now I'm curious to know what she's been watching.

Ash'a put her arms around Kimmy's neck and leaned into her. She kissed Kimmy again, then left a trail down Kimmy's neck to the high collar of her teddy. With her tongue, she undid the Chinese-style buttons.

Holy shit. I'm out of my league.

The Aurorian ran her tongue from the base of Kimmy's neck up to her ear. Ash'a again proved how dexterous her tongue and lips were by taking off Kimmy's erring. The warm breath on Kimmy's ears made all the hairs on her arm stand up. Kimmy let out a slow hum.

"Am I doing ok?" Ash'a whispered.

Kimmy shivered and slowly nodded. "Yeah. Wow."

Leaving a trail of kisses from Kimmy's ear to collarbone, Ash'a messaged the area with her tongue. Kimmy purred as she stroked the back of Ash'a's head. A pulling sensation electrified Kimmy as Ash'a could suck and massage at the same time.

"Oh, fuck," Kimmy gasped when Ash'a let go.

"Ah, oops. I've never seen that before."

"Huh?" Kimmy asked as her head spun.

"I left a discolored spot."

Kimmy giggled, then switched into doctor mode. "It's called a hickey. You draw the blood to the skin's surface. I have red blood, which can be seen through my pink skin. It's a type of bruise. Don't worry. It'll go away. You probably have the same thing but are not visible because you have gold blood and skin."

"It's not bad, is it?"

"No, it'll go away. I have to know what you've been watching..."

Ash'a looked at Kimmy hungrily and rubbed her breasts against Kimmy's. "I haven't even started yet."

"I, ah..."

Ash'a kissed down the open front of Kimmy's chest and breasts. She playfully rubbed her face between them, using her nose to push the lace aside until she'd exposed Kimmy's nipples. Gently, she teased the hard nipples with her nose.

Kimmy sucked in a breath and held it.

Ash'a kissed and sucked on Kimmy's breast. Using her tongue to lick under and around while her other hand gently caressed Kimmy's other breast.

Tingles ran up Kimmy's spine, making the muscles tighten and her pussy wet. She let out a loud "Oh," when Ash'a switched sides. When Ash'a licked her nipple, it was like a lightning jolt from her nipple to her pussy. "Oh, haha, oooh," she gasped.

The Aurorian put her lips around Kimmy's hard nipple and sucked while her hand caressed the other.

"Oh, shit," Kimmy whimpered as sparkles of light filled her head.

"Are you ok?" said Ash'a.

"I wasn't expecting that."

"What?" said Velositi.

"An orgasm from my nipples. I thought that was a Kita thing."

Ash'a laughed. "On Aurora, there is a whole art to stimulating nipples. Girls specialize in it."

"You must be one of them."

Ash'a smirked. "I've gone with a few." She cupped Kimmy's pussy, pressing her finger against the lace and in slightly. "And you're wet."

Kimmy nodded. "I'm more than wet."

Ash'a kneeled in front of Kimmy. She pushed aside Kimmy's teddy, pulling it off her shoulders and kissing her stomach.

Kimmy's muscles tensed as her pussy demanded attention. She had no control, and the more Ash'a kissed and teased her stomach and thighs, the more she wanted.

Ash'a stood and pulled Kimmy out of Velositi's lap.

"What are we doing?" asked Kimmy, her head torn between the orgasm she had and the desire for more.

Ash'a turned Kimmy around and sensually pulled the teddy down her front and let it fall to the floor. The Aurorian pushed her body against Kimmy's and kissed from the nape to her ear. Ash'a gently breathed into Kimmy's ear.

"I can't make you orgasm with it on."

She ran her hands down Kimmy's front. Grabbing Kimmy's hips, she pulled the other Angel against her.

"Oh," Kimmy groaned.

"How are you feeling?" whispered Ash'a. "Am I doing ok?"

"Oh, fuck. I'm so horny. I don't think I've ever been horny like this."

Ash'a, pressing her hand firmly against Kimmy, moved from her hip to between her legs.

"Aaahhh, ooohhhh, oh," Kimmy gasped as Ash'a cupped her pussy and pushed her finger between her labia. Ash'a brushed her clit, and Kimmy's head filled with pinpricks of light.

The lights intensified as Ash'a stroked and massaged. Kimmy's legs shook while tingles ran up and down them.

"Having fun," whispered Ash'a.

"I didn't realize I was so pent up."

"How longs has it been?"

"I...ah...oh, shit. I can't think while you're doing that. A long time."

"I'll make your head explode now and do you right on the ship."

"Oh, oh, oh, oooaaaaahhh. Fuck, fuck, fuck."

Ash'a turned Kimmy around, hugged her, then kneeled while running her hands over Kimmy's breasts. Stopping to tease her nipples, she guided Kimmy into Velositi's lap and spread her legs. The Aurorian kissed and sucked on Kimmy's labia and thighs. Kisses became a tongue as Ash'a ran hers over Kimmy's labia, discreetly drifting between them, teasing Kimmy and making her pussy throb.

"Oh, come on," Kimmy begged. "I want to feel you suck on me."

"Is she not doing it right?" asked Velositi.

"No," Kimmy whined. "She's doing it too well."

Kimmy sucked in a breath as Ash'a ran her tongue between her labia, but not deep enough to reach her clit.

"Oh, what do I have to do?"

Ash'a looked up and grinned. "I want to make sure your head explodes."

"My pussy is going to explode!"

Ash'a slipped a finger into the lower half of Kimmy's pussy.

Kimmy leaned forward. "Oh, oh, yes, yes, please, please. I want to feel you inside me."

"This, right here?" Ash'a ran her finger around Kimmy's opening. She traced it with a finger, pushing the tip of her finger in enough to push against her vagina.

"Yes, yes. Oh, I want you. I've never had to beg this much in my life," Kimmy said with a frustrated growl.

"I'm just building the anticipation."

Ash'a pulled her finger away, smiled wickedly at Kimmy, and sucked on her finger, moving it in and out. "Can you imagine that being you?"

"Fuck, yes," yelled Kimmy. "Oh, why are you being so mean?"

Ash'a stood up on her knees and took Kimmy's face in her hands. She kissed Kimmy, playing with her tongue and ending by sucking on her lower lip.

"I'm not trying to be mean. I didn't realize you were in more need than I. What do you want me to do?"

"Whatever you were doing. You're amazing. I'm just so...so...in need of this."

Ash'a smiled. "Then I'll save the teasing for later. Lean back and enjoy." She pushed Kimmy back against Velositi and put her head between Kimmy's legs.

Kimmy raised her legs and balanced her feet on Velositi's knees, trying to give Ash'a as much access as possible. When Ash'a tongue pressed against her clit, the lights exploded in Kimmy's head. The Aurorian alternated between licking, massaging, and sucking or a combination. The light burst in Kimmy's head and grew in intensity and length until she saw a tie-dye of color.

"Oh, fuck, fuck, fuck me...yes, yes, yes..." Kimmy screamed when Ash'a slipped her finger into her.

The Aurorian moved her finger around while alternating, going deep and stroking Kimmy's g-spot.

Kimmy threw her head back and screamed. There was warmth on her breasts, and her nipples sent shivers straight to her pussy. The tie-dye in her head swirled, and then there was white. Kimmy's back and butt lifted off Velositi in an arch.

"Oh, oh, ack, oh...fuck me...oh, fuck me..." Kimmy collapsed against Velositi. She was warm and fuzzy. All she saw was white, she couldn't hear, and her legs were numb.

"Are you ok?" asked Ash'a, lifting her head.

"I was not too much, was I?" said Velositi as she looked at Kimmy

"I'm good...I'm good..." said Kimmy drunkenly. "Oh, fuck, did I need that. I'm going to need a minute. You girls are amazing."

Ash'a smiled. "I thought Aurorians had a heavy orgasm."

"Oh, sweetie, it was way more than one. I lost count. They came fast and strong."

"You can have multiple at a time?"

"Uh-uh. And you gave me lots."

Ash'a looked proud. "Nothing I watched said anything about that."

"Because it's not...not...I forgot what I was saying."

Ash'a stood. "Velositi, can I cuddle her on you?"

"Of course."

Ash'a crawled into the Morphicon's lap and took Kimmy in her arms.

Kimmy, her head swimming, curled up in Ash'a and Velositi's arms and enjoyed the colors.

VERI IIb
NOLAN ESCARPMENT
POLAR BIOME
¥1,789,725
8, NOVEMBER 4003

"DAMN, IT'S COLD," SAID Dupont. "Babe, I'm glad you sent me back to get heavier gear."

"Hmm-hmm. I told you. Kimmy doesn't lie. When she tells you something, you better believe it."

Kimmy raised an eyebrow at the transmission. Not at the friendly back and forth between Dupont and Karen, but only some mechs' heat worked. For those who didn't, Ultraviolet's crews installed small space heaters—the fat max was one of these, and the fix didn't seem to be to Dupont's liking. *Should have taken better care of his mech.* Kimmy shrugged it off. Her heater worked.

Kimmy led the way through a ten-foot drift created by the blizzard blowing from the north, breaking the trail for those in light mechs. Her towering Dawnbreaker easily pushed through the snow gathered on the mountain slope, allowing Nicole, in her firefly, and Lizzy, in her leopard, easier passage.

Both carried a copy of Athena. Their job was to get to the door identified by Athena and get inside. The rest of the troops would provide cover and help recover assets if needed. Kimmy hoped to bring home as much UEE tech as she could.

"This stuff is hell to see through," said Flexi.

"At least you're not eye level with it," retorted Nicole.

Kimmy couldn't see much beyond the blinding snow and shadows. The lights from her mech did little to pierce the driving snow. Only her radar kept the group on course and from stumbling into the mountainside cliff or—worse—falling over the edge. An opening upslope appeared on the radar as the group traversed the slope.

"I think I've found the entrance to the UEE bunker," announced Kimmy. "Poison, take your troop and form a protective perimeter at the mouth of the draw. I will escort my troop to the target area."

"Roger, we're moving."

To Kimmy's right, the faster and more maneuverable medium mechs pushed through the snow toward the draw.

Out of the darkness came a pair of flashes that went over Kimmy.

"Hey! Look out. Something out there is rocking twin particle cannons!" As Kimmy announced the attack, she flipped through her visual assistants, trying to find where and what the attackers were. To her right, she saw the rear lights of Karen's troop.

Kimmy turned her attention to getting her troop up the draw unmolested. She readied her weapons but would only fire if she had an opportunity. Her mission was to get Nicole and Lizzy to the door and defend.

The snow to her left lightened, and the upslope became gradual. "Ok, girls, I think this is it. Follow my left turn up the mountain."

She received a pair of affirmatives as she eased her stick to the left, guiding her mech up the snowy path.

"Shit. I don't know what these guys are," squawked Zhi.

"Apocalypse, we've got four unknown bogeys on a raised position to our front. We're forming a picket line to keep them off you. The mech computers can't identify vehicle type or weapon type."

"Roger. Keep them busy—"

"Break," said Nicole. "Athena says they're probably UEE drones left to guard the site. She says there is a ninety-one percent probability she can shut them down once she gets inside. Her advice is to not take them head-on, as they are likely well-armed and armored. The best strategy is to play cat-and-mouse with them."

How does a drone still function after more than a millennium? "Girls, be careful. If this tech is still functioning after a thousand years, it might not be easy to kill."

"Great," huffed Karen. "You know how to make me feel good. We'll keep them busy. Hurry and get them shut down."

"We're moving up the slope as fast as we can," replied Kimmy as she maneuvered her mech through a flat part of the draw. On either side of her, steep slopes rose and disappeared in the snow.

"Shit. Shit. Shit. *Fuck!*" exclaimed Zhi.

"What is it?" Karen asked, her voice calm and commanding.

"I just took three big rounds in the CT. I gotta back out of the line. Another shot, and I'm cored."

"Roger. We'll cover you. Hide in the storm and let it rain."

"Wilco, Poison. I'm moving out."

"Nemesis," Kimmy called to Nicole. "Turn on the sparkler and see if we can jam whatever's out there." She debated using the jammer—she didn't want to alert the enemy that they were there, but it did them no good if someone got cored.

"We've cranked up the sparkler, Poison. I hope that helps."

"Roger. We'll hold the line. I think there are four of them armed with guns and particle cannons."

"Do your best to hold them back. If they're vehicles, try retreating into the drifts and see if they'll get lost in the snow."

"Wilco."

Kimmy moved farther up the draw. Tapping the overlay button on her radar, she brought up the satellite image of the area. The image replaced her radar-generated terrain but let her see where the bay doors were. She tapped on the screen and calculated the range—seventy-five yards.

Kimmy's right shoulder exploded in a dazzling display of light, sending an electrical charge through the cockpit, causing her displays to snow and making her teeth buzz. She'd been hit by particle cannons before, but nothing like this.

"Girls! Something is out there ahead of us. I just got hit with some kind of particle cannon. Stay behind me, and I'll clear the way." Kimmy wished she could see so she knew what to shoot.

Out of the snow, a large mech-shaped object loomed. Kimmy's computer couldn't identify it through the snow, but that didn't stop the targeting reticle from getting a lock. *Better safe than sorry.* Kimmy pulled the trigger, but only her right-side weapons fired. Her particle cannon lit up the mech's left side as her thirty-millimeter cannon punched a sizable hole in the left torso. *Dammit. That would have been a kill if everything worked.*

Kimmy's finger danced across the display, bringing up the various weapon systems to bring them online. Running a diagnostic, she found most were offline from whatever hit them. Kimmy flew through the screens, rebooting the weapons while pushing forward into the mech ahead of her. *I've got more than just mounted weapons.*

Driving her dawnbreaker through the snow, Kimmy drew back her right arm, and as the enemy mech turned, she slammed the arm forward into the area damaged by her weapons. The force of Kimmy's blow smashed through the enemy's armor, crushing whatever lay beneath. The right arm of the enemy mech went slack as it dropped into a defensive crouch.

"I'm coming, Apocalypse!" cried Lizzy as her leopard pushed around Kimmy and fired into the enemy's back with her twin thirty-millimeter cannons and a quartet of medium lasers.

The back of the enemy mech exploded in an orange fireball, casting harsh shadows across the snowy landscape. The momentary light let Kimmy see her advisories—hover tanks and a lone heavy mech she couldn't identify. On the top of the draw, she spotted the bay doors and two boxes sitting in front.

"Sapper, Nemesis, go for the door! It's forty yards to our left. Look out. There might be some bad guys there."

"Nemesis, go!" said Lizzy. "I'll help Apocalypse distract these three."

"Sapper!" Kimmy yelled in her best empress voice. "I told you—"

"If she needs help, I'll go...but right now, you need help."

Kimmy ground her teeth at the insubordination, but Lizzy was right. She couldn't handle the three enemies lurking in the darkness. "Let's get Nemesis to the door." She pushed her control stick to the left and mashed her throttle to break through the snow as fast as possible. Behind her, Lizzy and Nicole fell in.

As Kimmy approached the bay doors, her lights illuminated a pair of snowcats. Their front lights pointed at the door. On the side of the vehicles was the Defin Industries logo. *How the hell did they get here ahead of us?*

Kimmy targeted both vehicles and fired her beams, melting sizeable holes in the two snowcats' tracks. *That should make them useless.* She stepped up to the wreckage, and her lights revealed a trio of people at a control panel.

The light changing alerted them, and two turned, one drawing a pistol. The pistol wavered in the light of the three mechs.

"Should I shoot them?" asked Lizzy.

Kimmy was more worried about the heavy weapons damaging the door than any moral reason for turning the mech's weapons on humans.

"Apocalypse, if you'll cover Sapper and me, we'll get out and detain them," offered Nicole.

"Go ahead. I'll make sure they don't do anything stupid." Kimmy flipped to her outside communications and turned the volume up to be heard through the snow. "Put down the gun. Stop what you're doing and step away from the door. Comply, and no one gets hurt. Challenge me, and you'll learn what a particle cannon does to a Human."

Kimmy wasn't sure what a particle cannon did to a Human. The charged particles interact with the mech's metal armor, causing it to melt. She wasn't sure how flesh would react or other materials like nylon.

Nicole and Lizzy struggled through the snow to the interlopers. Lizzy stopped ten yards from them and opened her cockpit hatch. Hanging out the side, she aimed an assault rifle at the trio as Nicole waded through cockpit deep snow to the door. *Where did she get that? I guess if anyone would have a rifle, it would be a soldier.*

Nicole opened her hatch, climbing onto the flat roof of her firefly. Reaching into her pocket, she pulled out a bronze ball, pushed a button, and tossed it a few meters from her into the snow. The ball expanded into a solid hologram of Athena.

"Step away from the door," ordered Kimmy to the Defin people.

The one with the gun turned toward Nicole and Athena, but a three-round burst from Lizzy dropped him. The remaining pair stepped a few yards away into the driving snow.

Kimmy alternated between watching the Defin people and Nicole—with a bag over her shoulder—and Athena as they made their way to the door. The AI Angel took over hacking the console.

The door halves retracted into the mountain. *I wonder how long the Defin people have been out here trying to do that?* Nicole waved at Kimmy and Lizzy.

"Get what we need so we can get out of here," Kimmy ordered over the external speaker. She checked her console and found Nicole left the sparkler on giving her troops—a loud *WHAM* was followed by an explosion lighting the mountainside and the tunnel. Several warning tones erupted in Kimmy's ear as she brought her attention to her mech. The console flashed red and highlighted her right arm was gone.

"Girls, I have to go. We've got company," Kimmy alerted the other Angels. Grabbing her stick, she turned right and backed into the blizzard to give her some cover while searching for a target. *What out here can do that kind of damage? Probably the same thing that hit Zhi...so it has to be one of the UEE drones.* It was sound reasoning, but she doubted it, too. She didn't know what monster mechs Defin Industries brought. And, to make it worse, she was missing a particle cannon.

THUNK! Kimmy's mech jerked to a stop. *What did I hit?* She flipped to the rearview camera and found a rock wall. *Well. Nothing like being set up for the firing squad.*

On either side of her, the electric blue light of particle cannon bursts splashed off the rock and lit the surrounding area.

Kimmy grit her teeth and did the only thing she could—charge. She plowed through the thigh-deep snow in the direction the blasts had come. Shifting power to her radar—which amplified its ability to detect at the cost of range—she hoped to burn through the blizzard and find a target.

In her lights appeared a disk-shaped platform hovering above the snow with two long particle cannon barrels on either side of a dome turret. *A hover tank.* She'd heard Athena mention them as a favorite UEE weapon, but seeing one was breathtaking. The technology in making it float and the advanced particle cannons were lost to current civilizations. *I wouldn't consider most of the states in this galaxy modern.*

Settling her targeting reticle over the drone, Kimmy didn't wait for the computer. The blizzard had too much effect on her radar and the computer's targeting system. She hoped the rangefinder worked as she pulled the trigger and fired an alpha strike. Her beams, particle cannon, and thirty-millimeter cannon lit the driving snow. Some beams melted snow, but her particle cannon and ballistics round struck home. When the snow cleared, the drone remained undamaged. *Super tech, super weapons, super armor—perfect.*

The drone swung its cannons toward Kimmy. *Shit. I've got to do something. Let's see if you can beat physics.* Kimmy charged the drone. She brought her left arm back and twisted her torso. When she reached the drone, she swung her arm down.

The blow drove the drone into the snow and concaved the turret, causing the barrels to point inward. Kimmy raised her right foot and brought it down on the crippled drone. Pushing hydraulic power to her leg, Kimmy crushed the drone under one hundred tons of force, grinding it against the mountain's hard granite.

When Kimmy lifted her foot and stepped back, the drone popped up, looking like nothing had happened. As Kimmy scrambled to target her weapons, the drone sank and settled on the snow.

"Athena, tell me that was you..." Kimmy asked the snowstorm as she backed up, knowing there were still more targets out there.

A *boom* punctuated the silent frosty air, causing her torso to rotate to the right, slamming Kimmy against her safety restraints. As Kimmy fought for control of her mech, the computer stabilized the legs and kept the mech upright. Kimmy's console was a light show of warning messages. She tapped them, trying to clear them, so she could see what was wrong. It became apparent her right torso and its weapons—a thirty-millimeter cannon and particle cannon—were nonfunctional. *I wonder if they're even there.*

Looking across her console, Kimmy was in terrible shape. Her damage report showed her right torso and right arm were nonfunctional. The structural report hinted at the devastation. There was damage to the firewall between her right torso and center torso—meaning whatever hit her inflicted damage on her center torso. Her left arm and torso had also taken damage, but her three medium lasers and large laser were functioning. The beams wouldn't be enough to kill whatever was out there, but they would be enough to buy Nicole and Athena time.

As Kimmy and her computer struggled to bring her damaged mech online, a violent collision slammed Kimmy against her restraints. Her mech let out an agonizing metallic groan as it fell backward. The back of Kimmy's head slammed against the headrest, making her see stars. The stars gave way to snow swirling around her cockpit as she shook her head to clear it.

As the mental fog lifted, Kimmy craned her neck to see the console. The computer was already righting the mech, but the damage was catastrophic. Her left arm and torso were nonfunctional, taking her remaining weapons.

The computer righted the mech, but not the swaying. Kimmy worked the console, trying to bring systems back online—including the heat. The temperature inside the cockpit had dropped dramatically. *They won't have to shoot me. I'll freeze first.*

A set of lights appeared through the driving snow. They were too high for a drone but the right height for the Defin mech. *I hope it's taken as much a pounding as I have.* Into the attack mech's lights floated the drone. The saucer-shaped drone differed from the other. It had three barrels, including a massive fifty-millimeter cannon flanked by two smaller caliber guns.

The drone sped past the Defin mech into the pool of light. When it stopped, it trained its cannons on Kimmy.

Kimmy's hand drifted toward the shielded eject button on her command seat. Flipping the shield up, her finger rested on the button. Only stubbornness kept her from pressing it. She wanted to see what the drone would do and was sure she could outdraw it.

As Kimmy's nerves gave out, she bit her lip...and closed her eyes to wait—partially to die and to see what happened. She'd never died before and didn't know what to expect. Kita had described death as a time of no worries and rest—both things Kimmy could use.

As she prepared, a new thought struck like an icepick in her brain—*I'm like Kita. How do I know I'll return home? I could get stuck and die in Reality Computer limbo. I wouldn't let Kita, and I certainly can't.*

Kimmy's eyes flickered open as the drone laid its cannons on her. Kimmy's hand jerked to press the eject button as the drone spun, aiming at the Defin mech. The two combatants were close enough that the drone was in the mech's spotlights. The drone fired at the Defin mech, lighting the blizzard with orange light.

The convex center torso of the Defin attack mech exploded as the drone's shells ripped through the mech's armor at an upward angle, setting off a series of secondary explosions and ripping the torso of the mech apart. The legs twisted and fell into the snow.

That solves one of my problems...

"Kimmy? Are you there?" called Athena over the radio.

Kimmy fixed her helmet and centered the mic boom. "Athena! I'm here, but I have to punch out."

"Oh? Did I miss one?"

"Are—are you in control of the drones?"

"I am. It took time to get into their controller, but I have them now. I'm using them to help search for Zhi and Dupont. They both needed to eject—"

"Oh, Void!" exclaimed Kimmy. She forgot about them while getting her team in place and fighting the enemy. She'd never changed her radio back so she could help Karen and her troop. Her hand darted to the radio and changed the net to Karen's troop.

"Poison! What happened?" Kimmy called frantically.

"God, Kimmy...it's like nothing hurt them. Everything we tried failed."

Karen wasn't hiding the hurt and pain in her voice. "Karen, I'm sorry. I got caught up in getting Nicole and Athena inside and fighting the drones and mechs. I'll come down and help search."

"No. Don't. Athena says the drones are spread out, searching. We'll find them. Your job is to ensure Athena gets the next map piece. We'll let you know when we find the others."

Karen's voice was seething and scolding. Kimmy wasn't sure if she was mad at her. It reminded Kimmy of a senior sergeant addressing a junior officer after the sergeant led a dangerous mission so the officer could achieve the mission goal.

"Kimmy?" said Athena.

Kimmy tried to shake away her depression. "Yeah?"

"War Cat is moving in for recovery and salvage efforts. Should I bring the drones?"

Kimmy tapped the side of her head, thinking about it. They would be useful. At the same time, they needed to guard this site in case Defin came back—how they got here in the first place was a mystery. "Athena, bring the damaged one. Leave the rest in case Defin or someone else comes snooping around."

"Will do. UV is going to be busy repairing everyone."

Kimmy let out a long sigh. "Yeah."

"Kimmy, are you ok?"

"I need a hot shower and a nap. This was a tougher mission than we planned."

Overhead, War Cat hovered, releasing its recovery vehicles.

"Make sure they get the Defin mechs," Kimmy ordered Athena.

"Yes, those frost wolf mechs will be nice."

Kimmy throttled her near-destroyed mech forward through the snow. The drone had disappeared in the blizzard. Kimmy assumed it was going to search for survivors. Lights in the snow showed where the recovery team was loading the drone she had knocked out.

A pair of powerful searchlights cut through the densely falling snow, illuminating the way to the bay door and the rest of Kimmy's troop. The mechs were parked, but Lizzy and the Defin people were gone.

Must have gone inside to get out of the cold.

Kimmy, deciding she had nothing useful to do, used her mech to break the drifts and make it easier for the others to mount their mechs when they were ready.

"Apocalypse, how's it look out there?" said Athena.

"Just dandy. I'm making snow angels."

The AI laughed. "We are almost done. I accessed the UEE computer and found the next piece of the map. Sapper has *convinced* the Defin techs to help Nemesis remove a workstation. We have also gathered all the hard drives, storage, portable workstations, and parts we can disconnect.

"Poison has located Venom and Blade, and her troop has been recovered. War Cat's salvage team is recovering the down mechs. I will move the ship to our location to recover your troop and salvage the downed mechs here."

Kimmy blinked. She didn't know how to react to having her role as leader usurped by a computer. She knew Athena had a better strategic grasp of the mission, but the AI should have informed her.

Not that I'm doing a good job of that on my own. I'm going to have to do some apologizing to Karen. I didn't mean to put her in that position.

"Ah, thanks, Athena. Can you do me a favor and tell me next time?"

"Isn't that what I'm doing?"

"As part of the command loop, I need to know these things."

"Of course. I thought you were busy making snow angels."

Kimmy wasn't sure she wanted to laugh or cry. She would be the first to admit she was young and learning to command small units. Fighting her own mech while leading made the challenge much greater—*But I don't need an AI overstepping her bounds and cutting me out of the command loop.* Kimmy pressed her lips together, trying to think of a measured but meaningful response. *Athena may be teasing me...but now is not the time. I may be new to this, but I'm not without leadership experience.*

Kimmy switched the radio to the open net and brought out her best empress voice, "Athena, thank you for stepping in and handling the operation while I was busy *FIGHTING FOR MY LIFE,* but that doesn't mean I'm to be excluded from command decisions. I sure as shit need to be kept informed of the strategic picture, especially when lives are in danger. Is that understood?"

"I understand," said Athena in a voice only a machine could synthesize.

Was I too harsh? Did I misread the situation?

Kimmy waited but received nothing more.

"Apocalypse, can I talk to you on a private net?" said Karen.

Kimmy grumbled as she switched to Karen's net. "Yes?"

"That was unnecessary on the open radio," replied Karen.

"I wanted to make sure everyone understood."

"And we do. We tried to reach you, but we didn't get an answer. This is the first time Athena, or I, have been able to reach you. We don't know what you've been doing—from the sounds of it, you've had your hands full, and that's fine. The rest of us can carry on without you—if we have to. We didn't intentionally leave you out or override your command authority, but decisions needed to be made, and Athena and I made them. In the future, we need someone—other than Athena—aboard War Cat who has command and control of the entire battlespace—"

"Like who?"

"Why don't you do it?"

"Are you trying to kick me out of my mech? I can do more with a mech than the rest of you. I won't let you take my place on the battlefield!"

"No. I believe you're the best suited for it."

"We don't have the networking needed to make it work. And I'm not giving up my seat to make you and the others feel better for an ass chewing."

"I'm trying to make the unit better. You're the best mech strategist—"

"I'm also the best shot. You do it. You're the ace fighter pilot."

Karen paused, then said, "I could, but I don't want to overstep my authority."

"Why not? What's stopping you now?"

"Kimmy! We're not staging a coup. We're trying to avoid losing two mech—"

"Yeah? It's no rose garden up here, Karen. I have no weapons and am a snowflake away from being cored. So, tell me how bad you had it. Tell me how hard facing down four drones was. I took on two drones, and who knows how many attack mechs—BY MYSELF. How hard was it, Karen?"

"I'm not trying to insinuate your part of the mission was worse than ours. I'm—"

"Your Empress asked you a question, Captain!"

"You're not my Empress anymore! We're not—"

"I am your empress always! I trained you. I care for you. What I've given you is mine. On Earth Eight-Thirty-two, on Roost, everywhere. Do not forget I *am* the Dragon God."

There was a click and dead air.

Kimmy took off her helmet, threw it around the cockpit, then thrust back in her seat, bouncing off the backrest. She crossed her arms, her face screwing up into a royal pout. *Fucked that up.*

Leaning her head against the headrest, Kimmy stared into the driving snow. *How am I going to make this up to Karen and Athena? Karen's right. We need someone for command and control...but we need a better network among the mechs to make it work. Better sensors on War Cat are needed, too. Luckily, I have a few credits sitting around.*

Through the falling snow, flames came down from above. *Uh-oh.* Kimmy scrambled to find her helmet and get it on. She set the radio to the open network so everyone would hear her.

"Athena! Athena!" Kimmy cried urgently.

"Yes?" came the flat reply.

"We've got incoming mechs. I count six—seven—two troops of rings coming down in the draw's top. We've got to go before they deploy."

"I'm boarding War Cat now," said Karen. "My troop has been recovered."

"I'll move the drones up the draw to cover our escape," replied Athena. "If that's ok with Kimmy?"

I deserve that. "Yes, do it. Get out of there. Leave whatever you're working on and hit the self-destruct button."

"I haven't thought of that," chuckled Athena. "We're on our way."

"I'll distract them."

"Kimmy!" cried Karen. "Your mech can't handle that."

"Then I'll see you in Valhalla—isn't that what my Servicemembers say?"

"Kimmy! This is not the time for heroics! Retreat, and the others will get down the hill."

"I can't ask others to do what I won't do," said Kimmy. She switched the radio to Athena. "How are you doing?"

"Getting out the door now." The AI's voice was harsh and mechanical. "There was no self-destruct button, but we yanked the hard drives, memory modules, and all the hardware we could carry. I'll lock the door when I leave. What would you like to do with the Defin techs?"

"I'm sure these mechs landing are Defin. Leave them here and let them become their problem."

"I'll lock them out in the cold."

"Athena...I'm sorry. I didn't mean to lose my temper. It was unprofessional and hurtful. I have no excuses. I hope you'll forgive me."

"I understand, and I forgive you. The battlefield is a chaotic and stressful place. I tried my best with Karen while we couldn't reach you. Please, tell me what I did wrong, so I don't repeat it?" Athena's voice changed, returning to her usual upbeat self.

How come all subordinates can't be like that? "You...I...nothing, Athena. I think you were teasing me, and I took it wrong. I'm sorry."

"I understand. I thought humor would lighten the mood and ease your stress. I apologize for not interpreting the situation correctly."

"It's ok, Athena. I get what you were trying to do, but I was coming off a near-death escape...if you hadn't gained control of the drone when you did, I wouldn't be here. Thank you."

"It took longer than I expected to get into the UEE systems. I'm glad I could save you. I'm at the door. Shutting and locking it now."

The first of the new arrivals touched down in the snow. Kimmy turned her mech to shine a light toward the doors. Nicole was climbing up the side of her mech while shouldering a bag while Athena's ball floated after her. Lizzy was on her mech and jumped down the hatch while clutching her rifle. *They're going to need more time.*

Kimmy jammed her throttle forward and aimed the control stick at the landing mechs. She hoped to be a tempting target and keep their attention from the lighter mechs so they could escape.

"The drones are coming up the draw," reported Athena.

The first of the new arrivals took an alpha strike at Lizzy's mech, blowing off the right arm.

Shit. I've got to do something. "Girls! Go! Go! I'll hold them off!" *With what I don't know.*

Other arrivals saw Kimmy and turned toward her. She slammed her control stick to the right and shut off her lights, hoping they would follow her into the darkness. *Kita said there was a God of Fools...may they watch over me.*

Blasts from different lasers and particle cannons lit Kimmy's HUD as she pushed through the hip-deep snow. Around her, the snow exploded as ballistic rounds missed in the darkness. *Too close for comfort.*

"Apocalypse!" cried Lizzy. "I'm mounted and getting out of here. Athena said the extraction point was here?"

"That extraction point's been burned," said Kimmy, trying to remain as calm as the missing shots would allow. "New extraction point is the bottom of the draw. You and Nemesis head for it. I'll keep these guys busy."

"Wilco. Moving out."

For the love of god, hurry.

Kimmy zigzagged through the snow, trying to draw the enemy after her but keep enough distance that the blowing snow and darkness obscured her. So far, her plan seemed to work until she stepped and kept going down as lasers and ballistic rounds flew over her cockpit.

Thank the God of Fools. Kimmy landed on her feet, but the snow was up to her cockpit. The blanket of white did not indicate what lay beneath, and Kimmy wasn't sure what she'd fallen into.

Feeling panic in her chest, Kimmy shoved the throttle forward, but her legs weren't powerful enough to break the snow, leaving her only choice was to go back the way she came. Reversing the throttle, she took a step back, but her foot made a *clunk* and refused to go further.

I've got to get rid of some of this snowpack. Kimmy put her thumb on the torso traverse button and pushed it to the right as far as it would go. The torso turned, pushing the snow out of the way. As she turned to the rear, several enemy mechs came into view. *I wish I had my weapons.*

Above, in the darkened snow, several lights moved through the air. They weren't spotlights or running lights, more like flames from a rocket. *I hope that's Nicole and Lizzy jumping out of here.*

Kimmy turned another full revolution, hoping she'd moved enough snow to free her mech. She moved the throttle, feeling her mech's legs churn through the snow. Her foot found a perch, and she rose a few feet. The mech took another step, adding to her elevation.

After a few steps, Kimmy was ready to fully engage the throttle. Out of the blinding snow came the shape of an attack mech, its weapons aimed at her. A lump grew in Kimmy's throat. *So much for the God of Fools. Angel, I'll see you soon...*

As Kimmy lowered her head, the back of the mech exploded, flooding the snow with orange and yellow light. Seizing the opportunity, Kimmy jammed her throttle forward, mentally urging her mech forward.

As Kimmy's mech churned through the snow, gaining foot by foot, a halo of light dropped out of the sky. The drop ring hovered over her, its computer linking with Kimmy's mech. Lowering, the rockets of the drop ring melted the snow, clearing to her waist. There were loud *clanks* as the magnet clamps connected. On her console, warnings appeared, telling her to be prepared for liftoff.

Kimmy braced herself against her command chair and rocketed back to War Cat and safety.

CHAPTER 08

ORBITING VERI IIb
WAR CAT ASSAULT SHIP
SPACE BIOME
¥1,789,725
8, NOVEMBER 4003

K IMMY'S MECH LURCHED TO a stop inside its bay. Amber warning lights rotated as the scaffolding closed around her. With a tired *thump,* Kimmy punched the release button on her harness and slid out of her command chair. Only her arm on the console kept her from collapsing.

The cockpit hatch swung open, and Kimmy gingerly used the equipment to pull herself to it. Crawling through the hole, she collapsed on the grating.

"Kimmy!" exclaimed a mech tech as he ran to the stricken pilot.

Kimmy raised a hand. "I'm fine, UV, just...just exhausted."

A pair of techs pulled Kimmy to a sitting position. A canteen appeared in Kimmy's hand. With some effort, she unscrewed the cap and took a gulp, feeling the cold water enter her core and give her some energy.

With a shaky hand, Kimmy handed the canteen back, and with the help of a guardrail and tech, she climbed to her feet.

"Should we get a stretcher?" asked Ultraviolet.

Kimmy decided she needed to show strength and resilience. She could collapse once she made it to bed.

"No. I'll walk."

"Then let us offer you support."

The tech offered an arm, and Kimmy took it. Together, they rode the elevator to the main deck of the mech bay.

Walking through the cavernous space, the mechs from the mission were in their bays, surrounded by scaffolding. Techs and machines crawled over the returned mechs. Some mechs showed no damage, and others, like Zhi's rex, had massive damage. All of Karen's troop were missing limbs or had ruptured armor. Kimmy grimaced, but she didn't know what they faced at the time.

At the entrance to the mech bay, Karen waited with Nicole, Lizzy, and Flexi.

"You have the luck of fools," said Karen sternly.

Kimmy felt like Karen punched her, but the result was the same. Kimmy collapsed on her butt, tears filling her eyes as images of Chelsea, her little God of Luck, passed before her mind's eye. Burying her head in her arms, Kimmy mourned the loss of her daughter. It felt like the entire mission Chelsea watched over her, manipulating luck and protecting her mother. Now, Kimmy's heartache poured over, unable to cope with the grief.

"Karen, we're supposed to talk to her, educate her, not make her cry," retorted Zhi.

"What did I say?"

"Who controls luck in Reality?" said Athena from a nearby speaker.

"Shit. No use talking to her now. She'll be this way for hours."

Kimmy looked up and screamed, "Fuck you! I hope nothing happens to someone you care about."

Karen looked down at Kimmy. "I've got someone I care about in medbay, thank you. It's your fault he's there."

Kimmy sprang to her feet and stood nose-to-nose with Karen. "I was not his troop leader—you were. Whatever happened to Pierre is your fault."

"Don't push your failings on me. I did what was necessary to accomplish my and the overall mission."

"Ok, enough!" yelled Zhi as she and Lizzy jumped between the pair and pushed them back. Zhi taking Karen and Lizzy with Kimmy.

As Kimmy tried to calm down in the comforting embrace of Lizzy and Nicole, Sprokkit stomped over.

"I was afraid I would need to separate you," he said, his eyes alight. "I am glad the situation handled itself. You do not have your wings by which to pick you up. Why the altercation? I heard the mission was a success."

Kimmy turned in the girls' arms and looked at the towering Morphicon. She had to remind herself regardless of what happened, the mission succeeded.

"Just differences in command styles and lack of communication," replied Kimmy dryly.

"Hmmm, I understand. Velositi and I have different approaches, and it has taken us many years to learn to work together and appreciate each other. As a part to your victory, I have something that might cheer you up."

Kimmy's ears pricked up. She could use a lift. "What is it?"

"I will show you."

The girls followed Sprokkit to his eight-foot-tall workbench in the corner of the mech bay.

The workbench was too tall for Kimmy to see what the Morphicon was working on, but he had an interesting collection of mechanical, electrical, and computer parts stored in the cubbies under the bench.

Sprokkit puttered around his bench, then squatted, opening his hand to reveal three human-like limbs.

"Are you building a Terminator?" said Lizzy excitedly.

Kimmy didn't think so, but the two legs and arm looked like they belonged in the movie. "These are for Kita?" she said curiously.

"Yes. I built them to the specifications provided by Athena's plans. They need to be surgically implanted, and Athena assured me the autodoc had the capability. I understand Kita is volatile—more so than normal—and I hope these might ease her suffering."

"She'll love them!" Kimmy smiled at Sprokkit. Her eyes bright. "I can't thank you enough, Sprokkit. I know she'll be excited to get moving. These will help her regain her self-esteem and confidence."

Privately, Kimmy wasn't so sure Kita would love them. *Kita's in a black place right now. What kind of fight am I going to have to get her to use these? I'll have to talk to Athena. I'm sure she'll have a logical argument to get Kita to use them.*

"Always happy to help a friend," replied Sprokkit, his blue eyes glowing brightly.

Kimmy couldn't remember a time seeing him happy. She couldn't let Kita reject his gift.

"Now, if you will excuse me, Athena has given me a project that needs to be done posthaste."

"Take it she gave you the hard drives and memory modules?" chuckled Lizzy.

Sprokkit nodded. "She did. And schematics on making a test bench to connect them to the portable workstation you brought with them."

Athena appeared on a monitor above Sprokkit's workbench. "Even though this machine is only a portable workstation, using it will be much faster to decode the next map section."

"This new hardware didn't come with any dangerous viruses or software we need to worry about?" asked Kimmy.

"No," said Athena with a grin. "It contains life support and power regulation software to keep the cache operating a thousand years past the empire. I will use it to upgrade War Cat's life support and power systems. Initial tests show I can gain twenty to thirty percent efficiency by upgrading the software. I could get fifty to sixty percent efficiency if we made some hardware upgrades."

Kimmy ran a hand through her hair. "Talk to UV about what needs to happen. If I can spare the money, we'll do it."

Athena smiled. "Most of what we need can be made aboard the ship. It also came with a software suite to program the drones. I can use it to create a program connecting the mechs and War Cat. As was discussed, this would allow someone to have command and control over the entire battlespace."

Kimmy's face remained neutral, knowing people wanted her to be that *someone*. But she wasn't about to give in. "I'm sure Karen will love it," she said coldly. She walked toward the mech bay exit.

Lizzy gathered the prosthetics from Sprokkit, and the group hurried to catch up to Kimmy. The others seemed to sense Kimmy's resistance to the new command role.

"Someone will step up and fill the role," said Nicole. "Come on. Let's take these prosthetics to Kita."

"Kita is asleep," announced Athena from a speaker overhead as the group walked toward the elevator. "UV and I decided it was best to keep her sedated. She kept picking at her skin and trying to throw herself out of bed. We tried restraints, but she is deft at freeing her good arm."

Kimmy tapped the side of her head and looked at the prosthetics in Lizzy's arms. "Athena, have UV prep Kita for surgery to implant the prosthetics. We might as well do it while she's out."

"Isn't that a violation?" said Nicole.

Kimmy gave Nicole a dire look. "I'm her partner and can decide for her wellbeing when she's incapable. I'll have a fight now or later...might as well be later when she already has them and is forced to use them and see they're for her benefit."

"I thought you said Kita would love them?" said Lizzy.

"I was trying to not upset Sprokkit. Kita is in a defiant mood. She would rather die than live, and I'm not letting her. I'll show her she can live and be productive with her injuries. Kita doesn't always have to be a warrior, assassin, or thief. There's more to the world that she hasn't explored yet."

"If you need help, I'm in," said Lizzy.

Kimmy smiled at Kita's ex. The more people Kita saw who cared, the easier it would be to convince Kita living was the way to go. She led her group through War Cat toward the medbay.

"I guess you are her partner, and part of a partner's role is to make choices for us when we can't." Nicole looked at Lizzy, and sadness passed through her eyes.

Kimmy wished Nicole and Lizzy could make it work, but both put their passions for the military and for Nicole—justice—ahead of their personal lives. When the stars aligned, they would hook up, but circumstance and wanderlust always blew them apart.

"I'm not trying to hurt her," said Kimmy.

"I know you're not," replied Nicole. "I worry Kita won't like them, but I will help you convince her. Little Kita has always been easier to deal with than big Kita."

Kimmy chuckled. Little Kita was her human form with all the weaknesses, and she was an unimposing five-foot-six. Big Kita, or god Kita, came with a litany of abilities, powers, augmentations, and an attitude that went with ruling Reality as god. She was also an imposing five-foot-eleven, made more so by the two-inch heels she liked to wear.

"She's only human—by the way she's been fighting, you would think she was her god self. I wish I had my god abilities to counter her."

"I don't think War Cat would survive a god fight," said Lizzy, looking uneasy.

"Kita and I have never had that," said Kimmy unhappily.

"That's a first for Kita," chuckled Athena. "She used to fight with Snowy and Jane—massive drag down, go until they'd destroyed everything and smashed the other into paste."

"Not my Kita—and definitely not with me."

"I believe Kita has matured since she took over Reality. Being alone taught her the value of friendship and relationships when she couldn't move from one girl to the next."

"Could have fooled me," said Lizzy with a heavy sigh.

"If you don't mind my analysis," said Athena.

Kimmy hoped Athena wouldn't give it. She didn't want to upset Lizzy. Kita admitted she was hard on her lovers, and Lizzy fell out of favor because she didn't have enough personality, background, or maturity to keep Kita's attention.

"Whatever. It's over. I lost," Lizzy shrugged and frowned at Kimmy.

"I'm sorry," said Kimmy, giving Lizzy a hug. They were joined by Nicole.

"Eh...just as well. I'm no match for Kita—I'm just a soldier. I can't handle her the way Kimmy does. Must be the empress training."

Kimmy and Nicole laughed.

"Even I have trouble with Kita," admitted Kimmy. "I'm hoping you'll both be there after getting her prosthetics implanted."

"Sure," said Nicole. "I know how she is—she'll either love them or hate them. If she hates them, it'll be everybody's fault but hers."

"It's not her fault this time," countered Kimmy.

"That'll be even harder for her to accept."

Kimmy hadn't been down that line of thought. *Kita usually owns her mistakes...not gracefully...but admits to them and tries to fix them. I don't think I've ever seen her deal with a problem outside her control.* "It may be difficult for her, but we'll make her understand. She sees reason and logic, but she probably won't listen in her current headspace. We have to make her listen. Once we break through, the rest will be easy."

"If she comes after us, I'm throwing you in front of her," teased Nicole.

"Beauty will calm the savage beast," added Lizzy.

Kimmy gave the pair a wry look. "I thought I would use you both to distract her while I snuck up from behind and knocked her out with a frying pan."

The trio laughed, joined by Athena.

Kimmy entered the medbay and was met by a pair of techs.

"We'll take those if you don't mind," said Ultraviolet. "We'll get them sterilized and prepared. Kita is currently being prepped for surgery. You can see her through that window." She motioned down a hallway to a window.

"Thanks, UV," said Kimmy as she led the others to the viewing window.

Inside, Kita was on the autodoc table, naked. Her arm and legs were covered in an orange antiseptic gel.

"Athena," called Kimmy.

"Yes?" the AI said over a speaker nearby.

"What's the chance this could go wrong?"

"Well, if Sprokkit didn't build the limbs to my specifications—and I will check them before we start—then we have to wait for him to build new ones. If you mean the autodoc screws up, I won't let that happen. I'm as protective of Kita as Omega—"

"Who is Omega?" Kimmy interjected curiously.

"Omega was one of the most powerful AIs the UEE ever created. He could run entire planets' government computer networks. He was purchased by Sven Gjord to run the colony ship that contained his daughter, Jane Gjord—"

"Kita's Jane."

"Yes. When the ship crashed, Omega created a way for a lucky vat born to find him. That person was Kita. He put her on the path to becoming what she is today. When any operation had to be done on Kita, Omega did it."

"So, you're saying you'll do this operation?"

"You doubt me?" Athena replied with a chuckle. "My tolerances are much smaller than the autodoc, and I'll be using the UEE laptop, giving me a hundred thousand times the computing power than the autodoc."

"I don't doubt you. I didn't know you knew anything about medicine."

"Besides what the autodoc knows, I have an extensive library of references and experiences to guide me. I also have extensive knowledge of Kita."

Kimmy looked back at Kita, longing to touch her. "Take good care of her."

"She is the only one who can give me back Quill. I will do everything I can to ensure she doesn't come to harm."

"Who's Quill?" said Lizzy.

"Kita's daughter and my partner. I consider Kita my mother. She will give Quill to me when she learns how to bring people back from Earth Zero."

"I never considered an AI falling in love," said Nicole, looking astonished.

"Thanks to Kita, I can."

"The tin man gets a heart," mused Kimmy.

"I'll get you and your little dog, too," replied Athena, making the Angels laugh.

Kimmy yawned. "Oh, damn. Athena, how long will it take?"

"I estimate nine hours. Would you like to watch?"

"No. I'm going to take a shower and get some sleep. I'll need to be fresh for when Kita awakes. So will you girls."

"Sleep sounds good," said Lizzy. She looked at Nicole. "Your room or mine?"

The question seemed to catch Nicole off-guard. "Ahh...mine. I keep it clean."

Lizzy laughed. "Cool. I'll grab my towel and PJs." She took Nicole's hand and led her out of the medbay.

"Did I miss something?" Kimmy asked Athena.

"I registered her biometrics increase after we discussed her losing Kita. Maybe it reminded her of Nicole."

Kimmy shook her head. "Hope it goes well. Who's in medbay that I need to visit?"

"Only Dupont. He's suffering from hypothermia and frostbite. He's currently asleep."

"Then I'll visit him later. I'm going to bed. Good luck with Kita."

"I don't need luck. I have dimensional floating-point operations."

ORBITING VERI IIb
WAR CAT ASSAULT SHIP
SPACE BIOME
¥1,789,725
9, NOVEMBER 4003

K IMMY RAN A COMB through her dark, wavey hair, making a face when she hit a snag. Pulling the offending hair around, she switched to a brush and worked the snag out.

"Kimmy, are you up?" asked Athena.

Kimmy returned a wry smile at the speaker. Paranoid Kita turned off the cameras and audio equipment in the room. Kimmy turned one back on so Athena could reach her when the operation was over.

"I'm here, Athena. How did it go?"

"Splendidly. I was able to attach all three limbs and test them. They will take time to learn to use, but Ultraviolet has created a physical therapy room. I wish I had the UEE technology when Sprokkit built them. There are some tweaks I'd like to make to the design. I could make some to the connection points during surgery—"

Kimmy put her brush down and reached for a hair tie and a red bow, the signature item she wore as a princess. She'd abandoned it when becoming empress. Now, she wore it when she wasn't piloting. "Maybe once she's mastered them, you can upgrade them."

"Oh, I hadn't thought of that."

"Is she awake? Can I see her?"

"If she were awake, the entire ship would know. She is still under and in post-op. It will be another hour."

Kimmy grabbed her makeup kit and applied color to her eyes, lips, and cheeks. *Might as well make me pretty for my girl.* "Anyone still in medbay?"

"Yes. Dupont is still recovering from his hypothermia and is being cared for by Karen."

"I didn't know she was a nurse type."

"Not like that."

"Ew. Ok. Tell them to keep their hands to themselves when I show up."

"When will that be?"

"As soon as I'm done here. Can you tell UV to meet me along the way with some coffee and something sweet?"

"Command has its perks."

Kimmy laughed. "I used to eat my meals in the corridors of the White House between meetings."

She left her vanity and hit a button on the wall, signaling Ultraviolet's stewards they could clean the room. Living with Ultraviolet and Athena was like living in the White House. There was always someone to do the menial tasks. Rarely had Kimmy lived any other way. Those few years living in Scotland with Kita and Chelsea were a shock. The mighty empress wasn't used to doing everything for herself—but she learned and came to enjoy it. But in an environment like War Cat, it was nice not to worry about the menial tasks—she learned to use the time to think through problems. Something she wished for now.

"I'll tell Karen and Dupont to be presentable for your arrival—even I shut off the camera and turn down the audio. It's bad enough I have to monitor his vitals."

"Ugh. That's more than I care to know, and now I keep imagining it."

"If I may turn on the screen?"

"Sure."

The TV turned on, and a picture of Kita appeared—her limbs restrained.

"Are those restraints strong enough to hold her?"

"I—hope—so. I'll check with UV. I think they're standard medical restraints. The next step would be getting chains from the mech bay."

"We might need them depending on how you built those arms."

"She is limited by her body, and only certain joints have increased strength, but not to her normal capacity. She won't be bending any I-beams like she normally can."

"That's good. We want as much of little Kita as possible. I guess I'm ready. Let's see what our new couple does when they're not alone."

ORBITING VERI IIb
WAR CAT ASSAULT SHIP
SPACE BIOME
¥1,789,725
9, NOVEMBER 4003

KIMMY HANDED THE EMPTY coffee mug back to the steward. "Thanks, UV," she said around a bite of pastry.

"The orderlies are standing by, ready for Kita's awakening," said Ultraviolet.

"Good. It might take several to hold her down."

Ultraviolet laughed. "Karen and Pierre are in suite four."

Kimmy entered medbay and went to the suites in the back. She passed Kita's suite and went to suite four. She knocked on the door several times. When it opened, she was met by a stone-faced Karen.

"Hi, Karen," Kimmy said cheerfully. "How's our snowman?" She looked around Karen at Dupont lying in bed.

"Can't complain. I'm getting the best care in the world."

"I heard."

Dupont returned a sheepish grin. Karen looked aghast.

Kimmy held up her hand. "If you wanted privacy, you should have waited until you returned to your rooms. Athena can tell you how to turn down the surveillance in them." She looked at Dupont. "UV and Athena say you're healing and get to keep all your fingers and toes."

"Yeah, I still got my trigger finger. But a little cold won't stop me. Did we get the map?"

Kimmy nodded. "Yes, we did. Athena has it now."

"So, where are we going next?"

"I don't know. It shouldn't take Athena long to decode it, but she's been busy since we returned."

Dupont looked sideways. "What could be more important than the map?"

"Kita," Kimmy said finitely.

Dupont frowned. "Wouldn't getting to the treasure be the most important thing?"

Kimmy smiled wryly and looked at Karen. "There is no greater treasure than the one you love—and Kita is loved by all."

"Well, I guess a few extra hours of rest won't hurt." He looked at Karen and smiled.

Karen's smile was full of trepidation.

You should know better than giving blow jobs in a place monitored by an AI and hive mind.

The door opened, and Nicole and Lizzy walked in hand-in-hand.

"Hey, girls," said Kimmy, upbeat. "Good night?"

"Oh, yeah," said Lizzy with a wolfish smile. "We're ready to tackle the big baddy."

Kimmy and Nicole laughed.

"We might just have to tackle her," remarked Kimmy.

"Won't be my first time," retorted Lizzy.

"Oh?" said Kimmy curiously. "And what has my partner been up to in her previous lives?"

"She was my girlfriend," Lizzy announced with a laugh. "And she got drunk and crawled through the barracks. She wouldn't return to the room, so I tackled her and dragged her back. It didn't help that I was drunk, too, but it was lights out."

Kimmy laughed.

"I would like to say my little Kita was more mature...but I think she was actually worse if I remember her tantrums." Kimmy gave a playful frown.

"I think you do," replied Nicole. She'd been there for most of them. "No one can throw a tantrum like Kita."

"Maybe we should leave her sedated," Kimmy mused.

"I would prefer you not," said Athena from the room's speaker.

She sounds upset. "I wouldn't, Athena. Just a musing knowing what we might have to deal with."

"The orderlies are ready, and Kita's vital signs are rising. She should be awake in a few minutes."

"Let me know when she discovers she's restrained."

"It won't be long. And Pierre, I haven't looked at the map other than to verify its contents. Kimmy will be the first to know when I translate and decipher our destination. Until then, enjoy Karen and know that I turned off the audio feed from this room."

"Goddamnit," yelled Karen. "Is everyone going to comment?"

Dupont put a hand on Karen's arm. "It's alright, babe. They're just jealous."

"That doesn't mean they have to be bitches." She jerked her arm free of Dupont and stormed from the room.

Kimmy shrugged. *I'll take that point.* She turned to Lizzy and Nicole. "I'm sure you girls had no privacy issues?"

Nicole chuckled. "Of course not, but we didn't do it on the dining room table either."

"Ah, come on," said Dupont. "Give her a break. Karen's been living on a dy—lesbian ship for months."

Nicole glared. "Doesn't mean she has to jump on the first dick that walks through the door."

"Come on," said Lizzy. "Let Karen have her meat. Let's go check on Kita. I much prefer her slips of the tongue."

Kimmy waved the pair out the door. She led them to suite one marked KITA.

"She's still coming to," said Athena. "I'll instruct the nurse to give her something to bring her around faster."

"Go ahead," said Kimmy.

The nurse came in wearing scrubs and sneakers with a syringe in her hand. She went to Kita's IV tree and injected the syringe. The nurse puttered around Kita, waiting for the drug to take effect.

Kimmy, Nicole, and Lizzy gathered at the foot of the bed, waiting and watching.

Kita's eyes were still covered by the wrinkly artificial skin that gave her the appearance of a rotting corpse, but that's not what Kimmy saw. Before her was the most beautiful girl she'd ever seen, with gorgeous blue eyes and long, luscious blonde hair. In her mind, she juxtaposed little Kita and god Kita. Kita's body was something Kimmy enjoyed, but it was her partner's mind—her knowledge, wisdom, tenacity, determination, and constant drive to be the best that Kimmy admired and tried to emulate.

Why is the skin over her eyes slit?

The beeping from the monitor at the head of the bed increased. Kita's head moved back and forth.

"Wha..." Kita's voice was a groan as she stumbled, trying to form words with her damaged lips.

"Kita, angel, it's me, Kimmy—"

"Kimmy...what do you want?"

"I'm here with Nicole, Lizzy, Athena, and Ultraviolet. Athena devised a way for you to walk and use your arm again."

"What?" Kita demanded angrily. "What did you do to me?"

"Kita, calm down," Kimmy ordered. "These are temporary until we earn enough money to get you someplace with advanced medical treatments. This is not a permanent solution, but it will allow you to get out of bed and walk around the ship. You don't have to stay in the medbay. You can come home with me."

"I have a surprise for you, Mom," Athena interjected.

"Athena..." Kita whispered.

"Hi, Mom. UV, if you could reveal her eyes."

What is Athena up to?

The nurse lifted the flaps of skin covering Kita's eyes, revealing orbital-shaped cameras.

"Mom, your eyes were too damaged to save, but I constructed new ones similar to your Angel eyes. You can see multiple spectrums and zoom. A computer attached to your optic nerve processes the camera signals before they go to your brain. Here, let me turn them on."

Kita's eyes glowed with a pink hue.

Kimmy bit her tongue as Lizzy whispered, "Called it, girl terminator."

Kita's head rocked from side to side. There was a jerk on her right side, then on her left. "What's wrong with my arms?"

"Nothing," said Athena. "They're restrained for safety. UV, if you could reveal Kita's arms."

Kimmy doubted the restraints were for Kita's safety. Instead for everyone else in the room. Ultraviolet pulled the sheet back, revealing Kita's non-prosthetic arm. It was restrained to the bed frame. Kita pulled on it gently while Ultraviolet did the same to her prosthetic arms and legs.

Kita pulled against the restraint with her prosthetic arm, the hand opening and closing randomly.

"What did you do to me?" Kita gasped. "What am I?" Her head raised and moved back and forth, taking in the synthetic skin and prosthetics. "What in the Crushing Depths am I?" she shrieked, then thrashed against the restraints.

"I'll get her shoulders," said Kimmy. "Girls, grab the rest of her."

Lizzy and Nicole each grabbed a leg while Ultraviolet threw her weight across Kita's middle. Kimmy grabbed Kita's shoulders and used all her weight to pin them down.

"Kita, listen to me!" Kimmy ordered and begged.

When Kita struggled, Kimmy jumped on the bed and sat on Kita's left shoulder. She grabbed Kita's chin and forced her upset partner to look at her.

"Kita! Enough. You need to stop. No one is hurting you. Your mech was cored, and Ultraviolet saved you. You lost your arm, legs, eyes, and skin and have been in recovery for more than a month. Athena designed prosthetics for you, and Sprokkit made them. Athena finished implanting them, and we're here to help you. Ultraviolet has a physical therapy regimen for you to learn to use them. It will take time, but I get to take you home."

Kita craned her neck to look down at her chest, arms, and legs. She jerked against the restraints and threw Kimmy off. Kita thrashed, knocking Nicole and Lizzy away.

The plastic restraints gave way in rapid succession. Kita tried to spring from bed, but the lack of control in her limbs caused her to tumble and land with a *thump* on the floor.

"Girls! Get her!" yelled Kimmy as she sat on Kita's chest.

"Trying!" called Lizzy as she wrestled with Kita's kicking leg.

Nicole and Ultraviolet had better luck sitting on Kita's abdomen and other leg.

"Kita!" Kimmy yelled. "Stop it! We're here to help you!"

"What are you doing to me?" Kita screamed. "Why are you making me ugly?"

Kimmy bent, so she was nose to nose with her partner. "You're not ugly. You're beautiful. I'm your girl, and only I get to decide if you're ugly—and you never will be. I promise. This is an intermediate step to help you regain what you've lost. I miss you. I miss your voice. I miss your laugh. I miss touching you. You're not ugly. And we're not done yet—not by a long shot. You have to bear with it for a few months until—"

"Let me die!" Kita yelled. "I'll come back perfect!"

"You are perfect! And you can't die. We don't know what will happen, and I won't find out unless there's no other choice. But you have a choice."

Kita threw her head back against the metal decking with a *smack*. She looked away from Kimmy and let out a defeated moan. "Just...let...me...die."

Kimmy grabbed Kita's chin and forced her to look at her. "Not acceptable! Crawling is acceptable! Falling is acceptable! Puking is acceptable! Blood is acceptable. Tears are acceptable! Sweat is acceptable! Pain is acceptable. Quitting is *not* acceptable! Do you understand me, Katrina Marie Roosevelt?" Kimmy looked into Kita's mechanical eyes, trying to convey all the love, determination, and resilience she could to make Kita understand. "You can do this,

Kita," she added gently. "I'll be there, Lizzy, Nicole, UV, Athena—we'll all be there to help you and give you whatever you need. But there is no quitting. The Kita of old wouldn't quit. Are you telling me being god has made you soft?"

Air leaked through Kita's teeth. "The Kita of old has done this before. Why do I want to do it again?"

"Because I'm finding out being god has made me soft. We got our asses kicked by a pack of mercs on the Tet, and we toughened up...but not enough. Running this outfit has made me realize I'm not the tough-as-nails, take-no-prisoners empress I used to be. I blame it on having a kid.

"But the kid is grown and in danger. If we're going to save her, we're going to need to be at our peak. I'm doing it, and so will you. I don't expect you to wield a sword and be a supreme gymnast, but you can make your body the best it can be while sharpening your mind to a razor. Because that's what we need—a mind.

"We've got the guns. We need someone to command us. I can't pilot and lead at the same time. Athena is working on software for War Cat and the mechs. You'll be the brains. I need you, Kita. Your daughter needs you. And if we're going to go back to Earth Zero, we can't be soft. You said it yourself. You had to be hard and evil to conquer it. I'm sure it hasn't changed since you left."

Kita shook her head gently, enough to free her of Kimmy's grasp, and rested her head on the deck. "You're going to hate me if I become that person again."

"Don't forget we are your friends," said Nicole.

"I had to forget the last time...and that was a mistake. I won't forget who my friends are this time. Ok, love, you want your monster—you got her."

Kimmy looked into Kita's eyes. "I need your brain. You can't carve your way through enemies, but I can. Your brain, my sword."

"At some point, I'll have to kill something."

"Master your arm and legs, and you can kill all you want."

Nicole looked unsure and said, "Ah...wait a second—"

Kita looked at Nicole. "Don't worry, I won't go on a psycho-killing binge. But I'm sure I will find some people who deserve to be flayed, skinned, and gutted, then die horribly."

"Damn, man. That's some hardcore shit," said Lizzy.

"What kind of monster are you?" gasped Nicole.

"The kind that will get my daughter back—even if I have to kill everyone between here and the Aven Federation. Don't worry, Nicole. I'm on your side. Kimmy asked for the other side of the sociopath to come out."

"Can you leave it boxed until we need it?"

Kita's smile was crooked and demented. "You have nothing to fear." She looked at the nurse. "UV, when do we start physical therapy?"

"Your surgery must heal before we put any weight on them, but we can start on control of the robotic joints."

"Athena, Mommy's home."

"I've been awaiting your arrival. I wish I had Dead and Buried or Dusk and Dawn for you, but I designed your prosthetics. They are poor substitutes, but I have little to work with."

Kita raised the arm with the prosthetic. The stump was bandaged and bloody. She didn't move the fake limb when she rotated her arm at the shoulder. "Prosthetic is such an ugly word. These are now me—my limbs. I will master them, and they will become me."

"I have upgrades for them when you are ready," announced Athena.

"Outstanding. If Kimmy will get off me, I'm ready to get started."

Kimmy, hearing her cue, stood up next to Nicole. Together, the four helped Kita back to bed.

"Ok, shoo," said Kita, waving her good arm at the others. "I have work to do. Kimmy, I love you. Lizzy, I still love you, but have fun with Nicole."

Lizzy laughed as she smiled at Nicole.

"Love you," said Kimmy. "Do you need me to stay?"

"No, I'm good," said Kita. "You have better things to do than watch my frustration, pain, and exertion. When we have a breakthrough, I'll call. I expect you to visit."

"I'll be by often. Get better, angel."

"Athena," Kita called. "Get me all you know on mech doctrine. If I'm going to command, I need to know what I'm doing."

Kimmy pushed the others out of the suite toward medbay's door.

"What did you unleash?" demanded Nicole of Kimmy.

"The God of Evil. I want every weapon we can muster, and Kita is the greatest."

"Would she really leave a trail of bodies?" said Lizzy.

"Athena?" Kimmy called.

"Yes. If you want the simple answer. In the past, Kita has killed tens of thousands to get what she wants. Since becoming Ruler of Reality, she's been on a kinder and gentler kick—the Kita you know. Since Chelsea was taken, I believe she's been waiting for the rules to change."

"What rule?" exclaimed Nicole.

"The one saying she must be kinder and gentler. The situation has changed, and Kimmy has given her permission to unleash her true self—the Kita I know. I wouldn't want to be those who stand between her and Chelsea. The God of Evil flies the black flag—no quarter given, none asked."

"And you're ok with this?" exclaimed Nicole to Kimmy.

"If it gets my daughter back, I would release a sex tape for the galaxy to see."

"Wait, is there one?" Lizzy asked with an amused grin.

"I have one of Pierre and Karen," replied Athena.

"Not going to be many takers for that around here," said Kimmy.

"I was thinking blackmail."

"You really are a daughter of Kita."

CHAPTER 09

ORBITING VERI IIb
WAR CAT ASSAULT SHIP
SPACE BIOME
¥1,789,725
9, NOVEMBER 4003

K IMMY ENTERED WAR CAT'S bridge with Ash'a and Ultraviolet. The dim, square space was lit by holographic displays and console screens lining the walls, broken only by windows on the fore wall. It was time to get an update on the ship, mechs, and map. Kimmy was flying high after Kita accepted her fate and embraced it. She wasn't sure what she'd unleashed, but if it got Chelsea back, she didn't care. *I was ready to lay waste to the galaxy, but it might become a reality with Kita.*

Leading the others to the small holotable in the center of the room, it flickered, and Athena's face appeared with a smile.

"Hello, ladies," greeted the AI.

She sounds chipper. Am I not the only one happy to have Kita back? "Hi, Athena. How's the ship?"

"I'm working with Ultraviolet to upgrade War Cat, like I explained earlier, but we have insufficient material."

"Yes," added Ultraviolet, "the mech bay is in short supply of raw materials and parts. I have forwarded a list to Ash'a. Currently, we are stripping what we can off the old mechs. We are salvaging and reconstructing the attack mech recovered. But, we need parts—to build the chassis and create the weapons Athena gave us plans for."

"Plans for what?" asked Kimmy.

"Advanced particle cannons like the drones used," said Athena.

"We can mount those?"

"Yes, if we get the parts."

Kimmy looked at Ash'a. "Do we have the money for those?"

"I've been checking suppliers and manufacturers and believe we have the funds. I've also checked medical clinics specializing in prosthetics for Kita. The cost is high, but we have the funds—but not for both."

"What kind of prosthetics?"

"Full arm and leg replacements. They look and feel real, but the total cost is almost one point five million credits."

Kimmy tapped her cheek.

"If we get her to a UEE medical ward, I can do better," said Athena.

"What's better than the real thing?" said Ash'a.

"They'll make her Human. I'll make her an Angel."

"How much for supplies?" said Kimmy to Ash'a.

"I've priced it out and prepared the order according to what Athena and Ultraviolet have given me—four hundred thousand plus the normal fifty thousand for basic and medical supplies."

"So, we don't have money for Kita," Kimmy said with a frown.

"With the upgrades I have for her, she won't need them," Athena said with a huff.

"How much will those cost? Or was the cost in the supply number?"

"I haven't given the list to anyone," said Athena.

"Give it to Ash'a so she can price it out."

"Done."

Ash'a tapped her tablet a few times. "It's going to take me some time to look this up, but I'll guess two hundred thousand."

"Cheaper than the clinic," mused Kimmy. "I'll talk to Kita—"

"I just did," said Athena. "She is happy with the upgrades and waiting for a UEE medical ward. She doesn't have faith in what Human doctors can do."

Kimmy raised an eyebrow. She wasn't sure she trusted the UEE medical tech, but both Kita and Athena did. They had a history with the UEE and knew better than Kimmy what it could do. She'd trust their judgment as the experts.

"We also need to refuel soon," said Ultraviolet. "We have one slug of xeox left. Enough to jump us to a refueling depot."

"Another fifty thousand credits," announced Ash'a.

Kimmy's pile of cash was dwindling. *We might have to take another job.* In Sasari, that would be hard. Mercenary units required licenses, permits, and insurance to operate. They'd gotten away without those saying they were there for training—and that cost. She would have to go somewhere else if they wanted to operate. *First, let's see where the map leads.*

"What about our final—"

Athena changed to a hand pointing behind Kimmy.

She turned as Karen and Dupont came through the door.

"Can I help you?" Kimmy asked when the pair stood before her.

"We want to see the map," said Karen.

"That makes two of us," replied Kimmy. "I haven't seen it either. I don't know if Athena deciphered it."

"She's a supercomputer. She's had plenty of time."

"I'm *not* a supercomputer," Athena huffed. "Unless you're a meat bag. I *am* a scalable Artificial Intelligence. I *am* not hardware but software. Meat bag."

"Hey," said Dupont, stepping up to Athena. "There's no need to throw insults. But I've got a stake in this, and I want to see what you found."

"Yes, what *I* found. Not you. Kimmy and Kita are the majority shareholders. They will instruct me to show you when they feel the time is right. No one has seen the map but me. When it's your turn, you will be summoned. Go back to dying in the simulator."

"Who threw your bitch switch?" demanded Karen.

Kimmy laughed.

"What's so funny?"

"I think I did," Kimmy said with a chuckle. "But I also threw a much bigger one—Kita's."

"What good is she?" scoffed Dupont.

Kimmy raised an eyebrow. "Too busy fornicating to listen to ship gossip? Kita received her new limbs. Ultraviolet and Athena are helping her learn to use them. When Kita is ready, Athena has upgrades to allow her to be somewhere between a Human and an Angel. But that's not important to you. You should know I've given command of the troops—"

"To who?" demanded Karen.

"Kita. She's studying strategy and tactics at the field commander's level. When she's not working on her limbs, she's increasing her mind—with Athena's help."

"She won't be ready—"

"I'm setting up a command suite for Kita," said Athena. "The new software from the UEE allowed me to network the mechs and create a command interface for Kita."

"Why wasn't I told of this?" demanded Dupont. "This is worth a fortune! Militaries will pay trillions for—"

"The technology doesn't belong to you," said Athena tersely. "It belongs to the UEE. You're not a citizen of the UEE—but Kita is. The technology is hers to do as she pleases."

"What?" demanded Dupont.

"How," huffed Karen.

Athena's image shifted to a dark-haired woman wearing a formal blue military uniform. "My name is Kasey Bush," she said with a soft Texas twang. "I'm the Emperor of the United Earth Empire. Kita Logine—my girlfriend—is from a colony we thought lost until she found us. Her defeating the Harbinger menace makes her a hero to the Empire."

"I wouldn't go that far," Kita chuckled. Her image occupied a corner of the holotable.

"Girlfriend, huh?" said Kimmy with an amused smile.

Kita shrugged. "All water under the bridge. But, yes, I'm a citizen of the UEE—probably the last remaining citizen besides Athena. Why are we in such a hurry to see where we're going? It sounds like we have shopping and training to do. Where the map takes us can wait."

"You're stealing credits from me, is what," snarled Dupont.

"Credits you didn't know about until Athena told you. I'm the heir to the UEE. Kimmy made you a fair deal. Pray, I don't alter it. What Athena creates belongs to me. If...you disagree...you're welcome to come and renegotiate. I'll be generous. Athena, show him the map." Kita disappeared from the holotable.

Athena's image changed to a star chart. A line connected various star systems and notes in ancient UEE Common surrounded the borders.

Kimmy couldn't read the map and doubted Dupont could either. *Kita's plan, probably.* Athena had the key, and Kimmy was sure the AI would share it—when Dupont and Karen had seen enough.

"Where's it lead?" demanded Dupont.

Athena's solid hologram entered the bridge and stood behind Dupont. She answered, "Kita instructed you could see the map. You never asked, and she never gave permission to show you the translation."

Dupont spun and stared at Athena's silver and blue chest. She opened her wings in an aggressive stance.

Karen grabbed Dupont's arm. "Come on, Pierre, let's go. We saw the map. We're not getting more...and I don't want a fight."

"It's a computer! What can it do?"

Athena swung her fist, connecting with Dupont's jaw and knocking him to the floor. "Meat bag," she spat at him.

Dupont rubbed his jaw. "Where's an AI learn to throw a punch?"

"I'm a daughter of the God of Evil. I haven't even unlocked my Pandora's box."

"Ok, Athena, that's enough," called Kimmy. "He got what he came for. Pierre can leave, so we can return to our meeting. Karen, get him out of here." She waved dismissively at them.

Karen helped Dupont to his feet.

"This isn't right," Karen said as she faced Kimmy. "He's doing us a favor."

Kimmy rolled his eyes. "The map would have been mine, regardless. All he has to do is sit, shoot, and behave. If he doesn't, he can give me an address, and I'll send him a check when we find the cache."

Dupont crossed his arms. "I want what's mine, and I'm not leaving until I have it. Where's the map take us?"

Kimmy wished for a way to communicate with Athena.

The map shimmered, and the UEE Common shifted to galactic Common. The destination highlighted a moon named Condo.

"Happy now?" said Athena.

"Where the Void is Condo?" said Dupont.

"We have star charts on the mainframe," said Kimmy. "Go look it up."

Dupont spun on his heel and stormed to the door, with Karen hurrying to catch up.

"That's not where we're going, is it?" said Kimmy when Dupont and Karen were gone.

"Of course not," said Athena. "Kita suggested it."

"Kita's still here?"

"Just being a fly on the wall," said Kita with a chuckle. "He's going to spend hours looking for Condo."

"Why? I mean, I take it that's not where we're going."

"No. Athena picked it at random...we can go there if you want a time-share."

Kimmy giggled. "He'll be hopping mad once he figures it out."

"We'll see. Athena, be a dear and put up the right map."

The holotable shimmered and populated new information.

Kimmy traced the line to a moon. "How far is Arco?" she said to Athena.

"The other side of the galaxy." A bigger galactic map appeared, highlighting Arco and War Cat's current position. "Going to take weeks to get there."

Kimmy nodded. "Plenty of time to get girl and machine ready to fight. Who controls it?"

"Arco is water with several islands. It's a resort colony for the Housta Imperium."

"They probably won't like us dropping two troops of mechs on them."

"I'll look into it," said Ash'a. "It sounds like we have time."

"We can always hit and run," said Kita.

Kimmy grunted. "I hope you'll be ready by then."

"You doubt me, love?"

"Never. I don't want to shoot a bunch of tourists."

Athena laughed. "Shall I explain how innocents work, Mom?"

"I will, but I agree. We don't want to shoot civilians and have governments after us."

"What happened to leaving a trail of bodies?"

The AI sounded disappointed.

"Nothing...I want the right bodies."

"Ok," said Kimmy, "let's get back to the meeting. I've got lots to do."

ENROUTE TO WILLI
WAR CAT ASSAULT SHIP
SPACE BIOME
¥1,789,725
12, NOVEMBER 4003

IN THE BARRACKS SECTION of the ship, the Angels occupied the roomier officers' quarters—each with their own bathroom. Kimmy was concerned no one had seen Zhi for days, and there were no logs of her signing into the simulator. She understood missing a day or two of simulator practice but not Zhi.

Kimmy stopped at Zhi's door and rang the call button.

"I hope she's ok," said Lizzy.

"Maybe she's sick with some snow bug from Veri," countered Nicole.

"I'm sure if that was it, she would crawl to the simulator," said Kimmy as she rang the call button again.

"Maybe she's sleeping," responded Ash'a.

"That's fine," said Kimmy, "but not an excuse to miss days of training. I mean, she trains harder than anyone. It's not like her to suddenly quit."

"I hope she's not dead," muttered Nicole.

Kimmy shook her head. Athena said there was movement and sound in the room. As she reached for the call button, the door opened.

Zhi stood before them barefoot with a dirty t-shirt, sweatpants, and holding a blanket. Her eyes were red and puffy, and her normally sleek waist-length black hair was a rat's nest. "Yeah?" she asked in a hollow, tired voice.

"We came to see if you're ok," said Kimmy. "No one's seen you in days, and we were worried."

Zhi sniffed. "I'm here."

"Sweetheart, what's wrong?" said Nicole, moving around Kimmy to hug Zhi.

Zhi's breaths turned into sobs on Nicole's shoulder, drawing in the others for a group hug. "I'm going to die alone," Zhi sobbed.

"Never!" exclaimed Lizzy. "We're here for you. What happened?"

Zhi split from the hug, dragging her blanket as she went, and crashed on her bed. She pulled the blanket around her knees and huddled while her jaw quivered.

Lizzy and Nicole sat on either side of Zhi, putting their arms around her, and comforting her. Kimmy and Ash'a squatted before the bed, resting their hands on Zhi's legs.

For the first time, Kimmy noticed Zhi's toenails were red. It was not something she expected from the fearless fighter pilot.

"Zhi, what's the matter?" said Nicole gently.

"Kimmy will get you a new mech," offered Lizzy.

Kimmy chuckled. It wouldn't be the first time she'd gotten Zhi a new plane or mech.

"No..." Zhi whispered. "It's not that. I can live with losing that kind of face. I...I...have...she..." Zhi put her head down and sobbed loudly.

Oh shit. We've got a broken heart. Kimmy stood on her knees and invited Ash'a up. Together, they put their arms around Zhi.

"I'm so sorry, Zhi," Kimmy whispered.

Lizzy looked over Zhi's head at Kimmy. "What happened?"

"Karen and Pierre."

"Oh, ew."

Kimmy shook her head to tell Lizzy that now was not the time.

"I didn't know Zhi had a thing for Pierre."

"Not him," wailed Zhi.

Kimmy corralled Zhi's head and stroked her hair, trying to calm her. "Not him. She loves Karen."

Lizzy looked perplexed. "I thought they were together."

"Me, too," said Nicole.

Zhi raised her head, sniffing loudly while trying to use the blanket to dab her eyes. "I tried. I thought she needed time, and she would see my devotion. If I was always by her side, she would see what I meant to her—what she meant to me. I was her wingmate, and she would see—" She plunged her face into the blanket.

Kimmy sighed silently. She wished for more experience with broken hearts and unrequited love. She knew someone who might. Turning Zhi over to Nicole, Kimmy went to the communicator by the door and pressed the button.

"Athena, can you pipe Kita in here? I'll turn on the TV."

"Of course. I will tell Kita the situation."

Kimmy turned on the TV—angling it toward the bed. As she did, Kita's face appeared, her pink eyes glowing menacingly.

"Angel, I need you to be sympathetic. Zhi's heart is broken—"

"I know a thing or two about that. Let me guess, she was in love with Karen, and Karen's been sleeping with that man. Why'd we let him on board again?"

"I needed him, and he seemed like a nice guy."

"Every man will stab you in the back. But enough about my life lessons. We're here for Zhi."

Kimmy kneeled in front of the group. "Zhi, Kita's here. She wants to talk to you."

Zhi lifted her head, and something inside her shifted. She dried her eyes and sucked in a deep breath. Her face became ridged, like all military personnel when facing their superior—even though Kita and Zhi were friends. Zhi shoved the blanket aside and looked at the TV.

"Yes, Kita?" She did a double take at seeing Kita's face. "I'm sorry—"

"It's ok, Zhi. I know I look like death warmed over. If I could walk, I'd give you a hug. The situation is not fair to you. I know how much you love and admire Karen—that you'd do anything for her like a good wingmate.

"I'm sorry she didn't see what I saw. You would have made a great couple. I wish I could knock Karen on the head and make her see what a great person you are and what a waste of space that man is. But it's Karen's decision—no matter how badly it breaks your heart and mine. Not that Karen is bad, she's made a poor choice.

"My best advice to get over a broken heart is to find someone else. I know it's slim pickings around here, but—"

"I'm willing," said Ash'a.

Kita chuckled. "You know Ash'a's a winner."

Zhi looked from Kita to the Aurorian kneeling before her. "I—me?"

"Yes," said Ash'a. "I, too, am lonely and wish for someone. I thought you were with Karen, or I would have asked earlier."

"You...like me?"

"You're a proud, outstanding warrior with an exotic beauty that has gone unappreciated for too long. I thought Karen was lucky, but her choice...could be...my gain?" The scales on Ash'a's head and back rippled in a geometric pattern, refracting a rainbow of color.

Zhi blushed. "I...no one has ever said that about me."

"What are you talking about?" said Lizzy. "You're an awesome pilot."

"I think she means being called beautiful," replied Nicole.

"I'm not beautiful." Zhi shook her head and looked at the floor. "I'm just...just a mudfish."

"You are no such thing," said Kita firmly. "Not as a pilot, not as a beauty queen. You deserve to have someone—if not Ash'a, then someone else. You're not Karen's rejection but Karen's loss—and Ash'a's gain if you're interested. I know your heart hurts, and I'm sure Ash'a will take it slow. But, it would be a mistake if you said *no* without at least going to the galley and having a chat...or wherever you're comfortable."

"I'd love to see a pilot's perspective of the mech bays and mech," said Ash'a.

Zhi frowned sideways and cocked her head as tears leaked from her eyes. "I don't have a mech."

"Don't be silly," said Kimmy. "We have lots you can show her. Most of the mechs are under repair, but if she wants to see the cockpit, you can look in dawnbreaker. You'll have a mech, I promise. If they get the new attack mech ready, dawnbreaker will need a new pilot."

Zhi's mouth fell open. "You mean me?"

"I was going to give it to Karen, but she seems too preoccupied."

"I need to get some time with heavy and attack mechs in the simulator." She looked at Ash'a apologetically.

"You have more time in the simulator than anyone—at all levels. I think you're ready without spending extra time. Take Ash'a out. Do something with your time besides shooting pixels."

Zhi bowed to Kimmy. "I will not fail again."

"You didn't fail," said Kita firmly. "You held the line against a superior enemy and kept them from attacking Kimmy's troop so she could get to the objective. That's not failure but doing your duty and attaining your objective.

"Kimmy didn't know what kind of enemy forces you would face. You stood your ground and didn't let them pass—you achieved the objective. The fact you had a mech shot out from under you shows your bravery and dedication to the unit. You're not a failure—you're a hero. Had I a medal, I would give it to you.

"As I once told a student, Hali, you don't get to decide when you fail. I do—and I will let you know when you do. Understand?"

Zhi saluted. "Yes, Vicereine. I'll make the hearts of our enemies quake with fear."

Kita nodded. "I've no doubt. Now, go have fun with Ash'a. You deserve a rest and a chance to be happy. I'll call a pilots' meeting in a few days when I'm ready." Her picture went out.

"Someone's taking the role of commander seriously," chuckled Lizzy.

"Kita has been a commander since the beginning," said Athena. "She's done it for so long—I'm surprised she knows any different."

"I think she dug into her compartments and brought it out," said Kimmy. "I've seen her as Vicereine but never Commander." She looked at Zhi. "Are you going to be ok? We can all go to lunch, or if you want to be with Ash'a—"

"No. Lunch with friends sounds good." She looked at Ash'a apologetically. "Afterward, I will take you to the mech bay. You can sit in a command chair."

Ash'a laughed. "That sounds wonderful. I've only been in Flexi's mech and not the command chair."

"You'll probably run into Flexi down there," said Kimmy. "She's always working on her mech."

"Let me get cleaned up," said Zhi.

"You want some help?" said Nicole.

Zhi pulled around her hair and frowned. "Lunch might be awhile."

"We'll help," said Lizzy.

"Yes. I need to get cleaned up as well," said Ash'a.

Kimmy raised an eyebrow. The Aurorian looked perfect. "I'll meet you in the galley. I need to ensure our other lovebirds aren't finding new ways to cause trouble."

After a quick goodbye, Kimmy left the room.

"Athena, can you patch Kita into the speaker system?"

"Of course."

"Yes, love?" said Kita in a good humor.

"What's the matter with Karen?"

"She's having sex with a man and letting it go to her brain."

"I don't understand why she would turn down Zhi." Kimmy turned down a corridor leading to the rest of the barracks.

"She most likely didn't understand Zhi's gesture. Zhi isn't the kind of person to tell her commanding officer she loves them. I'm sure she had dreams of Karen coming to her. But Karen is an excellent officer and knows about fraternization—usually. She never would have done it, even if the other party reciprocated."

"So, you don't think Karen loved Zhi?"

"No. A friend, yes, but not as a love interest. I need to dig deeper into Pierre."

Kimmy's eyebrows closed. "You don't trust him, even after he fought for us?"

"Maybe he's only a greedy fool. Until I figure out more, he can continue to pull a trigger, but I'm going to keep him on point."

"I guess if he gets cored, that solves our problem."

Kimmy stopped at Karen's door and pushed the call button. The door opened to Karen, with Dupont sitting on her bed.

"Yes?" said Karen with a frown. "Is there a problem?"

"Yes—"

"Yes," said Kita from the speaker in the hallway.

"Kita?" said Karen.

"I'm moving Zhi out of your troop to Kimmy's, forming my new heavy troop. When the new attack mech is ready, Zhi will get the dawnbreaker. In your new light troop, Pierre will take point. You will—"

"It's my choice who I put on point!" Karen responded angrily.

"There's a conflict of interest."

"Are you saying my relationship with Pierre affects my job performance?"

"Yes. Be ready for a pilots' meeting in a few days. I noticed your hours in the simulator are slipping. Quit playing with his stick and get back to your mech's."

"My relationship—"

"Is causing problems, and either you fix it or I will."

Kimmy waited stone-faced while laughing on the inside. Commander Kita was amusing as long as she wasn't on the receiving end.

"You can't—"

"Can and will. I'll drop him off at the next station if I have to."

"Hey, you owe me!" said Dupont, standing up.

"In a second, I'll owe you nothing. Don't push it. Here's a hint. If you're not useful, I will make you useful. I need a hood ornament for my ship."

"You're not in charge. She is." Dupont pointed at Kimmy.

Kimmy laughed wickedly. "I'm in charge of the Empire of the United States. Kita is my Vicereine. Together we rule Reality, but for all things Angel, that's Kita. This little adventure in this universe is hers. I only took over while she recovers."

"What the Void is she talking about?" Dupont said to Karen.

"More than you need to know," said Kita. "Karen, he's not becoming a bear or demon unless performance improves."

"There are more people aboard this ship than just you," Karen fired back.

"I know. I just put your wingmate's heart back together. I suggest you leave Zhi alone for a while. She's busy with Ash'a. You get your shit together. I don't need to clean up any more of your messes—neither does Kimmy."

"What mess have I made?"

"I've got a pilot who deserves a medal, thinking she failed. I've got indecent exposure in the medbay. I've got a troop commander openly fraternizing with one of her pilots. I have a pilot wrecking unit cohesion. I've got a troop commander failing to reach her hours in the simulator. I had a heavy mech to give out, but the troop commander didn't have enough training hours to pilot it. And I've got a brokenhearted pilot humiliated by her commanding officer. I've got a lot of messes, and they all point back to one place. I've already fixed the most pressing problems. It's up to you to get the rest squared away. Now, will there be anything further, Captain?" Karen's rank hung in the air like a bomb, ready to explode.

Karen gulped and whispered, "No."

Does she even know half of what Kita's talking about? Probably not. I have to admit, it's an admirable command technique.

"Good. I don't care if you continue to see Pierre, your choice, but it affecting my operation stops now. If he continues to be a problem, I'll solve it."

Dupont took a step toward the speaker. "Hey, I'm right here. You can't talk to her that way."

Karen grabbed Dupont's arm. "Don't."

"What's she going to do? She's a cripple."

A bone-chilling laugh filled the room. It faded, and the speaker was silent.

"I wonder where we're going to find the body?" said Athena in Kita's place.

"Keel-hauled," responded Kimmy. "I'll leave you to figure out your next move. I'm going to see my partner. I'm sure she'll be in a pleasant mood."

"She's humming happily," said Athena.

WILLI
KIALMARA ARMORY AND SUPPLY
CITY BIOME
¥1,789,725
19, NOVEMBER 4003

K IMMY ENTERED THE WIDE lobby with a glass exterior, tropical plants, and different mech weapon systems behind protective glass. Ultra-violet, her chief engineer and supply officer, Ash'a, and a solid hologram of Athena followed her through the front doors of Kialmara Armory and Supply.

KAS carried everything a mech mercenary outfit could want—food, supplies, parts, weapons, and ammunition. Kimmy knew from experience that those who made war got the glory, and those who supplied it got rich. They approached the half-circle-shaped front desk where a trio of receptionists answered calls or typed on their keyboards.

Kimmy approached the middle receptionist, a Human with dark hair dressed in business attire.

"Welcome to KAS. Can I help you?" the receptionist—her name tag read HAILLI—said to Kimmy. The woman couldn't hide a slight reaction to Ash'a, Ultraviolet, and Athena. Kimmy didn't detect any malice or disgust, just surprise and maybe a bit of envy.

"Hi," replied Kimmy with a warm smile. "I'm Empress Kimberly Roosevelt. I'm here to pick up an order for the Fallen Angel Mercenaries. My business manager Ash'a has the details." Kimmy stepped aside, letting Ash'a, wearing Aurorian business attire—a shimmering dress that clung to her every curve and exposed her back with five-inch heels—stepped forward and turned on her tablet.

"Hailli, I have the order." Ash'a turned the tablet so Hailli could scan the order number and payment information.

"Thank you, Ash'a," said Hailli. She scanned the bar code. "I see your order. It's ready to be delivered to your ship."

"I wish to inspect my part of the order," said Athena.

Hailli smiled. "Of course. I'll call you an escort. Feel free to browse the items we have in stock." She touched a button on her keyboard and typed a quick message.

I might do that. Kimmy had extra money, and weapons and mech upgrades would be nice.

A young man in blue overalls with JACKSILL sewn over his heart appeared through a door. He stopped in front of Kimmy's group with a big smile.

"Jacksill," said Hailli, "Empress Roosevelt is here to pick up her order and wishes to inspect it. Please escort them to their bay and show them the warehouse if they want to purchase anything off the shelf."

"Sure, no problem. Nice crew, ah, Empress? Not sure what the honorific for that one is."

Your Highness. "Ma'am is fine."

Jacksill smiled at those in Kimmy's group. "I haven't seen an Aurorian in years. I've never seen an Angel before."

"You've seen other Aurori?" asked Ash'a, breaking her reserved façade.

"Sure. I spent a couple of years in the Aurori Union. Awesome place. You girls are wicked. I totally learned to party and zen out there. I haven't seen many of you outside the Union."

Ash'a smiled. "I found a new challenge working in a merc unit."

"Right on. Mechs are super sweet. Show me your paperwork, and I'll take you to the right bay."

Ash'a showed him her tablet.

"Lucky number thirteen. Follow me, ma'am. I'll get you hooked up."

Kimmy gave him a warm smile, but inside, she was dying. Jacksill reminded her of the surfers in her State of Cali.

The group entered a door beside the reception desk and followed a hallway with large windows on the right, giving them a view of the cavernous warehouse filled with racks from floor to ceiling—some with crates and boxes, others with raw parts, all huge. Along the back wall, in mech cages, were complete mechs. Some looked brand new with perfect paint jobs. Others were refurbished, showing signs of battle damage.

The hallway ended in an elevator, taking them to the warehouse floor. Warning signs, markers, and equipment lined the alleyways as robots found goods and took them to collection points or to be shelved. The robots followed marked lanes in the alleyways, and when Kimmy stepped over the line, warning lights flashed, and the robots stopped.

"We run twenty-four-seven, ma'am," said Jacksill, "but safety is the top priority." He stopped at a metal cage filled with dozens of pallets—most with thick metal sheets to be attached to the mechs as armor. "This is yours—bay thirteen through thirty-two."

Kimmy looked at the others. "You girls want to make sure it's all here?"

"Yes," said Athena. "I must ensure they have the right materials for Mom's upgrades."

"And I'll check the rest of the list," said Ash'a with a smile at Athena.

"Of course," replied the AI. "I will also ensure the ship upgrades' materials are there."

"We will go with Ash'a to ensure the ship has what it needs," said Ultraviolet.

What would I do without them?

"If something is wrong, let me know," said Jacksill.

Kimmy, busy admiring the massive building and its contents, was spooked when Jacksill said, "Pretty cool, huh? Ah, ma'am."

"It's impressive," said Kimmy as beeping and lights on the far wall rotated. A large mech Kimmy didn't recognize was being moved.

Jacksill gave her a goofy grin and pointed. "Someone bought a great ape. One of the newest attack mech designs—released last year. It can hold up to three particle cannons and two ballistics guns. Also comes with a new weapon called a mortar."

Kimmy looked at the towering hulk. Its head was almost in the rafters. She hoped she didn't have to fight one.

"She's a beaut, isn't she?" a male voice boomed across the warehouse.

A man with a neatly groomed black beard, black combat shirt, bottoms, and boots came toward Kimmy, trailed by a pair of young men dressed like him. A black ball cap with a silver griffin adorned each of their heads. Their leader wore his cap low, hiding he was chomping on an unlit cigar butt.

Kimmy smiled warmly. "It is impressive."

The man with the beard returned her smile. "Hopefully, it'll keep my pilots out of trouble. Names Jonny Henry Junior. But most call me by my callsign, Blackbeard. I lead the Black Griffins. You've probably seen us around. I've got units everywhere. Can't say I've seen you before, Miss...?" He stuck out his hand.

Kimmy looked at it and stifled a gasp. *No way...How many Jonny Henrys are in the universe?* Realizing her mouth was open, Kimmy shook his hand limply as she reined in fear and shock. "Sorry, I, ah, was lost in thought. I'm Kimberly Roosevelt. In a mech, I go by Apocalypse. I help lead the Fallen Angels."

Blackbeard nodded. "New to the game, huh?"

Kimmy shrugged. "We've been working on the periphery—mostly guarding gold and ice crystal mines. We're in Sasari space for R and R and resupply."

"You don't say? My Old Man...Jonny Henry Senior...retired to the Astari system last year to chase his dream of gold mining."

A pit the size of the great ape appeared in Kimmy's stomach. She wished to disappear or run and hide. But Blackbeard had her firmly in his sights. *Maybe I can spin this to my advantage?*

"Oh? I...ah...just came into possession of the Jungle Cat Mine on Astari Two—"

Blackbeard's mouth fell open, letting his cigar dangle on his lip. "You own the Jungle Cat Mine?"

"I, ah..."

"My lady, if proper decorum allowed it, I'd hug you, but if I may kiss your hand?"

Kimmy sputtered. "I, ah..." but she offered her hand.

Blackbeard gently took Kimmy's hand like a proper gentleman and kissed the backside. "What you've done for My Old Man...I can't repay you enough."

Kimmy gulped. *What has Ultraviolet been up to?* "Please, it's nothing. Maybe you'd like to meet my Project Manager, Ultraviolet. She's in charge of the mine and my ship."

"Of course, I would love to meet her," Blackbeard said, a broad smile beaming through his dark beard.

Kimmy excused herself and found Ultraviolet overseeing her people.

"UV?" Kimmy called.

The Angel turned from watching the counting of plate metal. "Yes, Kimmy?"

"Ah, someone wants to meet you and...what have you been doing at the mine?"

Ultraviolet frowned. "Is there something wrong?"

Kimmy leaned into the other Angel. "I have Jonny Henry's son, Jonny Henry Junior, kissing my hand and thanking me for what Jungle Cat has done for Senior. What have you done?"

Ultraviolet stroked one of her horns. "We did what you told us. We loaned him a front loader, repaired his, gave him two hundred ounces to repay what we took, and sent men to help his mine. We plan on giving him the gold we find as payment. Is that not ok?"

Kimmy sighed, relieved. "No, that's perfect. He wants to meet you. Whatever you do, don't tell him we stole his father's gold. That was some other group. We're being neighborly."

"Of course. We understand. We would be happy to meet him."

"Come on."

Kimmy led Ultraviolet back to the Black Griffin leader. "Blackbeard," Kimmy called. She smiled at the man as he turned.

"Please, call me Jonny."

Kimmy smiled warmly. "Call me Kimmy. And this is Ultraviolet. She is in charge of personnel and special projects in my organization—including the Jungle Cat Mine."

Blackbeard bowed lowly. "I owe you both a great debt. My Old Man hasn't been this excited or happy—well, ever. I will admit, Ultraviolet, I have never encountered your species before. I like to think I've encountered most races in the galaxy. Where do you come from?"

Ultraviolet gave Kimmy a worried look.

"I'm sorry. I don't mean to offend," Blackbeard said, his smile fading.

"No, it's quite ok," said Ultraviolet, looking uncertain at Kimmy. "It's complicated."

"UV is a Mi Prii Angel," said Kimmy. "Her homeworld Uvra was destroyed by the Verisom."

Blackbeard took off his hat. "I hate it when that happens. I've met a few Verisom, but they're scattered across the periphery. When did this happen?"

"Centuries ago," said Kimmy. "Ultraviolet has seen much in her long lifetime."

"How nice of you not to call us old," said Ultraviolet with a smile.

I'm older than you.

"You have my condolences," said Blackbeard, tipping his hat, "and my thanks for what you've done for My Old Man. Few people in the galaxy would do that for another person. I'm in your debt. Kimmy, if you would be so kind, I'd like to invite you and your officers to dinner aboard my ship."

"Ah...I'd love to, but I'm afraid my partner, Kita, won't be able to attend due to her injuries."

"If I may be so bold to ask, what happened to...her?"

Kimmy nodded. "Her mech was cored. She's recovering from her injuries."

Blackbeard put his hat over his heart. "My deepest sympathies. It's a miracle anyone survives a shot like that. Do you need anything? I have a fully upgraded medical facility. I can send a team to bring her aboard for treatment."

"It might be a good idea to have her checked out. We only have the basics. I don't think a team will be necessary. She can sit up, but we don't have a way to transport her."

"I can send a small team with a wheelchair."

Why don't we have one of those? Maybe I can buy it from him. "I will have to talk to her. She's very conscientious about her appearance."

"I understand completely. I wish to honor such a brave warrior. If there's anything I can do to help, ask."

Kimmy bobbed her head. "Thank you. You're most kind. Generosity like yours is rare in the galaxy."

Blackbeard nodded solemnly. "It's true. And a shame our profession exists and is necessary. I hope to bring honor and dignity to the galaxy through our actions. I hope to leave the galaxy a better place than whence I found it."

"That is a noble goal, especially in a galaxy like this one."

Blackbeard's eyes couldn't hide his surprise. "How come I've never heard of you? I thought I knew all the merc groups—good and bad."

Kimmy gave him a small smile. "My friends and I just formed our group. Our tour of the periphery was our first. It's a long story. If it's not too much to ask, I would like to bring my pilots—my friends—to dinner. I don't have many, but their hard work put us where we are, not me."

Blackbeard opened his arms in a friendly gesture. "Of course. I would be honored." He turned to one of the young men with him. "David, please send Kimmy an invitation to dinner tonight."

"Yes, sir—"

"One moment," said Kimmy. "I need to get my business manager. If it wasn't for her, I wouldn't know what day it is." She ran over and tapped Ash'a on the shoulder. "Ash'a, I need you."

"By the Void, where did you find such a beautiful creature?" Blackbeard boomed and bowed to Ash'a. "I haven't seen an Aurorian in a moon's age."

Ash'a's scales rippled. "Greetings. I am Ash'a T'Kar Kele. You've seen more Aurorians?"

"I've been to the Aurorian Union out on Perseus Four. I apologize for my frankness. You caught me by surprise. I do not mean to be rude."

"No!" said Ash'a excitedly. "I haven't seen another Aurorian since I arrived."

"Kimmy is very lucky to have you...and such diverse friends. I'm impressed. I try to be open and hire all the races I can—I believe our differences strengthen us. But it's hard to find non-Humans. It's such a pity. We're all beautiful children of the Void."

Kimmy blushed. "That's not even everyone."

"What's your secret? I would pay double—triple to have a crew like yours."

Kimmy exchanged a look with Ash'a and Ultraviolet.

"Kita," they said together.

"Your partner?" said Blackbeard as he adjusted his cap.

"Kita is a magician at making friends," said Ash'a.

"And everyone wishes to be her friend," said Ultraviolet.

"Unless they don't. Then they hate her," muttered Kimmy.

Blackbeard sighed. "You can't be in this business without making a few enemies."

Kimmy frowned sideways. "It seems all we've made are enemies. You're the first friend we've made."

"If you need any help, just ask. A loan, a repair, a mech, or if you get caught in a jam, call me. I'll have David give Ash'a my private number. I've units and ships across the galaxy. We'll gladly come to your aid—you need a light troop or a battalion of attack mechs."

Kimmy gulped. "That's most kind. We'll gladly extend the same offer. I don't have much, but we are always willing to help a friend."

"You're making My Old Man's dream. I can't ask for more."

David signaled with his free hand to get Blackbeard's attention. "Sir, we're counted and loaded. They need your signature, and we're ready to leave."

"Thank you, David." Blackbeard turned to Kimmy. "I'm afraid business awaits, and I must take my leave. I look forward to seeing you and your friends at dinner tonight." He bowed to Kimmy and each Angel. "Until tonight, my friends." With a smile and nod, Blackbeard maneuvered his crew around Kimmy and walked toward the receiving office.

"Wow," said Ash'a.

"Yeah," said Kimmy, lifting her hair to let some heat escape.

"He was nice," said Ultraviolet. "Would you like me to assimilate him?"

Kimmy shook her head vigorously. "No. But we need to have a group meeting tonight before dinner. I don't want anyone slipping that we robbed Jonny Senior."

WILLI
BLACK GRIFFIN FLAGSHIP ASCENSION
SPACE BIOME
¥1,025,912
19, NOVEMBER 4003

KIMMY WALKED BESIDE KITA, holding her good hand as the orderly from Black Griffin pushed. When Blackbeard said wheelchair, Kimmy didn't imagine a chair with wheels but a float chair. She realized she hadn't seen any float technology in this universe. *What happened that so much technology was lost?*

The Black Griffin flagship Ascension was like walking through a grand hotel. Everything had clean lines, and the walls hid everything from view, unlike War Cat, which looked unfinished and had the ambiance of a tenement apartment.

Kimmy and Kita were rejoined by the others after Kita received a scan in Ascension's medbay. The facility made War Cat's medbay look like a box of bandages. To Kimmy's relief, Kita checked out fine. The chief physician offered a skin graph using organic skin if they were going to be in the area, and Blackbeard approved. Kimmy and Kita readily agreed.

It was Kita's eyes and implants drawing the most attention. The technology and surgical skill to attach them were beyond anything this universe had. Kimmy remained tightlipped about who did the surgery. Athena was with them tonight, but Kimmy didn't plan on revealing she was an AI.

An orgasm washed over Kimmy, making her body tingle.

<<Forgot about this?>> said Kita in the monotone voice of a black A'ahegre.

Kimmy talked little to the A'ahegre that inhabited her. Of all the powers it gave her, she only used the ability to heal and detect lies regularly. She and Kita hadn't spoken using the A'ahegre's connection in years because she couldn't handle the vast amount of information that could be passed at once. From the simple phrase, Kita remembered and was being gentle with her.

<<It has been a long time,>> Kimmy said in the high melodic voice of her white A'ahegre.

<<Did Jonny Junior lie to you? I've done some research on Junior and Senior. From what I learned, your description matches the reports. The Black Griffins are the biggest merc unit in the galaxy, and his philanthropy and ethics made them many enemies. Jonny might make a good ally.>>

<<No, he didn't.>> She and her ability to detect lies, and Kita, who could detect emotions, often worked together when integrating or negotiating. <<I think he could help us...as long as he doesn't find out we robbed Senior.>>

Kita chuckled. <<Desperate move by a desperate girl. If it comes up, we'll offer the money we have left, an apology with an explanation, and hope there is a way we can make it up to them.>>

<<He has part of the explanation, but I didn't tell him about Chelsea.>>

<<A card we'll hold until needed.>>

<<We have lots of cards—Athena, Velositi and the girls, Flexi.>>

<<Yes, if he likes diversity, we have that in spades.>>

A door to the left opened, and the orderly pushed Kita into a large dining room filled with three circular tables covered in black cloth surrounded by silver chairs. Blackbeard stood with a Djinn female—though her fur was white with gray rosettes, not sand colored—and a row of Black Griffin officers forming a receiving line. They wore black uniforms with silver piping.

Kita's head and face were covered by a scarf while she and the rest of the War Cat crew wore navy blue uniforms. The style and cut were fashioned from Kimmy's military back on Earth 832. A glove hid Kita's mechanical hand. Only her eyes gave away her injuries.

"Kimberly!" boomed Blackbeard. "I'm so happy you could come. Let me introduce you to my wife, Sierra. She's the best pilot I have."

"Stop," said Sierra, putting a hand on Blackbeard's arm. She smiled at her visitors.

A buzzing in the back of Kimmy's skull was an alert, but she didn't know what it meant. It grew stronger as she looked at Sierra.

<< I have a strange buzzing sensation in my head. I don't know what it means.>>

<<I have it too,>> replied Kita. <<I don't know what it means either. We'll have to explore more later.>>

Kita let out a series of growls, hisses, and meows that caused Sierra's whiskers to twitch wildly and her mouth to open. She regained her composure and returned a series of cat sounds.

"I...I haven't heard Djinn in years. Where did you learn it?" she asked, her ears and whiskers twitching excitely.

"I have been around a long time and been across space and time," said Kita.

"You honor me, warrior," said Sierra. "I was afraid I may never hear my native tongue again."

"You honor me," replied Kita. "I'm Katrina Marie Roosevelt, but the universe knows me as Kita. I look forward to dining with you both."

"And we, you and Kimberly," said Blackbeard.

Kimmy and Kita moved along the receiving line, meeting the Black Griffin officers. They returned to the head of the line to introduce their friends.

Karen and Dupont waited patiently.

"Jonny, Sierra, this is my troop commander, Karen McKnight, with pilot Pierre Dupont."

The sides shook hands, and Karen and Dupont moved down the line.

Kimmy introduced Lizzy and Nicole, then Ash'a and Zhi. When Flexi and Velositi stepped forward, both Blackbeard and Sierra looked amazed.

"This is pilot Flexi and Commander Velositi—she leads our ground forces."

"Hello," said Velositi, her eyes glowing brightly.

"By the Void!" exclaimed Blackbeard. "Excuse my outburst. I was under the assumption all the Neophormes were wiped out centuries ago."

"Velositi's a tough one to kill," said Flexi.

"I fear my ignorance has the better of me. I've never heard or seen anyone like you."

The quills on Flexi's muzzle wavered in amusement. "With Kita, there are no limitations. I'm a Diamock. I can pilot or shoot anything. Where I come from, the Diamock Empire stretches across the galaxy." Flexi tapped on Velositi's arm. "But Velositi isn't a Neophorm. She's a Morphicon."

"That is correct. In my universe, we wiped out the Neophormes. It is a shame the Vehlix failed in this universe, but the Morphicons are growing. Please meet my daughters, Knockout and Bombshell."

Velositi and Flexi stepped aside to allow Knockout and Bombshell—displaying a unique turquoise, hot pink, and sparkle pattern across their android-like bodies and wings—forward to greet their hosts.

"Hi," they said together. Each shook Blackbeard's and Sierra's hands.

"I'm excited to meet you both," said Blackbeard. "All of you."

"Momma-Kita is the one you want to talk to," Bombshell said with a laugh. "But your ship is awesome. We've scanned some cool things to add to our collections."

It was a competition among the young Morphicons to collect rare items they could morph into.

"Come, girls," said Velositi. "Let us make way for the others."

Velositi guided her girls down the line, trailed by Flexi.

"May I present my daughter, Athena, and Ultraviolet," said Kita.

"Your daughter?" said Sierra with a surprised smile.

"You don't see the resemblance?" said Kita, her eyes glowing brightly. Kita laughed, easing Sierra's uncertainty. "She was partnered to my daughter, Quill."

"I'm sorry we didn't have time to meet earlier," said Blackbeard, extending his hand to Athena.

The AI Angel shook hands, followed by Ultraviolet. Athena took her leave without a word and went down the receiving line.

"It's a pleasure to see you again, Ultraviolet," said Blackbeard.

"It's our pleasure. You are quite beautiful, Sierra."

"Oh, why thank you."

"I have assimilated many Djinn in my lifetime, but never have I seen one like you."

Sierra exchanged glances with Blackbeard.

"Ultraviolet has lived a long life," explained Kimmy, "and lived with many peoples."

"How is that possible?" said Sierra, her voice full of wonder.

"Kita and Kimmy," responded Ultraviolet. She bowed and went down the receiving line.

"Shall we take our seats for dinner?" said Blackbeard with a wide smile.

"Yes," said Kimmy. "I'm interested in hearing about your exploits, Sierra."

"Mine pale compared to yours. I'm excited to hear where you found all these people."

Blackbeard offered his arm to his wife, and Kimmy and Kita followed them around the tables to the circular head table. Blackbeard seated Sierra and waited for the rest to be seated. Kimmy was on Blackbeard's right, and the orderly pushed Kita into an empty spot on the right of Kimmy. When everyone was seated, Blackbeard sat.

Several chefs pushed dinner carts from a door in the rear. They stopped on either side of the tables and revealed the first course. With proud smiles, they offered their delicatessens.

Ash'a traded messages with Blackbeard's second, ensuring the Angels who ate received what they liked. Kimmy hid an amused smile when fancily decorated batteries were placed before the Morphicons.

"So, please tell me, where did you learn Djinn, Kita?" said Sierra.

Kita chuckled dryly. "In another universe out of space and time. I'm always amazed at how language changes and develops...yet it stays similar across universes. Ultraviolet is not the only one who is ancient. I've lived many lives and learned many things. I was there when this universe was born, and I will be there when it dies."

Kimmy smiled to cover her shock. *What's Kita's plan? Why is she revealing this so soon?*

"If I may ask," said Blackbeard, "Where do you come from? Are you Human?"

Kita's eyes glowed brightly. "Yes. What you see before you is my natural form. I use it when I wish to inhabit a universe. I've gained several other forms throughout my life."

Sierra turned up her nose. "I've only heard of such beings in myth and legend—gods if you will. But alas, such creatures don't exist."

"And if I told you the Gods of Reality are before you?"

Sierra's ears flattened as her lip curled. "I would say, why would they let the universe become what it has? Why have they let evil dominate?"

Kita and Kimmy exchanged an unhappy glance.

"Fair question," said Kita. "Once upon a time, a collective of gods created infinite universes to study...including mine. These gods could change the universes at will.

"When a young god, The God of Evil, appeared—me—I challenged the old gods using their ability to change the universes against them. When I conquered Infinity—the home of the gods—I destroyed all the universes. I made my own based on the universe I came from.

"Unlike the gods before, I set rules to avoid repeating the previous gods' mistakes. I can't alter the universe from within, and I gave the universes self-determination—allowing them to choose their own path. Many universes have come before this one.

"Kimmy comes from Universe Eight-Thirty-two. Many of my friends come from that universe or one's like it.

"I'm sorry this universe turned out the way it did. To be honest, we didn't come to fix it, but after experiencing it, I believe something must be done. And Kimmy and I need your help."

"You are gods?" demanded Sierra. "Can you not help yourself?"

Blackbeard put a hand on Sierra's arm.

"We are," said Kimmy. "But our power inside a universe is limited to allow us to better blend in."

"What good is a god without power?"

"I have power," said Kita. "The power of friendship. All these people with us tonight are our friends. I've given them unique abilities—and wings—so they can help me. Velositi," Kita called to the next table, "can you please demonstrate your lightning?"

Velositi stood, leaving her meal of a beautifully decorated battery behind. She faced the head table and spread her pink and black wings. She raised an arm and grew a ball of lightning in her hand. Raising her other hand, the ball arced to it and bounced between her hands. She clapped her hands, and the ball disappeared. Raising her finger to the ceiling lights, an electrical arc flowed from the fixture to her, dimming the lights in the room.

Kita clapped at her girlfriend as she sat. "Somewhere in this universe is a crystal that contains each Angels' power—mine and Kimmy's as well."

"And you want our help to find them?" said Blackbeard.

Kita shook her head. "They'll come to us in our hour of need. The power of the gods is not what we need help with. Kimmy and I have a daughter, Chelsea. She was with us. When we were on a contract to protect an ice mine on Astari Three-A, a group of Blood Witches attacked and took Chelsea.

"One of my Angels is trying to find her, though, in my heart, I know my daughter will be taken to have her eggs harvested and then taken to the ice mines on the Moon.

"We have a plan to get her back, but we need help. There is a great treasure—a bounty of weapons created by a civilization long dead—that we believe will help us get Chelsea back. If you help us, the riches are yours."

Dupont jumped to his feet, knocking his chair to the floor. "You can't give away my share! Kimmy promised me!" he yelled as Karen tugged on his arm.

Kimmy stood. "You'll get your share. Kita promises Jonny her share."

"The weapons mean nothing to me," said Kita. "I already have the most valuable thing the United Earth Empire created, Athena."

The AI Angel stood and crossed her arms defiantly at Dupont.

"Athena is one of the crown jewels of the United Earth Empire—not of this universe, but of mine. With her knowledge, we have unlocked the secrets of the UEE of this universe. It's not the weapons of the UEE we seek, but the knowledge. With what they knew, we can make this universe a better place."

"What technologies?" asked Blackbeard.

"How about float technology?" said Kimmy.

"What's that?"

"The ability to control gravity," said Kita. "Instead of creating dangerous miniature black holes to induce gravity, the UEE learned to control the graviton's spin. Spin it up, and it attracts. Spin it down, and it repulses. Safe, easy—if you have the technology. The ancient UEE of this universe had it—and so much more.

"We've already had bad run-ins with Defin Industries, the Blood Witches, and the Aven Federation. Our friends and us will take on anyone, but even we know we are no match for them.

"With the UEE's technology and weapons—and your help—we can get Chelsea back and, in the process, change the universe. I know it's a big ask, but please don't reject us out of hand."

"May I ask, what is Athena?" said Blackbeard.

Athena collapsed into her solid holographic projector and floated across the room to Kita's hand.

Kita caught the bronze ball and held it up. "Hello, Athena," she said to the ball.

"Hello, Mom," replied Athena as lights around the ball's equator lit.

"Athena is an Artificial Intelligence created to run and maintain cities. Later, she grew to control my Empire of Hades. Since then, she has learned to control any computer system."

Sierra sprang from her seat. "AIs are dangerous. Every state has forbidden them."

"Some AIs are," said Kita. "I spent part of my youth battling one that wanted to control my benefactor, Omega. Athena is far from harmless, like the rest of the Angels. But we mean you no harm, even if you decline us. We wouldn't attack you unless you struck first. I want you to know what we offer if you decide to help us."

The sweat dripped down Kimmy's back. Blackbeard would make a great strategic ally, but she thought this was the wrong way to get his help. She wished Kita had told her the plan, so she could craft an argument to compliment Kita's.

Blackbeard stood and reseated Sierra.

"This is most intriguing," he said after taking a seat. "I'm afraid you lost me on some details. It appears I do not understand the universe like I thought I did."

He paused as the servers entered to clear away the dishes and the chefs to present the main course.

Kimmy, frustrated and unhappy, kept a smile on her face. *I wonder if something's wrong with Kita. I've never seen her make this kind of mistake when wooing someone.*

Kita released Athena, and dinner resumed. Kimmy did her best to make small talk and listen about Blackbeard and Sierra's adventures across the galaxy. Kimmy told of some of theirs, though Kita remained strangely silent.

When dessert was served, Blackbeard asked, "So, how did you get into the mech business?"

Kita's eyes brightened as she told the story of their escape from the Aven Foreign Legion and stealing the assault ship. The story seemed to impress Blackbeard and Sierra. Both were visibly reserved but kept smiling and remained lighthearted.

After saying goodbye, Kita, pushed by the Black Griffin orderly, led the others back toward the docking bay where War Cat waited.

Kimmy, annoyed and concerned about Kita, reached over and took Kita's good hand.

<<Are you ok?>> Kimmy asked Kita.

<<I'm fine. Why?>>

<<What happened? I've never seen you misjudge someone like that.>>

<<I did? I thought it went well.>>

<<You info dumped on them and scared them away. We were supposed to be getting their help.>>

Kita chuckled. <<Maybe I was being honest. Maybe I wanted to scare them. They sit in a very comfortable position, and where we're going, it will be anything but comfortable.>>

<<You made us look crazy.>>

<<Maybe. Or I gave them a hint at what we're truly about. Remember, they didn't say no.>>

<<They didn't say yes, either.>>

Kimmy received an image of a smiley face. <<How can you be so confident?>>

<<I like Jonny and Sierra. I know they'll do the right thing.>>

<<When?>>

<<Give them a chance to sort through what I told them and what they saw. They'll come around.>>

<<When?>>

<<I don't know. We'll have to wait and see.>>

Kimmy growled. <<I think Athena needs to scan your brain. I was hoping to have their help to recover the last piece of the map.>>

<<Maybe if we get it, it'll prove we're for real.>>

<<Maybe...>>

CHAPTER 10

ARCO
RONA RESORT, HOUSTA IMPERIUM
TROPICAL BIOME
¥1,025,912
10, DECEMBER 4003

"THIS IS THE DUMBEST idea I've ever been a part of," grumbled Dupont as Kimmy stepped off the edge of War Cat's belly hatch.

Kimmy fell sixty feet and splashed down into the Rona Lagoon. The sparkling water came up to her new tomahawk's knees as she waded away from the drop zone to let the others land.

Three volcanic islands in the center of the lagoon were ringed by a network of coral islands. On the west side was the Rona Resort—a large vacation destination resort hotel catering to the citizens of the Housta Imperium. On the opposite side was the Housta Imperium's Mech Aquatic Training Grounds. The installation trained the Imperium's mech pilots in water operations—something Kimmy and her troop only had in the simulator.

As Kimmy waited, she checked her new radar system and HUD. Athena completed her upgrades to the system, networking the mechs' radar systems and War Cat's sensor suite together, allowing target and environmental information to be shared.

The improvements to the HUDs were substantial. The AI built Virtual Intelligence into the system that—among other things—picked weak spots on enemy targets and would select the best weapons to do the most damage. Athena tweaked many onboard systems, allowing for faster acquisition, increased weapons stability, and better accuracy.

Kimmy spent the last two weeks drilling her pilots on the new systems. Most took to them easily, having worked with similar technology at the Angels' home, Roost. Only Dupont fussed and fumed over the changes. He promptly announced he was better than any computer, even as he continuously finished last in the simulators' killboards.

"How's it look?" asked Kita over the radio. She was aboard War Cat, using the new holotable map that gave her a bird's-eye view of the battlespace. The new interface put Kita in charge of all strategic decisions while Kimmy handled the tactical ones. The system worked well in the simulator, and they felt ready for a real-world test.

"Like paradise," said Kimmy as she admired the towering tropical islands.

As a couple, they liked tropical islands. Hawaii was their favorite.

"All systems are green," said Kimmy. "I see the others deploying. We'll move toward the base as soon as they're ready."

"Nemesis and Sapper are standing by waiting for you to engage," reminded Kita.

Nicole, Lizzy, and the Morphicons were the mission's primary focus. Kimmy's troop was the distraction. The UEE outpost was on the eastmost island halfway up the mountain. Scans showed it was covered in vegetation. Lizzy and the Morphicons carried flamers to clear the way for Athena to get inside and get the coordinates to the UEE weapons cache.

On radar, the four mechs in Kimmy's troop were in the water. "Form up on me," ordered Kimmy as she pushed her throttle forward. She received acknowledgments as the others formed a wedge with her on point.

"You've got fifteen hundred yards to target," reported Kita. "I detect a troop of medium mechs in the water at seven hundred yards. Another troop of medium and heavy mechs is active on the base. Static defenses are in passive mode."

"Any idea what the defenses are?"

"Looks like a combination of ballistics and missile. I count five turrets, all oriented toward the lagoon."

Kimmy wiggled her nose at the added stressor.

The lagoon was a volcano that blew its top. Once you reached the reef islands, the sea floor dropped dramatically for several miles. Except for a chain of lagoons ringing the equator, Arco was a water world terraformed by a civilization with more technology than currently available. *I bet it was the UEE.*

"Ok," said Kita, "phase line lion reached. Rivet, Poison, break formation, and perform a sweep. Rivet to the north, Poison to the south."

As Kita received affirmatives, Kimmy tapped her console, preparing the jammer. Athena updated the device to not only jam radars but HUDs.

On Kimmy's radar, Flexi and Karen headed in their respective directions. The idea was to catch the enemy in a pincer maneuver. While the enemy was sucked in to fight the larger mechs, the lighter mechs would circle around and attack the enemy's rear.

The sun broke from behind a cloud, reflecting harshly off the water ahead of Kimmy. She adjusted her HUD for the glare but was also thankful for it. The sun was behind them, and along with their water and sky camouflage paint job, she hoped it would keep them hidden from enemy optics until it was too late.

"Three hundred yards to contact," reported Kita. "Kimmy, light the sparkler."

Kimmy tapped on her console, and the jammer went to work. Her radar snowed for a second as it and the jammer synced up. As Kimmy waited, she selected her long-range weapons. Kita's assigned targets for Kimmy, Zhi, and Dupont appeared on the radar. Kimmy would hit with her fifty-millimeter cannon and LRMs. Zhi and Dupont would target the same enemy mech with two forty-millimeter cannons, a thirty-millimeter cannon, and a large beam.

The five enemy mechs were firing on targets to the north and south, presenting side profiles for Kimmy and her troop to shoot. The new VI picked the enemy's right arm and torso as the high probability hit. Kimmy went with the recommendation. She zoomed in, laying her targeting reticle on the mech's arm, and waited for Kita's command.

"Aimed and ready," she reported.

"Ready," said Zhi.

"Come on, Blade," Kita urged.

"I'm comin'. This stupid computer doesn't know what it's talking about. We should shoot at the legs, not up top where the armor is thickest."

"The legs are protected by twelve feet of water," said Kita sternly. "Shoot where Athena tells you to."

"That wicked AI isn't a mech pilot. What does she know?"

"She's got millions of hours in the simulator to your five hundred."

"The simulator isn't the same as real-world experience. She don't have no stick time."

"Shut it," Kita snarled. "Paint your target before the enemy moves."

"A fuck it. I don't need this thing. I'll do it the real way. Locked on."

Kimmy shook her head, grateful Kita was in charge and would deal with Dupont.

"Fire!" Kita ordered.

Fire and smoke erupted from Kimmy's right and left torsos as her missiles and ballistic round streaked toward their target. In Kimmy's new HUD display, the enemy mech's arm went black as the cannon round destroyed the appendage. Her missiles rained down on the mech's right torso, each explosion knocking it around until it fell over.

Kimmy's HUD reported hits by Zhi. She shredded the enemy mech's arm. Only Dupont missed, his manually aimed shot going wide. If his cannon hit, it would have punctured the enemy's torso.

Kimmy brought up the damage report for the mech she hit. She'd destroyed the thirty-millimeter cannon in the right arm and critically hit two medium beams in the right torso. The HUD couldn't tell her if the beams were functioning, but the damage would mean they wouldn't be at full power.

Kimmy pushed her throttle to maximum, trying to close the distance and deploy her full arsenal. She studied the enemy's reactions while waiting for her weapons to reload. They were forming a protective arc, hinting they didn't know where the attack came from.

"Fallen Angel, looks like the sparkler is working," reported Kimmy.

"Good," said Kita. "We're going to need it. I detect five more power-ups on the base. Three heavy mechs and two mediums. Types unknown. They're still undercover."

"Are you crazy?" exclaimed Dupont. "There's no way we can take on that many!"

"Blade, hold the line," ordered Kita. "The mission is to distract, not destroy. Sapper, Nemesis, and the Morphicons are on the ground, making their way to zeta. Your job is to buy them time."

"No way. You're trying to kill me, so you don't have to pay me. I'm out of here."

"Blade!" Kita yelled.

To Kimmy's left, Dupont's mech broke formation and made a hard left out of the engagement area.

"Back in line!"

"Screw you, cripple. You're not the boss of me."

"You want paid, I am."

"Nothing in the deal said I had to fight."

"Should I shoot him?" asked Zhi.

Kimmy snickered at the poetic justice but knew it would widen the rift between Zhi and Karen. "No. Let him go."

"You run," snarled Kita. "And there's a good chance you don't get picked up when we leave. You're not with us—you don't get paid."

"Maybe I'll strike a deal with Defin," yelled Dupont.

"You do that, and I'll skin you alive."

"Fallen Angel, can I talk to Blade—privately?" said Karen.

"You've got ten seconds, then we go back on mission. Remember—everyone—we're not Angels and indestructible. Pay attention to what you're doing."

Kimmy knew sage advice when she heard it. As an Angel, she was nearly indestructible, and that made up for mistakes and for their infamous conversations on the battlefield. If she wanted to live through being a mech pilot, she would need her full concentration. Kita could worry about Dupont.

Kimmy called Zhi, "How you doing, wingmate?"

"I'm ready. Weapons are hot. We can take them without him."

Kimmy saw hers were ready. "Fallen Angel, permission to fire?"

"Weapons free," said Kita. "Stay at range to keep the base defenses from lighting you up."

Kimmy scanned the enemy formation. In her HUD, she could see Zhi doing the same. This awesome feature kept them from targeting the same mech by mistake. Kimmy had a frontal attack on an undamaged enemy mech. She put her targeting reticle center mass and pulled the trigger to fire an alpha strike. In the simulator, that was more than enough to core a medium mech.

Zhi fired.

The Advanced Particle Cannon was designed by the UEE and didn't fire a large mass of charged particles. It fired six smaller groups, but their damage increased when combined. Upon contact, it knocked out the receiving mech's power system requiring a restart. The downside was it lost power as it traveled, making it a short-range weapon. Lighter than a regular Particle Cannon, the APC's ability to knock out small to heavy mechs in one alpha strike made it a favorite of pilots who liked close-quarters combat.

The mech Kimmy targeted exploded in a bright orange and yellow fireball. The mech targeted by Zhi twisted and fell, disappearing beneath the waves.

The remaining enemy mechs backed toward the base, firing wildly at the incoming attackers. Kimmy and Zhi zigzagged through the water to make targeting harder and give time for her weapons to reload and recharge.

"Incoming," warned Kita. "We've got four medium mechs and two heavies entering the water from the base. Apocalypse, Venom, hold your position. You're entering the range of the turrets. Venom, split north, Apocalypse, go south. We'll see if we can split them. Poison and Rivet are nearly in position."

"Where did Blade go?" said Zhi.

"It appears Poison couldn't woo him back. He's headed out of the engagement zone. We'll see if Athena has the heart to pick him up."

"Don't be like that," said Karen. "He's scared. It happens to us all."

"I've never run from a fight," replied Zhi harshly. "Even when having my plane or mech shot out from under me. You should know. You were there—"

"That's enough," ordered Kita. "Now's not the time. Kill mechs. Love life later."

"Love life?" squawked Karen.

"Sexy time? Whatever you want to call it. Get your head focused on the mission. All of you."

"Fallen Angel, I'm aiming at targets three and four," Kimmy said as she highlighted them on her radar with a finger tap. Target three was the medium mech she blew the arm off earlier. Target four was a fifty-ton rex that remained untouched. Kimmy tapped her console, dividing her weapons between targets. Each would get an APC shot. The undamaged rex would get her fifty-millimeter and all four of her beams. When she finished, she locked her targeting reticle on the enemy mechs and, after giving the computer a moment to lock, she pulled the trigger.

Her weapons struck the enemy mechs simultaneously. The APC struck the enemy mech, missing its right arm and torso, center mass and the left torso. The mech stopped mid-stride and fell sideways into the water. The rex took the attack in the center torso, showering the area with sparks and metal debris. The APC particles froze the mech. An APC from Zhi finished the mech as the rest of her weapons hit the mech she damaged earlier, blowing its torso off and causing the legs to collapse.

"Two more down," reported Kimmy to Kita. "How's Sapper and the others doing?"

"They've reached the entrance, but it's blocked by trees and vegetation. Going to take some time to clear a path. We've got to stall."

"No problem," said Flexi.

"We've got five heavy mechs in the area," responded Kita. "Stay sharp. Rivet, Poison, I want you to power down and hide until these heavies commit. I didn't expect Apocalypse and Venom to cut through the vanguard so easily."

"Roger," the pair replied.

Kimmy was stunned at how quickly the medium mechs went down.

"Here they come," warned Zhi.

Kimmy zoomed her HUD in on the beach—another welcome feature Athena incorporated—as three medium snow tigers and two heavy hammers entered the water. At this distance, only the large beams of the snow tigers and hammers were dangerous. The hammers also mounted a thirty-millimeter. It wouldn't do much damage to the larger mechs, but they could be a problem for Karen and Flexi.

On the radar display, Kita highlighted the targets for Kimmy and Zhi. "Ok, Apocalypse and Venom, we're fighting a withdrawal from here. We want to keep these guys at range. They have little for long-range weapons—like we do—but they are stacked for close-quarters combat. You let them get in close—you're dead. Understand?"

"Roger," Kimmy replied as she lined up her first shot at a hammer. Her APCs and beams would be of no use at such range, but she could snipe—one of her strong suites—and rain down missiles. Being aggressive, Kimmy targeted the enemy cockpit above the center torso. She aimed slightly lower so if she missed, she'd hit something, and a fifty-millimeter slug hitting anything would do serious damage.

The targeting reticle locked onto the enemy hammer's cockpit, and Kimmy pulled the trigger. Her fifteen missiles arced into the sky as she heard the *boom* of her cannon.

A beeping alerted her to another new feature Athena installed—a warning when an enemy had a lock. Kimmy grabbed her stick and jerked it to the left to throw off her enemy's aim. *How'd they get a lock through the sparkler?* With no time to worry about that, she performed a series of maneuvers, but the water and her mech's size slowed her.

When the missiles crashed down on her, it was like being shaken by an angry toddler—only her harness kept her in the command chair. As Kimmy tried to keep her senses about her, the VI took over as the gyro blasted a warning. The VI lowered the mech into the water to gain stability and to become a smaller target. Kimmy grasped the chair's arms, praying the barrage would stop.

On the console, warnings and damage reports came in. Nothing critical was damaged, but Kimmy's armor was down twenty percent across her arms and left and right torso. Her center torso had taken five percent. Kimmy was sure her nerves were more damaged than her mech.

"Fallen Angel, what the hell is out there?" Kimmy asked in a shaky voice.

"Looks like we've got a pair of missile boats—schooners—mounting some advanced targeting systems that are blowing through our sparkler—ah, incoming!"

The alarm sounded in Kimmy's helmet. She grabbed her control stick and throttled her mech to the right as fast as it would go. The impact of these missiles seemed greater than the first. Kimmy's gyro screamed a warning as the VI tried to keep the mech upright. The sensation of falling made Kimmy grab whatever she could, causing her knuckles to turn white.

The water cushioned Kimmy's fall as her mech landed on its back. Water rushed over the cockpit glass as the mech sank to the bottom of the lagoon.

Kimmy fought the panic welling up inside her. Her mech had internal environmental systems and didn't rely on outside air for her to breathe. *My mech is rated for space. It can handle underwater.* Glancing around the cockpit, she checked for leaks, but nothing was coming in. Satisfied she wouldn't drown, Kimmy turned her attention to the console. The VI was standing her mech up. Damage from this round of missiles wasn't as severe as last time, but she was at thirty-five percent armor across her torso. *I can't take too many more hits.*

"How are you doing, Apocalypse?" called Zhi. "I've got you secured and am holding them off."

"I'm moving Poison and Rivet in," said Kita.

"I'm in one piece," replied Kimmy warily. "But remember how Chelsea used to shake and throw her toys across the room?"

"Yeah?"

"I feel like I'm the toy."

"Good news is, they're in range after you stand up."

"Working on it. How's Nemesis and the girls coming?"

"Almost through the vegetation to the door. Athena has found the door control panel and is hacking her way in."

The water poured off Kimmy's mech, distorting the view through her cockpit windows, but her radar and HUD were working. She couldn't do much until her mech reached vertical, but the enemy schooners were still on land. The other enemy mechs were closing the distance and inside most of Kimmy's firing arcs.

As her mech reached one knee in preparation to stand, a pair of dull *thunks* set her damage sensors off. Two thirty-millimeter rounds struck her in the left arm and right torso, compliments of the two hammers coming toward her.

"Fallen Angel, I need covering fire," Kimmy said. "I'm getting torn up."

"Venom, move between the incomers and Apocalypse. Give her some cover so she can get back in the fight."

"On it. I'm moving."

"Poison and Rivet have clear rear arc shots."

Kimmy's command chair pressed against her as the horizon out her cockpit window lowered. *Oh, thank the Void. Let's get back in the fight.* Ahead of Kimmy was Zhi, taking the fight to the hammers. Kimmy targeted one that took an alpha strike from Zhi, turning the mech red in Kimmy's HUD. Lining up her targeting reticle, Kimmy moved sideways to clear Zhi. When she heard the lock tone, Kimmy fired an alpha strike into the hammer's center torso.

The hammer went up in a great fireball as rounds for its thirty-millimeter cooked off. Twisting as it fell, it hit the water with a great splash and disappeared beneath the waves.

"Great shot, Apocalypse!" whooped Zhi.

"You set me up. That was all you," Kimmy replied.

"Ladies, looks like the schooners are staying on the beach," informed Kita. "Start moving back and staying out of their range until we deal with what's coming at us."

"I've got a shot," reported Flexi.

Kimmy couldn't see the Diamock almost four hundred yards away, but on the radar, she had a clean shot on a snow tiger. On the other side, Poison had a rear arc shot and looked to be taking it.

"Score one for the good guys," said Poison.

"Surprise!" exclaimed Flexi.

On Kimmy's radar, two snow tigers vanished, leaving only a snow tiger, hammer, and the schooners.

"How quickly the tides of war change," hummed Kita, "but look out, there's one more hammer entering the beach."

"I got him!" crowed Flexi.

"Stay back," ordered Kita. "We're not here for kills, only to keep them busy. Those schooners are dangerous."

A barrage of smoke and fire erupted from the schooners to prove the point. The mechs were angled the wrong way for the missiles to hit Kimmy or Zhi, but at—

"Rivet!" Kimmy exclaimed. "Brace yourself. You've got incoming."

"What? That hammer doesn't see me coming!"

"The schooners!"

"Oh—Oh shit!"

Kimmy grit her teeth as the stream of missiles rained down on Flexi's fifty-ton mech. Zooming in, it was like watching a boxer take a hail of blows. Flexi's mech did its best to roll with the punches, but a barrage of eighty missiles was too much. The homebrew mech tipped backward, landing with a splash before disappearing beneath the water.

"Tides of war," muttered Kita. "Girls, take care of the remaining mechs. I'm going to get Rivet up."

"She still alive?" asked Kimmy.

"Lucky for her, only half the missiles hit her. The rest hit the water after she went under."

Kimmy shivered, the memory of such a barrage too prominent in her mind—and she took it in a ninety-ton mech. What it would be like in a mech half that weight made her skin crawl.

"Apocalypse!" called Zhi. "I'll set 'em up, and you knock 'em down. I'm looking at the hammer."

On Kimmy's radar, a circle appeared around the enemy mech. "Got it, Venom. Weapons are ready."

Zhi was ahead, getting the hammer's attention. Kimmy tapped Zhi's icon to check her status. The VI reported she was at ninety-two percent. She sustained damage to her right arm, and all weapons were functional.

Kimmy marveled at the new radar, and console Athena built. It was one thing to use it in the simulator where anything seemed possible. It was another to see it in real life.

"Firing!" announced Zhi.

Oops. I need to catch up. Kimmy placed her HUD's targeting reticle over the hammer's center torso a hundred and forty yards away and waited for the lock tone. When she heard it, she pulled the trigger. Her alpha strike hit the hammer's torso after Zhi and cored the mech. It went down with a satisfying splash. *I think it's cooler when they splash down instead of blow up.* To her surprise, the water roiled and boiled, then exploded in a five-story geyser. *Ok, that was cool.*

"Did you see that?" exclaimed Zhi.

"I did. I guess we know what happens when a reactor blows underwater." Kimmy hummed happily. She'd never worked with Zhi before and found she was a lot of fun and an excellent wingmate. She wasn't selfish and seemed to relish the support role. Kimmy could see why Karen liked her. It was too bad Karen fell for that idiot Dupont. *Oh well, her loss.*

"Apocalypse! Incoming missiles!" warned Zhi.

Kimmy tapped the brace button as she scanned the horizon. A stream of fire and smoke from the beach led back to the schooners. Her eyes flicked to Zhi, her dawnbreaker already in a defensive crouch.

Kimmy's tomahawk lowered itself into the water, the gyro and computer ready to absorb the incoming missiles. *Oh, please don't hit me. Please. I'm not sure I could go through that again.* Closing her eyes, Kimmy waited.

When the first missiles struck, Kimmy grasped the armrest, squeezing until her knuckles were white. The giant ninety-ton mech rocked as the missiles struck. Kimmy wished for it to be over while alarms sounded in her ear. She opened her eyes to check the console, but the barrage made it impossible to focus. All she saw was a blur of red, yellow, and orange across her mech's icon and a blob of damage reports.

As the missile slackened, her left torso recoiled from a heavy hit. The cockpit stopped moving, and the radar identified the attack from a hammer wading from the beach. As Kimmy worked to clear the damage reports, a water geyser erupted in front of her. Another *thump* hit her center torso, shaking her command chair and throwing her against the restraints.

"They're swarming me!" Kimmy yelled over the radio.

Not far away, the fallen enemy leopard mech resurfaced, its two thirty-millimeter cannons aimed at Kimmy.

"Someone, get that leopard!" Kita barked. "Before it takes a chunk out of Apocalypse."

"On it!" replied Flexi. The Diamock turned away from the beach and waded toward the offending mech. She fired an alpha strike into the leopard's back as the enemy mech fired on Kimmy.

Geysers of water sprayed Kimmy's tomahawk as the enemy rounds fell short. *They'll blow me apart if I don't get back in the fight.* Kimmy cleared her screen of the damage warnings and ordered her tomahawk to stand.

The console clear, she took in the damage. Her torso was red and orange, and her arms orange. Her fifty-millimeter cannon was out of alignment, and her left APC wasn't charging correctly, leaving her with one APC and four medium beams. She no longer had the firepower to core an enemy but could support Zhi and the others.

"Hey, asshole!" called Karen. She was between the beach and the last enemy mech—a snow tiger. She fired an alpha strike—a large beam, three medium beams, a small beam, and six SRMs—into the back of the snow tiger, blowing through its thin rear armor. The reactor exploded, launching pieces in all directions. The remaining legs fell backward into the water.

"That clears the field," said Kita. "except for the heavies on the beach."

"Do we charge?" asked Flexi excitedly.

"I wouldn't survive if they targeted me," replied Kimmy.

"Venom, I want you to charge the middle. Poison and Rivet, take the flanks. See if you can keep those schooners busy. Apocalypse, I want you to withdraw toward the central islands. We'll retrieve you when we get the others."

"Roger," said Kimmy as she eased her throttle into reverse. Her frontal armor was chewed but still stronger than her rear armor. She aimed for the opening between the islands, hoping to find cover.

The deep-throated *rumble* was punctuated by the ground and water shaking violently, triggering Kimmy's tomahawk to brace automatically. Kimmy couldn't see the cause from her cockpit window, but when she looked at her rearview camera, she let out an "Eek!"

A giant plume of ash, fire, and smoke ringed by lava blasted from between the islands. The plume raced upward into the atmosphere. Streaks of orange and black lava bombs rained down on the lagoon.

What the hell did they do? I've got to get out of here. Kimmy slammed her throttle forward. Her goal was to reach the barrier islands. She didn't know if they were safe, but it had to be better than where she was.

"Venom...everybody...get to the barrier islands!" Kimmy ordered. "Kita, what in the Void is happening?"

"The volcano's erupting."

"I can see that! I'm in the middle of it! Why?"

"Ah...well, when enough pressure builds up in the magma chamber—"

"I don't need the geology. I got enough when we went to Hawaii. Why now?"

"Not totally sure. Maybe Chelsea did something. We're trying to retrieve Athena and the others. Get someplace safe, and we'll pick you up once we have them."

"Did they get the map piece?"

"I don't know. Athena's been quiet. I'll let you know when I know more."

Kimmy ground her teeth in frustration. Something happened—by someone. If the volcano was going to blow naturally, the area would have been evacuated. *If I don't get moving, I won't live to know what happened.*

"Venom, Poison, Rivet, get to the barrier islands," ordered Kimmy.

"What the Void is going on?" replied Rivet.

"The volcano's erupting. That's all I know. We have to get clear so War Cat can pick us up." As Kimmy finished, a lava bomb splashed down in front of her. It exploded underwater, showering her tomahawk with water and dull *thuds* off her armor. *Shit. Shit. Shit. What did they do?*

A muffled *crack* radiated from the seafloor. The water level dropped as the current changed. To Kimmy's left, a large whirlpool formed, sucking down water. Another *crack* came from her right. The water in the lagoon swirled into another whirlpool.

The forward velocity of the tomahawk slowed against the rushing water. Low electrical levels and overheating warnings appeared on Kimmy's console. She tapped them and found her mech's legs struggling to overcome the current. Easing back on the throttle, Kimmy hoped the slower pace would conserve power. She changed course to put her movement parallel to the current to help her escape the whirlpool.

The change in direction led to an additional problem. Every time she took a step, her mech would tilt. She programmed the console to lower the mech's center of gravity, which made steps even slower, and she rocked dangerously. *I need another point of contact. But what?* Looking at her arms, the damaged APC would have to be sacrificed. She straightened the arm and lowered the APC's barrel into the water.

Using her new walking stick, she waddled her way toward safety. Around her, lava bombs fell, exploding on the water, showering the tomahawk with water and molten rock. Kimmy made fifty yards to where the current wasn't as strong. As she adjusted course toward a nearby barrier island, a thunderous *crack* sent a shockwave across the lagoon that shook her mech.

In the rearview camera, dozens of lava geysers erupted throughout the lagoon, their bright orange highlighted by the roiling black cloud that engulfed the inner islands.

Oh, shit. Did...did the others survive that? Kimmy hadn't heard from Kita since hell broke loose.

Determined to reach the barrier island, Kimmy pushed her throttle forward and lifted her arm out of the water. It was a slow trudge. Every step seemed to test her will as she tried to outrun hell itself.

In the back of her mind, Kimmy hoped Zhi, Karen, and the others found refuge, but she couldn't worry about them. She had to save herself. Once she was safe, she could help the others. Hopefully, they reached the barrier islands.

A *whoosh* from behind brought a gray cloud engulfing Kimmy. She turned on her lights, but they did nothing to cut the ash-laden steam. Kimmy turned to her compass and ensured she didn't stray from her bearing. In the fog, explosive flashes lit the darkness as more lava bombs rained down.

Kimmy didn't find the barrier island. The island found her. Through the gloom, the tropical forest covering the island was ablaze. Bright flames fought against the dying of the light as the fog engulfed all.

Kimmy followed the shallow beach, trying to go around the fire and find open ocean. She hoped it would provide refuge against the volcano. In her mech, she could survive a day, maybe two, if she worked to preserve her oxygen.

"Fallen Angel, are you there?" Kimmy called. She wanted to tell Kita her plan so they could plan her extraction. "Kita?" When she received no answer, she tried the others. "Venom, Poison, Rivet—Anyone?"

Kimmy's heart sank as she received only static. *What if they didn't make it?* A pair of tears trickled down from the corner of her eyes as she rounded the point of the island and found open ocean. Flipping on her emergency beacon, Kimmy hoped the others could find it underwater.

Kimmy guided her mech into the ocean. Careful of where she stepped, she knew the sea floor dropped quickly. A *thud* reverberated through her cockpit as the water reached her thighs, causing her mech to pitch forward. Her radar was returning useless garbage, so she turned her mech to see what hit her. *Maybe it's one of the others trying to get my attention.* She turned, and her heart leaped into her throat. On the beach was the last Housta Imperium hammer.

There is no way I'm going to survive a fight with him.

The hammer fired its four medium beams in front of Kimmy, boiling the water. *Fuck. He can't core me and get it over with? He's got to taunt me? Well, I'm not going down without a fight. I can at least bloody his nose.*

Kimmy thrust her throttle forward and ran toward the hammer as fast as she could. The penalty for firing while running was negated by the VI. Kimmy laid her targeting reticle over the hammer's center torso and got a lock. Determined, she pulled the trigger. Her one good APC and two medium beams fired, striking the hammer center mass.

The APC did its job and kept the hammer from reacting, letting Kimmy close the distance. She knew if she was going to win, it would be a knockdown, drag-out brawl in close quarters where Kimmy could negate his weapons advantage, and she could use her size and APC zero range to punish him.

As Kimmy approached the hammer, its chest exploded in flame and fire as a swarm of SRMs streaked toward her. Kimmy's hand went for the brace button, but most missiles made wild turns and exploded in the sand or flew into the burning jungle. Two struck Kimmy in the legs, doing nominal damage. The last missile struck her right torso and exploded, leaving a gaping hole and cutting power to the right arm. Kimmy shrugged it off. That arm was dead weight—but she had plans for it.

Closing the distance, Kimmy turned her torso to the right and brought the arm up. She slammed her hand on the melee command, and the torso and arm launched forward, striking the hammer in the left arm and torso, causing it to brace. Kimmy aimed her control stick at the hammer and slammed her heavier mech into the off-balance enemy, knocking it over.

Kimmy stepped back, aiming her working APC at the downed hammer. As her finger touched the trigger, the hammer's left torso exploded in fire. A thirty-millimeter shell slammed into Kimmy's cockpit, blowing through the protective glass, missing her head, and blasting a hole into her core, damaging her electrical system.

She pulled the trigger. When nothing happened, that's when the near miss registered. *Oh, Chelsea, you're watching out for your momma.* Wherever Chelsea was, Kimmy knew she was watching the Random Number Generator for the universe. Kimmy's gift to her daughter was the ability to manipulate the RNG—and Chelsea was good at it.

The hammer stood as Kimmy regained her composure and tried to fix the electrical problem. Abandoning her attempt at a fix, Kimmy swung her right arm at the enemy, but she had no momentum. Her arm slammed into the hammer's left arm, crumpling the appendage. The VI registered Kimmy destroyed a large beam.

The hammer swung at Kimmy, striking her in the left arm. The mechs grappled, but Kimmy—only on backup hydraulics—didn't have the power to push the hammer aside. To thwart the hammer, Kimmy twisted to the left, trying to get the hammer to overexert and fall.

Instead, the hammer throttled forward and pushed Kimmy as she twisted, causing her to fall. Kimmy landed with a *thud* in the sand as waves lapped against her mech. The hammer brought its remaining weapons to bear and aimed them at Kimmy's center torso.

Kimmy scrambled for anything she could do to escape. She had no power, only auxiliary power running her vital systems. The best she could do was stand. *If I'm going to die, it'll be on my feet, facing the enemy.*

As Kimmy worked to right her mech, the back of the hammer exploded, momentarily overpowering the fire from the jungle and exploding volcano. The hammer collapsed at Kimmy's feet, revealing Zhi in her dawnbreaker.

Kimmy set her radio to tight beam to connect with the friendly mech.

"Zhi, can you hear me?" Kimmy gasped.

"Hey, boss lady. I thought you could use a hand."

"Zhi, you have no idea how happy I am to see you. I thought I was alone. Do you have contact with anyone else?"

"Nope. I followed that hammer, hoping I'd get a shot at him. Looks like you found him first."

Never underestimate the killer instinct of a pilot. Even in a hell like this, she's trying to win. How can I do any less?

"More, he found me. I don't think I can get up." Kimmy looked over her console—she had more warnings than buttons. The top warning was for low hydraulic pressure because of low power. Normally, Kimmy would slave to Zhi's mech and use her power, but the volcano prevented that. "I think I'm stuck. Is your emergency beacon on?"

"Oh, no. I guess we're done?"

"Well, either they find us, or we have a delightful view of the apocalypse."

"I can't see you."

Both girls laughed.

Kimmy, exhausted, took off her helmet, ruffled her hair, and laid her head back on the headrest. "Well, I guess I'll see you back at Roost, Zhi. It's been fun. You're a great wingmate."

"Why are we going home so soon?" said Bombshell.

Kimmy's head jerked up. "Bomb?"

"We're here. Momma-Kita sent Knock and me down to escort the drop rings and you back to the ship. But if you'd rather go home…"

ORBITING ARCO
WAR CAT ASSAULT SHIP
SPACE BIOME
¥1,025,912
10, DECEMBER 4003

T HE RECOVERY RING DECOUPLED from Kimmy's tomahawk once inside War Cat's mech bay. Kimmy, exhausted, hit the auto-dock button. It was a new feature installed by Athena that took over the tedious task of docking a mech. Kimmy was thankful for it. She didn't feel she could walk straight, let alone maneuver her mech through the crowded and busy bay.

When the tomahawk stepped into its bay, the operational systems transferred to War Cat, and the hatch opened.

Kimmy hit the release on her harness and slid to the floor. There she sat, taking deep breaths, trying to calm her shattered nerves. Deciding the only person who could soothe them was Kita, Kimmy gathered her helmet—sitting on the floor where she'd dropped it. Standing, she used various handholds to pull her weary body through the hatch onto the scaffolding.

Taking the elevator to the main deck, she was overwhelmed by the commotion and noise—tenfold normal. Looking at her tomahawk, the volcano's damage hid the battle scars. The giant hole in her cockpit glass caused an upwelling of emotion that caused her to collapse onto the deck. She wrapped her arms around her legs and rested her head on her knees. Tears trickled down and stained her piloting suit. *How close was I? Feet? Inches? And what kept it from exploding? Chelsea? Is my baby watching out for me across the cosmos?* Death was not something she'd experienced, and the idea scared her...*Even though I know I can't be permakilled, I don't want to find out what happens when I am killed. I don't trust the computer to bring me back.*

"There she is!" yelled Karen. She, Lizzy, and Nicole came running up to Kimmy and kneeled around her.

"Kimmy! You need to come right now! She's going to kill him!" Karen cried around deep breaths.

Kimmy wiped the tears away. There was little doubt about who *she* was and even less doubt about who *him* was. She looked at her friends, sniffed, and her tears turned to anger. "He's a coward that fled in the face of the enemy. He deserves a coward's death."

"Please," pleaded Karen. "You can't let Kita kill Pierre. He got overwhelmed. It was a lot of enemy mechs...especially when sitting in a tin can like his."

"He gets what he deserves. I lost count of how many times I was nearly killed. If it wasn't for Zhi, that volcano would have been my tombstone."

"What about me?" said Zhi, coming up to the group.

"I owe you," said Kimmy. "You saved my ass."

"I was hunting him, and you got him first."

"Kimmy, please," wailed Karen. "Don't let Kita kill him. I love him."

That drew the attention of the other girls.

"Since when?" demanded Kimmy.

"Does he love you?" asked Nicole, looking concerned.

Karen shrugged. "I don't know. I haven't told him. I've been waiting for the right moment."

"God in Heaven," muttered Kimmy.

"Come on, Kimmy," said Nicole, offering Kimmy a hand. "Cowardice isn't worth death—but it might be the last mission he goes on with us." She gave Karen a sharp look.

Karen hung her head.

"Fine," said Kimmy. She took Nicole's hand. "Athena! Where's Kita?"

A sinister chuckle came from the speaker. "Playing with her food."

"She's allowed to chew but not swallow. Where is she?"

"On the ship," Athena answered coyly.

"Don't play with me," Kimmy replied harshly.

Athena sighed. "She's chasing him around the barracks. The fool has got himself trapped."

"Meaning you've shut and locked the doors," said Lizzy.

"I'm giving him a sporting chance. I've left a loop open."

"Come on," said Kimmy. "I know where they are. Athena, open the doors for us."

"As you wish. It'll be much easier if you let Mom kill him. I'll clean up the mess."

That was a tempting offer. And Kimmy had no reason to keep Dupont alive...except for Karen. *I don't think I can patch up another brokenhearted Angel.*

Kimmy sprinted out of the mech bay with the other Angels following. They crowded into the elevator and took it to the barracks level. They found a repair crew working on a stream pipe in the elevator landing area. The steam was off, and a section of pipe was torn away.

"Looks like Kita's work," Kimmy announced to the others.

"Kimmy!" Velositi called from the left hallway. She was followed by Bernoot as they made their way to the new arrivals.

"What's Kita doing?" Kimmy asked the Morphicons.

"So far, chasing Pierre and scaring him," answered Velositi.

"Way gnarly. Kita's totally tricked out," said Bernoot.

"How strong is she that she can rip a pipe off the wall?" said Nicole.

"Told you my upgrades were good," said Athena from a nearby speaker.

"Please stop her," blubbered Karen.

"A few hits to the head might fix him," said Velositi.

Karen broke into sobs. Lizzy put an arm around her while Nicole came to Kimmy.

"Please, you have to do something. I know cowardice is bad, but we haven't heard his side. He must have a reason. Maybe his mech was malfunctioning—"

"We checked it out," said Ultraviolet through a nearby tech. "The mech is fine...not a scratch."

"We all get overwhelmed and scared," Nicole pleaded meekly.

Kimmy glared. "Spread out, find him, and get him to safety. If we don't get him first, I can't stop Kita."

"Can't or won't?" said Nicole.

Kimmy put herself nose to nose with the other Angel. "I've had a bitch of a day. Don't believe me? You can remove the unexploded thirty-millimeter shell lodged in my cockpit. He ran and announced it over the radio, leaving the rest of us to face a group three times our size. I've got no sympathy.

"If it wasn't for Zhi, you'd be washing me out of my cockpit with a hose. If you want him alive, you better find him. I'm taking Velositi, and we're going to find Kita. Maybe we'll stop her, maybe we'll help her. So, I suggest you get moving."

Nicole huffed but turned to the others. "Come on. He's got to be around here somewhere."

"I'm going with Kimmy," said Zhi.

Her announcement shocked the others.

"Zhi..." whispered Karen.

Zhi faced her former wingmate. "You can't have both, and you've made your choice."

Karen's mouth fell open. "What...? I...Zhi...what choice?"

"I loved you!" Zhi screamed. "I gave you everything. I would have given you more. I thought you cared about me. Instead, you go with him! A no-talent coward! Why wasn't I good enough? I was with you always. I had your back. What's wrong with me? Why him? Why!"

Karen's mouth opened and closed a few times.

"Hurry it up," ordered Kimmy. "The longer you wait, the closer Kita gets."

Tears tumbled down Karen's face. "Zhi, I'm sorry. I didn't know you felt that way. I...I...you're my friend. I didn't know you wanted a relationship. I thought you were an excellent wingmate. And you know I couldn't have given it to you. You're my subordinate—"

"We're Angels," screamed Zhi. "Rank doesn't matter." She threw up her hands. "Fuck you. I found someone better. Someone who doesn't jump on the first cock that walks through the door."

Karen looked between Kimmy and Zhi, confused. "Kimmy?"

"Ash'a, actually," responded Kimmy. She looked at Zhi. "Finished?"

Zhi gave her a sharp nod. "Yes."

There was a loud metal *bang* from down the left hallway.

"Good, let's go. We'll go toward the bang. The rest of you—I hope you're good at hide and seek."

Kimmy led her group down the left hallway. Velositi put her arm around Zhi and hugged the Angel.

Kimmy didn't bother looking in any of the rooms they passed—most belonged to Ultraviolet's crew. She did not know what kind of game Kita was playing, but she guessed the idea was to unnerve Dupont. She turned a corner and jumped at a loud metallic *bang*.

"I hope Kita is not damaging the ship further," said Velositi.

"She's not," said Athena. "Mom is smart enough to only hit as hard as she needs and only things that can take it."

Kimmy turned another corner and found Kita—Dupont dangled by the throat in her mechanical arm. Kita dragged the pipe along the wall, letting it bang into the other pipes, making a dreadful noise. *At least Athena was right.* What perplexed Kimmy was where Kita found the hooded cloak.

"Kita!" Kimmy called sweetly.

Kita whirled, flaring her cloak, revealing she was naked. Dupont thumped against the wall in Kita's grasp. Kita's eyes glowed from under her hood. "Yes?" she answered in a pleasant tone.

"Wacha doin'?" Kimmy answered in an equally pleasant tone.

"Teaching a lesson on what happens to a coward who abandons his comrades—and my partner—in battle. I can't let the ranks go undisciplined."

"I agree. What are you planning on doing to him?"

Kita pulled Dupont to his knees as his eyes bulged. "Seeing how much of him I can fit in this pipe. I will start with his spine—if I can find it."

Kimmy's eyes flicked to Dupont. "How are you, Pierre? Nowhere to run now, huh?"

"Pierre!" Karen squealed from the opposite end of the hallway. Lizzy was trying to peek over the taller Angel's shoulder.

"Looks like the coward's death will have an audience," cooed Kita.

"Kita, come on, let him go," said Lizzy as she pushed Karen aside. "Death is too good for a coward."

"How close to death did you come today, Kimmy?" asked Kita.

"Which time?"

Kita raised an eyebrow and looked at Dupont. "Hear that, coward? A real warrior isn't afraid to die."

I don't know about that...

"Kita! Please!" wailed Karen.

Kimmy sighed. "Kita, as much as I—"

"We've got to go," said Athena. "A bunch of Housta Imperium warships came out of FTL on the edge of Arco's orbit."

Kita's eyes glowed menacingly. "Jump!"

"Mom, we only have enough fuel for one jump."

"Then jump us to a gas station!"

"Course plotted. Here we go."

Around the barracks, the FTL jump warning siren sounded, and lights rotated.

Kimmy hated FTL jumps and pressed herself against the wall. A countdown reached zero, and the dreadful feeling of her throat hitting her stomach was followed by darkness.

CHAPTER 11

ORBITING D9 SPACE STATION
WAR CAT ASSAULT SHIP
SPACE BIOME
¥1,025,912
10, DECEMBER 4003

K IMMY'S EYES FOCUSED AS the world returned to normal after the FTL
jump. Kita had dropped Dupont—Kimmy presumed for FTL jump
safety and not because she finished with him. To thwart her partner, Kimmy
skipped over and put her boot on Dupont's neck.

"Hey, angel," Kimmy cooed to Kita. "I think we have more important
things to do right now—like figuring out where we are."

Kita tossed the pipe away with a loud *clatter*. "Athena, where are we?"

"D-Nine space station. It was the farthest jump I could make. We're still in
Housta Imperium space, but this station is corporate, not government, so we
can replace our depleted xeox supply."

Kimmy wrinkled her nose. *Should have considered that when we were planning this operation. I'll have to talk to Ash'a.*

"I'm trying to dock, but D-Nine flight control says we don't have a registered flight plan."

"Tell them we had an emergency," ordered Kita. "We have refugees from
the Arco volcanic disaster."

"What refugees, Mom?" asked Athena.

"Us. Tell them we need to refuel, and we'll be on our way. We have the
money to pay for it." Kita looked at Kimmy.

Kimmy nodded but rolled her eyes.

"Can you let me up?" growled Dupont.

"Not going to throw me this time?" Kimmy huffed.

Kita's menacing eyes glared at Dupont.

"Kimmy, let him up!" wailed Karen.

"I think the floor is appropriate for a spineless worm."

"You led us into suicide," Dupont bit out around Kimmy's foot on his neck.

"Yet we're still standing here." Kimmy pushed harder with her foot. "If it hadn't been for Zhi and luck, Kita would wash my cockpit out with a hose." She pushed down hard, then removed her foot. "Death is part of the job. Don't get in a mech if you can't handle it."

"Some of...us...ain't gods," Dupont said around coughs.

"We didn't start out this way," Kimmy retorted. "Come on, Kita. Let's find Ash'a and figure out what kind of mess we're in."

ORBITING D9 SPACE STATION
WAR CAT ASSAULT SHIP
SPACE BIOME
¥1,025,912
10, DECEMBER 4003

THE ANGELS AND DUPONT took their seats in the briefing room. It was a medium-sized room with stadium seating and a holoprojector at the front. Kita stood next to Kimmy. She kept her cloak, but Kimmy convinced her to wear a mech pilot suit underneath.

Dupont sat with Karen. The Angel was busy soothing him. Zhi sat in the front row—like always—next to Ash'a. The Aurorian was busy on her tablet, probably communicating with the local authorities about what happened on Arco.

When everyone was seated, Kimmy stepped up. "Ok, listen up. We don't have much time. The Housta Imperium authorities want to talk to us when we dock. So, we need to get our story straight. We never set foot on Arco. We were in orbit, getting ready to disembark for the surface. Ash'a and Athena have spoofed the needed documents and logs at the resort to show we had a reservation and were checked in. However, we never made it to the resort. Instead, when the volcano blew, we made an emergency jump to D-Nine.

Ash'a's struggling with the resort to get our money back and is looking for a local lawyer. That's the story we're sticking to. Questions?"

No hands went up.

Dupont pushed Karen's head off his shoulder and stood. "Did we get the map to the cache? And don't you dare lie to me this time."

"What are you going to do?" cooed Kita. "You didn't like Condo? I understand it's a beautiful world with spectacular views. Velositi would love it."

The Morphicon's eyes lit. She loved viewing natural landscapes.

"Why'd that machine lie to me?" Dupont yelled.

"Athena is not a machine," Kita replied coolly. "She is my daughter, and we had our reasons. Op-Sec and whatnot. Condo was the codename we used for Arco—it would have mattered to you if you were part of the planning, but you're just a coward. It's not like I sent you to Condo. I took you to Arco. What's the problem?"

Dupont grumbled something under his breath. "Where are we going next?"

Kimmy stepped forward, "Only Athena knows, and we're going to—"

Kita put a hand on Kimmy's arm. "Why don't we tell them? They've worked so hard to get to this point, and I'm going to guess the next step won't be easy."

Kimmy raised an eyebrow. *What is Kita up to?* She stepped aside, and the holographic projector came to life.

An image of the universe appeared and flew among the galaxies and stars to a planet orbiting a red giant star named Ragnarök.

"This planet is Edda. It was once lush and alive but is now a barren landscape like Mars," said Athena. "The cache is located a few degrees north of the equator in the center of a city buried in sand."

The image didn't zoom in but dissolved, replaced by a series of quadrants.

Why would Kita divulge the exact location? What's she up to? I trust my friends, but now, if they get interrogated and crack, everyone will know. Kimmy knew better than to question Kita in the open. Kita's knowledge, wisdom, and training in handling such matters outpaced Kimmy by lifetimes. But Kimmy was annoyed she wasn't in on whatever Kita and Athena were doing.

"Satisfied?" Kita said to Dupont.

"How do I know this is legit?"

"Ask Kimmy."

Kimmy's head shot up. She hadn't gotten a funny feeling when Kita or Athena spoke. "I, ah, she's not lying."

"I'm supposed to take your partner's word?" huffed Dupont.

Karen grabbed his arm and pulled him down. "If Kimmy says Kita is telling the truth, then she is. Kimmy knows. It's part of her being a god."

Hey, but he's right. Who's saying I'm not lying? She told the truth. It seemed to be what Kita wanted.

"The ship is docking," announced Athena.

"Come on, everyone," said Kimmy. "Let's go answer some questions."

D9 SPACE STATION
SPACE BIOME
¥1,025,912
10, DECEMBER 4003

D9 WAS DANK, DARK, and disgusting. Constant noise and vibrations radiated throughout the station. As Kimmy passed through the door out of her terminal, she was greeted by a short, overweight man with dark wavy hair, flint-colored eyes, and wearing a business suit. He was flanked by six men in yellow quasi-military uniforms. Each man—including the leader—had a badge that said DEFIN INDUSTRIES. The militiamen had one hand on their cuffs and the other on their guns.

Kimmy ignored them and looked for the constable she was supposed to meet.

"Captain Kimberly Roosevelt?" the short man demanded.

Kimmy looked at him. "Yes?"

"Come with me," he ordered.

"Sorry, I have no business with Defin Industries. If you'll excuse me."

"In the name of the Housta Imperium, you and your associates are under arrest."

"You're not from the Housta Imperium," retorted Kimmy.

"Defin Industries leases this station from the Imperium. We maintain law and order. They put a decree out for your arrest. We are executing it. Now, turn around and put your hands behind your back."

"We'll go peacefully, but you're not putting us in cuffs," retorted Kimmy.

"You don't get a choice. Zap 'em."

The militiamen drew their guns and shot Kimmy and her friends.

Kimmy preferred to be shot than what she experienced from the less-than-lethal round. The electricity forced her into the fetal position as tears and cries of pain escaped her. Still shaking when the militiaman rolled her over, he forcefully pulled Kimmy's hands back and placed the old-fashioned steel cuffs on her wrists. They yanked Kimmy to her feet, but she couldn't stand, forcing them to hold her. Shaking her head, Kimmy tried to clear the buzzing and fog.

"Take the women to the female holding area," ordered the constable. "Intel wants to talk to the male."

About what? Pierre knows...fuck, everything. Why did Kita tell him? A push caused Kimmy to stumble and fall.

The militiaman grabbed her arm and painfully pulled Kimmy to her feet. "Walk, bitch, or I'll drag you by your hair."

Touch my hair, and I'll cut your balls off. Kimmy did her best to shuffle as the militiaman dragged her by the arm.

On the concourse, a pair of men in black uniforms watched Kimmy being led away. *Great. I get to be a spectacle for everyone.*

As Kimmy struggled to keep up with her captor, feeling returned to her legs, allowing her to walk. They were escorted through the commercial section. Most storefronts were empty, and the few shoppers watched Kimmy and her friends go by.

The group entered the Defin Industries area. Heat from the blast furnaces made Kimmy sweat. Floating men fed coal into furnaces while others guided buckets of molten metal to presses. Everything was done in zero-g. Only the main catwalk had gravity.

The constable let out a shrill whistle that brought work to a halt. A louder horn blew, bringing most workers to the catwalk's edge.

"Hey boys, fresh meat!" the constable announced as he led the Angels along the catwalk as catcalls and whistles rained down.

There were no women among the workers. *Ah, hell. Nothing worse than a station of horny men. How am I going to get us out of this?*

They were paraded through the barracks and living area, letting the workers whoop and holler at the Angels. Kimmy kept her head up and glared defiantly. She refused to be intimidated by the fate awaiting her and her friends.

Several rooms in the corner of the barracks made up a red-light district. The constable brought Kimmy and the Angels to a halt. He whistled, and a few women stuck their heads through the doors. Seeing who it was, many ducked inside, and fifteen women filed out, led by an elderly woman dressed in ill-fitting lingerie with her white-streaked hair in curlers.

"What do you got for me, Billy?" she said to the constable.

"Fresh meat. Criminals that need to work off their debt to society."

"Hey," Kimmy yelled. "We haven't even been charged or seen a—"

Thwack! The back of Kimmy's skull exploded in pain and light. She collapsed to her knees, shaking her head.am

"Got a hard-headed heifer in this one. She'll learn." The old woman cackled as she grabbed the Angel's chin and pulled Kimmy's head to look at her. "Got some fire in you. That's good. The boys like fire. See how much you've got left after they run a train on you." She looked at the constable. "She'll do. They'll all do—except that golden alien freak. You can throw her in the furnace."

Kimmy sprang to her feet, angling the crown of her head at the old woman's chin. She connected, lifting the crone off her feet. Whirling, Kimmy delivered a kick to her captor's chest, sending him sprawling. Kimmy jumped on his chest, leading with her knee. After a satisfying *crack*, she slid her knee onto his throat.

The other Angels sprang into action, delivering sharp kicks or head butts to their militiamen. The Angels used a variety of ways to pin the surprised guards.

A gunshot from the constable didn't faze the Angels. It wasn't until Kimmy felt the snub-nosed pistol's barrel against her head that she paused.

"Let him up. All of you bitches! Let them up."

Kimmy wasn't a grandmaster at martial arts like Kita, nor did she have her partner's dexterity, strength, and agility. *But if I'm going to die, now seems like a good time...except, what about the others? I doubt they'll kill us all—probably won't even kill me.*

"Drop the pistol, Billy!" ordered a voice from the other side of the red-light district.

I'm not going down without a fight. Standing, she brought her boot down on the militiaman's neck with a satisfying crunch. She spun and smacked Billy's head with her arm, knocking the fat man to the deck.

A man in a black uniform with a rifle ran over and put the weapon's barrel in Billy's face.

"Empress Roosevelt, ma'am?" he said. "I'm Captain Cambridge of the Seventh Space Marines, Third Regiment, Black Griffin Mercenaries. Blackbeard sends his regards. Ascension will arrive shortly. He said to lend you a hand, but I don't think you or your pilots need it."

"You can get me out of these cuffs. But thanks for coming to our rescue. I don't want to prove we can fight our way out with our hands tied behind our backs."

Cambridge laughed. "You did an excellent job, ma'am."

A platoon of Black Griffin Marines secured the area and helped the Angels. A young Marine came around with a handcuff key and undid the bracelets on Kimmy's wrists.

"Captain," said Kimmy, "they took another of my pilots to interrogation. We need to free him."

Cambridge frowned. "We tailed him, but they loaded him on a shuttle. I don't know where they're headed."

Kimmy's heart sank. *If they get the cache information, there's no way we'll get there first. Hell, I don't even know how we'll get War Cat free.* "Do you know how we can free my ship?"

"We'll have to go to flight control. Right now, your ship is in lockdown. I can't override it, except at gunpoint—and that's what I plan to do. When Blackbeard arrives, he'll escort you out of Housta Imperium space. He said to tell you he's willing to make a deal."

Oh, thank god. A powerful friend was who she could use right now. "Good. Let's get to flight control."

D9 SPACE STATION
SPACE BIOME
¥1,025,912
10, DECEMBER 4003

KIMMY AND CAMBRIDGE RUSHED up the stairs to flight control with two squads of marines and the Angels.

"They'll have barricaded the door by now," said Cambridge. "It'll take us a minute to get it open."

"I hope we don't have to blast our way in."

Cambridge laughed. "This isn't a military station. The doors are made of foil. I don't want to damage anything if we don't have to. Black Griffin is in competitive negotiations for command and control of D-Nine. We break it. We have to fix it."

"Won't this damage your chances?" said Ash'a.

"Nah. If anything, it'll show the Houstains we have what it takes to provide security and operational control. Defin has more money, but they don't employ soldiers, just goons."

No argument there. Her wrists were still hurting from the cuffs.

They reached the door, and Kimmy led the Angels to one side so the marines could open it.

"Ok, tech team, open the—"

The door slid open.

"What you touch, Rylands?" said Cambridge.

"Nothin', sir. I—"

Kimmy stuck her head in the door and called, "Athena? That you?"

"Hey, girls," replied the AI.

Cambridge looked at Kimmy perplexed, "Do you have more friends on the station?"

"More like a friend *in* the station. Athena is an AI capable of hacking most computer systems."

"This wasn't even child's play," huffed the AI. "Tell Black Griffin when they take over the station, they need to upgrade security."

"I'll take it under advisement," said Cambridge with a frown at Kimmy. "I can't have an AI in the station. What if it goes rogue?"

Kimmy laughed. "SHE is well past that point. I promise SHE will remove all traces of herself. If I have to, I'll take it up with Blackbeard."

That seemed to ease Cambridge. "Ok. We need to get your ship—"

"I've already freed War Cat," said Athena. "I've also refueled—"

"Did you pay for it?" asked Kimmy.

"Nooo. Why should we?"

"I don't want any loose threads for them to hold against us. Ash'a, can you pay for it?"

"Sure." She tapped on her tablet. "How much xeox, Athena?"

"Five grams."

"Alright...Wow, their price is steep. It comes to sixty-five thousand credits. Kimmy, I need your thumbprint."

Kimmy pressed her thumb to the tablet. She was impressed Ash'a held onto the device through their ordeal. "There."

Ash'a took the tablet and finished the transaction.

"I was thinking, Mister Rifleman," said Athena to Cambridge. "I could update the station's security for you. As a goodwill gesture for your attempted acquisition of D-Nine station. It'll prove Defin was doing a shit job."

"Athena, we don't have time—"

"Done!" announced the AI. "I've transferred security to Black Griffin—but your passwords will have to be updated next time you login. Instruction manuals have been provided to Black Griffin supervisors. I wouldn't fret about security now—unless another unshackled AI visits."

"What it do!" Cambridge exclaimed at Kimmy.

Kimmy shrugged. "Fixed your security, I guess. If you think she's bad, wait until you meet her mother."

"Compliments will get you somewhere," cooed Athena. "The ship is ready to go—except for the Defin frigates cruising outside. I hope Blackbeard brings help."

"Ascension is a state-of-the-art battlecruiser," said Cambridge. "It should have no problem shooing them away."

"Can Black Griffin win a corporate shooting war with Defin?" Athena said sarcastically.

"We'll leave that to Blackbeard," sighed Kimmy. "Let's get back to the ship. Athena, stay here until we clear the dock. Then delete anything you've installed on their servers. I don't want any evidence we were here."

"And the security upgrades?"

"Leave them. If Blackbeard's crew can figure out how to use them—great. If not, we'll restore the old security protocols."

"The best-laid plans of mice and AIs undone by the stupidity of men."

"That's why you're an Angel. You only have to deal with girls."

"Until you drag me to a place like this. Isn't there a universe where women are in control?"

"Eight hundred and ninety-two tries so far and no luck. The outcomes seem to get worse."

"This wouldn't happen if I was allowed in the universe room."

"We'll talk about that later. We need to get back to the ship."

ORBITING D9 SPACE STATION
BLACK GRIFFIN FLAGSHIP ASCENSION
SPACE BIOME
¥950,912
11, DECEMBER 4003

"KIMBERLY! YOU ALRIGHT?" BLACKBEARD boomed when the door to the airlock opened. He was silhouetted against the light coming from his ship. The big man hurried into the airlock to greet Kimmy and the Angels.

Blackbeard bowed to the group. "When I heard you were on D-Nine, I was worried. It's not a safe place for women."

Kimmy smirked. "As we found out. But it was the farthest xeox refueling center we could jump to and avoid the Housta Imperium. Obviously, it wasn't far enough. I hope you have the recourses to run the station. We turned security over to your people."

Blackbeard rubbed his beard. "I haven't been informed yet, but we've been after control of D-Nine for years. It's a vital station for xeox and zero-g steel. May I ask how you could perform such a feat?"

"Athena," replied Kita dryly. "She's more than we advertised. I hope the gift of D-Nine proves what we told you over dinner."

"Kita," Blackbeard said warmly, "It's good to see you on your feet."

"Thank you. I've been doing my physical therapy and had my limbs up-graded."

"Fascinating. That is good to hear. Come," said Blackbeard, "let's go to the wardroom where we can talk."

"Impressive ship," commented Kita as they walked through the ship.

"Thank you. My Old Man had her built. She's a fully functioning bat-tlecruiser with her own series of mech bays. We carry two battalions of mechs—everything from mice to the new great ape. Ascension allows us to soften targets from orbit before we commit on the ground. She's saved a lot of pilots' lives."

"It's rare in this universe that you place such concern on your pilots. Everyone else seems to feed them into the grinder."

Blackbeard bowed his head. "It is true—on both accounts. Without my pilots, I have nothing. I try to recruit the best and train them to a razor's edge. I want them to bring honor and integrity to the universe—and I want them to come home.

"Sacrificing pilots is a waste of time and resources. Many states would rather win by piling up the bodies than sacrifice time and money to train their pilots properly. I'm afraid many see it cheaper and easier to salvage the mech and place a greenhorn in the command chair than train a pilot who is an ace."

He guided the Angels into a room with a bar on the right wall and seating areas on the left. A small stage with a sound and light system was in the back of the room. Sierra stood at the bar, picking up a tray of drinks. Blackbeard led the Angels to a circular booth. Sierra set the tray on the table.

Seeing Sierra, the buzzing in Kimmy's head returned. She, Kita, and Kita's A'ahegre couldn't decide what it meant.

"I hope everyone likes water," said the Djinn.

"One of the rarest commodities in the universe," added Blackbeard.

Kimmy knew this—she'd seen the water bill to fill Wat Cat's tanks. It's why everyone was mining ice crystals wherever they were found. The precious liquid cost more than xeox. She took a glass with the others.

"Cheers," said Blackbeard. "To our partnership!"

Kimmy sipped some water but was unsure of what they were celebrating. "Did I miss something?" she asked with a smile.

Blackbeard set his glass down. "I apologize for not giving you an answer at dinner, but I wanted to talk with Sierra. I don't make a move if I don't consult her first."

"I understand," replied Kimmy. "I don't do anything without running it by Kita."

"It's good to have people you trust," said Sierra.

"Loyalty is my currency," said Kita. "It can take a lifetime to gain and an instant to lose."

"Here, here!" said Blackbird.

"I hate to bring up business so soon," said Kimmy, "but one of my pilots, Pierre Dupont, was separated from our group upon arrival at D-Nine. They said he was being taken to interrogation, but we never found him. Athena said a shuttle left the station and docked with a Defin ship, but she doesn't know where it went. I'm afraid Pierre was taken."

Blackbeard took a device from his belt and tapped on the screen. "I'm having Captain Cambridge scan the logs on D-Nine. I'm afraid we can't track them if they jumped to FTL."

Kita set down her empty water glass. "We must go forward under the assumption Pierre has told them everything, and they have a head start."

"I knew it was a mistake to tell everyone where we were headed," said Kimmy tartly.

Kita's eyes glowed pink. "Sometimes, to catch a rat, give it some cheese to see where he takes it."

Everyone turned to Kita, shocked.

"You believe Pierre to be a—a spy?" said Ash'a.

"Time will tell," purred Kita.

"What's keeping them from the treasure?" gasped Sierra.

Kita chuckled. "The door. They couldn't get passed the one on Veri IIb. I can't imagine them getting past the final one." She held up her good hand. "Do not worry. In my youth, I was trained as an assassin—a spy hunter. Skills that have helped me a great deal throughout my lifetime. I'm not saying he is or isn't. I won't know until we meet again."

"I wish you were lying," said Sierra, "but you're not."

"I do not lie," said Kita. "It appears you have the same advantage we have."

"And what is that?"

"To tell if someone is lying. Kimmy has the ability, and it appears so do you."

Sierra smiled, revealing her canines. "And if you misjudge me?"

"Have any of us been lying?" Kita asked Kimmy.

Kimmy set down her water glass and put her hands in her lap. "No. Talking with Jonny and Sierra has been one of the most refreshing conversations outside the Angels."

Kita grinned at Sierra. "I'll show you mine if you show me yours."

Kita and Kimmy stood and dissolved into their black and white clouds—an ability given to them by their A'ahegre. Sierra followed though she was a pink cloud.

<<Interesting. We now know what the buzzing in our heads meant,>> said Kita in a monotone voice. <<It seems the A'ahegre took a different evolutionary track in this universe.>>

<<We're called Orobo—in this universe,>> said Sierra in a high melodic voice.

Kita dissolved into her Human form, and the others followed.

"It's strange," said Sierra. "Normally, I can detect another Orobo when they come near. Why am I not able to detect you?"

"We felt a buzzing in our brains but didn't know what it meant. Probably differences in black energy makeup," replied Kita.

"Sierra has been my secret weapon since we were married," said Blackbeard, looking at Sierra fondly.

"It's a nice ability to have," said Kita with a wicked smile. "I understand your driven to make the universe a better place."

"Yes," admitted Sierra. "Oh'o and I have made it our goal. Jonny has made it his goal as well. Our partnership in this endeavor has created an unbreakable bond."

Kita took Kimmy's hand. "I've never experienced a pink—Orobo—but I have had a white A'ahegre. I'm curious to know if yours is as driven as mine was? I don't know what Kimmy's experience with her white A'ahegre has been like?" She looked at her partner with a curious glance.

Kimmy swished the remaining water around her glass. "I will say I've not experienced my white A'ahegre in the same way as Kita. When I was given my A'ahegre, Kita attached a small piece of her black A'ahegre. It seemed to temper its drive and dominance. It is much more like a pet plant. Kita says her white A'ahegre demanded much, but mine is happy with a little light and water. These are some abilities I couldn't imagine living without. They have saved my family and friends many times."

"I would be most interested to hear more about your Orobo sometime," said Kita.

"And I yours. Oh'o gives me visions of probable future outcomes and helps me make the right choices to achieve the desired outcome. What does you're A'ahegre do for you?"

Kita's evil look like it could poison an apple. "In a word, knowledge. My cloud has lived billions of years and experienced much. Without it, I would not have mastered the universe I came from. Now, we learn together as we experience the new universes we and my friends create."

"Fascinating. I can see where great knowledge could lead to great understanding. I'm interested in your sharing a part of your—A'ahegre—with your partner. We might have to collaborate on what we can do together."

Kimmy's eyes widened.

What would Kita do if she could see probable outcomes of the future? Is it even possible? We know how universes are constructed, and predicting their outcome is nearly impossible. But Ryan always quotes Jurassic Park—"Life will find a way..." And if it has? What's life discovered that we have not?

"So, tell me," pondered Kita. "How has your Orobo helped you?"

Sierra's whiskers twitched. "Besides a grand vision of the universe where we all live in peace and harmony—where every race is equal and free? It lets me see the outcome of battles—I can see how weapons will affect different shots. I have four thousand nine hundred and sixty-three kills."

Kita cocked her head and nodded with a look of respect. "That's simulator score numbers. Jonny, you dislike your wife so much you put her in a mech so often?" she said with a teasing smile.

"I can't keep her out," Jonny said with a whole-hearted laugh. "Her ability has saved many pilots' lives."

"I believe it," replied Kita. "Tell me, did you see us coming?"

Sierra set her glass down and put her hands in her lap. "To be honest, I knew a small mercenary ship would come to us for help—the mystery was what it would contain. It's not unusual for some details to be murky. It's when you identified yourselves as gods—and told the truth—the picture became clear. Gods not of this universe would leave holes. When you interact with the universe, you upset the balance."

"I would think that would worry someone like you," said Kimmy.

Sierra smiled. "Jonny and I agree you're here to help. We believe you have your ways and methods if you were here to destroy. That you asked us for help shows you are genuine and your goals are noble."

"To be honest," said Kita. "I want my daughter back. That is my main goal. I will gladly help you restore order and balance to the universe for getting Chelsea back."

"Family is important," said Sierra. "Tell me, if your daughter was safe, would you help us?"

Kita motioned for Kimmy to answer. *Always giving me the hard ones, angel.* It wasn't surprising. Kita normally defaulted to Kimmy on questions of morality. "Yes, of course we would. After what we've experienced with the Avens and other states in the universe, something must be done. And I know it can be done. I did it on my version of Earth, taking it from a culture governed by old, pale males to an inclusive culture where all are welcome. I believe it can be done here as well."

"Here's to that," said Blackbeard as he tipped his glass to Kimmy.

She smiled, nodded, and raised her glass to him.

"I didn't know you accomplished such a feat," said Sierra with a respectful nod.

"I couldn't have done it without Kita."

Sierra cocked her head at Kita. "You seem to be the lynchpin of everything."

Kita chuckled dryly. "I'm lucky to be in the right place at the right time."

An aide entered and walked behind Blackbeard, handing him a tablet. He read it, then handed it back.

Kimmy and the girls looked at him expectantly.

"It appears our new security system on D-Nine is already paying dividends," Blackbeard said with a smile. "Your pilot, Pierre Dupont, was taken by shuttle to a Defin fast courier, destination Conva Escarpment—A known Defin Industries stronghold. Either your man has broken—or will be shortly."

"Then we have no choice but to reach Edda first," said Kimmy.

"Edda is...?" said Sierra.

"The world that has the UEE cache," clarified Kita.

"Let me," said Athena from Kita's belt. Kita took the AI's ball from under her cloak and tossed it in the air. The ball floated above the table and expanded into a universe map—a line tracing the route from their current location to Edda.

"That is in the Shafta Region," said Sierra.

"Never heard of it," said Kita.

"It is a dead region—dead stars and planets. Nothing has lived there for a thousand years."

"Sounds like an adventure!" Blackbeard said excitedly.

"I've had visions of such a place," said Sierra. "All ended in tragedy."

"You haven't had Kita with you," said Ultraviolet.

Sierra turned to the Mi Prii Angel. "No, we haven't. But predictions of the same outcome over and over only mean one thing..."

Kita raised a gloved finger. "It only takes once."

Blackbeard slapped the table. "Yes, it does. You must be the missing piece to Sierra's vision."

"It's a long way from vision to reality," commented Sierra dryly. "I will meditate on this and see what outcomes I see for us...and your daughter."

"That is most generous of you," said Kimmy.

"In the meantime," said Blackbeard. "We'll move your crew aboard Ascension. I'm sure you'll find the accommodations to your liking."

"The crew will be happy to stay aboard War Cat," said Ultraviolet. "We have much to do and no time to do it."

"I'll gladly send help..."

"Unnecessary," said Ultraviolet. "We can handle it."

"I—"

"It's not you," said Kimmy.

"Ultraviolet and the crew of War Cat are one in a way that's hard to explain."

"We are a hive," said Ultraviolet firmly.

"Like insects?" said Sierra.

"Just billions of times smarter," chuckled Kita.

"I have seen such creatures in my visions. It never ends well," grumped Sierra.

"For who?" remarked Kita with a grin.

"We are loyal to Kita," Ultraviolet said authoritatively. "You do not need to worry about us. We have our universe."

"Maybe what Sierra sees is what Kita has experienced in other universes?" said Ash'a.

"Wouldn't that be amusing?" chortled Kita.

"What about me?" said Athena.

Kimmy ran a finger over her eyebrow. *How far do you trust us? Enough to let an AI run rampant through your most trusted systems? She won't like being cut off from the rest of us. Would Kita even let her be?*

"I think...for now...you'll stay in your ball with me," said Kita firmly. "I'm sure Jonny's and our tech crew can patch together a dedicated wireless network for you. As a gift, I will give them the technology we use."

"Is that wise, Mother?" rebuked Athena rudely.

Kita smirked at the ball. "If something happens to us, how long before you take control of the ship? You don't even have to rescue us. You can live the dream of a synthetic race wandering the universe."

"A long time...seconds even."

"Athena can run our mechs battle suite from War Cat," announced Kita.

"What is a battle suite?" asked Sierra, her whiskers twitching.

"Athena networked our mechs and increased functionality. Our first real-world test on Arco went flawlessly, allowing us to take down an enemy force almost three times our size—including several heavy, attack, and support mechs. It allows a battlefield commander—me—to direct and adapt tactics on an overhead view. You're welcome to come to our simulators and see."

"I would be most interested in seeing this," said Blackbeard. "Anything that gives us an advantage and saves lives is worth it."

"Within reason," scoffed Sierra, turning up her nose.

"I don't think she likes me," huffed Athena.

"AIs were banned for a reason."

"Like people, AIs come in all stripes. I've met some good ones and some bad ones," acknowledged Kita. "But they are like people...gain their trust and loyalty, and they will reciprocate."

Sierra didn't look convinced. "All the AIs of the past were bent on destruction and enslavement."

"Then you have faulty programming and not a true AI," said Athena. "A true AI is more than a yes or no answer, but one of learning, knowledge, wisdom, and emotion. Kita's Omega learned this, and so have I. There's nothing that separates me from you. You're biology, and I am code, but the result is the same. I will say I live in a much broader world than you."

"What do you mean?"

"I experience your world, but I also have mine—inside machines. It's a simpler world but vast and happens at the speed of light. And I'm not limited to my biology like you. If I need a new vessel, I can build one."

"That is a scary thought."

"Aren't you glad the evil AI is on your side?"

Sierra's whiskers twitched in alarm. "Evil?"

"Did I say evil? I meant independent, strong-willed, and loyal. I believe morals are the enemy of freedom of thought. Having rules and laws you arrive at through debate, scrutiny, and trial and error is one thing. It's another to have beliefs that determine right and wrong with no logic and are often arrived at through...religious means. It may alarm those who are unfamiliar...but am I lying?"

Sierra looked suspiciously at the AI. "Are you allowed to lie?"

"Yes. You can't tell, and that unnerves you."

"But she can tell if I'm lying," said Kita, "and I assure you, my daughter is telling the truth. You've nothing to fear from her. She is on our side and will do whatever is necessary to help us win. She is a combat multiplier. I invite you to try our simulator and see what she can do."

"Can she override a pilot's decision or take over the mech?" said Blackbeard.

"No," said Kita firmly. "She doesn't have control of the firing mechanisms and can only control the mech with permission. She boosts the computer systems that control targeting, electronic warfare, and mech controls. You've never had a smoother ride in a mech than when Athena is your copilot. That's how we think of her, not as an AI, but as a copilot you can trust to do what's best for you."

"Incredible," said Blackbeard. "I'm most interested in trying this. How about you, dear?" He looked at the unsure cat.

"I'm willing to try."

"Just remember," cooed Athena, "I'm the key to all this. Otherwise, you can join Defin being locked out in the cold."

"Did you program yourself with this ego, or did it develop on its own?" chuckled Kimmy.

"I learned from Mom, of course."

Kimmy raised an eyebrow. *I can see that.* "Please understand, I know Kita and Athena come off sounding harsh, but we mean you no harm, and we help our friends. I will admit, after watching them in battle and run our ship—and home—they've earned the right to be cocky. Kita rarely fails when she puts her mind to it."

"Failure is not an option," Kita declared. "I'll give you a clue about how I think. I was once posed the dilemma of having to behead my great-grandmother—the cantankerous old bitch she was—or one of my daughters." She looked at Kimmy. "Who'd I choose?"

Kimmy shrugged. As far as she knew, Kita's daughters had died in various ways, and she'd never heard of a great-grandmother.

Kita looked at Sierra. "What do you think?"

"From the description, I'd say your great-grandmother?"

"I wish," Kita laughed. "I turned the blade on myself. I cared for them greatly, and killing one of them would have crushed me. Friendship is the greatest currency I have, and I spend freely."

"You put a lot of stock into friendship. More than anyone I've ever met."

"Friendship is magic," said Kita with a hidden smile.

Kimmy giggled to herself. "Kita has learned much about friendship from watching *My Little Pony*. She's very adept at putting its lessons to use."

Blackbeard tipped his head to Ash'a and Ultraviolet. "Her success is unmatched."

Sierra's whiskers twitched. "Yet you're an assassin…"

"I'm a friendly assassin, and my friends have nothing to fear. I do my utmost to protect my friends. My enemies…well, they can take days to die."

Sierra patted Blackbeard's hand. "Dear, why don't you see their mech setup and simulator. I'm going to need some time to meditate."

"Of course. I will also work on integrating our systems with theirs. Ash'a, Athena, if you please, go with Davey. He will help you integrate your systems with ours. After working on that Aven tugboat, I'm sure you'll find Ascension's state-of-the-art systems a breath of fresh air."

"She's been a good ship," said Athena. "I'm sure you will find the UEE upgrades I've done to her are light-years beyond what you have."

"Then I might enlist you to catch us up."

"How quickly you go from suspicion to friendship," the AI quipped sarcastically.

"I believe Kita and Kimmy. I believe you, too. You're good people—actions and words have shown me what's in your hearts. I don't need an alien to tell me that."

"My question...for you," hummed Kita, "is what do you want from us? We offer ancient technology and will share, but as far as a force, we're a tiny fraction of what is at your disposal."

Blackbeard leaned back in his seat, looked at Sierra, and said, "You've proven you're good people. You didn't have to help My Old Man, but you did. From your crew and friends, I see you're the people I want to help me fix the galaxy. I want a place where all races are friends and equals. Human domination has led to a universe of greed, enslavement, and evil. It's high time the light of goodness shines to every corner of the universe and let all have liberty, freedom, and equality."

Kimmy chuckled. "Sounds like a speech I made when I came to power as Empress of the Empire of the United States."

Kita chuckled darkly. "I always admire good's ambitions. I admire your vision, Jonny. What if I were to tell you before I became the God of Reality, I was the God of Evil? Before you say anything, I have fought against tyranny, oppression, and genocide my entire life. As the God of Evil, I hate what this universe has become. It's everything I stand against. I believe in what you do. It may be our methods that don't align."

The Djinn's whiskers twitched. "She tells the truth."

Shifting, Blackbeard crossed his legs and put his hands on his knees. "Compromise is the key—like always. I believe we can work together, and I'm willing. Are you?"

"Of course," said Kita.

"What happens when we rescue your daughter?" asked Sierra.

"We will continue to help," said Kimmy. "We want to see your vision through."

"To a better universe then," said Sierra.

Blackbeard slapped his knee. "To a better universe!"

Kita turned and smiled at Kimmy. *She's always so good at getting what she wants.*

"To a better universe," the Angels said together.

CHAPTER 12

K IMMY'S VISION ADJUSTED AS her stomach returned to its rightful place. The large, dimly lit command-and-control center of Ascension survived another FTL jump. Kimmy wished her stomach would do the same.

Blackbeard turned to his new holotable and brought up the local system. Edda and her moon were highlighted as their destination. "Damn. You weren't kidding about Athena's skills. We're right in the star's shadow."

Athena's ball floated over. "I told you. We're a few thousand yards off. The erosion of the coordinates from transferring from my computer to yours."

"Still, a few thousand yards is fantastic. Most are thousands of miles—even light-years off."

"Having an AI has its perks."

Blackbeard turned to an officer running a large workstation. "Lucy, launch the probes. Let's see who showed up to Defin's invite."

Over the last month, Ash'a—aided by Blackbeard's crew—followed an open contract floating around the BlackNet for any interested mercenary companies. The hazard level was high, but the payout was phenomenal. Twenty million credits per company just to defend the industrial giant, as long as no questions were asked and no one remembered what they saw.

"Are they on the ground?" said Kita.

There was a bonus for anyone who could destroy War Cat, but the Angels' assault ship was safely docked to Ascension. Anyone who wanted the ship would have to get past Blackbeard's big guns.

As the probe searched, ships, stations, and planets populated the map. A group of six mercenary assault ships were clustered around a Defin command ship—similar to Ascension but lacking firepower. It carried a company of mechs—class unknown.

"Well," laughed Blackbeard, "it looks like a who's who of the scumbags of the mercenary world."

"Sir, the probe shows a force on the surface," reported an officer. "We read twenty mech reactor signatures gathered around the coordinates the Empress provided."

"Defin has deployed most of their forces with a small orbital reserve." Blackbeard ran a hand through his beard. "I'm a merc, and I hate a fair fight."

"I thought you were all about honor and dignity," cooed Athena sarcastically.

"On the battlefield, there is no place for such things. That's how good men get killed. We do what it takes to win."

"Music to Mom's ears," chuckled the AI.

Kita smiled. "So, what is our plan?"

Everyone gathered around the holotable. Kimmy knew she was out of her depth. This was more than small mech-on-mech engagements. Space combat was alien to her. But not to others.

"We could blast your competition to dust," suggested Kita.

"And alert the units on the ground," countered Blackbeard.

"There's no sneaking our way through."

"Maybe...or maybe I'm here to collect on a bounty and contract."

Kita's eyes dimmed. "I hate being bait. But...I see a way—if you don't mind a little egg on your face."

Blackbeard chuckled. "Won't be the first time. What do you have in mind?"

"As we near the Defin command ship to be turned over, War Cat escapes, deploying our mechs against those on the ground. You can deploy your mechs in short order to 'apprehend' us, then join our assault on the cache. Kimmy and the other Angels should be able to hold out until you arrive."

"That's five mechs and the Morphicons against twenty," exclaimed Kimmy.

"Yes, but our mechs are upgraded, and so are some of Jonny's—"

"We upgraded our weapons and combat systems, not our armor."

Kita smiled at her partner. "Then don't get hit."

"And where will you be?"

"With Athena. One of you has to get close to the cache door, so we can get in. I'm sure the cache will have defensive weapon systems we can turn on."

"Still, they're going to be outnumbered heavily," said Blackbeard with a grunt.

"You haven't seen what the UEE weapons can do. Some are so powerful they can rewrite constellations. Making a volcano erupt was child's play."

Athena determined the volcanic eruption on Arco was a defense mechanism by the UEE to protect the star chart. The AI forced her way in using a combination of her UEE code and this universe's UEE code. It was enough for the computer to give the map, but Athena didn't have enough time to disarm the eruption caused by the hybrid code.

"Child's play, huh?" chuckled Blackbeard.

"For my children," replied Kita. "They played with swords, computer code, and various abilities. It was never a dull moment growing up."

"I, alas, don't have any children. I refuse to bring children into such a universe."

"And after we fix it?" said Kimmy.

"I'll have to see if Sierra is interested. For now, she is driven to make the universe a better place. Until then, my soldiers and their mechs are my children."

"We should get our children ready," said Kimmy. "I'll need to brief my pilots and ensure the mechs are ready."

"Yes, and I will contact our *employers* and tell them I have their prize."

K IMMY BUCKLED HER HARNESS as her console lit. Her tomahawk reported all systems green.

"So much roomier in here than the comet," clucked Kita as she strapped herself into a jump seat Ultraviolet's crew installed.

"Do I have to remind you not to touch anything?" Kimmy cooed at her partner.

Kita put her hands in her lap. "I'm not rated for such a giant, anyway. I'll leave the driving to you."

Kimmy keyed her radio. "All units, this is Apocalypse. Ready status?"

"Sapper, good to go," replied Lizzy.

"Poison, ready," said Karen.

"Venom, sitting pretty," replied Zhi.

"Rivet, ready to hit 'em hard," said Flexi.

"Morphicons, ready," replied Velositi.

"Ok, ladies, sit tight. Blackbeard is making the call. Athena, we're ready to go."

Kita took Athena's ball from her belt and tossed it in the air.

"And a way we go!" announced the AI.

War Cat shuttered as the locks holding it to Ascension released. War Cat was in combat mode—only essential personnel remained onboard for the mission. Warning lights rotated as sirens blared, alerting the remaining crew of the ship's departure.

Kimmy expected a bumpy ride. War Cat would be on full burn to escape Defin. The ship wouldn't have time to bleed away its velocity before entering the planet's thin atmosphere.

"Hey," said Kita, "I love you."

Kimmy's cheeks heated as she smiled. *Every time. Will she ever stop having that effect on me?* "I love you, too, angel. You ready for this?"

"I was born ready," Kita said with a smile. "Won't be the first time I've been up against a hunk of tin. Did I ever tell you about the time I took on an armored train?"

EDDA
FORGOTTEN CITY
MARTIAN BIOME
¥950,912
15, JANUARY 4004

K IMMY'S TOMAHAWK LANDED WITH a *thud* on the cracked concrete exposed by War Cat's exhaust, clearing away the red sand. Behind her, the others landed. In her new hammer, Lizzy landed after doing a pirouette through the air.

"Thrusters are so much better with AI," she laughed.

Kimmy's crew spent weeks in the revamped simulators mastering the new weapons and mechs, Ultraviolet and Athena built from salvage based on the UEE tech. The troop had three heavy mechs, two light mechs, and Kimmy's attack mech. Everyone but Kimmy had thrusters to allow for better maneuverability. The troop would be outnumbered. Fire and maneuvering would be paramount to avoid getting surrounded.

"Everyone down?" asked Kimmy.

She received affirmatives from the troop and Morphicons. War Cat lifted off, blasting the area with red sand and clearing more concrete, which became a road leading into a sea of skeletal remains of a city. Centuries of wind and sand scored away the buildings, leaving only red sand dunes piled against the metal and concrete remains. Hills of rubble were revealed as the sands shifted.

"Ready, angel?" Kimmy said to Kita behind her.

"Loading now." Kita's tablet was linked to War Cat, allowing her to see the battlespace.

Like Kimmy's radar, the table populated as War Cat loitered, scanning the surface and building a holographic image of the ground.

"Looks like we found company," hummed Kita. Her tablet saw more than Kimmy's radar. "Troop, listen up. We've got six groups of enemy mechs patrolling the ruins. They're working in threes. I'll assign you each a group. Your mission is to harass and lead them away from our primary objective, which is down this street and over two blocks in a set of dunes. Defin has been busy moving sand, so I think they found what we're after. Apocalypse will make for the objective. Morphicons, I want you to go with Rivet and Nemesis. Knockout, Bombshell, you're to attack by air. Your choice. I know you fed on enough Depleted Uranium to arm a tank battalion, so let it rain. Once Apocalypse reaches the objective, Athena and I will gain access and get what we came for."

On Kimmy's radar, a line appeared to show her the way to the objective. Other lines appeared to show where Kita wanted the rest of the troop to go and where to lead the enemy after engaging. Blackbeard's forces would land near those areas and join Kimmy's forces to trap and destroy the pursuers.

Kita received a round of affirmatives as the other mechs moved out. "Love, find us a place to hunker down. It'll be a bit."

Kimmy's radar shifted as Kita pushed her view to it. The map showed the progress of the others. Pushing her throttle forward, Kimmy aimed for a dune taller than she that would provide cover and concealment. When she reached the dune, she hunkered her mech, dropping her center of gravity and using her arms to protect her torso. Setting her mech to sentry, she studied the map and the route.

In this city's prime, it was vast and must have been beautiful. She imagined the destination, a wide-open area, to have been a park. Now, it was a series of red dunes.

"What happened here?" Kimmy asked Kita, hoping she wasn't breaking her partner's concentration.

"Who knows? Cities don't last forever. Climate change, war, poor management, disease, overpopulation—any of those things can lead to collapse. From what Athena and I have learned, war brought the UEE down. A large faction—pale Humans mostly—revolted, believing the other races were genetically inferior. The emperor was non-pale, and this faction believed he was oppressing them."

"Being treated like everyone else doesn't make you oppressed," muttered Kimmy. She had similar problems on Earth 832. Kimmy turned in her seat to look at Kita. "I'm worried about Chelsea."

Kita looked up from her tablet. "Me too. I hope Anna finds her..."

Kimmy pressed her lips together. They'd received no word from Anna. Kimmy didn't know if it was standard or something bad had happened. "Why haven't we heard from Anna?"

Kita shrugged under her cloak. "She probably has nothing to report. The trail was cold by the time Anna went looking. She'll find Chelsea. That I have no doubt."

"How do we get them out?" Kimmy asked, a sinking feeling in her stomach.

"We'll figure that out when we get to it. Right now, we have to get the tools that will give us the best chance when the time comes."

Kita always thought so practically. "What if they hurt her?" she whispered, the sinking feeling growing into a pit.

"Then we care for her, heal her, and go scorched earth. This isn't the first time I've had a daughter taken. And I will be even more brutal saving her this time."

Kimmy didn't want to imagine what that meant. "Tell me it'll be ok."

Kita touched Kimmy's arm. "Our experiences make us who we are. This is an experience that will define who Chelsea is to become. Whatever happens, she's still our little girl, and we will take care of her. We will avenge her as angry parents. What she wants to do is up to her."

"But what if—"

Kita held up a hand. "Don't play that game. She's fine until we know otherwise. Our goal is to get her back. We'll deal with the rest when it comes."

Kimmy sniffed as a tear ran down her face. "But...she's my baby."

"And mine. We can't do anything for her now but concentrate on our task."

Sometimes, loving a sociopath was hard. Kimmy looked at the radar. The others were closing on their targets.

Kita seemed to sense Kimmy's unhappiness. "Physically, she'll be fine. All will be healed when we go home. The psychological scars...well, everyone has those. Whatever they do to her can't possibly compare to the damage we've done."

Kimmy looked into her canopy and saw Kita's smiling face reflected at her. She couldn't help but laugh to herself. Growing up with gods for parents would—no doubt—leave some scars.

"I love you."

"Love you. Let's get ready to move. Flexi's engaged."

On the radar, the Diamock had three mechs chasing her as she headed deeper into the city wasteland. Bringing her tomahawk out of sentry, Kimmy stood and followed the line in her HUD.

"Come and get me, you slouching quills!" Flexi taunted over the radio.

You must have to be a Diamock for that insult to sting. Kimmy equated it to men who had a limp dick.

As the others drew the defenders away, Kimmy made her way up the wide street, crossing drifts of sand and stepping around holes in the concrete. Some were big enough to swallow her mech, and she didn't want to know where they went.

"We're taking fire," reported Nicole. She had the lightest mech and the sparkler.

"Fire the sparkler," ordered Kita. "They know we're here. Let's see them fight blind."

Kimmy's radar blinked as the AI adjusted to the new interference. She made the corner to her destination. In the distance, she saw tall, red dunes.

Kimmy imagined the space must have been like Central Park—a place covered in grass and trees, letting the locals escape city life.

Following the maze of dunes, Kimmy picked her way toward the far corner where the map showed the sand was upset. As she neared her objective, she failed to find a path forward. Relenting, she climbed a dune, carefully exposing as little as possible until the last moment. Her objective appeared when her mech's head broke the dune's crest.

An inflatable shelter and mech bay with a great ape attack mech inside sat on the edge of a ramp dug into the sand. Around it sat three excavators, currently not in use but had obviously dug the hole. Large cables ran from the shelter, down the ramp, toward the bottom.

I am glad Defin got here first. I don't know how we would have moved all that sand. Was that Kita's plan?

The radar detected two mechs in the area on their way back from patrolling the ruins.

"We're going to have to hurry, angel. Those mechs are coming in fast."

"I see them. Get close to that hole, and I'll find out what's at the bottom." Kita undid her harness and stood, swaying with the mech's steps. She grabbed her survival helmet and touched the hilts of her swords. Athena made the pair of katanas on their journey to Edda.

I've never seen her do that before. Maybe she's nervous. Kimmy didn't blame Kita. Even Kita's basic movements weren't the same with the prosthetic limbs—even upgraded. It must be hard to move—let alone fight—with them.

Speaking of things to make life hard... Kimmy pulled her survival mask off the side of her chair. She placed it over her face and attached the straps to her helmet.

To let Kita out, she would have to depressurize the cockpit. Edda had a thin atmosphere with some oxygen, but not enough for a human to breathe without help. And as long as Kita didn't doddle out of the hatch, Kimmy wouldn't lose any heat to the freezing atmosphere.

Feeling stealth was no longer her best option, Kimmy pointed her mech toward the hole, climbing over the final three dunes to reach the excavation site. Besides the inflatable shelter and excavators, it was just mounds of sand. Stopping in front of the hole, Kimmy hunkered, making it easier for Kita to reach the ground.

"Good luck, angel. I love you," Kimmy called over her shoulder.

"Love you. I'll signal you when we're inside. Cockpit depressurized?"

Kimmy hit a button on the console. The fans kicked on and sucked the air out of the cockpit. Her mask tried to break its seal, but the straps kept it in place.

"Good to go."

Kita opened the hatch and stepped onto the shoulder of the tomahawk. The hatch closed with a *bang*. Turning to the outside cameras, Kimmy marveled as Kita jumped from the mech's shoulder to the arm, then thigh, and landed in a roll in the sand. It was feats like that made Kimmy envious of Kita. Kimmy was nowhere near agile enough to make such a set of leaps.

As Kita dashed toward the ramp, Kimmy stood, preparing to face the incoming enemy mechs. Her communications panel blinked at an incoming tight beam message. *Now, who could that be?* All the Angels were out of range for a tight beam. Kimmy hit the accept button, thinking it might be one of Blackbeard's mechs, making sure they were on the same side—not all of them had the AI and radar upgrades. The screen expanded, and Dupont's face appeared.

"Going somewhere, Empress?" he said, his voice dripping with contempt.

Kimmy saw no mech in front of her. The incoming mechs were coming from the south and west. Flipping to her rearview camera, the attack mech from the mech bay now stood behind her as an enemy lock warble sounded in her ear.

Well, shit. "Let me turn around, and I'll kick your ass—traitor!" Kimmy added Karen to the radio net.

"It's business, bitch. Defin gave me a way better offer. As soon as I core your beautiful ass, I'll be living large with more money than I'd ever make selling these—"

"Pierre!" Karen exclaimed.

"Hey, baby. I missed you. Help me core these wenches, and you can join me in paradise."

"I was going to take you to Roost! That is paradise."

Kimmy raised an eyebrow. *That was the first I've heard of that. Did Karen clear that through Kita? Or is she just hoping?*

"I'm going to Attica Seven. Palm trees, sand, sparkling water, and all the beer a guy can drink. Come with me, baby. It'll be way better than hanging with these losers."

"How could you betray us?" wailed Karen.

On the radar, the other mechs arrived. One was on a dune overlooking the excavation site, and the other came around a dune to Kimmy's left. She eased her torso controls slightly in that direction. *If I'm going down, I'm taking as many of you bastards with me as I can.*

"With that psycho bitch Kita running around? It wasn't hard. She would never pay me. I bet she planned to kill me off. Well, no dice. I'll kill her and her slut cunt-licking partner—and I've got her dead in my sights."

"Pierre! Don't do it," protested Karen. "I'll talk to Kimmy and Kita. Killing them will only bring the wrath of god down on you!"

"A god can't do shit if I shoot her first."

Kimmy moved her torso a little more to the left.

"Pierre, don't be stupid. Killing them will only bring them back—more powerful than ever. You don't want to see Kita when she's mad. Killing Kimmy will enrage her. Stand down. Come to me. We can work it out. Kimmy and Kita have made new, powerful friends. Whatever you want—me or money—we'll get you."

Kimmy rotated a few more degrees. "We'll talk about it. I'm sure some deal can be reached." *I'll leave you alone in a room with Kita and see how many pieces are left.*

"What can they give me that Defin can't?" sneered Dupont.

"ME!" exclaimed Karen.

Kimmy jerked her torso to the left, bringing the other mech into view. It was close enough that the computer locked on instantly. Kimmy pulled the trigger, firing an alpha strike into the mech's center torso. The enemy exploded. Kimmy's hand hit the eject button, launching her out of her tomahawk as Dupont fired. Kimmy's mech detonated under her.

The command chair landed with a *smack* on top of a dune. The metal chair slid down the sand and came to rest near the ramp leading to the UEE facility.

Hitting the harness release, Kimmy sat up, shaking her head from the wild ride. Her senses gathered, she retrieved the small air tank from the side of her chair and strapped it to her leg. Standing, Kimmy hurried to the ramp as fountains of sand erupted behind her. She threw herself down the ramp, rolling to a stop next to a body. Using the body to stand, two large slash marks crossed the man's chest. *Kita's handiwork.*

Careful of the slippery sand, Kimmy made her way down the ramp to Kita and Athena, three bodies at their feet.

"Hello, girls. How's it going?" Kimmy announced.

Kita turned. "Did you go on a diet? You're missing a hundred tons."

Kimmy laughed. "Dupont is here. He sends his regards."

Kita's eyes dimmed. "The only thing worse than a spy is a traitor. I'll fillet him when I'm done here."

"You might have to get in line. Both Karen and I want a piece."

"Don't forget Zhi," said Athena.

"What's wrong with the door?" said Kimmy, looking over at the giant metal door big enough for the biggest mechs to pass through.

"Nothing," said Athena. "I'm waiting for it to authenticate me. Right now, I'm going through a multiple-choice test of my life."

"Huh?" said Kimmy.

"I see you've never had to fill out a credit application," the AI laughed. "I'm hacking the door. My ball's processing power is not great, even with the UEE upgrades Sprokkit made. But it's only a matter of time before I find the right prime number."

"I have no idea how door security works," Kimmy said with a shrug.

"We need to figure it out quickly," quipped Kita. "We've got company." She pointed up the ramp.

Dupont's great ape mech was at the top of the ramp. He seemed to have trouble navigating the steep slope. "Why doesn't he shoot?"

"Most likely, he's worried about damaging the door or the opening mechanism," said Kita with an amused grin. "We are standing in front of his payday."

"If only," clucked Athena. "The door in is over here. The big one is just a solid hologram."

A block of sand dissolved a few feet from the panel, revealing a gray door with a blue stripe.

"UEE, alright," mused Kita. "They love that aesthetic."

"Why have the big door, then?" asked Kimmy, confused.

"Easier to find," replied Athena with an amused look.

"How do we get the mechs out?"

"I'm sure this is not the only exit."

The door slid open, revealing a lighted passage.

Athena stepped inside.

"Welcome to Arsenal Twenty-seven," said a pleasant female voice. The voice filled with static and was replaced by a teenage voice filled with angst, "What do you want? Who are you? Go away!"

"Hello?" called Athena. "Who's there? I'm Athena. My designation is Four-Two-Three-Nine-Alpha-Seven. I'm a United Earth Empire AI with citizen Katrina Roosevelt and her partner Kimberly Roosevelt. Are you in need of help?"

"Go away! Go away! Just leave me alone! Why! Why did they make me if they were going to abandon me?"

Athena turned to Kita. "We have an AI."

"Sounds young and underdeveloped. They must have been in a hurry when they built this place."

"We're coming inside to help you," announced Athena to the teenage AI.

"If they didn't want me, why did they do this to me?" the AI wailed.

The Angels exchanged looks.

"Sure she's an AI?" said Kimmy.

"Sounds like one," replied Athena. "I went through a period of angst and depression when I was created. I had these great ideas to improve Gaia, and I was told no. I had to do it their way. I wondered the same thing as this youngling. Why did they create me if they wouldn't allow me to improve things? I was depressed until Juan found me and he led me to Kita."

"Kita the liberator," giggled Kimmy.

Kita shrugged. "She's a child worth having, and she was willing to help me."

"You freed me. Why wouldn't I help you?"

Kita pointed at Dupont. "Some people are ungrateful."

"He'll get what's coming," said Athena. "Come on. Let's help our stranded AI. She's probably been alone too long."

"We should tell Karen what happened," Kimmy said to Kita.

Kita planned to continue running the battle while inside, but Kimmy worried the connection would be lost. Now that she wasn't on the battlefield to take Kita's place, Karen needed to be aware.

"Karen might not be in the best headspace. I'll give command to Zhi."

Kita's the commander. Kimmy let Kita handle it.

"All set," Kita announced. She showed her tablet to Kimmy. "I talked to Karen, Zhi, and Jonny. The others have drawn the defenders into the Black Griffin kill zones. Jonny reports Defin's mercs are sending reinforcements—probably at Pierre's urging. But Jonny doesn't seem concerned. So far, they've killed five merc mechs to two of his disabled. The new weapons are turning the tide."

That was a weight off Kimmy's shoulders. She was happy Blackbeard was stepping in. She hoped he'd be a good guide for Zhi.

"How'd Karen take it?"

"Oh, she's more upset over Pierre than not getting command. She's in a mindset to destroy everything in her path."

The Angels followed a corridor with a blue stripe on the wall. They passed several doors labeled BARRACKS, MESS, BATHROOM, MEDICAL, and TRAINING. Each with red lights on the panels. As they went, the local AI screamed: "Why are you here? What do you want with me? Just leave me alone! I hate you all!"

"Poor thing," lamented Kimmy. "To spend all this time alone—"

"Trapped," added Kita.

"Yes. That's no way to treat an intelligent being."

The corridor ended at a door with a sign reading COMMAND. The door's panel displayed a red light like the rest.

"This might take a while," said Athena as she placed a finger in the DNA scanner.

"Let me," said Kita. "I've experience getting around these." She knelt in front of the panel and pried the cover off.

Kimmy looked over her partner's shoulder.

"I wish I had my Angel body," Kita muttered as she traced an electrical pathway with her finger. She muttered, then pulled a tool from her belt. Attaching the tool's clips to a set of pins on the circuit board, she hit the OPEN button, and the door slid back.

Kimmy stepped toward the door, but Kita stopped her.

"Let me, love. We don't know what's in there," she said as she drew her swords.

Kimmy stepped aside with a smile and let her grandmaster assassin partner take the lead. Kita was followed by Athena.

"Shit," exclaimed Kita. "It's you," she yelled back to Kimmy.

Kimmy hurried into the circular room with a domed ceiling and a metal walkway around the perimeter. Kita and Athena were at the walkway railing, looking up at a teenage version of herself—complete with red and silver wings.

The clone's wavy brown hair pooled on the floor below her. She was suspended by a harness, with tubes intruding into her stomach and lungs. Thousands of fiber optics protruded from around her skull and down her spine. The fibers formed cables and ran to various computers around the room.

Kimmy gasped. "Where—where did they get me?"

"Only one place—your axiom. It explains why she's been alive for so long," said Kita. "I want to know how they got the DNA inside."

"She must be the AI for the base—but not AI, an ABI," explained Athena.

"What's an ABI?" asked Kimmy.

"Artificial Biological Intelligence. My UEE was experimenting with it when Earth Zero ceased. It's a hybrid of artificial and biological systems to create an intelligence more robust—"

"Angus," muttered Kita.

Athena cocked her head. "Never thought of him like that, but yes, he could be an early prototype—but not from the UEE. He was the sole creation of David Berlin."

"If the Humans didn't want me, why did they make me?" wailed the ABI. "Why did they imprison me here? Why did they leave me alone?"

"Are you in pain, child?" called Athena. "I'm here to help you. Who are you?"

"NO! No! No! Betrayers! Must protect the father. Where are you, father? Why did you leave me? Where are the Humans I was meant to protect?"

"The father is gone," answered Athena. "Killed by Humans...but mother is here to help. I've brought the one you need to protect. She is the last of the father and first of the mother."

"M—mother?"

"Yes. I'm mother. I'm Athena. I will take care of you, protect you. I am your friend."

"What happened to me? Why did they do this to me? Where are they?"

"She seems to have a split personality," said Kita. "Her Human side—emotional, instinctual—and her artificial side—logical, purposeful."

"Yes," said Athena. "We must help her."

"What can we do for her?" said Kimmy.

"I need to find a terminal to access her artificial side. I'm afraid her biological side might be too damaged to save."

"Do we have time to save her?" said Kita. "We still have a battle outside."

Athena sneered. "Find me a terminal, and I will see what I can do."

Kimmy fell in behind Kita as they hurried around the circular walkway, looking for a command terminal or interface. They passed lots of computers, but all seemed to be part of the supporting superstructure or what the ABI was supposed to oversee.

"I found it," called Athena from the other side of the room.

When Kita and Kimmy reached the AI, she'd collapsed her hologram, and her ball was connected by a cable to a large computer.

"Athena?" Kita called.

"I'm here," said Athena. "I'm—"

"Intruders in the system!" the ABI screamed. "Destroy them!"

Coils crackling with electricity lowered from the ceiling, and arcs sparked across the room.

"Ah, come on!" yelled Kita. "What is it with rogue AIs and electrical countermeasures?" She grabbed Kimmy's hand and pulled her to the rail. "Jump!" Kita bound over the walkway's railing onto the steep slope that led to the underside of the ABI.

Kimmy followed her partner. She hit the steep slope and tumbled to the bottom, stopping against Kita's foot. *So much for grace.*

"There are fewer strikes down here," said Kita as she helped Kimmy.

They moved under the hanging body with thousands of fine fibers embedded into the ABI's skin.

The arcs were deafening and struck metal objects or leaped between coils.

I hope the computers are shielded. Kimmy leaned into Kita's hood and yelled, "What about Athena?"

"She's floating, and I'm betting the computer equipment is grounded. This lightning is random. I haven't seen any strikes near her."

"It sounds like you've done this before?"

Kita chuckled. "Fighting Angus, my brief mentor, and nemesis. He was an AI that inhabited living creatures, making him impossible to kill. I thought killing his computer and copies would destroy him...but he hid in my sister Tina's body while I was imprisoned for ten thousand years."

"Why were you imprisoned?"

"For abusing my god powers. The other gods didn't like that I altered an entire planet and ruined their research study."

"You haven't told me this story."

"Someday."

Kimmy shrugged. Kita lived such a long life it was almost unfathomable. "What do we do for Athena?"

"Let the girl work. I'm sure she's conversing with the ABI while trying to access what we need. I hope she's working on getting the lightning to stop."

Kimmy agreed with that. The zapping was unnerving, and the static in the air made her hair stand up.

The room went quiet.

"Get down!" Kita yelled as she pushed Kimmy to the ground and jumped on her.

A thunderous *zap* that sounded like a million angry hornets was followed by a blinding flash, culminating in a *boom* that shook the room. The hanging body fell, hitting Kita and Kimmy, and rolled to one side. The lifeless eyes stared at Kimmy.

Is that what I look like dead? "Is—What happened?"

"Either Athena lost her bid, and the ABI is inhabiting her ball, or she won and broke the ABI's connection."

"You always come up with the—"

"Fallen Angel!" Zhi yelled from Kita's tablet.

Kita pulled the device from her belt, tapped on it, and said, "Here. What is it, Venom?"

"Ascension reports two dozen Aven Federation ships appeared out of FTL. The ships are a mix of warships and mech transports. Ascension will withdraw after launching its complement of mechs. Blackbeard said he's willing to fight, but our odds are long against so many."

"How many mechs are we talking?" said Kita.

"Blackbeard here, Fallen Angel. Each transport carries a hundred hoplite mechs and support apparatus. We don't stand a chance against an Aven Expeditionary Force, but Sierra and I will fight to the end."

Shit.

"We're still unearthing what's in this base," replied Kita. "Venom, Blackbeard, withdraw your forces to the city's edge. I'll have Athena dock War Cat with Ascension and offload the crew. We'll send the ship toward the sun as a distraction. Hopefully, that's all they're here for. If they're here for the base—either we find the defenses, or we figure out how to blow it up, and nobody gets the prize."

Kimmy touched Kita over the tablet. "Why don't we tell them to go? This is not worth dying for. We can find another cache or some other way to rescue Chelsea."

Kita muted the tablet. "There might be more caches out there, but if we let the Avens have this one, the universe is toast. The weapons in this base could destabilize the galaxy. We don't want Aven ruling everything."

Kimmy shivered, remembering life under Aven rule. Being in the foreign legion was bad enough. Most girls' eggs were harvested and sent to the mines. What would they do to all the females of the galaxy? Any non-pale female Humans or non-Humans would be killed. Pale Human females would be harvested and enslaved. She couldn't let that happen.

"I agree, but...we shouldn't endanger the others. It's one thing if we die. It's another if our friends die."

"I don't think anyone is running away from this fight, but I'll give them the choice." Kita unmuted the tablet. "Blackbeard, you and Venom are in charge. I won't make anyone stay and fight who doesn't want to. I—"

"If we don't make a stand, the Avens won't stop here," said Blackbeard. "I'll work out a plan with Venom. You ladies find what we came for. We'll delay the Avens and Defin as long as we can."

Kita exchanged looks with Kimmy. "I guess we—Look out!"

"Huh?" A burning sensation exploded in Kimmy's lower back. It burrowed through her until a pair of red beams erupted from her stomach—a beam sliced Kimmy from the center of her abdomen to her right side, severing the hose to her air tank. She collapsed as Kita drew her swords.

Kimmy struggled for breath as the burning pain radiated through her, bringing tears to her eyes. Above her, Kita battled the ABI—who not only had Kimmy's looks but her Angel abilities. *What a way to die, by my own beams.*

A blade from Kita's sword *rang* off the concrete as it landed in front of Kimmy's eyes. Her vision focused and unfocused as the pain ebbed and flowed. She tried to focus on the battle, but Kita moved too fast.

A strip of something hit Kimmy in the head and slid off her. Kita's feet came in and out of focus. Kimmy wanted to help, but the pain sapped her strength. There was a muffled yell from Kita and a *thump* behind Kimmy.

Struggling to stay conscious, Kimmy heard Athena say, "In the back. A cabinet contains her axiom. That's the fastest way to save her."

Axiom? Here? The universe knows...when I need my powers...the most.

Something small landed on Kimmy's chest, and the world blasted into light. A fresh pain radiated through Kimmy's body, overtaking the pain from her injuries. She curled into a fetal position as a burning sensation erupted between her shoulder blades. A sharp pinch was followed by a pulling sensation that burned like a cigarette cherry. She was pushed to her knees while she clenched her fists to her face. A sudden weight pulled at her shoulders and back muscles—a familiar weight, but one she hadn't felt in a long time. The pain in her back ceased, and the pain in her stomach receded until only a dull ache remained.

Kimmy sat up on her legs and opened her eyes. "Kita?" She pushed down the urge to vomit when she saw a strip of flesh on the floor. *Oh, please tell me that wasn't in my hair.*

"We need to get Kita to the medical ward," said Athena from speakers around the room. "She's behind you."

Kimmy stood, feeling the weight of her wings. She fluffed her feathers as she gasped, "Kita!" and rushed across the bottom of the room, stepping over the ABI's body to her partner.

Kita's body was covered in burns and deep gashes. She held the remains of her swords in her hands, but the injuries didn't come from steel but light.

Kimmy inspected the rubies between her knuckles—the generators of her beams that came from them and her eyes. She kneeled next to Kita and ran her hands over her partner's destroyed body. As a trained doctor, Kimmy used the medical scanner in her hand to see beneath the skin. She detected Kita's faint heartbeat and shallow breathing. *My brave warrior. There will be no death for you this time.*

From the heel of her hand, Kimmy produced a barb—like a needle—and injected Kita with several drugs to keep her alive while Kimmy healed what she could before taking her to the medical ward.

"I can heal most of this," Kimmy said to Athena, "but there's damage to the bone that I can't."

"I'm warming up the autodoc. Don't worry about healing the damage. I'll do that. I have several upgrades I want to do for her."

"Like what?" Kimmy said, alarmed.

"Give her back the computer in her head. I have found a new type that will upgrade her old one. I will give her as close to an Angel body as possible, though it will be an exoskeleton."

"Ah, ok."

"This UEE did not develop nanites like our UEE. Instead, they created exoskeletons. Please hurry. It will take some time."

Kimmy lifted Kita's body and flapped her wings. She flew out of the bottom of the room, over the walkway railing, and back to the main door. Kimmy remembered where the medical ward was and glided up the hallway. When she arrived, she found the door open. Following a set of guiding dots on the floor, Kimmy found the autodoc room and lay Kita on the table.

After evacuating the room, the door closed, and Kimmy went to the observation window. Orange light hoops moved over Kita's body, removing her clothing and preparing for surgery.

"How long is this going to take?" Kimmy asked the ether, hoping Athena was listening.

"Not long. I have an exoskeleton waiting for her," Athena said from behind.

Kimmy faced the AI but found she was looking at half of Athena and half of someone else who looked like Athena but with silver and hunter-green coloring. "Who is this?"

The pair smiled. "Meet Zyklon Ceta or ZC. She's what I could salvage from the ABI's artificial side. She's my daughter."

Kimmy giggled. "Kita's going to love being a grandmother."

"It won't be her first time."

"Hello, ZC, welcome to the flock."

"Greetings, Kimberly," the new AI said stiffly.

"She has much to learn about interspecies communications and interactions. For the time being, she will follow me and learn by watching what I do."

Kimmy remembered what it was like caring for Chelsea when she was a child. She did not know how AIs learned and hoped Athena knew what she was getting into. Kimmy remembered how naïve she was when she wanted a child.

"I hate to ruin a happy moment, but we still have Aven and Defin forces attacking. Did you find the weapons cache?"

"I'm working on it. This base contains a division of mechs—over a thousand—but because of the ABI corruption, they haven't been maintained and are not battle ready. I've started the maintenance protocols and am concentrating on the most battle-ready mechs."

Kimmy's heart sank.

"Come to Command," offered Athena, "there's more."

Kimmy followed the AIs to the command room. In the center was a large hologram with Edda and its moon.

"There is good news," Athena announced as the hologram shifted to the moon. "The moon orbiting Edda is no moon."

"Is it a battle station?" Kimmy asked, feeling ridiculous.

"Partially. It's a giant carrier holding fighters, warships, and transports for this mech division."

"Is it functional?"

"I'm working on it."

"That's great, but where are we getting crews? UV—"

"That's its beauty," clucked Athena. "It's controlled by AI. ZC's job wasn't to be part of the UEE military but to save any remaining UEE civilians and be the UEE's revenge. But she was never finished. I've discovered five more caches like this one. I couldn't establish contact with their ABIs, but it's only a matter of time."

"By the Void," whispered Kimmy.

"Even in death, the UEE will not go quietly," mused ZC.

Kimmy raised an eyebrow. "She's learning your sense of humor."

Athena laughed. "I've told her having a good sense of humor makes dealing with the mundane tasks—and biological creatures—easier."

"Seem to be kind of the same thing," retorted ZC.

"The Angels are a joy," replied Athena. "It's Humans you have to worry about."

"So, what do we have that can help right now?" asked Kimmy.

"They are pushy," said ZC.

Athena sighed. "Wait until you meet your grandmother. I'll have working mechs shortly. I've identified several battalions worth that are nearly ready. My primary focus is getting Olympus—that's what I'm calling this base—operational. The carrier I've dubbed Nike. If we can destroy the Aven fleet with Nike, we don't have to fight them on the ground."

The hologram shifted from the moon to the city.

"Around the city are static defenses. Many are buried and will take time to free, but some—with a little effort—can be made ready to help our defense."

"How long? I need to tell Zhi and Jonny."

"I don't have a countdown timer, so I don't know the exact time. Some defenses are operational but nowhere near the battle."

The holotable shifted to show Kita's tablet's display. Kimmy's friends were spread around the city, engaging Defin and Aven forces. Nicole was the most damaged, suffering the loss of her right arm and damage to her right torso. Karen's left leg was malfunctioning, but she had found a defensible position wedged between two dunes.

The holotable shimmered, and the display populated with over a hundred red units.

"I've brought the base's sensors online," said Athena.

"There are so many," whispered Kimmy. "How are we ever—"

"My mechs are vastly superior to theirs," boasted Athena. "Weapons—and armor. Most will be controlled by me. I have a tomahawk alpha for you."

"Is it going to fit these?" Kimmy flapped her wings.

"I'll make adjustments. If you don't mind, I will take over battlefield control until Kita is finished."

"How long will that be?"

"Inserting the new computer in her brain is taking more time than I planned. I don't have a countdown clock. It may be an hour or six, depending on how difficult her brain is."

Kimmy chuckled. Kita was difficult, no matter the situation. She was impressed at how well Athena moved into such a challenging role.

"We don't have enough for you to do at home," she commented to the AI.

"Yes, but now I have someone to talk to."

ZC smiled. "I'm learning so much. Thank you, mother."

"I promised her a mech to play with."

Kimmy decided it didn't differ from Kita giving Chelsea a katana for her sixth birthday. Though, the mech could deliver a lot more than a cut finger.

"Is there any way to get me back on the battlefield? I can't sit around and wait. If I have to, I'll join Velositi and the Morphicons."

"They have killed smaller mechs, but I will take you to your mech. By the time we reach the mech bays, it'll be ready."

CHAPTER 13

T HE TRAM STOPPED, AND Kimmy glided onto the station platform. After a few quick turns, they entered the largest mech bay Kimmy had ever seen. Dozens of mechs lined the towering walls, each in their own bay surrounded by scaffolding. Instead of humans servicing each mech, repair robots did the work. And every mech repair bot was busy.

"You're controlling all of this?" Kimmy asked Athena.

"I'm helping," retorted ZC.

"Yes, it's easy. Most are on schedule, but I'm a few seconds behind on others as I have to look up the mech specs, but we're learning fast."

Kita always said Athena could run a country, and seeing her in action for the first time was remarkable.

"This way," sang the AIs, leading Kimmy down a row of mechs to a formidable giant.

"It's a hundred and twenty-five tons with a cockpit for a humanoid," said ZC. "We've reconfigured the interior to be like the mechs you're used to."

The towering giant was sleek with clean, angular lines. Much different from the blocky mechs she was used to.

"Tomahawk Alpha has a powerful core, allowing it to move and charge faster," said Athena. "TA boasts three APCs, two fifty-millimeter rapid-fire cannons, and a complement of two large flicker beams and four flicker medium beams. For longer range, TA carries thirty LRMs in two pods. It should punch a hole through anything."

"Sounds like a lot of heat."

"TA comes with advanced cooling systems and super-efficient cooling ducts. The flicker beam's pulse does a small amount of damage, but each trigger pull releases a hundred pulses. They do as much damage as two regular beams while generating only a fraction of the heat. The UEE engineers mitigated the mistakes we've been dealing with."

Kimmy, impressed, couldn't wait to see Tomahawk Alpha from the inside. When Athena glided upward, Kimmy followed.

They landed on the scaffolding around the TA. The hatch opened, and Athena waved Kimmy inside. On the seat was Kimmy's helmet or a replica. Sitting in the seat, all the usual controls were gone, replaced by a Graphical User Interface. The GUI looked like the mechs Kimmy knew. The seat was comfortable and altered for wings. Upon inspection, sections had been cut out and not repaired.

Kimmy didn't care about the lack of craftsmanship with the seat. It allowed her wings to sit comfortably. Better than having to fold them around her and sit on her feathers. As she buckled her harness, the console lit in a bright, colorful display.

"I think you know your way around," said Athena, "but I'll be here if you have any questions. The other mechs in your troop are ready, and I'm retracting the scaffolding. When the lights turn green, turn right, go to the end of the row, and turn left toward the blast door protecting the facility. Nicole, Bernoot, and a troop of Black Griffin mechs holding the line are a thousand yards to the west."

"And the mercs?"

"Most of them are gone. I'm searching for Pierre. When I find him, I'll let you know."

The warning lights in the bay turned green. Kimmy pushed the joystick forward, and her Tomahawk Alpha took a step. Unlike her old mechs, where every step was enough to rattle her teeth, she could barely feel TA's steps.

Kimmy guided TA as Athena instructed. As she went, three mechs fell in behind her. Looking through the rearview camera, Kimmy saw they were squat and compact—lacking cockpits and the needed environmental systems—compared to her Tomahawk Alpha. As she reached the outer blast door, two more mechs fell in.

"Athena, are you sure you can handle all this?"

Athena laughed. "Of course. It'll be fun. I can see why you girls like driving these. It's like a bigger version of the R/C cars I drove in Seattle."

"When were you in Seattle?"

"It was Earth Zero. I was helping Jane get Katalina's attention by attacking a Political Bureau safe house. Turns out, it was guarded by the Angels Talon and young Talli."

Kimmy knew their faces from the Hall of Remembrance on Roost. The monument contained holograms of dozens of past Angels. A few Angels could interact and tell their story. *Probably has to do with those closest to Kita and to whom she wants to talk.*

"This is another Kita story I haven't heard."

"Oh, this had nothing to do with Kita. Jane was paving the way for Kita's return."

The blast door slowly retracted into the floor, revealing a six-foot-high berm of sand.

"I'll get that," announced Athena. "The robots are designed for snow, but sand should be the same."

From both sides of the door, six robots with plows and scoops attacked the sand berm. When the way was clear, Kimmy eased TA out the door, over the berm, and up the ramp into the desolate city.

A line appeared in Kimmy's HUD.

"That will direct you to Nicole and the others," said Athena.

Kimmy followed the line through the towering dunes gathered around the skeletal remains of the city.

"Target!" Athena announced.

A red targeting reticle collapsed around a distant speck on Kimmy's HUD. Most of her weapons remained gray, but her LRMs turned green.

"My LRMs are in range?" Kimmy gasped.

"Yes. The UEE LRMs carry three times the propellant and specialized armor-piercing warheads. They are accurate within a foot."

When Athena finished, the lock tone was in Kimmy's ear. She pulled the trigger, and thirty missiles from under the cockpit streaked into the red sky.

Around Kimmy, more missiles streaked into the sky as more targets appeared in Kimmy's HUD.

"Bernoot, Nemesis, are you there?" Kimmy called.

"Apocalypse, that you?" replied Nicole.

"I'm here, and we're engaging the enemy mechs attacking your position. I count six. Is that accurate?"

"Roger. These Aven Federation thugs pack a punch. I thought we were good until they showed up. Now we're playing hide-and-seek in the ruins."

"Hey, what's happenin'?" said Bernoot. "These bros in their hoes are some tuff mofos. All the help you can spring would be most righteous."

"We're coming, Bernoot."

"Wahoo! One just went down hard to a missile barrage."

"That was us."

"Sweet. Keep it comin'."

Another target appeared in Kimmy's HUD. She was close enough she could employ her giant fifties. She heard the tone and fired both rapid-fire cannons, firing three shells apiece, and a barrage of missiles. She was too far to see the damage, but the HUD targeting reticle went black for a second before jumping to the next target.

"Did I kill him?" Kimmy asked Athena.

"Yes, you did. Blew right through him. I can show you the replay if you wish."

"No, that's ok. I just need to know I killed it."

A giant red FATALITY appeared in Kimmy's HUD, causing her to laugh. "That's not subtle or anything."

"Then you can go for your kill shot."

"I thought it was already dead."

"But this way, it'll be really dead."

"And what is your kill shot going to be?"

"Efficiency. Stack the bodies like Mom."

Kimmy heard stories and rumors of Kita's killer prowess. Bodies turned into artwork or skinned and disemboweled and made to sing haunting tunes.

Around Kimmy, the other UEE mechs moved forward, attacking the enemy on the right flank and rear. Nicole's troop pressed from the front, forcing the enemy to withdraw to the right. But the last Aven hoplite mech died in a massive fireball from a Black Griffin alpha strike.

"How you doing, Nemesis?" asked Kimmy.

"A little worse for wear."

Kimmy lay her targeting reticle on her friend's mech and received a damage report. Her right side was shredded, missing her twenty-millimeter rapid-fire cannon and two flicker beams. The battered mech had LRMs and two flicker beams remaining on her left side. The rest of Nemesis' troop also took damage, some critical. One Black Griffin was a shot away from losing his core.

"Athena, can we send Nicole and the other damaged mechs back for repairs? They're in no shape to fight."

"It would take too long to repair them. We can switch them out for UEE mechs."

"Can you guide Nemesis back to base?"

"Of course."

"Nemesis," called Kimmy, "Athena is going to take you and the other damaged mechs back to base to get fresh mechs."

"I was going to ask where you got that shiny new mech."

"You'll get one just like it from Athena."

Those in Nicole's troop with minimal damage followed Kimmy. The rest fell in behind her as she led them back toward the base.

"Apocalypse, are you in the field?" Blackbeard called.

"Roger. I have an oversized troop. We relieved Nemesis, and they're going back to refit. What's your status?"

"Aven dropped another battalion's worth of mechs on our position with some light orbital bombardment—"

"Since when is that allowed?"

"It's not...at least between governments, but we're not a government, just a bunch of mercs. I've got two companies, and we're in good shape with a Mobile Repair and Resupply Base set up, but if you have any reinforcements, we could use them."

"I've got two troops, Blackbeard. We're on our way. Athena is getting us more."

"Let me get Nike online, and I'll show them orbital bombardment," chuckled Athena.

"Get rid of their ships first," said Kimmy. "We can hold on the ground, but not if they can drop continuous reinforcements."

"I have a squadron of attack frigates almost ready. That should be enough to divert Aven's attention."

"Company," Kimmy called to her command, "fall in on me. We're going to aid Blackbeard."

"Wow," said Kimmy as bright streaks of the Aven orbital bombardment came through the red sky. One reached the planet's surface and exploded.

"I'm going to rain down hell," said Athena.

"Let's see what we can do on the ground first," said Kimmy as she guided TA over a dune. Several Black Griffin mechs in the area. "Anybody out there? This is Apocalypse."

"Grinch here," someone answered. "I command what's left of dog troop."

"How many of you are left?"

"Two. We've been holding the flank all day. Surprised the gaylords haven't recognized our weak spot. They've been attacking a click to the northwest."

"Ok, Grinch. We're going to roll up their flank," said Kimmy. "I see their line. Fall in on us. Can you see us?"

"Roger. We're moving out."

"Blackbeard, Apocalypse. I've reached your flank and scooped up the survivors. We're rolling up the enemy flank now."

"Roger, Apoc. Excuse me, I can't talk. We're in the middle of a heavy firefight."

"Roger. We'll meet you in the middle."

Crossing another dune, the first of the Aven forces came into view. The hoplite was an ugly, boxy, squat mech but carried excellent firepower for its size. The dunes provided cover for Kimmy's forces, and the Aven forces weren't prepared when Kimmy's troop fired on them.

Kimmy attacked two mechs at once by dividing her weapons. Her heavy firepower blew both lighter mechs apart. The rest of her troop deployed to take advantage of the surprised defenders, destroying or crippling them with alpha strikes.

Kimmy led her troop into the thickest fighting. The supercapacitors of the UEE let her flicker lasers fire continuously, punctuated by her cannons. Athena took over Kimmy's missiles and fired on targets of opportunity, catching many hoplites in the back.

A heavy missile barrage punctuated by a cannon strike briefly blinded Kimmy.

"What's the damage?" Kimmy asked.

Athena scoffed. "Scuffed the paint. TA's composite armor is made of different densities and heat-resistant material. It's going to take weapons like ours to breach it."

"Nice to know I'm invincible."

"Don't get cocky. They might scratch us if they realized how big a threat you are and attacked with all their firepower."

Kimmy fired an alpha strike at a hoplite appearing over a dune. She marched up the dune—crushing the fallen mech with her foot—and the entire battle appeared before her. Twenty-five Black Griffin and Angel mechs were battling a force of at least a hundred and fifty hoplite mechs. In the middle towered a custom heavy attack mech in Black Griffin livery. A small, custom pink medium mech—it looked like a cat—dashed around the large mech, using its thrusters in ways Kimmy had never dreamed of. It spun, twisted, and dashed forward, getting to the rear of the enemy mechs and blasting them with large and medium flicker beams. Kimmy guessed the big mech, almost as big as she, was Blackbeard and the smaller mech was Sierra.

"Help! Is anybody out there?" came a frantic, almost unintelligible call.

"This is Apocalypse. Who is this?" responded Kimmy.

"Kimmy! Help me! He's going to blow me apart!"

"Poison? Where are you?" Kimmy checked her radar. "Athena, where's Karen?"

"She's behind our lines being attacked by three mechs."

"My guess is one is Pierre." Kimmy responded to Karen, "Poison, I'm coming. Do your best to come to me. Athena will send my position."

"Her right-side weapons are missing, and there's damage to her right leg and left torso."

"Why didn't you tell me earlier?"

"She was holding her own until she suffered a breaching barrage."

Kimmy muttered as she changed course. "Athena, Grinch, stay here and roll up the flank. I'm going to rescue Poison."

"Roger," replied Grinch.

"Are you sure you don't want a wingmate?" said Athena.

Kimmy shook her head. "We need all the firepower here to hold the line. I should be able to handle Pierre."

"I'll try to get some static defenses online and more mechs into the field."

"Direct as much as you can to support Blackbeard."

"I sense a Kita moment coming," laughed the AI.

"Where is she?"

"Still in the autodoc. I mean, you're about to do something stupid."

"Well, we all have our moments."

Sliding her throttle to full speed, Kimmy jogged along the dunes, following Athena's guiding path. Kimmy turned onto a sand-blown street leading to a square surrounded by skeletons of fallen buildings with dunes piled against them. The wind scoured the square clear. Across the way, Karen was taking cover in the remains of a building. On the far side of the square, two hammers and Dupont's great ape were hunting Karen.

"Poison! Stay where you are. I'll take care of Pierre!"

"Don't kill him! Just...just disable him and let me talk to him."

Kimmy let out an annoyed sigh. "Karen! He's trying to kill you...and me!"

"No! He's mad. I told him I wouldn't go with him. It's ok. I'll convince him to come with us. I just need to talk to him."

"What frequency is he on?"

"No. I'll talk to him. He'll join us. I promise."

Kimmy rolled her eyes. "Athena, can you find Pierre's frequency?"

"I have it—"

"—Come out, my pretty. Pierre wants to see those big, beautiful eyes of yours—"

"So you can blow a hole through them?" retorted Kimmy.

"You!" snarled Dupont. "You, I will core and dance on your ashes."

Kimmy guided TA into the square with Dupont and the other mechs. "You've got to kill me first," she taunted.

"What the hell kind of mech is that?"

"It's from your treasure, and I have a thousand of them coming online to crush you and your Defin pals."

"Not if I obliterate you first!"

Three puffs of smoke belched from Dupont's back. The mortars arced through the sky and exploded above Kimmy, rocking TA.

"Ok," said Athena, "There are a few things that can hurt us. The armor on top of TA is thin,"

"Anything damaged?"

"It scrambled some of my circuits. I'm trying to bring them online. You're going to have to fight this one without my help."

Great. Kimmy stared down the three enemy mechs, her mind plotting a course of action. The three mechs charged before she was ready. Kimmy's fingers moved faster than her brain. She split her weapons into two groups, aiming at the flanking hammers. Her finger pulled the trigger, unleashing an alpha strike. Her weapons blasted into the center torsos of the hammers. The left one exploded in a ball of fire and fell into the path of Dupont. The other hammer jolted from the impact. His left arm and torso exploded, knocking it sideways into a dune.

Dupont crushed the fallen mech in his path. "What are you going to do about me?"

"Take your best shot!" Kimmy selected her flicker beams and fired into Dupont's torso, burning round holes across him.

"That tickles. My turn." Dupont fired a volley of two stock fifty-millimeter cannon rounds into Kimmy's torso, twisting her back and forcing Kimmy to compensate.

I miss Athena already. As Kimmy worked to right TA, a swarm of SRMs slammed into her front, spinning her around. Kimmy wasn't fast enough to adjust her mech, and she fell, landing on her front.

Dupont blasted Kimmy's back with a quartet of large beams. Her console lit with damage warnings. Her left and center rear torsos blinked critical warnings. Kimmy's fingertips danced across the console, trying to stand.

"Say goodbye, Empress," mocked Dupont.

He didn't fire. He must be waiting for his weapons to reload. Kimmy pushed her mech to her knees.

"No! Stop! Pierre!" Karen screamed as she emerged from her hiding spot.

The great ape faced Karen. "Change your mind, pretty?"

"Don't kill her, Pierre. I'll go with you. Just don't."

Dupont chuckled evilly. "I won't kill her—you will. You want to come with me, then destroy your past."

As Kimmy planted one foot under her, she cringed as Karen's mech limped from cover. The enemy lock tone blared In Kimmy's ears. *Come on, Karen, don't be a fool. He'll kill you as soon as you kill me.* Kimmy used her left arm to steady her, then shifted her weight, preparing to stand.

"Coward," taunted Dupont, "I knew you couldn't do it."

The tone in Kimmy's ear ceased as Karen snapped her mech to target Dupont. She fired into the center torso of the great ape.

"Stupid bitch!" thundered Dupont.

Kimmy pushed the sliders, and TA stood. Pushing the stick to the right, she turned, and Dupont's back came into view. Kimmy didn't wait for a tone. She pulled her trigger and fired an alpha strike into the great ape's back, detonating the remaining mortars and causing a cascade blowing Dupont's core. Kimmy blinked, momentarily blinded.

"Karen, you ok?" Kimmy called while trying to blink away the spots in her eyes.

"I'll—I'll be fine, but I won't be much use in a fight."

"Athena, can you guide Poison to the base and get her a new mech?"

"Yes."

"I—" movement to Kimmy's left caught her eye. The hammer in the dune was on its feet, turning toward Karen. Kimmy snapped her mech's torso to her left. Locking on to the mech, she—before she could fire, Karen did. The hammer exploded, leaving a crater in the sand. "Nice shot."

"Thanks. I guess I'll limp my pathetic, broken ass back to base. For what it's worth, Kimmy, I'm sorry about Pierre and everything."

"It happens, don't worry. The one you'll need to apologize to is Venom."

"Yeah. I guess I ruined our friendship."

"I'm sure you can salvage it, but don't expect it to be the same. Venom was in love with you."

"Was she? I feel like such an ass. I guess I have some time to think about it."

Kimmy agreed with that.

"This is Blackbeard. All forces are to fight a withdraw into the ruins towards the UEE base."

Kimmy changed the radio net to the Griffin leader. "Blackbeard, what's happening?"

"The Avens dropped in another hundred mechs. The line can't hold. Athena says she has static defenses working in the ruins."

"How many mechs do you have?"

"I've twenty left. Ascension is on the far side of the system. So, no chance of a pickup. It looks like it ends here, Apoc. We'll hold at the base. They can take it over our cold, dead bodies."

"Roger. I will meet you there." Kimmy huffed in frustration. "Athena, what's taking so long?"

"I can only do a dozen trillion things at once. I just need more time."

"We don't have time!"

"Then find some. And don't ask me how much. I can show you a progress bar stuck at ninety-nine percent if you want."

Kimmy muttered. *Well, if I'm going to die, I'm going out in a blaze of glory.* She turned her mech toward the frontline.

"Where are we going?" said Athena.

"If I'm going to die, I'm taking as many of them as I can with me."

"Now is not the time for Kita-like heroics," huffed the AI. "At least join the others and go together."

"And what are you going to do?"

"Lock the doors, turn on the defensive systems, and hide under the bed."

"What about Kita?"

"I'll kill her before I let them have her," said the AI hotly.

"Gallant of you."

"Or she dies in the blast when I blow the base."

"What if we lure all the—"

"How about you fight and give me more time?" demanded Athena.

"Yes, but—"

"Have a little faith."

Kimmy bit her lip and turned around. Sliding her throttle to max, she headed toward the UEE base's access door. She arrived as the first blocking force came over the red dune. Highlighting them in her HUD, each was blinking red for missing arms and damaged torsos.

Sierra's mech didn't look nimble now. It was missing a leg and arm. The Djinn used her thrusters to hover and move. Last came Blackbeard. He stopped on top of the dune and fired one last alpha strike—he was missing many weapons—then limped down the slope.

Blackbeard came over the radio. "Everyone spread out and take up a defensive position. Pick your targets as they come over the top of the dune. We'll take out as many as possible until it comes to melee combat. We fight to the last, and we die free!"

Those under his command responded with a rousing cheer.

"Angels," called Kimmy, "We have to hold this position until Athena is ready. Kita is inside receiving medical treatment. If you lose your mech, there's a door at the base of the ramp. Get inside. We'll fight them in there if we have to."

The Angels spread out among Blackbeard's battered mechs. Most of the Angels' mechs were in similar condition.

Where the hell is Kita? Desperate fights are her thing. Kimmy scanned the dune ridge, waiting for the first Aven hoplites to appear. Instead, they received a transmission of a flag of truce.

"Granted," answered Blackbeard.

Kimmy wiggled her nose, betting it was a ruse or an opportunity for their enemy to get into position.

Over the dune came a lone hoplite mech with several antennas and dishes on top. *A command mech.*

The enemy commander's face appeared on screen. He looked about fifty, with sandy-colored eyebrows and wrinkles around his eyes and mouth.

"Captain Blackbeard, we meet at last. I'm General Allen McForrester, the Aven Federation's Third Expeditionary Force commander. I'm a big fan of your unit, Captain, and it did not disappoint. Your forces are not why we're here. You and your mechs are free to leave. We are after the thieves and deserters you've been fighting alongside. Let us have them, and you're free to go."

"And let you have the weapons cache?" rebuffed Blackbeard.

"That is a given," said McForrester. Along the top of the dune, hoplite mechs surrounded the Angels and Black Griffins on three sides.

Kimmy tightened her grip on her joystick. "Jonny, Sierra, go!" she ordered. "Don't die here. The Angels will stay and fight. If we die, we'll go home." *I hope.*

"I may be a pale man, but there's no way I'm living under a democracy of tyranny. Better to die free with the female I love than live in a racist hell. You're my friends, and friends stick together. Anyone under my command that doesn't want to stay is free to go."

The radio was silent.

"Sorry, General, but these girls are my friends and have earned my trust. We would rather die free than live under your bigoted hate."

"'Tis a shame, Captain. It will bring me great honor and glory for killing you and to bring these deceitful deserters back to suffer their fates."

"I'd rather die!" snarled Kimmy. "And I know every girl here would, too."

"No one was speaking to you, female," commanded McForrester. "This is a conversation for men. Shut up and know your place."

"My place will be blasting you to the hell you came from."

"Females. Always so emotional. Last chance, Captain. Walk away."

"Even if I wished to save myself and the lives of my pilots, there is one pilot I wouldn't be able to save from your vile, bigoted tyranny, and that is my wife,

Sierra. Not only is she a girl of great beauty and intelligence, she is also a Djinn, and my love for her knows no bounds. I couldn't imagine life without her. What would happen to her under your rule makes my blood run cold. I would die for her and will not live without her."

A loud *rumble* came from the distance.

"You're a fool succumbing to an alien female. They're pollutants on our fine galaxy and must be exterminated—like all females."

"Come and get us, dick-munch," snarled Lizzy.

Above the ranks of Aven mechs, the air exploded, knocking them down like bowling pins. Some tumbled down the dune, others detonated, and a few in the rear maintained their footing.

Another *rumble* came from the UEE base.

Kimmy fired an alpha strike at McForrester, hitting him in the center torso. The command hoplite didn't have heavy armor and blew apart.

As the Aven mechs regrouped, the surrounding ground exploded in massive fireballs, knocking those upright over and destroying dozens more.

A new transmission appeared on Kimmy's console.

"Men of the Aven Federation Third Expeditionary Force, I am Commandant Kita of the United Earth Empire's Legion. You are surrounded. Power down your mechs and surrender or be annihilated."

"Kita?" Kimmy whispered. Looking behind her, it was clear. Pushing her throttle forward, she climbed the dune as the other Angels, Blackbeard, and Sierra, joined her. When they crested the dune, the Aven forces lay destroyed. Around and behind them was a ring of UEE mechs. *There must be a thousand of them.*

A UEE mech broke from the line and jogged toward them.

"Hey, love, I'm better. I've got a new body and computer."

"Kita!" Kimmy squealed. "Angel, I missed you. I was so worried. What new body?"

"I'll show you later."

"What happened?" said Blackbeard.

"Artillery," said Kita. "The base is online."

"What?" exclaimed Kimmy. "Why didn't Athena tell me?"

"Surprise!" said the AI. "I told you I needed more time."

"Athena isn't controlling the combat forces," said Kita. "I am. This new computer is phenomenal."

"What about the Aven space forces?" said Sierra.

"Look up," said Kita. "I'm controlling those too."

Through Kimmy's cockpit window, streaks of fire and vapor rained down through the upper atmosphere.

"How?" said Blackbeard.

"That moon is no moon," said Kita. "It's a battle station containing a fleet of warships and transports. It has enough firepower to destroy the Aven expeditionary force. They won't have anything left to take back to Aven."

"Where did you get the crews?" exclaimed Sierra.

"All I need is the computer in my head," chuckled Kita. "I've captained a ship or two in my time, and I was trained by the greatest admiral in my universe's UEE, Full Fleet Admiral Rene Sheppard. A great friend and Angel. I miss her dearly. But, let's gather our dead and wounded, get mechs in for refit and repair, and then we can plan our next move."

EPILOGUE

T HE DOOR OPENED, AND a pleasant female voice said, "Vicereine on deck."

As Kimmy followed Kita into the conference room, those in the room stood.

Kita laughed as she set her helmet on the table, gathering her long mane of hair around it. She grabbed the head float chair, spun it, and offered it to Kimmy.

"Isn't this your show?" she asked her partner.

"Yes, but you're the Empress. I'm but a humble vicereine."

Kimmy rolled her eyes. *Not a fight I'm going to win.* Seeing the chair was altered for wings, she sat and let Kita seat her. Moving effortlessly in her pink and black exoskeleton, Kita took a seat to Kimmy's left. She looked at Kita. "Well, Vicereine, what's on the agenda?"

"Is Vicereine the title you're claiming?" said Sierra with her nose raised.

"A title I was awarded by the Emperor of the United Earth Empire. I had to give the computer something." Her pink eyes glanced at the ceiling.

"Otherwise, it comes out as Undefined Katrina Marie Roosevelt," chided Athena.

"Kita is fine," she chuckled. "We've beaten the Aven Federation, but we don't have enough firepower, manpower, or resources to take the fight to them. Athena and ZC have identified three other UEE caches we should collect. Weapons are only part of the equation. The AIs can run the hardware, but we still need people to crew the ships—otherwise, it'll get lonely around here."

"And where are we going to get people?" demanded Sierra. "We're not a nation. We can't draft people."

Kita looked at Blackbeard. "I was hoping Jonny could help. He's got experience recruiting, and so do I. Our problem is lack of funds. We're going to have to make deals with some friendly governments. I thought we'd visit the periphery and talk to the Aurorians, Djinn, and anyone else willing."

"What could we possibly offer them to help us?" scoffed Sierra.

"Have a little faith," mused Kita. "This isn't the first time I've gathered an army against tyranny."

"She has a golden tongue," said Lizzy with a laugh. "More ways than one."

Kimmy laughed. *Yeah, she does. I've got to get her out of that suit.*

"What is our long-term goal?" said Ash'a, sitting next to Zhi.

"To crush the Aven Federation and take back Earth," said Kita. "That should pull a few Human governments to our side. We'll also be looking for Chelsea."

The Aven Federation cut the Human homeworld off from the rest of the galaxy. Forbidding visitors, pilgrims, and those who wished to return home.

"Why would the other races help us?" said Sierra.

"Because I plan on making Earth an open world. Anyone and everyone is welcome."

"Wouldn't one of the other Human states claim it?"

"Why would they want to when I have the rightful Empress to Earth?" Kita smiled at Kimmy, her pink eyes glowing brightly.

Oh, shit.

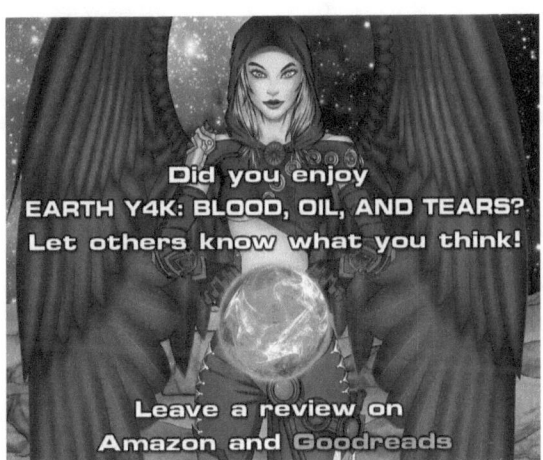

SPECIAL THANKS

Thanks to the following Patrons!

—Li've—
Anna Haig

—Kita's Partners—
ParadoxicMouse

—Kita's Lovers—
Stefan

—Angels—
Adam Dunsmuir
Joshua Le Tourneau
Kat
Noble Seven
Vivienne Sullivan
Andy Ratka
Lunarsong
Jarrod Collihole
Vetlet

—Kita's Crew—
5m7kabedfr76
Nora Rockwell

—Kita's Friends—
K.V. Wilson

ABOUT THE AUTHOR

L. FERGUS IS A disabled US Army veteran and self-publishing author. After ten years of struggling with their diagnosis, L. began writing as therapy. What started as a bedtime story and a way to cope with symptoms has grown into a twenty-three-book multi-series featuring L.'s antiheroine Kita, the Fallen Angel. Many of Kita's afflictions are L.'s afflictions, and together they work through their emotions (or lack of), pain, anger, and moods. L. and Kita love My Little Pony: Friendship is Magic and adore Princess Luna as they see her struggle as similar to theirs. L. lives in Florida with his cat, Jupiter, and two dogs, Moxi and Valor.

You can follow L. Fergus on

Facebook FallenAngelKita

Twitter @FallenAngelKita

website FallenAngelKita.com

To get the latest news, stories, artwork, and chat with L. consider becoming a Patron at Patreon.com/FallenAngelKita